Alex Keegan has worked for the RAF, in direct selling and as a computer consultant. He gave up a sixty-thousand-pound salary to take a degree in psychology and sociobiology. He took up writing seriously after being involved in the Clapham Rail Disaster and now lives in Southampton with his wife and their two young children. A committed runner, he is a UK top-thirty veteran sprinter.

Alex Keegan's previous Caz Flood novels, *Cuckoo* and *Vulture*, are both available from Headline.

Also by Alex Keegan

Cuckoo
Vulture

Kingfisher

A Caz Flood Mystery

Alex Keegan

HEADLINE

First published in 1995
by HEADLINE BOOK PUBLISHING

First published in paperback in 1996
by HEADLINE BOOK PUBLISHING

10 9 8 7 6 5 4 3 2 1

All characters in this publication are fictitious and any resemblance to real persons, living or dead, is purely coincidental.

ISBN 0 7472 4826 5

Printed and bound in Great Britain by
Cox & Wyman Ltd, Reading, Berks

HEADLINE BOOK PUBLISHING
A division of Hodder Headline PLC
338 Euston Road
London NW1 3BH

For
Toby and Claire

ACKNOWLEDGEMENTS

I would like to express my gratitude to the County Engineers of East and West Sussex, particularly Chris Barnard and Dick Roberts, for their theoretical knowledge, their help and guidance, and the loan of a hard hat.

Special thanks must go to Peter L. who has never heard of anyone called Mariella.

Very few people understand absolute darkness.

It is not the awesome black of a night in the forest;
for in the forest there may be a distant moon, the stars,
the faint but crept reflections of invisible towns.

It is not a dark cupboard, no matter how black,
because outside you know that there is light.
And no matter how deep, how cold, it is not a cave,
for a cave has its way back to the world and its
secret living phosphorescence.

Real darkness is an absolute, absolute nothing.
This darkness is a total of absence of light energy,
a pit thrust deep into the earth when nothing, nothing,
nothing is, where one sense is so completely removed
from the sighted that the other senses rebel.

Where smell rebels because what is smelt
should also be, where touch rebels
and screams its fear because what is felt must be there,
where hearing rebels
as the echoes and echoes grow, taunting, taunting;
you are powerless, are frightened, you are open to me.
Now, you realise you are mine.

Listen to my voice. Listen. I have you.

Kingfisher

One

Flood looked out from her flat window and down at Brighton. At eight o'clock it had been overcast, a faint drizzle washing the street, but now the sun was out. It was a little limp maybe, but definitely out. It was nine o'clock, New Year's Day. She finished the last of her coffee and grabbed her car keys. She could hear the voices of her father, her running coach and her conscience in debate.

'Always start the year with January, Flood.'

'And always start January with the first.'

'You will have a hangover, Flood, so you get out there by five past nine, get in the car, drive out of Brighton, and get a long run in.'

'Fifteen miles on the Downs should do the trick, Caz. Nice 'n' steady.'

She had rolled naked from her bed at twenty minutes to nine. She had creaked through to the kitchen, flicked on the kettle and slapped two pieces of bread into the toaster, virtually without breaking her stride. Then she had gone back through to her bedroom, said good morning to her only surviving fluffy pink pig and nipped into the en-suite bathroom. After using the loo she had thrown cold water into her face. *Then* she had risked looking into the mirror. It was not a pretty sight.

She had run wet fingers through her hair – it had looked more grey than blonde but she blamed the light – then she had leaned forward towards the analytical glass to begin damage assessment.

Her eyes had started out that colour green – so far so good – but her tongue definitely hadn't. The tongue she could see had to be someone else's but why she'd eaten it, she had not the faintest idea. From what Caz could remember, *her* tongue was pink. She wondered how well this furry yellow one would work. It was eight forty-five. She coughed once. Time was marching on. She decided she might as well give it a little try. Her first words were croaks. 'DC Flood . . .'

She was a little surprised, but the tongue worked. It wasn't all that different from her old one. She squinted into the mirror. 'Kathy Flood, you are *disgusting*. Is this the face of an England runner?'

She pulled her lower eyelids down, thinking, 'Oh, God!' There was definitely white there, plus a faintish tinge of yellow and just a few red, wriggly blood vessels. And New Year's resolution number one was?

As she walked back into the bedroom, she reminded herself. 'I have given up drink. I *will* not drink. I *do* not drink.' She sat on the bed and slipped on a pair of white underpants. Then she picked up her running kit and headed for the food.

'I have given up drink. I will not drink. I do not drink,' she said as she arrived in the kitchen. The toast popped.

She flicked the kettle back on.

'I will not drink until after the London Marathon.'

She poured water on to instant coffee.

'I'll only drink for special occasions.'

A thin smear of Flora on the toast, a little honey.

'A little wine, maybe, if I'm out, but *only* if it's with a meal and then only on Saturdays.'

Caz looked into the fridge. There was no milk. She slammed the door. 'Shit!'

She had decided not to swear in 1993. That resolution was gone and it wasn't even nine o'clock. She sipped black coffee, thinking, 'That's pathetic, Flood, even for you!' The coffee was too hot. She blew into the mug and decided to look on the bright side. This was really a good sign. She should let some promises go early and focus on the important ones.

With her black coffee she clarified her first resolution. 'No excessive drinking and no drinking alone, except weekends, i.e. Friday, Saturday or Sunday; unless I'm celebrating a big arrest or I'm out on a date.' She decided to write it down before she went out.

Caz was waking up. She went over to the NAD CD player and buttoned it on. There was a compact disc already in, so she pushed 'play' to see what it was. It was the Pogues – Jeez! she must have been really pissed last night. There was a piece of toast in her mouth and her legs were high in the air as she wriggled into her Lycra bottoms. The band was digging in. She managed to take 'Fairytale of New York' as she pulled on her Helly top, but she had to press 'track' to skip the next two songs. She finished her toast listening to 'The Irish Rover'. Then she went back into the kitchen to dump her empty mug.

Up on her notice board was her running number for a race near Fareham; scheduled for the coming Sunday. Alongside that was a list of the UK Women's 1992 Top Ten for eight hundred metres, and next to that, a picture of a sun-drenched Club la Santa, Lanzarote.

There was nothing else pinned up except two postcards, one from the Florida Keys, the other from Portugal. She untacked one card and read the message again. It was a flight number, a time and a request for a lift from the airport. Val had signed it with a smiley which she took to mean they were probably all right. There was a little hormonal squirt somewhere inside her and she felt randy. She'd wash his car tomorrow.

The other card was from Plantation Key, a little south of Miami. Caz didn't take that one down but she knew the message by heart. It was unsigned but had begun *Dera Caz*. If she was sober, the little spelling error kept her awake nights. The message on the reverse of the card said, *Weather fabulous. Winter here is expensive. Keep well. Hope we don't meet in '93.*

Eventually she was going to have to tell her boss, DI Tom MacInnes. That was one of the troubles with being a copper, especially a very junior *female* detective constable – even if your mail was marked personal, you couldn't keep your serial killers to yourself.

Two

It was when Caz threw open the doors to her lock-up at the top of the next street that she knew 1993 was going to be her year. When you go to bed owning a twelve-year-old battered MGB and the morning brings you a brand new British Racing Green Mazda MX5 and they've fixed it up with a walnut dash and it's yours, and you really don't owe a penny on it, and you don't have to think about MOTs for three years, and . . .

She stared into the garage, still not quite believing it. Around her head she could feel blunted alcohol buzzing. She wasn't at her sharpest and possibly still illegal, so she closed her eyes, and shook her head awake. Her ponytail flicked twice and her head rang, but when she opened her eyes, the Mazda was still there. All she could say was, 'Wow! It's real.' She climbed in.

As she drove out of the lock-up, Caz was unable to resist a single sudden press of the accelerator, just to hear the unfettered bbbrrampp!! of the MX5's engine. She was grinning as she dropped down the street. As she reached Kings Parade, she stopped briefly, then she swung the car left, raunching the engine again just to see what it felt like. With the windows down, she purred along the seafront's empty dual carriageway into the town centre, then north via the Old Steine, through

Withdene and Westdene, and out of town on the A23.

After Patcham, the A23 ducked underneath a bridge, the slick of the Brighton & Hove bypass flacking overhead. Then the road followed the railway and a few farms before splitting at the village of Pyecombe. This was where Caz parked up before stretching at the side of her car and then jogging across a field to find the South Downs Way.

Once on the Way, Caz went east, heading for Ditchling Beacon. To her left, she saw two windmills, one black, one white, Jack and Jill. Then the track veered sharply and she was running north, towards them. Then she swung right again, trees to her left, the chalk and gravel beneath her feet, the sun high and white.

It normally took at least fifteen minutes before the rhythm of her running settled into her. Until that happened she was just running and looking. Then her body would finally concede that she wasn't going to stop and it would switch into its beautiful economic mode, carrying her along smoothly and effortlessly. Then she would be part of the world she cut through. This was the feeling she looked for.

High up to her right the sun was barely lemon, the sky greyer than blue. Away to her left the land fell away sharply and further out were roads, farms, little villages, tossed green and something unarguably English. *Now* she was part of it all. Now she cruised.

Caz was breaking rules. She was running alone, she was on the Downs without extra clothing and she had gone running without telling anyone her route. She would have jumped on someone else getting into trouble doing exactly what she was doing, but what Caz was doing was within *her* rules. She was travelling a straightforward out and back route, was never more than a mile from a road, and tucked into her waistband for personal protection was a short, diamond-handled leather riding crop.

Caz was running on flint; on the rounded edge of something ancient and primitive. Her own edge was self-made. She could not feel too safe and she would not let herself be too comfortable. When she had been running steadily for half an hour she began to look forward to the challenge of the winding upward slopes. When these came, she pushed herself harder, revelling in the minor battle between her muscles and her mind. Now she was beginning to work, she took the riding crop from her belt and carried it, cobra-black, balanced easily in the palm of her hand in lightly closed fingers.

The heat in her thighs was a forge; blunting everything bad that had ever threatened her but honing *her*, leaving her sharp. The pain gave Caz her sharpness. At the point on each hill – fifty yards to go – where lactic acid began to bite into her quads, the hardness she sought was crystally obvious, etched by effort into each green focused eye. She would never be alone, never a victim and never without her edge. Not as long as she could run and not as long as she carried the black whip, light, subtle, balanced in her fist. Ready.

Caz was back at the car in the very late morning and rolling back into Brighton just after twelve o'clock. She had run the Downs Way until she could see Lewes spread before her, then she had turned and come back easily except for one or two hammered hills.

She parked the car outside the flat and when she got in she poked her head out of her first-floor window to look down at the little beast. The tiny rush of joy she felt was close to sexual and she thought she would go for a drive in the afternoon.

She bathed – more usually she would shower – and she wallowed there in a slightly ludicrous pink froth listening to Harry Chapin aching through the flat from the stereo in the lounge. She had a tall glass of Mosel Saar Ruwer Kabinet on the bathside (it was only one glass) and she let Harry's voice roll over her, slowly making her sad. She thought about her fella and gave out a little sigh. She needed Val to be back.

After her bath, Caz strolled through the flat. She was wearing an extra-large T-shirt sprayed orange and yellow and demanding *Independencia!* She had poured another cool glass of the German wine and swapped the Harry Chapin CD for Joe Cocker. When she came out of the kitchen she had a crispbread spread with peppered brie and the postcard from the Florida Keys. She picked up the phone to ring Tom MacInnes.

The DI's phone rang out in an empty room. Caz waited for an answering machine to cut in. When none did, she counted another ten rings, cut the call and dialled the nick. Joe Cocker barrelled out 'Delta Lady' while she listened to fifteen more rings. Finally, a voice answered.

'John Street.'

'Caz Flood. Is DI MacInnes there?'

'He's off-duty today.'

'I know that. Is he in?'

'What do you think?'

'Is that Bob Allen? Stop fuckin' round, Sarge.'

'OK, Flood. Putting you through.'

After two clicks, she heard Tom's voice. He sounded frail. 'Hello, Caz.'

'How about lunch?' she said softly.

'Your place or mine?' he said, just a little brighter.

Three

Tom MacInnes was waiting behind Hannington's department store; outside Donatello's and underneath a turquoise and white awning. In the summer, eight tables would be squeezed under the striped cover and with the walls of the restaurant rolled back, the smell of buttered garlic would sizzle into the street. Right now, though, the one thing the place definitely *didn't* need was cooling down.

The DI looked slightly weary. He was cold, his fleshless frame feeling the day's chill, but when Caz skipped towards him, five minutes late, he smiled genuinely at her. She was grinning, only vaguely apologetic.

'Let me guess,' the DI said. 'Parking, right?'

'This *is* Brighton, boss!'

'You could have walked from your place.'

'I'm a runner. I *hate* walking.'

They went inside. As Caz passed by the older man he touched her briefly on the shoulder. It was a quiet Friday. The place was almost empty. They took a table near the door and Caz sat with her back to the wall. When the DI suggested a whisky she nodded. Then she took out the postcard and laid it in front of him.

'This is what?'

'A postcard,' Caz said slowly. She looked up. 'From a man who likes the Florida Keys.'

A waiter had come to them, gone away and brought back two menus and two double whiskies. The DI's was with ice; Caz's was drowned in Canada Dry. The waiter had returned later with a half-litre flask of Chianti and a flat pizza-sliced serving of garlic bread, exactly as the DC had requested. Then later he brought them Tagliatelle Donatello, off-white, flecked with ham and petits pois. When the main course arrived, Tom MacInnes finally passed the postcard back to Caz. For more than ten minutes he had stared at the picture, read the message, stared at the picture again. He took a deep breath. 'From a friend of yours, right?'

'You think so, Tom?'

'A diver maybe. Someone taking in the sun.'

'But nothing to be done about it?'

'There is nothing to be done. What happens, happens.'

MacInnes stared at Caz for an extra second then looked down at his steaming dish. When he glanced up again, Caz was waiting, her first rolled forkful of pasta poised. His eyes locked into hers. They looked old but then a little hardness returned. Suddenly he grinned and reached out for his glass of red wine. He lifted it.

'To you, Detective! *Salut!*'

Caz picked up her wine glass, waved it, then drank. She shouldn't be doing this, she said. When her DI asked why, she told him about Sunday's race.

'You fit enough to win it, Flood?'

'Second, third, maybe, Tom, but I'm not racing. I'm taking DS Mason round. See if we can't drag him under forty minutes for the first time.'

'You two are sorted now?' MacInnes said.

'It's OK,' Caz said. 'Like breaking forty minutes. Not great but OK.'

'I've had a shite time at the office t'day,' the DI said.

It was supposed to be a quiet Friday but at least half a dozen extra uniforms had been told to put their hangovers on hold and turn in. New Year's Eve had brought the usual spate of broken windows, pissed-in doorways and scratched cars, but the night had started with at least five burglaries, a couple of domestics and a ram-raid in Western Road.

'I'd've said it was fairly quiet, but on top've all that we had two hit-'n'-run drinkers last night and two missing persons that we can't write off.'

'Wonderful!' Caz said. 'And I pulled Saturday thinking I'd get a light one.'

'You were nearly in today, lass.'

'Even more wonderful.'

'We rang your place. You were out.'

'I went running on the Downs. Glad I did now.'

'Don't be. One of the missing persons is a mate of yours.'

Caz stopped eating, suddenly embarrassed, as if she should be ashamed for not knowing.

'A lady called Claire Cook-Bullen. Apparently you know her, at least, according to her husband you do. He rang John Street about eleven, said they'd had a door-slammer of a row in the afternoon. She went out just after six. Told him she was going for a twelve-mile run and she'd be late.'

'She's a fair runner, sir. Into half-marathons and marathons. I think I met the husband once. Is his name David?'

'Daniel. He asked for you in person. Someone said you'd gone away for Christmas but were in Saturday. First-off he said he'd leave it until then but he rang back within five minutes and said he wanted to come in to make it official.'

'Did he say why?'

'Just that he felt bad. Jim Greaves spoke to him. Apparently he was white as a sheet and looked like he was about to throw up.'

'You said there were two walk-offs?'

MacInnes took another mouthful of wine. 'Yeah. Girl named Petula Walters. Eighteen. Went out about half nine. Told her mother she was going to a party in Shoreham, never came home. Trouble is, the mother hadn't actually asked whose party it was. The girl is probably shacked up with her boyfriend somewhere, doesn't even know people are worried. Either that, or she went up to the smoke to try out Trafalgar Square.'

'Who's on it?'

'DS Reid, Billy Tingle and Dibben.'

'Moira Dibben?'

'Thought we'd keep her busy, you know. And it won't hurt to let her work with Billy for a couple o' days.'

'So what they doing? Working out from the girl's house, friends, work-mates?'

'No other way. It's dead slow too. Looks like the mother never had a clue what her daughter did with her evenings.'

'Father?'

'Did a runner years back. Last known address was in South Wales.'

'Sounds like a lot of fun.'

'Now you know why Billy Tingle and Moira are on it! You can work with me and Bob Moore on one of the hit-and-runs. There's a bit of real investigation in there, I reckon. Should suit you down to the ground.'

'When did Bob Moore get back?' Caz asked.

'Tuesday,' the DI said. 'Told me he's looking forward to working with you again. Happy?'

'Oh, I can't wait!' Caz said. She looked like she was going to sulk, so Tom spoke again. 'The guy doesn't like women bobbies, Caz. But you've had two good scores since you started. He'll come round. He's a bit short-sighted but in the end he's a good copper. Give him a break.'

'You know me, Tom.'

'That's my problem, Flood. I know you too well.'

She ignored him and waved at a waiter, who bobbed his head and came over, wiping his hands on a napkin. She ordered a liqueur coffee. When it came she sipped it sensuously, its dark brown sweetness biting with Italian brandy. MacInnes went for another couple of Bells. When they'd finished, Caz said she was over the limit so she might as well walk up to the nick with him, take a quick look at the Cook Report. MacInnes didn't even notice the joke.

'I was hopin' you'd say that, lass. That way you get Sunday off.'

'Oh, thank you, sir!' Caz said. She tried to look pissed off but she couldn't do it. Sniffing round a few cases would shorten Friday and Saturday. Come Sunday evening they'd need a tug-of-war team to drag her out of Valerie's bed. *Then* she wouldn't want to work.

They cut through Hannington's when they left the restaurant, crossed North Street and went down through Castle Square to the Old Steine. As they were passing the Pavilion, Caz checked something out with the DI. 'Tom, you said Claire Bullen went out to do a twelve-mile run.'

'Daniel Bullen said.'

'Do we know her route?'

'He said she went to a sports centre and ran from there. Shoreham way. It'll be in the file.'

'Oh, right,' Caz said. She was wondering which sports centre and which short, sharp four-miler route there was near. Caz had run more than a few times with Claire Cook-Bullen. Claire would be blown away in an eight-hundred-metre race – she simply didn't have enough leg speed. In a 10K she'd be off the pace and at least a minute behind Caz, but in a half-marathon – like last year's IBM at Portsmouth – she could run Caz very close. She was a long long-distance runner, the further the better. In a marathon she was fifteen minutes quicker than Caz's best. If she'd had that extra bit of sheer leg speed she might've made international. She was about the same age as Caz and they had talked training regimes once or twice. Thursdays very hard, Caz had suggested to her. 'Not far, save your knees,' she'd said, 'but make every mile really hard.'

Claire had been working on sustained speed now for six months. The last time they'd met she was still doing 'four fast' every Thursday night. That was *Thursday* night. If she wanted to, Claire Cook-Bullen could be out the front door and back in half an hour, including her warm-down stretches. So what did she do for the rest of the evening?

Caz had been silent for five minutes, striding out next to the DI's tipper-tapper walk. They were turning on to Edward Street and leaning into its shallow hill when she spoke. She coughed. Then she asked the DI about the Bullens' marriage.

MacInnes shrugged. 'The husband said it was fine. Just the usual rows, he said. He said they rowed a bit about how much time she devoted to her training but that otherwise they were all right.'

'But she went out for a few hours every Thursday night?'

'Yes. And Sundays. And Tuesdays. Always from the sports centre. Monday, Wednesday, Friday she just went for an easy jog from the house. What d'you want to know for?'

'Professional jealousy, Tom. Claire Bullen was getting quicker. I was just wondering about her training schedule.'

'And ah'm a teapot!' MacInnes said.

Four

A busy-quiet Bank Holiday Friday afternoon in John Street nick meant an empty canteen, a half-full car park and door clangs that echoed down yellow corridors. The place was like a morgue. If there really were extra bodies drafted in, then every one of them was out cruising in a panda or knocking doors. It was one a.m. with daylight. Quiet.

They'd gone in the front and turned down in the general direction of the DI's office. Caz had stopped off five doors before Tom MacInnes as he walked quickly on and she had clicked into an office which was empty but still faintly hummed with the echo of earlier activity. A fax machine buzzed electricity and a single sheet of paper was slowly curling in its out-tray. On Jim Greaves' desk an ashtray still smelt of cigarette heat and his discarded dog-end. Two plastic coffee cups were upended on a brown melamine tray and a thin spill of the drink was slowly cooling, slowly congealing, waiting for the cleaning lady. Home. Shame about the ciggie smell but what the hell.

There was one note in Caz's slot, Moira Dibben asking her to get in touch. 'I'm off till Monday, Caz, but I'd really appreciate a call. Come round for a takeaway?'

There was nothing on the hit-and-runs on any of the DCs' desks and nothing in the computer room where most of the time she hung out with Moira. Caz went to Bob Moore's desk but there were no files there either. She was just about to swear when the phone pinged next to her. She had picked it up before it rang. 'Tom?'

'Come round,' he said.

The two hit-and-runs had happened in the early hours. Their one had been in West Street just after half past two. All the witnesses had been post-midnight drunk but four of them had managed to dive out of the way of a speeding Cavalier SRi. The car had come down Queen's Road at 'at least sixty and going like fuck'. It had swerved round the clock tower at the end of North Road and 'come fuckin' straight at us'. It was red, dark blue, green and black. The revellers were all from the same high street bank and the one witness with a decent view, a man of twenty-five called Roland Prout – the only one who didn't manage to jump out of the way and might actually have seen the colour – had been thrown on to the bonnet and over the top of the car. He was now in intensive care at the General with multiple fractures, serious internal injuries and severe shock. It might not yet happen but they could be looking at causing death by dangerous driving.

'There was headlight glass at the scene and rubber from the bumper, but not enough paint for Forensics to guarantee us a colour. Dark's the best bet. If it's a Cavalier, that narrows the odds down to about fifty thousand to one.'

'No one saw the number, the driver?'

'They were all pissed. One of them thought the driver was a fat guy.'

'What does that make it – thirty thousand to one?'

'If we're lucky,' MacInnes said. He picked up a Yellow Pages and passed it to Caz. '*If* it was a Cavalier.' He grinned. 'Feelin' lucky, Flood?'

Five

Most of the local car showrooms were open but their repair shops were not. It was a Bank Holiday. It seemed that Joe Public liked to spend a morning at Do It All and an afternoon trying to make a level shelf somewhere. But if he wasn't, he went out, trying to avoid old films. Like as not he'd wander into the nearest car showroom, 'just browsing' but aware that a new car now was *this year's model.* 'We do all right,' one manager said, 'but forget about the service shop. We're open for parts tomorrow but repairs don't start back till Monday.'

Caz prepared a situation summary for Saturday's and Monday's morning briefings. The best way to get the word into all the repair garages was via the foot patrols and the pandas. The local area bobbies knew who to see and what to say and they also knew which garages were likely to be iffy and which ones the CID should take a bit more of an interest in. There were more than enough bent garages to chase after – and they were just the ones they knew about.

Tom MacInnes was working on the two 'missing persons'. Neither of them were seen as vulnerables so they were low priority. The DI was going through the motions, just keeping Friday flowing. When Caz rang through to check out the other hit-and-run he was bored and testy.

'You're on the twenty-colour SRi, Flood.'

'I know that, sir. But I'm preparing something for the beats. We might as well kill two birds with one stone.'

'Give me a second.'

Caz waited, pulling out Moira's note while she counted seventeen.

The DI came back on the line. 'A Sierra, dark-coloured. Nothing but skid marks left behind. Oh, and some kid with a broken leg.'

'A kid.'

'Fifteen. On her way home from a rave party. Do you believe that?'

'Where was the accident, Tom?'

'On the A27, not far from the Albion's ground. Girl crossing the road on a zebra. Car didn't see 'em. They were both wearing dark clothes.'

'Them?'

'Girl that was hit was with a friend. Friend was older – nearly sixteen apparently. She panicked and just sat there screaming until a car stopped. She said half a dozen motors came past but they just slowed down and went round them. The drivers were probably pissed – too scared to stop. The guy who eventually helped had been drinking too, but at least he had a bit of humanity. So did the Traffic when it turned out. They took a statement off him and told him to fuck off home quick.'

'What time was this?'

'About three in the morning. The accident was about quarter to, ten to; not long after the ram-raid.'

'Not the car used?'

'No, we got that on video. Three blokes in a Range Rover.

Nicked of course. All wearing balaclavas. One of the shites waved at the cameras.'

'Who's on that one?'

'Bob Moore wanted it. But he wanted a crack at one of the hit-'n'-runs too. Must be a glutton for punishment.'

'Must want to be an inspector!' Caz said.

'Well he c'n have this seat whenever he wants it,' MacInnes said. He sounded like he meant it.

'What shall I say to the beats?' Caz said.

'Any repairs to Fords, Escorts and Sierras in particular. Anything at all done to the front end of a Vauxhall, especially the headlight. Add something about unusual customers or anyone who acts suspiciously when they call. I want every place seen twice a day for the next fortnight. And they're to go inside and look themselves. Say that.'

Caz typed out the notes for roll-call and left the sheet with the duty sergeant. As well as her Catalonian rebel T-shirt, she was wearing skin-tight black lycra bottoms with a red guardsman stripe down the outside that stopped just above a pair of Nike Airs, not her favourite shoes but OK on the street. The desk sergeant clearly didn't approve. He gave Caz a withering look but took the paperwork. Caz could have ignored him but instead she said, 'Like the treads, Bob?'

'You're joking,' the sergeant said, 'you look like Max fuckin' Wall.'

'No, I don't,' Caz said, 'I've got a much better arse.'

She belled Moira Dibben and made out like she was *incredibly* busy but yeah, how about she dropped round at half seven? Moira said that would be great, Billy was doing an extra late so she'd be at a loose end.

'D'you want to stay in or d'you fancy going out?' Caz asked.

'I need to tell you something,' Moira said slowly.

'So we stay in, then? Shall I bring a pizza?'

'Nah,' Moira said. She paused, sounding as if she really didn't fancy the pizza. 'Nah, let's go out somewhere. I think I need cheering up.'

'See you at seven thirty, then, Mo.'

'Thanks, Caz.'

Caz left the nick and walked back into town. Moira had sounded a little bit odd but Caz figured that she'd find out why in the evening. Her car was fifteen minutes over when she got to it but there was no ticket, so she said a little thank you to the sky, got in and drove off, heading for Shoreham. She was trying to think if there was a sports centre there.

The traffic was fairly light as Caz drove her MX5 along the seafront at Hove, past Portslade-by-Sea and Southwick. She was on the A259 to South Lancing with Shoreham to her left when she crossed what used to be the old chain bridge over the Adur. As she dropped down on the Lancing side, she saw some public loos and what looked like a leisure centre to her right. She turned off opposite some mud flats and a dozen or so houseboats and pulled up on gravel outside the building.

The centre was locked up. A sign on the door said Adur Outdoor Activities Centre and another quick look made it clear that wherever Claire Cook-Bullen changed for running, it wasn't here. It was just possible that Claire used the public toilets – a man would – but in winter darkness they wouldn't look the safest of places. Caz decided no, then she turned her back and jogged up to the bridge to take a look at the houseboats and the river.

Shoreham-by-Sea was a peninsula about a mile and a half long and a few precarious feet above a spring tide. Caz had the sudden thought that if global warming ever did its worst, the houseboats looked underpriced.

Running round Shoreham looked to be about a three-miler, ideal for the flat-out part of Claire's run. If there was somewhere in Southwick to get changed, Claire would've been doing five miles max. She could jog from where she left her gear, cross the bridge, hammer round the island and jog back. And there were streetlights. It was a fair bet.

Caz had an old battered briefcase in the boot of the MX5. It was long since past its sell-by date but at least the combination lock still worked. She clicked the tumblers on to 7-4-7 and flicked open the lid. Inside, in what she called her box of tricks, were various useful items – Ordnance Survey maps and some A to Zs, a couple of torches, a screech alarm and an illegal can of Mace. In a separate box she had tools – some of which were legal – a tow rope, a spare fan belt, a few fuses and a surveyor's foldable wire ladder. Right now she was after the maps.

There were two places where Claire Bullen might have changed; a community centre between North Street and Western Road, and a bit further away, Southwick Sports Centre. The sports centre was two right turns off the coast road and about a two-mile jog from the Norfolk Bridge where Caz had parked earlier. If Caz's first guess at Claire's fast workout proved to be correct, then Claire was doing seven miles rather than the bare four, but that wouldn't be surprising, distance runners always did too much. Caz felt lucky. She went straight there.

Six

Southwick Sports Centre was just off Old Barn Way. It looked typical seventies, concrete and other aggregates split by ugly steel windows. It only had the one squash court so there were less than the usual number of XR3s parked in the car park. At the back of the building there was a recreation ground with enough grass for Claire Bullen to have worked on her leg speed doing hard four-hundred reps. Not that those reps were very likely, Caz thought. Claire Bullen was old school, piling on mile after mile, typically substituting quantity for quality. Caz had been surprised when she'd agreed to even *try* some fast four-milers. Claire was a long-distance runner and most of the long-distance types Caz knew thought that speed was something you ate.

Caz had clocked the distance from the river to the sports centre on the MX5's trip meter. Car mileometers were notoriously inaccurate, but the two miles each way suggested by the Mazda made up the total of seven miles that Caz had guessed at earlier. The warm-up jog towards the bridge at Shoreham wouldn't have been the greatest, but at least it would all have been on lit roads. Evening running in the winter was never easy but, boring or not, Caz knew that Claire would have chosen something like it for safety.

She went into the reception. There was a woman in her early forties taking admission money from behind a slatted perspex screen. She wore some sort of uniform and had the air that people working around fitness sometimes have – as if just *working* there and wearing the uniform would somehow shift the pounds. Still, she had a nice face.

'Step?' the woman said. A big smile.

'Pardon?'

'Step aerobics, right? You look worked out.'

'Actually . . .' Caz fished out her warrant card. A smaller smile.

'Oh,' said the receptionist, 'you don't look like a policewoman.'

'Don't I?' Caz said innocently. 'What does one look like, then?'

The receptionist's name was Brenda Whent. She didn't usually do Thursday nights, she told Caz, but, as it happened, last night she'd had to cover for her mate. 'This Claire, she's the same build as you?'

'Yes, but she's got short dark hair.'

'And thirty years old?'

'Ish.'

'Can you give me a sec? I've a feeling she's a member here. I don't know her myself, but a woman a bit like that came through about half six yesterday. She didn't book any of the courts.'

'She wouldn't,' Caz said.

When Brenda came back she had company, another forty-something who said her name was Mrs Euston. Claire Cook-Bullen had a family membership, she explained – with Mr D. Bullen. It was cheaper that way. The manageress smiled. 'Claire runs with Worthing. She's a really good runner. If I remember, she came second in the Chichester Half-Marathon last year.'

'That sounds like Claire.'

'And she was here last night,' Mrs Euston said. 'Most Thursdays she goes for a run. She likes to get out of the centre by seven o'clock and she gets back just before eight. I think she really has a go at it, because she's always shattered when she gets back.'

The woman made a face which indicated that she thought Claire Bullen was totally deranged. Caz felt vaguely miffed. 'That's why she's good,' she said, barely hiding her sarcasm. 'It's called training.' Then she softened and managed a faint smile. 'I don't suppose you would know what car she drives?'

'No,' Euston said. She glanced at the receptionist. 'Unless it's a Metro. I vaguely remember a yellow Metro, but I wouldn't want you to take that as gospel.'

Caz nodded, then she spoke to the receptionist again. 'Last night, Brenda, were you on the gate at eight o'clock?'

'I was working all evening.'

'And you saw Claire?'

'I told you. I saw her when she came in at half past six. But if you're asking me if I saw her when she went off on this run of hers or when she came back in, then you've got me. It's far too busy in the early evening. I can't remember.'

'Not to worry,' Caz said. 'I doubt it matters much anyway. This is just routine at the moment.'

Euston coughed slightly, then she leaned into Brenda Whent's space, smiling hopefully at Caz. 'Er . . . You never said what the problem was . . .'

Caz smiled back.

'No, I didn't, did I?'

Seven

It was half past four and miserably dark. Caz had two choices – go see Daniel Cook now and rush back for a shower about six o'clock before going on to Moira's, or slope off home and have a hot bath and a stretch. The second alternative sounded much the better bet, along with the third possibility which was to say 'stuff Cook' and wait for his wife's 'Dear John' to arrive. She idly wondered what the boyfriend was like.

Daniel Cook was an OK sort of bloke, not a runner but reasonably fit. Caz was trying to remember his face. She had a vague feeling he still played Sunday park soccer or something. Really, she didn't fancy going over to see him, but in a fit of decency she thought she'd start the year off with a good deed. Cook's place, she decided, so instead of continuing along the seafront to Hove she swung left and headed for Hangleton.

The Cook-Bullens had a big, pricey-looking house which backed on to West Hove Golf Course. It looked a few years old and had a few too many bedrooms for a couple without kids, but no doubt every bedroom had an en-suite. Caz pulled up in their drive behind a black Golf GTi parked next to – *surprise!* – a yellow Metro. She grinned, immediately glad she'd driven over. So Claire Bullen was no longer a missing person, or a runaway. She was just a dirty stop-out with a bit on the side.

Caz pressed the doorbell, idly tensing and flexing her calves while she listened to some awful electronic tune. There was no answer. She pressed the bell again. Another naff tune buzzed in the hall. Then there were footsteps in the hallway, a man's outline through frosted glass. The door opened. Dan Cook, unshaven and hollow-eyed. 'Oh,' he said, 'you. Any news?'

Caz was slightly taken aback. 'News? I thought . . . Isn't Claire here?'

'You'd better come in,' he said.

They went through a hall decorated with green and gold flock wallpaper, the carpets patterned and clashing. The lounge was finished to much the same effect, as if the Cook-Bullens had bought the place off a tasteless middle-aged couple and had never bothered to redecorate. There was a large green three-piece with gilded trim, a teak nest of tables spread with slate coasters and a huge antiqued globe that Caz just knew would contain drinks. A G-Plan cabinet in one corner revealed a newish TV and a brand-new video through open doors. On its top was a framed wedding shot of Daniel and Claire. Claire was smiling.

Despite the wedding photograph, the house just didn't seem to belong to Claire Bullen. The only other allusion to her was the clutter of silver running trophies on the mantelpiece and a single photograph, Claire with two other lady runners, the threesome proudly holding up their London Marathon medals and smiling self-consciously at the camera.

'Is that the London?' Caz said, pointedly looking at the picture.

'Nineteen ninety-one,' Cook said. 'She never stops talking

about it. She was the first lady home for her running club.'

'What time did she do?' Caz asked.

'I don't know.'

'Was it sub-three hours?'

'It might've been,' Cook said. He went to the window, staring out at nothing. 'But then I wouldn't know, would I? I wasn't there.' He was close to the windowpane. He stayed there, his breath condensing on the glass, facing the darkness, his face reflecting from it. His voice faltered. 'I didn't go down to London that weekend. I don't like Claire going out every night and she knows it. Since she got serious about her training, I never see her. That's what we were rowing about. It was New Year's Eve and I thought we were going out. When she told me she was off running, I told her to fuck off and not come back.' He turned round, close to tears. 'But I never meant it. It was a heat-of-the-moment thing. Claire said that running was the most important thing in her life.'

Caz glanced away awkwardly, 'But she didn't take the car?'

'No, she left it in the drive. She usually takes it, but every now and then, when she wants to run some extra miles, she leaves it here and jogs down to Southwick with a change of clothes in a little haversack. It depends on her schedule. One of the girls usually gives her a lift back.'

Caz was on edge. She felt the need to move. If she was on duty and Cook broke down, that was just part of the job, but she was off duty and the husband of a vague friend was close to blubbering. That she didn't want. She coughed. 'Would you mind if I looked around, Dan?'

'At what?' he said.

'Anything, everything,' Caz said. 'Just while I'm thinking. Sometimes you get a feel for things by just wandering around. It helps me to ask the right questions.'

'What sort of questions?'

'I'm not sure,' Caz said. 'That's why I want to wander around.'

'D'you want a drink?' Cook said.

'Yeah, fine,' Caz said. 'I'll have whatever you're having.'

'I'm drinking vodka and black.'

'*Vodka* and black?'

'You want something different?'

'No, vodka's fine,' Caz said.

Cook went to the kitsch globe, opened it, and pulled out a bottle of Stolichnaya and two tall, thin glasses. While he poured, Caz asked him if he knew any of Claire's running routes.

'I didn't want to know,' he said. 'So I never asked.' He waved a bottle of cordial at her. 'How much black?'

'Same again,' Caz said.

'So you don't know where Claire ran last night?' Caz asked after the first sip of her drink. She could feel the vodka in her stomach and a rush of the fruitiness in her nose.

'To Southwick. The sports centre.'

'But you don't know the exact route.'

'No, I don't,' Cook said. He looked grim. 'Before last night, it didn't matter all that much. I didn't give a shit where she went.'

Caz took a little more of her drink. The blackcurrant cordial was so strong that she was able to make it stick to the sides of the glass as she swirled the purple gently. It was bad news, another one of those deadly 'get you pissed while you're not looking' drinks. Dan Cook might want to drink himself into a stupor but Caz didn't. She suggested tea.

'And would you mind if I popped upstairs while you make it, Dan? Is that OK?'

'Is this your little wander?'

'If you like.'

Cook swallowed the rest of his vodka. 'Our bedroom is at the front,' he said. 'Claire's got a little office in the room above the front door.'

'I'll take a quick look up there, then,' Caz said. She was still hesitant, though she wasn't really sure why. She muttered a vague little 'Yes?' still looking for some sort of permission to pry.

'If you keep asking, you'll never get anything done,' Cook said, digging out a smile from his reserves. 'Off you go. I'll give you a shout when the tea is mashed.'

Eight

Upstairs there was a lot more of the same décor, almost everything floral, green-brown bland, mismatched and depressing. All the paintwork was a dull four-year-old cream and the lampshades looked like they'd been rescued from a late fifties Wimpey. Downstairs, Caz had thought how nothing of Claire Bullen showed in the furnishings. Now she realised that there was nothing here that echoed Daniel either.

She poked her head around the toilet door to more of the same. The loo seat lid had a pink ribbed cotton cover that matched the pedestal and bath mats. Even the spare loo roll was covered by the skirt of a plastic doll-dancer who stared maniacally with tiny, beady eyes. Arggh!

The larger back bedroom presumably had a pleasant open view over the links but right now the browny curtains were pulled together. Caz peaked through, looking down on to a long manicured garden lit by the house lights and a Victorian streetlamp. Unbelievably, as Caz got used to the half-darkness, she could see a little wishing-well and a scattering of garden gnomes circling a red and white spotted concrete mushroom. A gnome on his own, presumably a loner or with BO, was sitting on the edge of a goldfish pond patiently fishing, his little Noddy cap dashingly askew. She did not believe this!

The room itself was fitted out as a single, with older, maybe just post-war furniture that smelled of almond polish and mothballs. There was nothing anywhere – inside a drawer, behind a door, under the bed or on top of the wardrobe. Caz took another look out of the window, shook her head and went out on to the landing.

The main bedroom was about fifteen by eighteen, menopausally pink and frilly, with the only plain carpet in the house, a deep beige pile. The cupboards down one wall looked builder-fitted, the only things in the room that were post-Beatles. Again, everything was empty, nothing in the drawers or cupboards except dust and the occasional dead fly. In the en-suite, an extra-length pink bath was dry, spotless and unused. There were two toothbrushes in a sparkling glass and a loofah, very dry, was balanced across the bath taps. As Caz left the room, she was frowning.

The next room was Daniel's. It had a dark, man's smell, the bed was half made and there were a few clothes that had been pulled together in a hasty pile before being kicked into a corner. There was an ordinary chest of drawers and a tall wardrobe, matching, with the same yellow-brownish plastic veneer, either top-end MFI or bin-end Habitat. The wardrobe contained three suits, a dozen shirts and a few ties, all hanging above a stack of jumpers, and a couple of pairs of shoes. It was very ordinary. The suit pockets were empty.

Some time in the recent past, the walls had been stripped for decorating, and even more recently it looked like Dan Cook had given up on the idea and slapped on some emulsion for the time being. On the wall by the single bed there was a brown-framed picture of a football team kitted out in green, and next to that a pennant, also green. The boys had been beaten Sunday

League cup finalists, 1990–91. Well, bully for them.

Caz looked for Daniel Cook on the team photograph. He was in the front row with a massive grin across his face, a white football plonked between his boots. She looked at the pennant then suddenly back at the team shot. The men were in classic pose, hands on knees, staring sternly at the camera, but Dan Cook, the long-haired ginger guy next to him and a dark-haired heavyweight the other side were less serious. Their arms were crossed, their hands on each other's knee. No wonder they were grinning! Real chaps, eh? Caz had no doubt they thought it was *terribly* funny. They probably did moonies out of the minibus window on the way back from a game too.

Dan Cook had got rid of the carpet during his decorating phase. On the bare boards to the side of the bed was a small portable TV balanced on a chair and at the other side was a three-shelf bookcase half filled with a couple of dozen books. *The Rise and Fall of the Third Reich* was on the same shelf as *The Hite Report* and *The Joy of Sex*, these squeezed in next to *The SAS Survival Guide*. On top of the bookcase was a pile of *Guns 'n' Ammo* and a stack of Terry Pratchett paperbacks. That figured.

Under Dan Cook's pillow were the latest two copies of *Playboy*. The heavier-duty stuff that Caz looked for was shoved under the mattress, not exactly hidden, just put away where Claire Cook-Bullen could never say that she had found it accidentally. Caz felt slightly annoyed. If Claire and her husband were so completely separate, why did they bother to stay together? Why not just make the break, take the pain and get on with their lives as newly detached thirty-somethings?

'Tea'll be two minutes!' Dan Cook shouted up the stairs.

Caz looked at the room, a lad's pad, and shouted back that she was just coming.

It was a white lie but who cared? She went into Claire's room.

Nine

Claire Bullen's room was cold and white. A narrow divan bed was covered with a white bedspread and in the room's corner, at the head of the bed, above the swell of the single pillow, was a spray of white cushions, laid gently against the wall. The floor's bare boards were glossed white and there was a white fluffed rug at the bedside.

The walls were white, stark white, layered emulsion over anaglypta, roller-spread so many times that the ripples and folds of the paper were now scarcely suggestions of the original pattern. A cheap desk of white melamine was jammed between the head of the bed and Claire's only other item of furniture, a white cupboard with silver handles, one door firmly blocked by the body of the desk. There was no chair, but when Caz opened the other wardrobe door, she found a white stool tucked neatly away beneath the hanging clothes, all casual, all soft, and every item either colourless white or relentless black.

The desk top, more bare white, was spotless, wiped clean, its only blemish a chip in one corner carefully replaced but leaving a triangular scar. There were two silver-handled drawers in each pedestal and the first one stuttered as Caz tried to open it. When she pulled a little harder, it opened a couple of inches. Inside, pens and pencils, scissors, Blu-Tack, drawing pins, a geometry set, an assortment of office tools. She felt vaguely unnerved and intrigued, but this was not the time to dwell on her feelings. Cook was about to call her downstairs so she'd have to go. There was always later. Shrugging her shoulders, she left the other drawers and went out on to the landing. As she emerged from Claire's clinical room, Daniel called up from below. She didn't bother to reply. Instead she showed herself at the top of the stairs, light from the open bathroom at her back. He was in the hall, looking up. She smiled.

'Could you turn off the bathroom light?' he said.

Over the tea, Caz asked about their marriage. This wasn't very official, she explained, but could Claire have stayed out deliberately or, maybe! – she sipped her tea – she was sorry to ask, but could she have left him for somebody else?

'No,' Cook said.

Caz was thinking of the separate rooms upstairs, the distinct, opposed personalities. 'How can you be so sure?' she said.

'We don't – can't – have that kind of problem,' Cook said heavily. 'Claire and I, we—' He put down his cup. Caz looked up. 'My, we . . .'

He stopped.

'You have separate bedrooms, Dan.'

'We always have had.'

'Always?'

'Yes. Look, the bedrooms are not important. I just want you to find Claire and bring her back. Is that too much to ask?'

'It doesn't work like that, Dan.'

'What d'you mean?'

'Claire's been gone twenty-two hours. If you allow that she

wasn't due back until ten or eleven o'clock, then she's only been missing *eighteen* hours. You said yourself that you'd had a big row. In official terms, Claire is not yet considered as a missing person. The police won't be looking for her yet, there's no reason. If we took every short-term disappearance seriously we'd be doing nothing else.'

'But you're here.'

'Because I know you and I know Claire.'

'But what if something's happened?'

'We've no reason to think it has, Dan. Claire is,what, twenty-eight, fit and healthy. She's intelligent. The two of you had a barney, she went off in a huff and she's stopped out to teach you a lesson. Believe me, we get this sort of thing all the time.'

'She might have been hit by a car. She could be lying in a ditch somewhere right now.'

'Yes, Dan. But she could also be sleeping off a bottle of wine or pouring out her troubles to her best friend over the kitchen table.'

Caz was thinking loosely something on the lines of 'Of course, she could be screwing the arse off her lover' as Daniel continued, telling her that Claire didn't have friends, she had never stayed out – ever – and that, he had to say it again, he *knew* she wouldn't have gone off with another man. Caz was hardly listening. Dan Cook's voice rambled up and down, the meaning being attended to by one of her mental lieutenants. There was a sudden, vivid, almost pornographic flash of Claire having sex. She was grinning, standing against something metal, a shadow moving over her, her eyes glinting . . .

'What?' Caz said.

'I said Claire and I have an understanding. I know – my . . .'

Caz dragged herself back, leaving Claire. As she did so,

the horniness of the image rushed away to something dark and sick. She shuddered.

Caz heard herself starting the year off with a mistake. 'I shouldn't . . .' she began. She stopped and looked at Daniel Cook. He looked grey and desperate. 'All I can say is, I'll see what I can find out.' There was a slight lift in his face. 'I'll see if I can persuade my boss to give me a bit of time to chase things up, but I can't promise much.'

'Just find her,' Cook said.

Caz looked at him again. Everything about him was limp and pathetic. The best she could say was, 'No promises, Dan.' Suddenly she wanted out of there. The grief she got from work was bad enough, but doing a 'foreigner' like this was close to stupid. If she had liked Dan Cook it might have been easier. She thought of the boys in the team minibus; the rugby songs on the way back from an away game; the smell of spilled Carlsbergs. There was this desperate urge to say something cruel and walk away from Daniel Cook. When she said, 'I'll do my best, Dan,' she knew then that she would regret it.

Ten

When Caz left Daniel Cook, she had to force herself to drive slowly away and not rush the MX5 up through the gears. She was so keen to get out of his house that the urge disturbed her, the exact emotion, the word for it, elusive. The place, its smell, its personality made her feel uncomfortable and she didn't know why.

She kept her speed down as she drove towards Hove and thought about the oddness of their place, the separateness of Claire and Daniel's lives, their room statements. He looked like a not uncommon man-boy, never fully matured yet functioning quite well in the adult world. Despite his good looks, dark, chunky, brown eyes, he seemed awkward, shy maybe, somehow lost. It didn't surprise Caz that he was desperate to find Claire; without her he probably didn't have a clue.

The scruffy industrial bits and pieces of Portslade-by-Sea went by on her right – definitely not the shots for postcards from the south coast – then she buzzed past the fat statue of Queen Victoria on her left. Almost home, she began to cheer up. She forgot about the Cook-Bullens and thought instead about a nice hot bath and an evening getting slowly pissed with Moira. When she pulled up outside her flat she suddenly felt warm.

She was short of time so she flicked on the taps, shot through to the kitchen, put just enough water in the kettle to boil and went through to the lounge. There was enough time to swap Joe Cocker for *Hot Rocks 2* then she went back to make an overstrong black coffee to take into the bathroom. She fancied a work-out but there was no time. She stripped while 'Jumpin' Jack Flash' finished and just managed a few ballistic stretches to 'Street-Fighting Man' while pouring pink bubble bath into the tap-fall. When she eased into the water she was forced to grin. It's impossible to be depressed sitting in a bath of Matey.

She felt even better once she climbed out of the bath water, better still as she rubbed herself pink with a towel, and not far off in a really good mood by the time she had sorted out her clothes and got dressed. When she left the flat, she was wearing her white Asics trainers, anti-fit Joe Bloggs jeans and a soft blue cotton shirt; but it was the long-sleeved loose-necked teddy underneath it all that made her feel so special. The white silk next to her talcumed skin felt gorgeous. Her hair she combed straight, parted slightly left of centre and thrown behind her shoulders. She was late, so stuff make-up. All *right*!

She got to Moira's smack on half past seven. The front door was open and Mo bawled, 'Come through!' before she could ring the bell. She was watching a video of *EastEnders*, eating Frazzles and drinking Fitou.

'Two minutes!' she said. 'This is just finishing. Have a glass of wine.'

Caz winced, filled the waiting glass, and sat down. On the TV, the Mitchell brothers were planning villainy of some sort in their garage. Their lock-up was built into the supports of a railway bridge but as far as Caz knew, you never heard passing trains. The brothers were meant to look hard, but Caz wondered if the programme's producer knew that they dressed and wore their hair in the uniform of the London gay scene. She thought idly about bent garages and the hit-and-runs.

'So,' Moira said. It was two or so minutes later but it felt like fifteen. 'Which brother do you fancy, Grant or the other one?'

'Neither,' Caz said. 'One's a nutter, the other one's fat.'

'Phil's not fat, he's cuddly.'

'He's fat.'

'Cuddly.'

Caz stood up, ready to leave. 'OK, Mo,' she said. She finished her wine. 'You're right, Phil Mitchell is cuddly.' She nodded towards the door. 'And Cyril Smith is just carrying a few pounds.'

Moira blanked her. 'Indian or Chinese?' she said.

Caz chose Indian. Moira chose the restaurant. It was a small place in Richmond Road with a sign outside, white light shining through blue perspex, declaring itself the Eastern Dream Tandoori. On the door a sign said, 'We Serve Carlsberg!'

'Come here a lot?' Caz asked.

'Me and Billy.'

Caz groaned.

There were plenty of tables free and they sat down to a dish of curried nibbles and a spotless tablecloth. A waiter hovered. 'Two laga?' Caz nodded and smiled.

'Cobbla and Carslsburr?'

'Cobra,' Caz said. She glanced at Moira. 'Two.'

The waiter dipped his head. 'Right off!'

'What's wrong with Carlsberg?' Moira said without looking up from the menu.

'What's wrong with Cobra?' Caz said.

'It's foreign!'

'Yer in a friggin' Indian restaurant, Mo.'

Moira was muttering, deciding between onion bhaji and aloo gobi. 'Don't mean I have t'drink their beer.'

'Why not?'

'Well, they're Indian – Pakistani, whatever. How'd they know how to make beer?'

Caz looked across. Moira looked up. She wasn't joking.

'Oh, give me strength!' Caz sighed just as the waiter returned.

They had poppadums, too many, freshly flashed in hot oil and served with an array of chutneys and raita. For starters, Caz had a taste of tandoori chicken, Moira had prawn boona. It was while they waited for their main courses that Moira told Caz she was three weeks late and worried. It was four and a half weeks since Moira had been with a guy who wouldn't take no for an answer. She had said nothing to Billy. She looked at Caz. What was she going to do?

'Have you been late before?'

'I'm *never* late, Caz.'

'Have you done a test?'

'I was too scared.'

'And what are you going to do?'

'Do?'

'If you're pregnant, Mo. What are you going to do?'

Moira crunched a mouthful of poppadum. 'I don't know, Caz,' she said. She cracked another wafer in half. 'I thought I'd talk to you . . .'

'Oh, great! Who am I, Claire Rayner?'

'It was just . . . well, you were there, Caz.'

'I was?'

'I mean, if it's not Billy's then it's Peter Mason's.'

'Oh, Christ, Moira. Why couldn't you just keep your knees together?'

'You know why, Caz.'

Caz softened. 'Yeah, OK, Mo. We'll work something out.'

Caz's Chicken Tikka Masala wasn't exactly adventurous. She skipped the rice and went for nan bread instead, dipping it into the sauce as she talked to Moira. Mo had ordered Lamb Jalfreezy, way too hot for Caz but apparently no problem to her mate.

Caz had to ask, but it *could* be Billy's, right? They *were* actually at it? Oh, yes, Moira told her – the night they'd got back from Southampton. Billy had been trying hard for a couple of weeks. That night she let him. She thought it was some kind of compensation, you know . . .

'You haven't said anything to Billy about Pete Mason?'

'Shit, no. Billy'd crack up.'

'Leave it that way.'

'But if I'm pregs, Caz, I'll have to talk to him.'

'And say what?'

'Well, I can hardly just . . .'

Caz pointed at Moira's glass. 'You want another one of those?'

'Why not?' Moira said.

Caz waved at a waiter. When she caught his eye, she raised the glass and held up a single finger.

Moira narrowed her eyes. 'Aren't you having another one?'

'I'm driving, Mo. And I thought you said this lot couldn't make beer?'

Moira sat up. 'I did. So why can't I have a Carlsberg?'

'*That's* beer?'

'It's closer than Cobbla,' Moira said.
'That's Albert Pinhead's fault,' Caz said flatly.
'What?'
'Looks like you're getting food delusions already.'

Eleven

Caz was in for eight fifteen the following morning, a quarter of an hour before the average Saturday start time, and three-quarters of an hour after Tom MacInnes. She had gone for an easy run at seven o'clock, nothing special, just a comfortable four-miler to start paying back the calories from last night's Indian.

The canteen was quiet and cold. Once the bodies arrived on shift and filled half the tables, it would be its normal smoke-ridden, back-chatting self, but now it was slightly 'cold grease', maybe a little fusty.

She grabbed half a dozen coffees and a wodge of sugar sachets, paid up and went up the back stairs to the computer rooms. She was still a touch early. As she came in, Bob Reid was just coming out, still the only detective to surface.

'Morning, Flood!' he said, too bright for a Saturday.

'Morning, Sarge,' Caz said, close to pleasantly.

Without asking, he took one of the drinks.

'Like a coffee, would you?' Caz said. The sarcasm was laid on with a trowel but wasted on Reid's disappearing back.

'There's a note on your desk,' he shouted back. Then a fit of remorse caught him. He half turned, raising the plastic cup. 'Oh, and thanks for the drink, Flood.'

'You're welcome,' Caz said. She grinned and walked backwards into the War Room.

The note was from Moira. 'Can we go out about half twelve?' By 'out', Moira meant to the chemist's. She had asked last night, desperately trying to make a joke of it, but aching for Caz to say yes. Caz had said, 'Ring me in the morning and we'll sort it out.' She didn't mind being moral support, but she thought the whole thing silly. It was a bit like a bloke being too embarrassed to buy condoms.

Caz crumpled the note up before binning it. 'Bloody hell, Moira. You *must* be uptight.' She did that just as the rabble bundled in, dirty-joking through the flapped double doors, led by Bob Saint. No Greavsie. Saint saw her straight away and spoke with a massive stupid grin.

'Fuh-lood!' he said, his arms out. 'We wuz just talking about you. Fancy going halves on a baby?'

'Yeah, sure, Bob,' Caz said. She lifted from the desk, waving the coffees at the crowd, not even a flicker in her face. She managed a tight little smile. 'Good idea,' she said sweetly. 'I'll get back to you next time I've got forty-five seconds spare.'

She offered out the tray and the coffees were gone in two seconds flat. She flicked her hips just enough, turned away and leered back over her shoulder, just for Saint. 'Nah, Bob. Let's make it a minute,' she said.

She was still smiling.

For the others she said, 'That way we can do it twice.'

It looked like being an average day.

Twelve

Bob Moore came through just before nine. Caz wasn't surprised to know that the DI had crawled in, but DS Moore was another matter – he wasn't exactly renowned for devotion to duty. After a second's double take, Caz put it down to 'course fever'. Maybe some super had given the DS delusions of grandeur. Maybe he *did* fancy the DI's job.

'Flood,' Moore said, leaving the ground rules to her.

'Hi, Sarge. How was the course?'

'Brilliant!' Moore said. 'What I don't know about scene of crimes . . .'

'Postage stamp?' Caz suggested.

'Gnat's dick.'

'That good, eh?'

'*That* good,' the sergeant said brightly. He was full of himself. Caz thought he might even have lost a few pounds.

DI MacInnes had decided to pull the two hit-and-run investigations together. Moore told Caz that really, it was the sensible thing to do, as most of the investigations could work in parallel. Caz said nothing.

'So, it's me and you, Flood. Monday we get Nick Berry and Julie Jones. That sound all right to you?'

'Sounds great, Sarge,' Caz said. Maybe it really *was* a new year.

Moore continued, 'The DI wants t'keep his dick in on all three investigations. It's the wrong car but he's not convinced that the hit-and-run up by the Albion isn't connected to the ram-raid in town. He wants us to concentrate on the two drive-offs while he has another look at the video of the Range Rover gang. I've already seen it. Some shit gave us the finger.'

'I heard,' Caz said.

'You what?'

'The DI mentioned it yesterday, Sarge.'

'Fuckin' charmin'!' Moore grunted. 'Why didn't you say, Flood?'

'Sorry, Sarge,' Caz said meekly, 'I was just being polite.' She smiled, a halfway gesture, but she couldn't help thinking, why didn't *MacInnes* say? This little awkwardness had been avoidable. Maybe he forgot.

Bob Moore shook his head. He looked like he wasn't sure whether to be pissed off or not. He dropped it. 'The foot soldiers and the pandas will be clocking the repair shops already, Bob Allen put the word out at parade this morning.' He scratched his belly. 'But not many are going to be open over the holiday. We might have to wait till Monday before we really get moving.'

'So what's on today, Sarge?'

'We go talk to the victims. They're both still in dock.'

Caz asked if they'd be coming back to the nick for lunchtime.

'Yeah, why?'

'Oh, nowt, Sarge. It's just that I'm supposed to be meeting Moira Dibben for a coffee.'

'We should be back in for twelve, Flood. Tell her half past. No, make an allowance for slack. Tell her one o'clock.'

Caz said thank you with a soft, controlled voice.

'Right!' Moore said sharply, puting a lid on it. 'My motor in ten minutes. One phone call and I'll be with you.'

'One each!' Caz said.

He was gone before she'd finished dialling Moira.

They left in Bob Moore's Sierra but went the long way round, heading up the A23. Before Caz had the chance to ask, the sergeant grunted, 'Wanna get my *Sporting Life*. Local shop . . .'

They stopped in a litter-strewn street, the few unopened shops hidden behind wire grilles. Moore got out, went into a newsagent's and came out with his newspapers and two bars of chocolate. As he lumped into his seat he grunted again.

'Say what you like about Pakis, Flood, but they never miss a trick. Patel was open at half five this morning and he never forgets anything.' He had placed two 'picnics' on the dash. 'One of those is yours,' he said. Caz looked at the chocolate. It was another ten seconds on her race time tomorrow but what the hell, if Moore could try, so could she. 'Cheers, Sarge,' she said.

They turned right down Viaduct Road, into a massive chamber of dark, dirty brick, sixty or seventy yards wide and fifty feet high. When Caz had been on the beat, the place had always given her the creeps. Even now, isolated from it, drifting through it in the car, she could still manage to make herself feel claustrophobic. They were effectively inside a bridge but her disquiet always made her feel slightly ridiculous. The space beneath the viaduct was like a cathedral. It was a hang-out for kids and winos at night and not the sort of place to wait about in, but why such a huge chamber should give her a sense of foreboding, she had no idea. She'd been *pot-holing* once, for Christ's sake! 'I hate this place!' she hissed.

'Knee-tremble alley?'

'It gives me the creeps.'

'I just worry about the creeps behind the pillars,' Moore said.

They took a couple of right and lefts, cruised along Elm Grove while they finished their chocolate, then a couple of turns got them into the hospital grounds. Moore parked in a slot marked DOCTOR and they went inside, Moore striding up to reception and Caz dawdling behind. She was looking at a display of florist's flowers when she noticed a sad, lost-looking man dressed in pyjamas and an ancient dressing gown. He was unbelievably thin, in some sort of wheeled chair with dark green vinyl seating. For the briefest of seconds he caught Caz's eye. He looked so lonely, Caz broke away, feeling slightly ashamed and taking a sudden intense interest in something over there.

After a couple of minutes, Moore came back.

'Prout is still in intensive care but he's awake. The girl is up on Orthopaedic Two. She's going home this morning, but we can see her. We'll leave Prout until later, he won't be rushing off.'

Thirteen

Jenny Fullerton was sitting up in bed, bright as a button, talking across the aisle to an old man with a grey face and thin silver hair. She was flushed with optimism, her cheeks tinted red and her blue eyes darting as she cracked rude jokes. She had a gold stud embedded in her nose.

'Ay-up!' she said, spotting them at the door. 'Piglets!' The old man chuckled, then winced with pain. She giggled. 'Hey, George! You watch that circumcision!'

Caz stopped just inside the door when Moore did, counting beds to be sure. They needn't have bothered.

'Stop playing with yer dick!' the girl shouted. 'I'm over 'ere!'

As they walked up the old man muttered, to no one in particular, 'It's a *hip replacement*, not a circumcision. It's a hip replacement . . .'

They arrived at Fullerton's bed. As they did so, she leaned out and around them, pursing her lips at the old man. 'We still on for tonight, George, yeah?' She winked and sat back, grinning at Caz. 'He's a sex fiend, you know; an animal. He can't get enough.'

Bob Moore was unmoved. He went formal. 'Jenny Fullerton?'

The girl threw back the bedclothes, revealing a plaster-cast and a nice line in black knickers. She trumpeted, 'Ta-rah!' She had NKOTB green-penned in 3-D all the way up her immobilised thigh.

Caz nodded. 'You're feeling OK, then?'

'Brill!'

Moore smiled. 'Good,' he said. 'Can we talk about Thursday night?'

'Fire away, mate.'

Moore stepped back and Caz took out her pocket book. 'It's Jenny, yeah? Can I have your full name?'

Jennifer Edwina Fullerton was a week off her fifteenth birthday, doing GCSEs at school (all right, not fantastic), and was going to do a B-TEC in Leisure Management at college rather than A levels.

'I'm the first one in our family ever to finish school and my mam wants me to do A levels and go to university. I told her, though, I want to manage a sports centre. I don't need to go to uni for that.'

She had been coming home with her mate. They were in a hurry. She had promised her mother she'd be home for two o'clock and it was half past already.

'We were just coming up to the top road and I was just ahead of Clare. We were, like, running up a side street. Just before I got to the road, some big motor went through, really belting. I only half saw it. I didn't notice the make, except it was big – like a Shogun or somethink. Then the car that hit me came. 'Cos I was attracted by the first car I didn't think. I ran straight in front. He swerved. I don't know how he managed to miss me, but he must have been a fucking good driver. I just sort of ran into the back of the car by the back wheel. I kind of spun round and ended up lying on the floor. When Clare came up I tried to get up and my leg just sort of went. There was this like "scrunk" sound and I fell back down. Until then it hadn't hurt.'

'Did you see the car that hit you?'

'No. He was like, *racing* the other car, the big one. Like I said, I was attracted by the first one and I wasn't looking.'

'You said you ran into the car by the back wheel . . .'

'Yeah.'

'So you must have seen it, the wheel, the back of the car.'

Jenny looked faintly annoyed. 'Have *you* ever been knocked down?'

Caz was taken slightly aback. 'Yes, as it happens.'

'Well you know what it's like, then,' Jenny said. 'Everythink sort of stopped. I was still thinking about the first car. These lights were like right on top of me and I thought. "Oh, fuck!" I suddenly felt *really* stupid. Then I thought, "Oh, I'm going to be run over." Then, when he kind of slewed round me, I thought, "Oh, wow, he's gonna miss me," then I thought, "Oh, not quite, I'm still going to get whacked." It's not frightening, you know. It's like it's already happened. Like a film.'

Caz was understanding. When she spoke again, she spoke slowly. 'OK, Jenny. No one's trying to give you a hard time. We'd like to find the driver of the car that knocked you down, that's all. We're just trying to make sure that you've thought of everything. If you'll—'

Sergeant Moore cut in suddenly, leaning in from behind Caz. 'Leave it out now, Flood. The kid's stressed.'

'I was just—'

'She's had *enough*, Flood!'

'That's about right,' Fullerton said. 'Your boss is bang on. I don't *know* anythink. Like I told you, the accident was all dreamy. If I've gotta guess what 'it me, it was a Ford – an Escort or a Sierra – but really, I don't care. It was just one of those things, you know?'

Fourteen

Sergeant Moore led the way out of the orthopaedic ward, his body language not offering his DC the chance to talk. Caz was more than a bit cheesed off. She knew enough to know that with the right kind of help Jenny Fullerton could have remembered more. There was uptight and uptight but the Fullerton girl was hardly bleeding from the ears.

The ICU was back down a flight of stairs and Moore was still a step ahead of her. Caz paused to speak but he moved on quickly. She let it go. By the time her sergeant was speaking to the ward sister she had relaxed again. It wasn't worth the aggro.

The sister was smart and confident, dark-eyed with dark brown hair bunned up under a white starched cap. She had that peculiar, superior, all-knowing air that calmed patients and disarmed coppers. She was insisting that Roland Prout was still vulnerable.

'And when I say five minutes, that is what I mean.'

She smiled at Sergeant Moore. It was a smile that said 'I'm stronger than you if push comes to shove.'

They went into a room with just two beds. One was empty, the other was filled with the wired up, drip-fixed, electrically monitored figure of Prout. The apparatus surrounding his body made Caz think bizarrely of Meccano sets and discarded puppets. To add to his troubles, Prout had a broken jaw. When he spoke to them it was through wired-together teeth.

'CID?'

'I'm DS Moore. This is DC Flood.'

'WDC.'

'We just say DC.'

Prout grunted and flicked his eyes at his restraints. Caz tried to imagine his pain; the worst kind, the all-over dull burn that denied any comfort. It was depressing just looking at him. Bob Moore spoke.

'Mr Prout, Roland. We won't disturb you for long. I just want to ask you a few questions. Where we can, we'll try to make them yes-no answers, all right?'

Prout ugged.

'Full name is Roland Vincent Prout?'

'Es.'

'You work at Barclays Bank?'

'Es. Com-buters.'

'Five years?'

'Es. Straight from college.'

'The accident . . .'

'Es?'

'What were you doing? On your way home from a night out?'

'New Year's Ee party.'

'New Year's Eve?'

'Ee.'

Moore left it. 'The car that hit you. Can you remember anything about it?'

'No.' It sounded bitter.

'Anything at all. The colour? The make? The driver?'

'No.' Prout paused. 'Was – in – Keen's – Road. Headlights full beam.'

'Queen's Road? The car's headlights were on full beam. You couldn't see anything?'

Prout nodded.

'Your friends, your colleagues? They thought the car might have been an SRi?'

'Could've bin anything. Could'n see . . .'

The DS wasn't overjoyed. He took a slow, deep breath before he spoke again. 'Can you tell us *anything*, Mr Prout?'

Prout made a deep, aching sound then gestured them to come closer. All his movements seemed deliberate, as if he was avoiding the risk of pain. Moore leaned towards him. Prout waved again and he leaned even closer, like a confessor to a dying man. Caz edged in behind, listening. Prout's voice was breathy, almost angry. He whispered at the DS. 'It's Roly,' he said. There was an odd look in his eyes. 'My name is Roly. As in Poly.'

Moore pulled quickly back. 'That's it?'

'That's it.'

Prout had obvious difficulty controlling all his facial muscles and spittle that had been building in front of his lower teeth now frothed out from behind his lips. He looked almost ashamed. Caz pulled a tissue from a pocket and offered to dab it away. He nodded his gratitude. With her eyes, she said 'no problem' and dabbed his chin. She felt him stiffen, then he relaxed. Then he whispered something. Caz couldn't quite hear, so she leaned in like Sergeant Moore. Roly's breath was slightly tart. This time she felt the little laugh in his whisper.

'I suppose,' he said, 'that a fuck is out of the question?'

The joke wasn't a new one but it was so unexpected, Caz didn't move. Then she recovered. Prout was grinning. She caught his eye and whispered back, 'Is that me?'

Her face flashed teeth, 'Or did you mean the sergeant?'

'Time to go, Flood,' Moore said.

Fifteen

The DS didn't say a word, either as they left the ward or as they strode towards his illegally parked car. Caz had the feeling that his mind was racing, that he was trying to work something out. She had the impression that his neck and ears were redder than usual but she wasn't sure.

She was at the passenger door when he went to open his. His head moved back slightly as if his thoughts had finally clicked into place.

'Right, then, Flood!' he said.

He drifted out of the hospital grounds slowly, driving deliberately, with that excess care that means 'let's chat'. He seemed to think that Jenny Fullerton was a dead end but that 'this Roland Pratt' was sitting on something. 'An' I don't mean his fuckin' bedpan . . .'

'So what's next, Sarge?'

'I suppose we'll have to talk to Fullerton's mate, the screamer. She lives out Shoreham way. We're going to have t'talk to all Prout's drinking buddies, whether we like it or not. They sound like a bunch of chinless wankers. They're all from Barclays so our best bet will be to interview them at the bank on Monday. You c'n do that. I'll see the girl.'

'Monday?'

'Yeah, Monday. Monday's soon enough.'

They came to a three-way junction just south of the hospital. Moore took the left-hand fork, a bus route that would take them in the direction of Brighton Marina.

'You in a hurry t'get back, Flood?'

'Not particularly, Sarge. Long as I'm back fer one.'

'Coffee then,' he said.

Moore knew an Italian restaurant down at the marina. A huge place, he told her, fancy enough to be a nightclub. He could get coffee there.

'Will they be open?' Caz asked.

'I said I can get coffee there.'

She left it.

They sat near a huge window waiting for cappuccinos. Moore seemed different. As yet, Caz hadn't figured *what* was different about him, but he was different. Outside, they could see the neat sea surrounding the private moorings, lapping against mainly empty berths. A bit of a wind was picking up and the glass calm of the harbour had been shattered, little patterns beginning in the water. A solitary white boat bobbed against corked ropes, looking slightly annoyed.

'Tom MacInnes says you did well on the Burke case, Flood.'

'OK, I guess.'

'He says I should try a bit harder with you.'

'It's a thought.'

'He thinks women coppers are useful. He doesn't think they should all be shipped off to Child Protection.'

'Child Protection's important.'

'D'you want t'do it?'

'No.'

'Not that important, then?'

'I just don't think it's me, Sarge. I don't know how I'd handle it.'

The coffees came. Froth had been spilled into Caz's saucer.

'I heard about that ruck you had with the DS in Southampton.'

'That's sorted now, Sarge. I just overreacted is all.'

'Like me and women coppers?'

'If you say so, Sarge.'

Moore sipped at his cappuccino. A little brown froth stayed on his upper lip. He tried again.

'The DI says I should try, Flood. So I'll try. How about starting today? New year, new broom? Worth a crack?'

Caz didn't believe a word Bob Moore was saying but she had nothing to lose. She smiled. She could lie with the best of them.

'I think it's a great idea, Sarge.' She stirred half a sachet of brown sugar into her coffee.

'You'll lose the froth!' Moore said.

Caz smiled. 'There's always more froth.'

Sixteen

On the way back to the nick, Bob Moore told Caz he was spinning plates. As well as his input on the two hit-and-runs he had a few old cases open and an ongoing investigation into organised burglary.

'There was an inspector on my course. He said that the Met have got this new targeting strategy. It's based on the old eighty-twenty idea. A few crims are responsible for a lot of crimes. The idea is to focus on them, and take them off the street. Stop wasting time on the tossers, the one-off chancers – they'll fuck up anyway. The crime stats are down to these nine-to-five villains. The idea is to nip their careers in the bud.'

'If you're that busy, Sarge, why take on the ram-raid as well?'

'Why not?'

'Well, you just said you've got a lot of plates to keep up.'

'Did I?'

'You did.'

'I just don't like the fuckers, and like this inspector said, one arrest clears up a lot of outstandings. You've got at least one nicked car, usually two, criminal damage, aggravated burglary and conspiracy to rob. Not only that, but some of these teams have baseball bats in back so we can throw in "offensive weapons" too.'

'I take the point.'

'They're fucking *scum*, Flood. They don't give a shit. It's money for drugs, whatever. I told you? One of the shites gave the finger to a security camera?'

'You said.'

'I'd like to snap the fucker's finger off, then get the little twat to eat it.'

'You don't approve then?'

Moore's face was flushed. He was staring at the road a little too hard. 'Ha bloody ha, Flood.' He glanced at her. 'No, I do *not* fuckin approve.'

Caz went with him. 'It's OK, Sarge. Neither do I. We're together on this one. Any time I can help. If I can help, you know?'

'I hope you mean that, Flood.'

'Why shouldn't I?' Caz said.

They were near enough to John Street to stop talking.

Seventeen

The DS drove the Sierra in through the automatic up-and-over door and into the basement car park. He stopped just inside. As the doors closed behind them, a shadow moved over the car.

'I've got nothing for you this afternoon, Flood,' Moore said. 'Maybe you'll get time to sort out your desk. Talk to me Monday afternoon about the bank crowd and we'll go from there.'

Caz got out and walked away. Behind, she heard the squeal of the Sierra's tyres as the DS went to park. Moore wasn't Tom MacInnes, she decided, but he wasn't actually biting her head off. It *might* work out.

It was eleven thirty so Caz telephoned Moira, hoping to drag the girl in a bit earlier and put her out of her misery. There was no quick answer so she put the phone on 'speaker' and let it ring. She sorted a few papers and wasted a minute but the phone still wasn't answered. She decided Moira must be in town, buying something to cheer herself up. Or maybe she was drifting past Mothercare, trying to look casual.

She was feeling spare, so she rang Daniel Cook's home number. When there was no answer there, she rang off in disgust. She had never worked out why CID worked Saturdays. Nothing *ever* got done.

Caz went down to the canteen for coffee, decided to stay down there and at the last minute bought an Eccles cake, *another* ten seconds on tomorrow's race!

Something about the cake, the currants, reminded her of a late night at the nick a few weeks back. She'd killed half an hour there with a DS from Southampton and she'd been trying to work out what made him tick. She had hated Peter Mason, attacked him, and now she owed him. And tomorrow she was supposed to be coaching him round a 10K road race near Fareham. It was a funny world.

Caz had been with Moira and Peter in a Southampton pub, taking a break on a case. She had said Peter was overweight and Moira had been incredulous. Caz had meant for a serious runner, but Moira wouldn't go with it. She thought it was an anorexic conspiracy. They were both mad, she had said, roughly as mad as her Billy.

Caz closed her eyes. She could see Moira's face, a beautiful, simple face. She saw it, remembered it, tracked with her 'morning-after' tears.

And now the poor, stupid, Catholic cow was pregnant, or soon would be – when pink turned to blue or a plastic slide showed more than a single stripe. She would recommend Predictor to Moira.

There was something ironic about the fact that you had to urinate on these things to get a result. In the last two minutes of hope you had to piss on your fingers and pray – the final indignity. The words 'pissed on' and 'fucked' now took on another, deeper, meaning. Caz shuddered. She felt sorry for Moira but all she could think was 'there but for the grace of God go I'. More than anything, except maybe dark, confined spaces, Caz feared pregnancy. It wasn't the thought of having a child, but the thought that she would lose control of her life, the thought that she would be slave to another's agenda. She awoke feeling sick. Poor Moira!

Caz went back upstairs, desperate for something to do to fill the next hour. When she found herself absent-mindedly tidying Bob Reid's desk she shrieked her dismay. If she'd had long fingernails she'd be sanding and polishing them now, prior to careful painting. Saturdays!

She went back to her desk, dug out Dan Cook's number and dialled him. Once again, there was no answer. It had occurred to her that Claire might have returned home or contacted Daniel to at least let him know she was OK. Yes, if she had, he *might* have rung in to let the station know, but he might not. She knew from experience that people often didn't bother.

She decided to buzz Tom MacInnes' office, curious to see if anything had come up on Walters, the other missing girl. When the DI's number rang unanswered, she suddenly understood the motivation for arson. She felt like setting fire to her desk just to get some *action* here. It was a quarter to one. That was *fifteen* minutes to one. She went downstairs to wait for Moira. As she walked down the stairs, she played around with the two-car race Jenny Fullerton had described. The second car, the one that had so nearly killed Jenny, she said was *racing* the other. Caz toyed with the idea that the second car was *chasing* the first. She arrived in the foyer muttering, 'Oh, and by the way, Jenny, it's *distracted* not attracted. You were *distracted* by the first car.'

She read every poster in the hall twice before Moira arrived. She read the Avocado 'wanted' ad a mere four times. When

Moira turned up at two minutes past one she took her head off at the knees.

'Fer fuck's *sake*, Mo. What time d'you call this? Some of us've got *work* t'do, you know!'

Eighteen

The preg-test pack cost ten quid. They went in the loos of the nearest pub to use it. Caz didn't actually go into the booth with Moira but she might just as well have. The running commentary, complete with sound effects, was graphic. Moira came out looking the other way, gave Caz the stick blind and went to wash her hands. By the time she'd dried them under the blower, the second blue stripe had appeared.

'Congratulations, Mo!' Caz said.

'Oh, shit!' Moira said.

They went upstairs to toast Albert Pinhead.

They weren't that far from the nick but they didn't expect to see any of the uniforms or CID. Most of the lads drank the cheap beer in the police social club. If they did go out – usually only the CID lads did – it would be across to The Grapes of Wrath. They were safe.

'What d'you want, Mo? Your usual?'

Moira sniffed. 'An orange juice, please.'

'You don't mind if I have *my* usual?'

'No,' Moira said. 'And have a big one for me.'

They sat down where the open door would hide them. Caz

asked her mate what did she think she would do?

'Get married, I suppose.'

'Married? But Mo, what if—'

'What if what, Caz? Billy wants to. What's the problem?'

Caz sipped at her Bells and Dry. 'Are you sure you want to – have – I mean, have you thought about any other way?'

Moira looked at her. 'Christ, Caz. You don't know me, do you?'

'What d'you mean?'

'I'm Catholic, Caz, but even if I wasn't, that's something I wouldn't do. What happens is meant to happen. If there's a little person inside me, then he's meant to be there. However he came about.'

'What do you mean, *he*?'

'Albert.'

'OK,' Caz said softly. She had never had to face something like this. She hoped she never would.

'And it's Billy's,' Moira said deliberately. 'I know it is.'

Caz nodded. There was nothing else to do or say. 'I'll get another round in,' she said quickly. She didn't bother to ask, same again?

When Caz came back, she thought Moira had a bit of a twinkle in her eye. She even thought a light flush had returned to her dusky cheeks. It was ludicrous. Moira could blossom, but it should take more than half an hour! She said so.

'It's been three *weeks*, dummy!' Moira said.

'I just—'

Moira cut in. 'Caz, I was duffed up before I took the test, you know . . .'

'Up the duff.'

'That's what I said.'

'Well, you're looking good on it, Mo.'

'Yeah, I am, aren't I?'

The whisky, on just a snacked breakfast and an Eccles cake was taking effect. Caz could feel its burn. She decided against any more. She shook her head at Moira, totally failing to understand.

Moira had obviously reconciled herself to her fate – and Billy's. It seemed that as soon she had made the decision, she was fine. Now she was planning a fat future, a string of off-white bambinos and a size sixteen wardrobe. Caz could hardly wait to see Billy's face.

'No,' Moira said when she asked, 'I *haven't* told him yet.'

Nineteen

Caz got back to John Street for half past two. There were a couple of voices in the back office behind the front desk, but other than that, the place was still a cheap version of *Beau Geste* meets the *Marie Celeste.*

She went back upstairs on the off-chance but it was just as cold and empty, stale even. As far as she could tell, no one had been in while she'd been out with Moira. Caz wasn't happy. She toyed with the idea of telephoning Dan Cook but instead she tried the DI.

He answered second ring. She stopped thinking of *Lost in Space.*

'Could I have a quick word, sir?'

'Come round,' MacInnes said.

She went the forty yards to Tom's office, tapped lightly and went in. He had a drink that looked suspiciously amber on his desk, about an inch of the liquid in the bottom of a plastic cup. There was an empty cellophane sandwich pack in the bin.

'Bakers,' he said when she looked. 'Prawn mayonnaise. You weren't around.' He raised the cup. 'And a Whyte and Mackay.'

'I had lunch with Moira Dibben,' Caz explained.

'She OK?'

'She's fine. Blossoming even.'
'Good t'hear it.'

She told MacInnes that there didn't seem to be any real work to do. The witness follow-ups on the hit-and-runs were chalked in for Monday and the round robin of all the repair shops couldn't start till then either.

'I was wondering if it would be all right to follow up on Claire Bullen, Tom. I know she's not an official missing person yet, but I told Dan Cook I'd help and I think I know roughly where Claire went running on Thursday night.'

'And where was that?'

'She runs a few fast miles on Thursdays. I know because I persuaded her to. I reckon the fast part of her run is on the island. I'm pretty sure she pushes it around Shoreham Beach.'

MacInnes looked doubtful. 'I thought she did a very long run on Thursdays. What d'you call it, LSD?'

'Long slow distance. She used to, but I persuaded her to change.'

'But she told her husband she'd be out for hours.'

'Well, that's the next thing, Tom. I think it's quite likely that Claire was playing away.'

'D'you know who with?'

'I don't even know if she was yet!'

'But you want to check something out this afternoon?'

'There's nothing doing here, Tom. So, I thought I could drive over to Southwick and run the course I think she used. I'd be in running kit, so I thought it would be a good idea to clear it with somebody. Otherwise it'd look like I'd bunked off for the afternoon. It looks like you and me are the only ones here, boss, so is it OK?'

'Take your radio. Remember what happened the last time!'

'It's OK?'

'Piss off, Flood.'

Caz got up to leave. As she went to turn away, MacInnes reached into a draw for his whisky.

She caught his eye, 'You up to anything tonight, Tom?'

'Nothin' special.'

'Fancy a bit more pasta?'

'Your place or mine?' he said.

'Mine,' she said, suddenly a lot brighter. 'Bring a decent Chianti and I'll do a Mia Cara special.'

'Half past seven?'

'You're psychic, Tom!'

MacInnes tried to look firm. 'Take yer fuckin' radio, Flood!'

'Yes, sir!' Caz said as she bounced out the door.

Twenty

She went back to her desk, wrapped up nothing, grabbed her Goretex and got out fast. Par for the course would be some desperately urgent phone-call the moment she reached the door. No way, she decided. She was about to score a few miles jogging on the firm's time so she went quickly, determined not to hear a phone if it rang.

When she got to the car park she nearly went looking for the old MG. The MX5 was still far too shiny to be hers but she managed to convince herself by rammpping the engine again and hearing the motor throb as she bubbled out the door. God, it was orgasmic!

Caz wanted to run while there was still some daylight so she got to Southwick as quickly as the traffic lights let her. When she reached the sports centre she parked up and went in, but despite flashing her warrant card and explaining why she was there, the jobsworth on the entrance insisted it was seventy pence to get in. Caz asked for a receipt.

She was in, changed and out in ten minutes, wearing her sub-four Lycra tights, a Helly Hansen top and a pair of white gloves. The shoes were her usual Asics. Even if she was only going for a jog, her feet deserved the best.

She started off slowly, realising that there was more than one way to get from the sports centre down to the Shoreham Road. She wasn't sure exactly what she was doing, just that it felt like a good idea. Putting herself into Claire's shoes (Nikes, if she remembered rightly) she went off the most direct way, on to Gardner Road and then two rights which dropped her on to the A259. She wasn't being too specific, just trying to pick up something, just trying to get a feel for those Thursday nights.

Once she was on the main coast road, Caz turned towards Worthing. She passed small shops, double-glazing outlets, a post office, a chippie. The going was tricky and would have been worse in the dark. There were kerbs to negotiate, side turnings, cracked pavings and the odd garage forecourt. Caz took it very carefully. She was only shuffling, probably somewhere around eight forty-five a mile, and her eyes were scanning the floor. She was thinking, thinking, trying to get a hold on Claire Cook-Bullen, what she did, how she ran, *where* she ran.

She got to the bridge over the Adur. On her left was a bungalow, a conversion. It was the building that once had housed the mechanism of the old chain bridge. Now it was a cute little place with a porthole view of the river. Caz stopped to enjoy the same view and stood looking out over the mud flats towards the hand-operated footbridge just downstream. Over to her right were a dozen or so houseboats. She was just about to continue running when she heard kids' voices, a clang of metal and then another voice, deeper, like someone shouting into a barrel.

She peered down over the edge of the bridge and saw nothing. Then she heard another clang and a prospective vandal's shout coming from beneath her. There was a gap in the traffic and she skipped across the road. This time, when she looked down she caught a glimpse of a head disappearing, up to no good. 'Bloody kids,' she thought as she dropped over the edge.

Under the bridge, before the land fell away down to sea level, the surface was sparse concrete giving way to stone-block walls. There were five kids, all in sloppy skateboarder's street gear; three about twelve or thirteen and one either underdeveloped or much younger. The fifth boy, noticeably older, was larger, almost as big as a man, a slow-talking awkward fifteen-or-so-year-old, the kind who hung around with younger kids because they'd talk to him. They had all been smoking. The oldest and the youngest lads still flaunted their cigarettes.

'Hi-yah, lads,' Caz said, 'what goes?'

''Oo's askin'?' the older one said.

'My name's Caz.'

'That's not a proper name.'

Caz grinned. 'It's short for castrate.'

'Yer what?'

She ignored him and looked at the young one; bags of street cred; baggy jeans, sloppy-top LA Raiders jacket with a hood, baseball cap reversed, Mike Jordan cross-trainers, the tongue outside the laces . . .

'Yo, Jordan. You gonna tell me what's goin' on?'

'Nowt.'

'So what's all the banging?'

'That wuz Freeko. He was just having a laugh.'

'Who's Freeko?'

One of the others said, 'Me.'Oo wants t'know?' Caz turned.

Freeko. A walking Olympus ad. Washington Redskins baseball cap, huge trainers, the rest 'red and grey baggy'. Caz grinned.

'I already said. My name's Caz. I was up on the bridge. Up there.' She pointed at the concrete above them. 'Whatever was banging frightened the shit out of me so I dropped in to take a look.'

'We were tryin' the lock out.'

'What lock?'

'The one on the trap door in the bridge. Some fucker's stuck a lock on it. That's where we usually keep our stash, you know.'

Caz went over. Above the boy was a dull metal door. She had to duck slightly to get a good look at it. It was pinned to a catch by a massive Chubb lock. There were faint marks where Freeko had been hitting it with a large spanner, but Freeko had been wasting his time. He could have hit it with a sledge-hammer, it wouldn't have given way. The only way through a lock like that was with bolt-cutters. Or the key, of course.

'We left our cigs in there,' Freeko said, matter-of-factly, 'last week. We used t'be able t'get in. It's a great den. I reckon the fuckin' council must've found out about our stash. Probably nicked our cigs then locked it up deliberate. Miserable bastards.'

'I don't suppose you *bought* the cigarettes?' Caz said.

'Oh, yeah, 'course we did. We been cleaning cars to earn the money. We're reglar citizens!'

Freeko thought this incredibly funny and so did the rest of the gang. He smirked, enjoying his minute in the limelight. 'We've tried t'get girls t'come down but they think it's too scary. You know . . .'

Caz shrugged and turned back to the oldest boy. He wasn't laughing. She went for him as he was the weakest.

'What's your name, bro?'

'Denny.'

'You must be the oldest, Denny. You, like, the leader, the gang boss?'

'Sort uv.'

'Does that mean you are?'

'Sort uv. But Nippy's the one with all the ideas.'

'Nippy's the Raider, yeah?'

'Yeah.'

'OK. Let's me and you have a quick word . . .'

Caz took Denny's arm and walked him away from the others. They stopped about a dozen feet away from the hatch, near the seaward edge of the bridge. Effectively, they had crossed the road and they were now directly underneath where Caz had earlier admired the view.

There was the obligatory smell of piss where they stood, but surprisingly, there was no graffiti. Caz made a big deal of laughing as she talked. She was aware of the rest of the gang watching them and she clenched her fist once, Black Panther-style, for their benefit. They looked vaguely impressed so she made up a few more neat moves. Whatever gang Caz was from, they'd seen nothing like it.

The young lieutenant in the Raiders gear was desperate to make an impression but right now all he could think to do was light up another cigarette and try to look mean. When Caz came back, Denny was in seventh heaven. She let him drift ahead so he could explain everything to the others. As he spoke he glanced over his shoulder at her.

'That Caz, she's a fuckin' *movie* agent! She's big mates with Sharon Stone *and* Bruce Willis!' He looked again. Caz glanced away. 'They're gonna do a fillum down here. This is the place where Stone has to, like, get away, by swinging underneath the bridge!'

Three of the boys took a quick look at Caz to weigh her up, then tucked their heads back into the huddle.

'Thing is, Caz says the place is, like, supposed t'be secret till the fillum comes out. She says she can get us Bruce Willis's pitcher.'

He looked back again and gave Caz a quick smile. Nippy's leadership ambitions were slowly moving westward.

'She tol' me another secret. When they do all the filming they're gonna want extras an' all the extras are gonna be picked from that Adur Outdoor Pursuits Club. She says the fillum's prob'ly this year, or beginnin' of next. She says that when they come t'pick the extras, if we're in the club, she c'n fix it so we get picked.'

Now four of them looked at Caz. She shrugged her shoulders and splayed her palms out, sort of, 'That's how it is.' Suddenly, the boys were high-fiving each other and slapping each other with their baseball caps. One had a sweatband she hadn't noticed before.

She walked over. 'So what's it t'be, lads? You on the team?'

'Sure, lady!' Nippy said.

'Right on!' Denny said.

'Yeah, right *on*!' the other three shouted together.

Caz grinned again. 'And are we OK about this lock? I mean, we going t'leave it alone now?'

The one with the headband laughed and said yes.

'Appreciated!' Caz said. Then she thought again about the headband.

'So what you called, bruth?'

'Jinky.'

'So, the head, Jinky, is that, like, street?'
'Don't know. I found it. Issabit Sly Stallone, d'yereckon?'
'Mind if I . . . ?'
'You wanna try it on?'
'I wouldn't mind, Jinky.'
'Are you *really* matey with Sharon Stone?'
Caz twisted her fingers. 'We're like that . . .'
Jinky pulled off the sweatband. Caz tried to take a while getting the towelling band just so. She wanted Jinky to say where he'd found it, but she was trying to sound as casual as she could. Kids like this were like quicksilver. One slip, one spill, and they would scatter.
'D'you wanna sell this, Jinky?'
''Ow much?'
'Oh, I don't know. You found it, right? A quid?'
'Fuck off! A fiver.'
'Where exactly d'you find it, Jinks?'
'Just by there. On the waste ground. Where the lorries park up.'
'Show me where, exactly, and I'll owe you a fiver.'
'Yer on!' Jinks said.
Jinky took Caz so she could see for herself. They walked less than forty yards up-river, back in daylight but somehow colder.
'By here, I reckon,' he said, then he suddenly changed his mind. 'No, it was by there!' He moved quickly across the gravel and just past an overturned oil drum. 'We were larking about. Nippy'd tipped the drum up. He was gointa roll it in the river but it was too heavy.'
'So this is where you found the sweatband?'
'Yeah.'

'You didn't find anything else, I suppose?'

'What d'you want to know for?'

'One of the film crew fell over here. He could've lost anything. We're just checking things out, playing safe, you know.'

'You mean the headband belongs t'someone *famous*?'

'No, he's just a cameraman.'

'Oh,' Jinky said slowly.

'It's really appreciated, though. We won't forget . . .'

'Oh, *right*!' Jinky said.

Caz dropped to her haunches, squatting like a peasant in a field. She was still waiting for something to come to her, some feeling, but nothing would. Her famous – some said infamous – intuition had deserted her. Even with the sweatband in her hand, she felt nothing, no darkness, no rush of danger, no fear. She felt lost. She had the peculiar idea that she *wanted* to get some awful sensation but there was nothing out there.

If Caz had been alone, maybe she would have tried to commune with Claire Bullen. She might have tried to send something out, some message on the ether. She might even have tried to 'use the force'.

But after the two jogged miles, she had stopped for too long and had cooled off too much. Now she was feeling the evening cold and the light sweat from her run was making her feel slightly pathetic, as if she was just about to go down with flu.

She felt awkward and anxious, like someone waiting for a phone to ring, but the more she tried to relax, the more obsessed she became with the complete lack in her gut of any significant feeling. The sensation, or rather the total lack of sensation, was so rare for Caz. The coolness and calmness surrounding the case was unnerving her as if somehow no news was bad news. The very ordinariness of everything she found disturbing, almost as if some worry, some clue to a horrible predicament involving Claire would come as a relief.

She was still squatting in the gravel and she lowered her hand to the ground to scoop up a little of the grey-white stone. Now she was closer to it, the earth smelt slightly of dripped diesel oil and of a faint and distant sea. She let the grit tumble through her spread fingers, one final stone sticking to her wedding finger, courtesy of a smear of diesel. There was a poem – was it Shakespeare? The words were as elusive as Claire Cook. *To see a world in a grain of sand, Infinity in an hour* . . . Close but not it. *Heaven in an hour? A flower?* Not that either.

She had let herself get cold and was now slightly unhappy. Now she was drifting so far out of it, she was redoing her A level English! Jesus!

'Hey! Hey!' It was Jinky, finally breaking the spell.

'I'm sorry,' Caz said. 'I was just . . .' She was drifting off again – was it Blake? – but Jinky dragged her back.

'Are you on sumthink, takin' a crap or what?' he said.

Twenty-One

Caz gave Jinky the emergency fiver she had tucked into a pocket in her Lycra pants. It was folded into a half-inch square. Jinky grinned and handed her the sweatband. He could probably buy a brand-new one for £1.95, but Caz couldn't have cared less. She was freezing now and needed to get back to the sports centre. The worst bit was that she couldn't push the run hard because it was so dodgy underfoot.

When she'd first talked to the boys Caz had used her own accent, part Wembley, but with a healthy dose of a well-spoken and insistent Herefordshire gran. That, with a two-year overlay of boarding school, three years of Merseyside, a couple of years in Europe and eighteen months with an American boyfriend, meant she was un-English enough to get away with sounding almost anything.

Her accent had started out just west of Ireland but had got as far as Iceland once she was into her stride. She was a fair actor and a good liar. By the time she had convinced Denny she was Steven Spielberg's buddy, she had drifted on to well-spoken New Hampshire and now, as she was about to say, '*I'll be back*,' she could probably have got away with a Louisiana drawl. Instead, as she said her goodbyes, she showed them how well she'd picked up talking like a Brit. They were impressed.

After she had been running for two or three minutes, Caz picked up the pace from a dead-slow nine-minute mile to a steady-jogged eight. First her sweaty clothes warmed up – one of the most disgusting sensations known to mankind – then a fresh flow of sweat began. The Helly Hansen thermal top was meant to wick away perspiration from the skin and it did just that, but only as far as the outer fibres and the now freezing night air. There it waited for her to stop.

She was thinking about the boys. They were average louts and, apart from Denny, not particularly stupid. She was glad she'd lied to them, if the lie got them through the front doors of the outdoor activity centre. She knew that if she'd directly suggested the place they'd have laughed in her face. The centre was for poofs, for tossers. If she *had* suggested it they would have asked her was she from the social or was she fuzz? They would probably try at least once, she reckoned, and she could have a quiet chat with the principal there. Four weeks and a couple of goes in a kayak and they would have forgotten about Bruce Willis and Sharon Stone. Nevertheless, she made a mental note to get the photos. She'd promised . . .

It was dark and awkward now, and Caz was unable to think clearly and run safely at the same time. When she passed shops, their candlelight blobbed on to the pavement but their faint help did not compete well with the needle attacks of oncoming car headlights, first starkly brightening her day, then leaving her hopelessly blacked out with shrunken pupils. She had taken to looking away in her attempt to preserve her night vision. Usually that was timed to coincide with a particularly nasty crack in the paving. She had tripped once already and had tweaked, nearly twisted, one ankle. The ankle was still vaguely sore from a fight a few weeks ago; this with a huge nutter, a rapist-murderer with a Mercury One-to-One line to God. The memory made adrenaline squirt somewhere but she still wondered why these 'in the know' people never got told by big G to simply give all their money away and go live on an island. Her ankles were important to her. For safety, she was now resorting to a running gait more like a trotting horse than an eight-hundred-metre hopeful. God had a lot to answer for. I mean, for starters, why hadn't he designed things so *women* came first?

Caz was wearing the sweatband rather than carry it and now she remembered why she had never bothered with them. Apart from looking tarty, they felt awful and gradually they seemed to tighten and tighten as the runner ran. They accumulated sweat too, and when they reached saturation point they would release great globules of stale salty water which would flap down into the eyes. She knew the growing tightness was an illusion but she had seen runners at the end of a marathon screaming to get them off. Why they had put them on in the first place was the real question. Caz didn't know whether to blame Sylvester Stallone or John McEnroe for that one.

Had Claire Cook-Bullen worn a headband? Caz couldn't remember. New joggers, especially fat ones, wore headbands. Not many serious runners did, but those that did weren't noticed after a while, they were like spectacles; part of the person.

She arrived back at the sports centre. The jobsworth was still on duty at the entrance. She asked for Brenda Whent and Mrs Euston.

'Tea break!' the jobsworth said, hardly looking at Caz.

Caz dropped her half-smile and took one deep breath. The JW got her drift. 'Er, right! I'll just, er, get them!'

'Why, thank you,' Caz said, the smile re-administered.

Euston and Whent came down together, Mrs Euston leading and arriving at the perspex window first. 'Ah! Detective Constable Flood!'

'Hello again,' Caz said. 'I was wondering . . .'

'More questions? Would you like to come in?'

'There's no need.'

Mrs Euston seemed disappointed. 'Oh! Then . . . ?'

'Mrs Cook-Bullen,' Caz said formally. 'You've already described her. Do you think you could do so again?'

'What for? Have you lost your notes or something?'

'No, Mrs Euston. We are just checking a few things out. You described Mrs Bullen's general appearance but do you remember her accessories? Shoes, gloves, that sort of thing? Do you know if she wore gloves, carried a Walkman, anything like that?'

Caz still wore the headband. It had just dripped a blob of cold sweat down her face.

'I don't think she had a walkman . . . I don't remember gloves . . .'

Look at my head, for God's sake. Did she wear one of these? This!

'We can't see their shoes, of course. Not from behind the counter . . .'

What about a fuckin' headband?

'No, I really don't remember anything else.'

No leading questions, Caz. Don't do it!

'I am sorry . . .'

'How about you, Mrs Whent? Can you remember anything else?'

Caz moved the headband slightly. It dripped on to the floor.

'No, I don't think so . . .'

'Nothing?'

'No . . .'

Caz lifted the band from her scalp, leaving a telltale ridge across her forehead. A bead of sweat formed at the bottom before blobbing on to the counter. She grimaced. 'Could Claire have worn one of these?'

'Oh, yeah,' Brenda said. 'I thought you all did.'

'I can't say I remember either way,' Mrs Euston said.

Twenty-Two

Caz grabbed her kit but didn't bother to shower and change, preferring the comforts of her own bathroom to the lottery of public ablutions. When she got in the Mazda she put a towel on the seat to protect her baby from all that nasty sweat. On the way to Inkerman Terrace she thought about sweatbands and pasta.

She had desperately wanted one or both of the women at the sports centre to spontaneously mention that Claire Bullen had worn a sweatband. Once prompted, they had given her one yes and one don't know. She was hardly any further down the line. She might strike lucky when she got on to Claire's club-mates, but finding them would be difficult. She could wait for Tuesday night and turn up at one of their club sessions, or she might get lucky on Sunday and bump into a few at the Stubbington 10K. She figured, pasta shells, cream, a lot of black pepper and then flakes of John West smoked tuna. Oh, and some niblet-sized Jolly Green Giant sweetcorn. One bottle of Il Grigio . . .

And she'd bought a couple of classical CDs. One was cheap, the other one had Nigel Kennedy on the cover. Vivaldi. It sounded like a sexually transmitted disease! *The Four Seasons* was all right, but when she wasn't paying attention, it was a bit like listening to the BBC test card.

She parked up, got out, and went in through the front door. There was still a very faint smell of paint when she went into her flat but it looked pretty good considering its history. Vincent the pig was on the sofa and next to him, suspiciously distant, was Victoria II, a blousy Miss Piggy type with a pink dress and frilly knickers. Caz wasn't stupid, if they hadn't been at it while she was out, then . . .

She bumped the NAD on as she went past, heading for the kitchen. When she came back out, she pressed 'open' and removed the Rolling Stones disc. She replaced it with Gary Glitter and the Glitter Band. She didn't *like* Gary Glitter, of course not, but sometimes, when she wanted cheering up, you know . . .

She had a quick shower, came out, dried, and grabbed a bottle of the best Chianti from under the bed. She used a corkscrew from the bedside cabinet, opened the bottle and left it to breathe while she got dressed.

Her stomach was still flat but maybe it wasn't *quite* as hard as she'd've liked. As she pulled on a pair of white bikini briefs, she heard the band singing, *Do you wanna touch me there?* She suddenly realised that in less than twenty-four hours she would be with Valerie again. Oh, yes please! She closed her eyes, thinking of him. Bits of her began to feel hotter than they should. She got dressed quickly.

When she came out of the bedroom, Caz was in another pair of Lycra tights, these navy blue and down to her calves, almost reaching the tops of a brand-new pair of padded white ultra-max socks. She wasn't wearing a bra and her top was a man-sized long-sleeved light blue cotton shirt which flapped loosely over her buttocks, partly obscuring her shape. Caz was comfortable and felt sexy but the look was meant to be desexed and casual. She had decided that a boyfriend would think her ravishing but that Tom MacInnes wouldn't. He would be on time. She poured herself a glass of the Chianti.

Tom arrived outside at seven twenty-eight, rang the door bell at seven twenty-nine and came through Caz's flat door at exactly seven thirty. He had brought a Bottoms Up bag. When Caz accepted it, pecking him on the cheek and laughing a thank you, he gruffed back that he hadn't bothered with wine.

'Ah know what'yer like, so I didna bother.'

She looked inside at a sealed bottle of White & Mackay, some Malvern still water and a bottle of low-calorie Canada Dry.

'Why low-cal, boss?'

'Yer a runner, aren't you?'

They went in and Caz sat the DI down on the sofa, shushing her two piggies to one end. Tom noticed the new addition to the family.

'I've called her Victoria Two,' Caz said. She was clacking open the whisky. 'Moira Dibben bought it for me for Christmas.'

'To keep Vincent company?'

'I guess. Anyway she *is* sweet.'

'But a bit of a tart?'

'They all are,' Caz said as she passed him his glass.

Tom MacInnes had bought Vincent for Caz. He had given it to her the day she moved back into the flat. At the time, the gesture had embarrassed him.

'You haven't bought any replacements yourself, Caz?'

'Not so far,' Caz said. 'I could, but I haven't touched the

insurance money yet. It's kind of nice to let the piggies just happen, you know? That way they mean more. Like Vincent and Victoria. They were both presents and they both mean a lot to me. If I was out in the Lanes or something and I saw a piggie I really liked, I'd buy it, but I'm not going to go out with a blank chequebook and *buy replacements* for my babies.'

'Of course not,' MacInnes said. He smiled and raised his glass.

'Cheers!' Caz said. 'Here's to nineteen ninety-three!'

Twenty-Three

Caz had wanted to talk about Claire Bullen over the pasta Mia Cara but Tom MacInnes had decided to talk about Jeremy Avocado. Caz had looked up, her eyelashes fluttering, waiting to see what Tom thought of her cooking, when he smiled the smile of someone bringing bad news.

'This postcard, Caz. It worries me. It *is* Avocado?'

'It has to be, Tom. I don't know anyone who lives in Florida and I don't know anyone who's on holiday there.'

'Couldn't it be an old mate?'

'Nothing's impossible, Tom, but you read the message. It's Avocado.'

'And you'd bet your life on it, right?'

'It's not funny, but yes, I would.'

'So what do you think we should do?'

Caz sipped her whisky and ginger. 'I don't see that we *can* do anything, Tom. Presumably *our* lot have told *their* lot that Avocado spent a fair bit of time in Florida. We know about him, Region knows about him, the Yard knows all about him and he's on the books at Special Branch. What else can we do?'

'You could tell them about the postcard!' MacInnes said softly.

'Shit, no!' Caz snapped back. 'They'll interview me and try to cover my back. I won't be able to get any real police work done.'

The DI nodded. 'That's what I thought . . . so?'

'So nothing. Some pro killer, *alleged* pro killer, *maybe* sends me a postcard. He's not threatening me. I'm not the only person who knows what he looks like. I don't think it matters.'

'So why did he send you the postcard?'

'I don't know. Perhaps he fancies me.'

'He's bent.'

'Maybe he swings both ways.'

'I'd still like to know why he wrote.'

'You and me both. Can we change the subject now?'

'OK,' MacInnes said. 'This pasta is gorgeous.'

'You like?'

He nodded.

Caz waited a few forkfuls then she looked up.

'Don't you want to ask me about Claire Cook-Bullen?'

'No.'

'Why not?'

MacInnes slurped at his wine and looked at Caz. 'Because . . . because; some woman who has a fancy man and doesn't come home one night doesn't make for a justifiable suspicion of foul play.' His grey eyes were watery but there was steel behind. 'You can roll with it because you're you, Caz – you'll get all your other things done! – but you know we can't treat walk-offs as serious unless we have just cause.'

'What if I said that I had a *feeling* . . .'

'Then I'd believe yer. But I could never sell it upstairs. You'd have to give me somethin' t'argue with.'

'But—'

'You know ah have't'say, "But nothin'," Caz. The other girl, the eighteen-year-old from Shoreham. She's borderline vulnerable and even that's a low-key investigation. We can't—'

Caz cut in sharply, 'Shoreham. I never thought . . . Tom . . .'

'What?'

'If Claire Bullen had gone missing, and was last seen in Shoreham, what would you think?'

'I'd think, coincidence. I might look the other way for an extra couple of hours but I'd still say, what *evidence* is there to suspect foul play?'

'There's evidence.'

'What?'

'Claire Bullen wore a headband. I found one on her route. I don't *know* it's hers but—'

'Where?'

'Underneath the old chain bridge where the 259 crosses the Adur. It's exactly the sort of place Claire would stop if she was taken short.'

'Short of breath?'

'Needed a pee . . .'

'Oh.'

'It's isolated. She could've—'

'Anything's possible, Caz, but you *know* I can't do anything.'

'I know.'

'So?'

'I promised Daniel Cook.'

MacInnes topped up both wine glasses, put the bottle down, then stopped, resting his elbows on the table with his hands folded beneath his chin. He looked like he was thinking. Eventually he spoke. 'Caz. You'll do what you have to do. Just make sure you keep on top of the live stuff and don't fall out with Bob Moore.'

Caz wasn't particularly overjoyed but she didn't see what else she could do or how the DI could do or say anything more until she turned something up. She knew she had to leave it. What concerned her more was the absence in her of any real feelings to do with the case. She was used to hunches when she worked, to sniffing things out, to gut feelings. Sometimes they were strong, sometimes not so, but the absolute factual and emotional emptiness surrounding Claire Cook-Bullen she found perverse and disconcerting. She told the DI.

'Well, that's to the good, surely, Caz?'

'You mean, no news is good news?'

'I guess.'

'I should feel that, Tom. I *want* to feel that. But what's weird is the absolute nothingness of my reactions. I *never* feel like that. It's as if Claire doesn't exist – and I don't mean she's gone – I mean like there's nothing anywhere, no hint of her, no nuance, nothing. It's like she's far away or hidden from me. Sometimes, like when I came across the headband, her headband, maybe, I wanted to get the vibes or whatever it is, but just nothing came. Absolutely nothing came . . .'

'And you're worried?'

'That something's happened to me. That I've lost it, the—'

'I've told you before, Caz. We don't have hunches any more—'

'We have computers?'

'Yes.'

'I know you *said* it, Tom. But I know you think it's bollocks!'

MacInnes grinned. When he picked up the bottle, it was empty.

'Can't a man get a drink around here?' he asked.

Twenty-Four

Caz stood up and switched on the coffee machine. Tom got up and went through to the lounge. She followed him and picked up the whisky on the way. She was trying to remember something she had once said to Tom about hunches; about how there was no such thing, how they were the product of unconscious analyses of information. And that was it, there was nothing to feel about Claire Bullen because she had no data. She had been in danger of believing her own publicity. She wasn't a water diviner; she didn't read tea leaves. She solved cases by looking at the evidence, by speaking to suspects. By sensing their lies and then tricking them into the truth.

Before she got pissed she thought she'd ring Daniel Cook.

It was half past eight on a Saturday night. He answered second ring.

'Dan? Hi! It's Kathy Flood. Any news?'

'Nothing.'

'Well, I haven't got far myself yet, but I would like a small favour.'

'Which is?'

'There's a picture of Claire in your front room, Claire and a couple of her mates after the London in ninety-one?'

'Yeah.'

'Could you pick it up and bring it to the phone?'

'What for?'

'I'll explain when you've got the picture.'

There was a clunk as Cook put the receiver down.

'Hello?'

'I'm still here, Dan.'

'So what d'you want?'

Caz waved at Tom MacInnes to relax. She would only be a minute.

'So what d'you want?'

'I'm sorry, Dan. I've got someone here. I need to know two things. One, do you know the other ladies in the picture? Two, what can you say about how Claire looks?'

'How she *looks*?'

'Is she knackered, what?'

'No. Well, yes, she must have *been* knackered but she's very happy.'

'And what's she wearing?'

'What? Running kit, a tracksuit, her medal.'

'On her head?'

'Nothing.'

Caz remembered the photograph. She had one more question.

'One last thing, Daniel. Claire's forehead. What does it look like?'

'Her forehead?'

'Yes.'

'Like a forehead. You can still see the marks from her sweatband.'

'A sweatband. Does Claire always wear one?'

'When she's running, yes.'

'I don't suppose you can remember the colour?'

'She's got a pink one. The rest are white. The pink one is in the wash. I know because I . . .'

Caz rang off after getting the names of Claire's marathon mates. No, Daniel *didn't* know their addresses; couldn't she look them up? Caz didn't bother to argue, but it was husbands who usually got listed in the phone book. The phone line echoed with long pauses and the far-off house felt cold and painfully empty. The ache got to Caz. Even though she didn't like him, she felt desperately sorry for Daniel Cook.

Later, when she got good-friends-very-slowly-pissed with Tom, he told her a little bit more about himself. His father was a short man too, he said, foreman in a mill that took the wool from the sheep's back and then took it on through every process until it became a blanket. They had lived in a cramped cottage, tied to the mill, in the middle of a terrace, one of four streets all linked absolutely to the job, the mill, the mill-owner. As Tom got quietly drunk, his English veneer slowly dissolved.

'Ma fairther wukked twelve oors a day. He played dominoes in the pub each night. He'd hev two pints, and a wee dram fer the walk haim. Muther wukked part-time in the mill, two oors ever'day and Saturdees. She brought up me an' two brothers. There were other bairns but they died.'

'And you became a policeman.'

'Aye. The mill closed. Ma fairther got another job – another mill, half way 'tween Brampton and Carlisle. Mill wasna fer me. I was always gon't'be a bobby. I joined as a cadet as soon as ah wuz old enough.'

'Do you see your family now?'

'Fairther an' Muther'r both deed, an' so's ma bruther Frank.

The youngest, James, he's in New Zealand. We write once or twice a year.'

The White & Mackay had rolled all over Caz. She now felt maudlin; sorry for Tom and vaguely sorry for herself. She knew from the last time they'd got pissed together that Tom had been divorced for fifteen years. He had told her then that he'd spent that fifteen years celibate. She couldn't even imagine that length of time, more than half her life, and to imagine that time, all that time, alone and loveless, made her feel desperately dark and achingly sad. Once, when she had stopped over at Tom's, he had warned her about being alone. His place was dark and real and when she had looked out at dawn breaking over the sea, she had said, 'This place is lovely, Tom.' But Tom had warned her then, that she was dangerously wrong. It was the *view* that was lovely, *outside* that she saw as special. He was alone and had been for fifteen years. He told her, the flat was empty.

Twenty-Five

Caz woke at five forty-five, fifteen seconds before her alarm. She hadn't got maniacally pissed with Tom MacInnes the night before, but they had downed almost all of his White & Mackay as well as the Il Grigio.

She was supposed to be running at ten thirty; nay, she was supposed to be *racing* at ten thirty. Right now, that was a not-very-funny joke. Her head thudded and she felt as if the cast of *Zulu* had been bivouacked in her mouth overnight. She wanted to quietly die but she couldn't; she had a schedule to meet and there was nothing for it but to crawl from her pit and face the music. She had promised a Southampton DS, that she would take him round the Stubbington 10K and finally get him under the forty-minute mark. Not so long ago Peter Mason had saved her life. He might or might not be a bastard but she owed him six point two-one miles all at faster than six-and-a-half-minute miling.

The alarm was on early so she could go out and run a few miles to shake away the poison from the night before. She was a slut, so she pulled on last night's underwear, the socks and the Lycra running tights. If she could have got away with it, she'd've worn the shirt as well. She couldn't, so she grabbed the first Asics top in the cupboard instead. The plan was to warm up, very gently, hammer a mile or so, then come back steady – say three to four miles *toto*, just enough to clear her head.

The Stubbington was always cold and *always* windy. Half the races seemed to be run in the rain, too – the price of being the first race of a new year. The weather due later over Stubbington was practising right now over Brighton and when Caz finally made it on to the street she had a momentary flash of sanity and almost turned back. Then a particularly loud pulse of blood clattered painfully into the back of her eyes. She set off, wincing, ready to take the agony.

By the bottom of Inkerman Terrace, Caz hated Brighton. She hated the rest of the world and she hated everything in it.

When she crossed the road and felt both the wind and the whipped-up sea spray smarting into her eyes, she hated running and being fit; she *loathed* aerobic work-outs, she *abhorred* stretch classes and she discounted forever absolutely anything that did not require a warm duvet and an extra pillow. She was soaking wet and freezing cold and wanted to die. Six hundred yards later she thought she was in heaven.

Caz was now pumping pure pleasure. The wet still lashed her face, her skin still stung, but now she was above everything, last of the brave, out there, sticking it to them, sticking it to God and the weather. She was grinning with pure, unadulterated, masochistic pride. God? No contest! He was outclassed and Caz knew it.

Caz was certain that only a runner could hope to understand her now – her holier-than-thou, absolute, masochistic glory of being cold and wet but still doing it. The glory came when the runner remembered the warm, slowly fattening alternatives. Caz revelled in the wet *because* she could still have been in bed – she took the pain and loved it precisely because she could be under the covers, sitting up with soft-boiled eggs, warm buttered toast and a cup of tea on a tray.

If the bed wasn't there, if the luxury wasn't there, Caz wouldn't be able to feel the sacrifice, her triumph over her softer side. Like Satan, she could put these weaker desires behind her but you needed the devil so you could see how very very *good* you were.

The cold helped Caz's head to clear and she thought briefly about work; about Daniel Cook and Claire Cook-Bullen. She still felt strangely uncomfortable about the whole affair as if something about the Cooks' dysfunctional relationship was somehow affecting her. It was as though their superficial normality and their underlying abnormality was rubbing off on her, tainting her. She suddenly felt that it was the very oddness of the Cook-Bullens that prevented her *feeling* for things in the case the way she usually did. She was annoyed with herself for ever getting involved. She didn't like Daniel Cook and she hardly knew Claire. As she kicked into her fast mile she thought how nice a result would be. Then she could forget the Cooks.

She was now up on the clifftop road out towards Rottingdean, approaching Roedean School for Young Ladies. Most cases you could pick up and put down; burglaries, shoplifting, robbery, even a lot of murders were forgettable. But there were some crimes, some cases that you couldn't isolate; crimes against kids and old ladies, the worst murders, blackmail, rape . . . Then you took home the smell, the taste, the distaste. Then the images haunted your ordinary days and your private nights. Then you heard the cackle of the sick and unrepentant, saw evil fleetingly in the people you loved. That was why Caz had never gone into Child Protection. She knew she would never handle it. She knew how many paedophiles got away with it. She knew that she would not be able to let them walk away. The knowledge frightened her.

Twenty-Six

Caz got to Stubbington just before ten o'clock but the car parking was a ten-minute walk out of town on the wrong side. She would have been late for her meeting with Peter Mason but he spotted her walking just ahead of him and caught her. 'I thought I was going t'be late,' he said, trotting up from behind. 'Fuckin' traffic's a nightmare! Feelin' fit?'

'You just do *not* want to know,' Caz said.

Peter Mason was a DS in Southampton. Caz had met him on a recent case, when she and Moira Dibben were looking for a particularly sick serial rapist. One night, Moira and Peter had gone out clubbing and later ended up in bed. The morning after, Moira's version of events had suggested date-rape, but there was no way she was going to come out and formally accuse a DS. Caz had lost it and had a go at Peter. She was lucky to keep her job. It was only after a time, when she was forced to work with him that she decided that maybe things were not quite so clear-cut. Peter was no gentleman, but Caz had eventually decided he was no rapist either. To think that, she had made herself move a long way in from right point in the battle against men. Now Moira was pregnant and Mason was in the frame as Daddy.

Caz had come to terms with whatever had gone on between Peter and Moira that night and she had come to some sort of understanding with Peter. In the end, Moira had made her own decisions and she was learning to live with them and her new perspective on life. She was going to have the baby and she was doing a good job of convincing herself it was Billy's. Maybe it was. *If* it was, then the pair of them would be OK and Billy would be in seventh heaven.

They were talking about the race. Caz had been miles away but Peter hadn't noticed. 'I cut right back on the booze, 'cept for Christmas Day. I ran a twenty-miler three weeks ago and sixteen the week after. On top of that I've been doing eight hundreds, Ks and mile reps like you suggested. I've lost nine pounds.'

'How about rest?' Caz said.

'Last Monday I did eight K reps, average time three minutes forty. I did some stretching Tuesday night, four miles in twenty-five minutes on Wednesday. Thursday and Saturday was rest. I jogged five on Friday.'

'What a *good* boy!'

'No. You were right. I've been fuckin' about at it for too long. It was about time I got my act together.'

'You're not wrong there!' Caz said quickly.

Caz had managed not to think about Valerie and Portugal but Peter inadvertently reminded her when he asked about her fella – when was he back? 'This afternoon,' Caz said. 'I'm picking him up from Gatwick.'

As they huddled ready for the start, it was not far off freezing. It would be about seventy in Portugal. Val was probably in an airport queue, still in his shorts and T-shirt. Life was a bitch sometimes.

Runners hyped up to do a fast one often blew it very early by starting too fast. The rule of thumb was that every second too fast in the first two Ks cost three seconds in the last two. She told Peter to take it easy. The hooter went. Straight away, Peter tried to shoot off. Caz chased after him. 'Fer fuck's sake, Peter!' she hissed. 'Cool it!'

They went past the first K marker in three minutes forty-seven seconds, just a touch fast. Peter was immediately worried. Caz told him not to panic. The second and third kilometres were more sensible and at halfway they had clocked 19.32, a whole twenty-eight seconds in hand.

It had started raining the moment the race hooter went, but neither Caz nor Peter were really aware of it. Caz was concentrating on helping the DS; he was concentrating on just keeping going. He had registered a personal best at halfway and again at five miles but now he was really hurting and was tempted to ease back.

Caz shouted at him, 'Winners always hurt!' and he kept going. When they reached the 9K marker, a little over half a mile to go, Caz's watch read 35.38. All Mason had to do now was keep it smooth and he was home free. When she told him, he grunted. It was all he could manage but there was a hardness in his eyes as he stared ahead.

Near the end of the race, they rounded a roundabout and could see the finish. As soon as he saw the clock, Mason kicked hard, his male power-muscles sending him surging ahead. At a push, Caz could have gone with him but she thought, what the fuck . . . She wound it up just enough to hold her position and went under the banner in 39.10, her slowest time for three years. Mason was lost in the crowd, four or five bodies ahead.

When she eventually found him, the DS was still showing off, his fists punching the air and his eyes silver with achievement. Someone shouted that the leading lady had clocked 35.20, nearly one and a half minutes slower than Caz's best time. She thought briefly about the forfeited prize money but then forgot about it and went to find the showers. After the finish, Peter Mason had been with a woman; shortish, with a sweet round face and dark curly hair. Caz guessed she was the wife and that they were having one more try. She was glad she hadn't been tempted to say anything about Moira.

In the showers, the faster ladies were already sluicing down. One called Celia smiled recognition at Caz. She was a short, slightly squat New Forest runner with a tinted skin that reminded Caz of Moira. Though she wasn't built for it, she nevertheless picked up medals. Caz admired her guts. No, she said, when asked; she hadn't been racing. She was taking a friend round. And how did the friend do?

'Broke forty!' Caz said, a wide grin cracking across her face. 'Had to pull him all the way round. Now the guy thinks he did it all by himself!'

Caz was covered in soap suds, wavelets of foam rolling deliciously down her body. She was suddenly aware of Valerie's homecoming and she closed her eyes for a second, the shower water beating into her. Oh! The run had honed her, toned her, tightened and stretched her. Now she felt so *gooood*! The hot water rattling into her shoulders plucked and teased at her nerve endings. If she'd been a man, right now she would have had a huge and embarrassing erection. Faintly flushed – it was the race – she left the showers with her towel wrapped round her. Twenty minutes later she was ready to drive to

Gatwick. She wondered what Valerie would say when he saw the MX5.

The rain had stopped and a sharp extra-lemon January sun lanced out of the clouds and shafted down to earth. Caz was tempted to pull the Mazda's top down but then decided she wasn't that lucky. She wound both windows open and sniffed the air, feeling for what was still good in the world. To her surprise, she had been sixth lady in the race and one of the girls in front of her was the first vet. She couldn't wait for the prize, but she'd picked up twenty-five quid for fifth senior.

She drove slowly out of the car park, looking for faces that she knew. Every time she saw one, she had to let go a little toot on the car's horn because no one looked for Caz's face behind the wheel of a nice tasty little green sports job. There were a few waves, the occasional shout and at least half a dozen heads shaken in disbelief. Caz lapped it up. Sod hiding any lights under bushels or 'pursuing the noiseless tenor of her way'; she wanted a few rooftops to shout from. What did they say – if you got it, flaunt it? Nah, Caz thought. If you got it, make them *eat* it!

Then she saw Janice Passfield, a vet from Totton, third today and just in front of Caz not so long back in a cross-country when Caz was a bit off-colour. Janice was a solid runner, really well worked out and very lean, but she hated speed work and still had to break through into the big time. When Caz tooted her, she waved back vaguely, as if she was wondering, who the hell is *that*?

Seeing Janice made Caz think about Claire Cook-Bullen. Then she saw a few Worthing ladies and some of the light went from her face. She pulled over, tight in to the left, to let the stream of cars squeeze past her, then she hailed the girls. A couple looked up and wandered over.

'Caz Flood,' she said, 'I—'

'What happened to you today?' one said. 'Did you run?'

'Yeah,' Caz said quickly. She didn't want to chat about running. 'Look, do any of you know Claire Cook-Bullen? I'm trying to get hold of her or one of the girls that ran the ninety-one London with her.'

'Ninety-one?'

'Don't ask now,' Caz said. 'One is called Frances Thomas, I think – blonde hair. The other one is shortish with short dark-brown hair. I think she's called Jane or Jenn. Don't know the surname.'

'It's Jane Roberts,' one of the two women said. 'She runs a fair bit with Claire. She's not as good as her but she hangs in there. Our coach reckons she shouldn't. He says she's doing too much; that she's overtraining. Leaving it on the track, he calls it.'

'Do you have her address?' Caz said hopefully.

'Do better'n that,' the woman said. 'She's here today. Come over to the club bus; she shouldn't be too long.'

Jane Roberts was already on the minibus. She hadn't bothered to shower and was struggling to swap her sweat-soaked running kit for something dry without waving her bits to the driver or the couple of laughing husbands stuck in the back. Caz said hello, ignoring the heaved-off vest. Was she Jane Roberts, Claire Cook-Bullen's friend?

'That's me, who wants to know?'

'Name's Flood.'

'Kathy Flood?'

'Yeah.'

'Did you run today?'

Caz changed the subject and while Jane tried to wriggle into some fresh gear she explained she needed a chat. Jane was distracted and miscalculated her changing routine. For a second and a half she was topless and the three men in the back cheered. One of the other women shouted, 'Oh, give it a rest will you? There's good boys.'

Jane looked quickly towards them. 'You would think by now that they'd've seen enough tits, wouldn't you?'

Then she turned to Caz. 'What's this chat about then?'

'Look,' Caz said a little too sharply. 'I've got to get up to Gatwick for three o'clock and I'm running late. D'you think I could ring you later? It's important, otherwise I wouldn't ask . . .'

Twenty-Seven

There were probably quicker ways, but Caz decided to go to the airport via Brighton. She knew the M27 and the A27 through Chichester and Arundel so well, there seemed little point in going cross-country with the chance of taking the wrong short cut and accidentally ending up in Obscurity-on-the-Wolds.

The motorway was busy-ish with people visiting their in-laws for Sunday lunch (or going out because their in-laws were coming round). The A27 had its fair share of missionaries and refugees too. Caz kept the MX5 at a steady eighty on the motorway, seventy-five on the dual carriageways and going on the narrow bits through Arundel.

As she bumped up to cross the concrete bridge in sight of the castle she remembered something about it being designed to move as it settled. DS Lindsell's brother was a bridge engineer with more letters after his name than in it. George had once told Caz that what his brother didn't know about bridges – including why they sometimes fell down – wasn't worth knowing. He also told Caz useless things like this bit of information about the Arundel bridge. George's delivery was nasal and flat and though he didn't try to be, he was hypnotically boring. Still, Caz thought, at least his brother wasn't a gynaecologist.

Caz stayed on the top road past Worthing and passed within a hundred yards of Dan Cook's place as she curved around Southwick. When she reached the ring road around the top of Brighton she followed it until she hit the A23, then turned off and purred up that, back up to seventy-five miles an hour as she headed for Crawley.

She got to the North Terminal not much after two. Valerie was due in to the South Terminal at five to three, if he wasn't late. He was flying charter so the 'if' was a bit superfluous. She parked up, then went to browse in the soft-toy shops. Along with Mickey Mouse and twelve different grades of teddy bear, Gatwick usually ran a nice line in pink pigs. She probably wouldn't buy one but she could have a little fondle.

Thirty minutes later she was drinking coffee in the South Terminal with Albert. Albert, a very trendy pig, she had named after a French guy she nearly went out with once, and Moira's sixteen cells. He wore dark glasses and the cutest waistcoat (this Albert), and unlike the original, he didn't slurp soup. She had another coffee.

There had been no loudspeaker announcements about flight delays and Caz thought it was just about time to move. Then she realised there had been no loudspeaker announcements *at all.* She looked up at a sign that said, 'No announcements, dummy' (almost) and cursed when she saw Valerie was going to be at least seventy-five minutes late.

The usual comment about here began with 'f' and ended 'uck' but Caz was too mellow, too optimistic to swear in front of little Albert. Instead she went to make a few phone calls, the DI, Moira, Jane Roberts if she was in. She tried Moira first, business and pleasure. Third ring she picked it up.

'Is that Momm-cee?'

'Fuck off, Flood!'

'Guess what?' Caz said.

'Er, Gatwick, coffee, flight's delayed, you bought a pig.'

'Jesus, Mo! You following me?'

'Special Branch. The guy with the orange shirt. You see him?'

'No.'

'Good, isn't he?'

Caz paused. 'You told Billy yet?'

'No, but we had a great bonk last night.'

'When're you going t'tell him?'

'When it feels right. I don't know. When he proposes, maybe.'

'You mean Billy Tingle *hasn't* proposed. You slipping, Moira?'

'Well . . . Last time we had a curry he said, "Mo-Mo—" '

'Mo-Mo?'

'That's right, Cazzy-Wazzy.'

Caz smothered a laugh. 'A curry?'

'And Billy said, "Mo-Mo, if we were engaged would I move into your place or would you move into mine?" Is that a proposal?'

'I'd say close, Mo.'

'Well, he's coming round this afternoon so I might get him to do it properly. See how it goes. I'd rather he'd already asked before he finds out about the little man.'

'Don't leave it too long, Mo.'

'I won't! You know I'm working with him tomorrow? There's this kid called Walters went AWOL New Year's Eve? We're on that one. It's not high-priority. She's prob'ly shacked up with some pimply kid and trying spliffs 'n' cider. Just didn't tell her mam.'

'Kids have got no idea . . .'

'Maybe. But sometimes they just get a bit drunk, forget to go home. Then they get too frightened to ring and the longer they leave it, the worse it gets. You know how it is, Caz.'

'When's Billy coming round?'

'Like now. He got an extra early today, finishing at two. He said he'd come straight here.'

'Tell him soon, Mo.'

'I said, *I* will!'

Caz heard a distant thumping.

'That's him now!' Moira said.

Caz tried to say a goodbye but Moira had already shouted, 'Just a minute!' and the phone had clunked down. She heard a faint 'Billeeee!', a muffled 'Hi-yah, Mo-Mo!', a few indistinct words and then the sound of the phone being picked up. 'You still there, Caz?'

'Yes, Mo-Mo!'

'Oh, piss off!' Moira said, then Billy's voice rattled in the background.

'Can I go now?' Caz said.

'Billy wants t'talk to you.'

There was a wait, two clunks and then Billy's voice.

'You all right, Flood?'

'Shouldn't I be?'

'You 'aven't 'eard yet, then. Your misper, that missing woman o'yours. She's turned up. Came home this morning, all muddy. Apparently she won't talk to her husband at all. She's just sitting there, covered in crap.'

'Fer fuck's sake! Is she all right?'

'Far's I know. They tried to contact you when the 'usband rung in. He did ask fer you but you were out. They tried MacInnes but he wasn't available eiver. So they sent Julie Jones round just t'see if the woman was OK. Julie couldn't get much sense out've 'er so in the end they got the family doctor round, gave 'er a shot and put 'er t'bed.'

Caz spoke slowly. 'Thanks, Billy, I . . .' There was the sound of a door closing in her ear.

'Caz?' Billy was suddenly hushed, conspiratorial. 'Caz?'

Caz responded in kind. 'Yes, Billy?'

'Moira's just gone through to the . . . kitchen.'

'Y-es . . .'

'Caz, I was goin' t'ask her. I was going t'ask if she would . . . if we could get engaged.' Nothing. Then, 'Caz? What d'you think?'

'I think she's just waiting to be asked, Billy. Go for it!'

'I will. Ta, Caz!'

'Nothing of it, Billy,' Caz said.

She had managed to be nice to Billy but the news about Claire Bullen had shaken her. Suddenly she felt her surroundings neon-harsh and intrusive. She was trying desperately to think, but the world around her flapped and sailed as she tried to get a grip. Claire Bullen was back? Mud? She put the phone down. Even as she did, she could hear Moira's voice squawking faintly, her lightweight last-minute cheerio dropping untended towards the floor.

For some reason, Caz felt sick.

Twenty-Eight

Valerie's plane landed at 16.04. The overhead monitors blipped and said so at 16.06. Caz left the café and walked to the Customs exits just after ten past, joining the mass of backs and straining necks waiting for the trolleys as they broke out. He came through well after the rush, bright and blue-eyed, pushing one of the trolleys and laughing at something the woman with him had just said. Caz felt the wrong kind of heat in her stomach. She stood stock still, her face in neutral. When he saw her he pointed and turned to the woman as if saying, 'She's over there!'

Caz waited passively as Valerie and the woman walked towards her. The woman was tall, a size ten-twelve, and her hair was blonde-to-red. She was in a slightly crinkled cream cotton suit and gave off an air of confidence, class even, like maybe she was an advertising exec, 'something in media', or an actress 'just doing a bit of TV'. Caz hated her. When she came closer and Caz could see her lovely light brown eyes, soft smile and great teeth she hated her even more. Valerie said 'Ca-zz!!' and leaned to peck her cheek. He smelt slightly different. Caz pulled away and offered her hand to the woman.

'Caz,' Val said brightly, *too* brightly as far as Caz was concerned, 'this is Mariella. We met on the plane.'

'Hello,' Caz said neutrally. She had meant to sound colder but Mariella was disarmingly nice.

'Nice to meet you. It's Caz isn't it? What's that short for?'

'Kathrine—'

'My middle name is Katarine. We have something in common.' The voice was painfully well schooled but there was just a hint of—

'Mariella is half-English,' Valerie said, suddenly deciding to push the trolley away from the crowd. 'She says the other half is all sorts of European but mainly Russian-Polish.'

'He has teased me a little. How I talk. I am still sometimes like my father.'

'Mariella works in London but she's got a place in Dorking. I said we could give her a lift.'

'You what?' Caz snapped.

'I said we could drop Mariella off on our way to Brighton. You did *bring* the car, didn't you?'

'Yes.'

'Well, that's all right, then.'

'Er, not exactly,' Caz said. She was looking forward to seeing him squirm. 'I came in my car. It's got two very small seats.'

Valerie's friend took it very well. 'Oh, really? Valerie told me that he had a wonderful old car, a Daimler. I presume he thought you would be—'

Caz smiled at Mariella but broke in all the same. 'One of Valerie's favourite sayings is "Never presume, always check".' She turned to watch his mind doing overtime. 'That is right, isn't it, Val?'

He nodded sheepishly but Mariella came to the rescue. 'This is really no problem. I can get a taxi or I can ring home and my husband will fetch me.'

Husband! How Caz liked that word!

'I suppose I could drop you home,' Caz said thoughtfully. 'I could come back for Valerie.' She caught a little twinkle in Mariella's eyes. 'I'm *sure* Valerie wouldn't mind.'

Valerie looked mortified. He had got off the plane a hot-shot hunk, neat motor waiting. Now he was a sidelined silly boy. Caz was feeling a little better. 'How about a drink?' she suggested. 'Mariella can make her phone calls and we can have a chinwag while we wait for her husband to arrive.' She was so pleased she'd stopped herself saying 'husband' with any emphasis. They went to the bar, the two women ahead and Valerie slinking behind with the trolley.

They talked jobs while Valerie was at the bar. 'Oh, no!' Mariella squealed at Caz's first guess. 'Definitely not!' She thought the idea of public relations *very* funny. 'You're not going to guess,' she said, 'so I'll tell you. I'm an engineer!'

Caz looked up to the bar. 'Valerie never puts enough Coke in with the Southern Comfort.'

'I'm into testing bridges for stress,' Mariella said, 'working out if they're still safe.'

'I wouldn't have thought—'

'What? Are you surprised to meet a woman who's an engineer?'

'I shouldn't be, but yes.'

'Don't apologise. It happens a lot to me. I just rectify the mistake and then I carry on with the job. I'm very good at it and even the most pig-headed man eventually discovers that.' She laughed, her long hair flashing back. 'And since I might be saving some of them upwards of fifty million dollars they tend to listen to me.'

'You did say *fifty* million dollars?'

'What my company investigates and analyses can mean the difference between demolishing a bridge and building a new one, or strengthening the old one. Sometimes we can tell them there's nothing at all needs to be done. So, for maybe a fee of fifty thousand dollars you save the cost of two bridges.'

'Two bridges?'

'Well, not quite, but demolition costs can be enormous too. That's another of my company's specialities.'

Valerie came back. Caz told Mariella that a detective sergeant she knew, DS Lindsell, had a brother in her line of work.

'You're joking!' Mariella said. 'Do you know his first name?'

Caz told her.

'Why, that's amazing,' Mariella replied. 'He set up our company. He's very well respected in the field. What he doesn't know about bridges—'

'—isn't worth knowing,' Caz said quickly. 'George already told me.'

'Well, what a coincidence.'

'Not really,' Caz said. 'I'm always meeting coppers.'

Valerie said, 'What are you two chatting about?'

'Mathematics,' Mariella said. 'More specifically, topology.'

Caz grinned at Valerie's expense. 'In case you don't know, Val, that's the study of shapes and space. We were trying to work out how to get two female executives, six suitcases and one male plonker in a two-seater sports car.'

'How big are the suitcases?' Valerie said.

Mariella was trying to persuade Caz that what she did wasn't *at all* boring. She went all over the world and she made decisions which cost or saved millions. And the stories! There were new guidelines in the UK which proved that half the bridges were incapable of carrying traffic – some were alleged to be unable to even carry their own weight.

'It's nonsense, of course. Like you can prove a bumblebee can't fly!'

Mariella bought the next round and they continued to chat, still about bridges. Caz was deliberately cool towards Valerie. Even if talking to a fellow passenger was completely innocent, the prat should've known better than to walk out of Customs looking so bloody happy. This was their reunion, for God's sake!

She mentioned the Arundel bridge, this thing that George had said about settling. Oh, yes, Mariella explained. The road above the hollow abutments was not fixed. It moved as the road subsided and could be jacked up out of the way for another layer of tarmac to be applied. It was cheap but it worked – a fine example of clever engineering.

'What's a hollow abutment?' Caz said, mock-thick.

Her new-found friend smiled. 'Another time, maybe. I'm telling you, Caz, it's not as boring as you think. It's really quite an exciting world. We should get together some time. I've got *lots* of funny stories. Ask me some time about the Medway Bridge.'

Caz offered to carry Val's flight bag when they finally left. It was her first gesture of reconciliation but she only made it after she had let him pre-pay their ticket so they could get out of the car park. He grunted but let her take the bag. Then he tried a little smile. Caz blew him a teaser's kiss.

Mariella's husband had arrived and had whisked Mariella away. He was the same height as her, dark hair, glasses and completely unmemorable. They had swapped addresses and promised to phone. Maybe they would, maybe they wouldn't – that was how these things were, but by the time they'd parted Caz had come round to really liking Mariella. She thought maybe a night out with the four of them might happen. At least, once Valerie had eaten enough humble pie . . .

When she got to the MX5, Caz walked past it deliberately. She noticed Val's sideways glance at it. She stopped as if she was taking a rest and asked did he like it?

'They're OK, I suppose,' Valerie said. 'But give me a refurbed Spitfire or a Sunbeam Alpine any day. Even an old MG like yours is worth doing up. Nah, it's a tart's car . . .'

'That,' Caz said slowly, 'is *this* tart's car.'

'What is?' Valerie said.

'The green MX5.'

'How many drinks have you had?'

'Enough to still be under the limit.' She went round and opened the boot.

'Are you serious?' Valerie said.

She opened the driver's door.

'You're serious . . . But how the hell did you . . . ?'

Caz got in and left him standing there, the boot and his mouth both wide open. Eventually she had to wind his window down and tell him to load up and get in. When he squeezed in, he acted like they were about to drive off in a stolen car. 'I'm staggered,' he said. 'Mind-boggling, what-the-fuck's-going-on-around-here staggered. I don't suppose you're going to explain?'

'Nope!' Caz said. Then she laughed and roared out of the bay, making the wheels squeak on the shiny floor.

Twenty-Nine

Valerie gave up. He had obviously decided to let Caz get whatever it was that was bugging her out of her system. Apart from saying, 'Lights!' as they pulled away from the car park, he was doing a good impression of a tortoise, his neck pulled into his shoulders, his arms folded across him. When they hit the A23 and Brighton was less than fifty quick miles away, Caz reached across to briefly touch his thigh.

'I missed you,' she said.

'Both hands on the wheel, Flood!' Valerie replied. A minute later he said, 'I missed you too. Can't we stop somewhere?'

She asked Valerie what he meant. Did he mean a pub? Was he hungry? No, Valerie said, he meant a hotel. Was he serious? Was he that desperate? Yes-no, Valerie said. He wanted them to be together tonight, now. It was just that maybe his place might not be a good idea, not first night back.

'Well, there's always the back seat of the—'

'What back seat?' he said.

'Point taken,' Caz said. Then she suggested her place.

But that wouldn't be right either. Even if her inspector didn't mind, it wouldn't be; it wouldn't be, would it?

'You're absolutely right,' Caz said, terribly seriously.

'There's only one thing for it, then – my flat!'

'I thought it was—'

'Fixed, yeah. Redecorated, yeah. I moved back in over a fortnight ago.'

'No problems?'

Caz ignored the fingers of cold that flashed through her.

'No, no problems,' she said.

'Well, if it's all right with you.'

Caz ran her hand lightly up the inside of Valerie's thigh.

'If it's *all right?* Jesus!'

'That's a yes, is it?' Valerie said. Caz glanced across. He was grinning like a cat.

'Arsehole!' she said.

When they got to Inkerman Terrace they found a parking place outside the flat, saw Mrs Lettice's curtains twitch the once, got out, got the cases and went upstairs. Caz let Valerie carry both cases to give herself the chance to scurry ahead and flick things on; the lights, the CD, the kettle, the bath. Some girls reckoned they liked their blokes rough and sweaty, as they came, but Caz had always preferred them just out of the bath and either talcumed or oiled-up.

She'd forgotten the last time she'd loaded the NAD, and Gary Glitter started singing, 'I'm the leader, the leader . . .' Shit! She'd been found out. She rushed through to press 're-set' and grab something else. 'Moira was round,' she said, red tinting her cheeks, 'It's hers . . .'

'Oh what a shame,' said Valerie, 'I'm quite partial to a bit of glam.'

Caz looked at him. He was standing just inside the open door with the cases either side of him. He was smiling softly. Glam rock? Valerie?

She thought, no, then maybe, but in the end she decided it was too late to tell the truth.

'Fancy *The Four Seasons*?' she said.

They compromised with some George Michael and while the kettle boiled, steamed like a mad thing, and then clicked off, they went at each other in the kitchen, Valerie, his backside against the stainless sink, one hand inside her jeans and lifting Caz as she tried to eat him. She was three-quarters undone when she remembered the bath.

'Fuck!' she said.

'That was the general idea!'

'The bath!' she said. 'Put me down!'

'Oh,' Valerie said.

She clipped together the top button of her fly and left. Then she leaned back and said, 'Tea. Strong please!'

The bath was only half-full. She must've been psychic when she put the taps on 'dribble'. She dug out an expensive girlie oil and slubbed it into the circular splash between the taps. The room immediately smelled gorgeous, somewhere between vanilla and roses – she liked the taste of vanilla – and she turned off the taps.

When she came into the kitchen with a bottle of Il Grigio, Valerie turned round and presented her with a tray complete with cups, saucers and milk jug. The tea bags in the cups spoiled it a bit but he was puffed up like he'd just built a fitted cupboard. 'Made the tea,' he said.

'Oh, well done!' Caz said. She uncorked the Chianti, sniffed, then put the bottle on the side to breathe. Valerie leaned awkwardly to kiss her and she kissed him back, eyeballing the tilting tea. 'Bath time,' she said.

Thirty

She let Valerie go to the bathroom first and gave him some time before she knocked and went in herself. He was already in the bath, lying back with a flannel floating modestly over his bits. She had a silk long thing on and it came to her that though they were both crazy for each other they had only ever stopped over once and maybe they were both just a little bit shy. It felt nice.

'Is there room for one more?' she said softly.

He sat forward, the flannel rising. She took off the kimono. As she slid in behind him, he said, 'Right there,' touching his neck.

'Here?' Caz said, thumbs in both sides.

'Uu-r-r-r-r-nnnn!' Valerie said.

Caz wriggled closer, her legs looped over Valerie's thighs, her feet between his legs, her smallish breasts occasionally touching his back as she worked. She started at the forehead, working her short-nailed fingertips in tiny circles, slowly backwards through his scalp. His hair was only damp so she lifted a cupped hand to wet him before adding some more oil. Now she pressed hard enough to make her fingers ache. Valerie groaned. Then she grabbed a handful of his light-brown hair and pulled. 'Oh, bia-beee!' he moaned.

When she had worked her way back as far as Valerie's crown, Caz shifted very slightly, the water squeaking between them, resting her arms on his body, the inside of her elbows pinching back his shoulders, the heels of her hands at the nape of his neck. Then she began to work her fingers at the base of his occipital bone, her thumbs down his medulla. The sounds he made were the human equivalent of purring.

At some time she whispered, 'More hot water!' and some time later she dropped back and tugged gently at his chin until he rested back against her, his oily head on her breasts. It was an old, very long bath but even so, Valerie's knees were tucked up and his feet were somewhere by the taps. 'I'll do your face,' she whispered, very, very, gently. Valerie nodded feebly, too relaxed to speak.

She pinched and stretched the skin around his chin, squeezed and pulled the skin around his eyes, pulled at his cheeks, his ears, his forehead, his nose, the line above his mouth. As she worked, Valerie aahhh-ed in some deep, sleep-ladenly vague way and when she reached his hairline and began slowly, methodically to sweep back his hair, hand over hand after hand, he snored, he actually snored.

She held him there quiet, gently stroking his fringe back towards his neck. The water cooled or they became accustomed to it, but their close-wrapped bodies kept them content. Caz lay very quiet, her man in her arms. It was so right, she felt like crying. Something like this was too rare to lose and too fragile to keep. She would let Valerie down so many times, like she had already let him down, and one day he would be gone. It was her clenched fist that woke him, his hair trapped between her fingers. She shook the thoughts away and told him to top up the heat again.

Thirty-One

When they eventually made it to bed, Valerie seemed to take his cue from Caz's slow, sensual approach. First they held each other, her head nestled in his neck, then they drank some wine, then Valerie used some oil to loosen Caz's back and legs. When, finally, the oozing sexuality of it all, Caz's rear, her long legs, the line of her back, finally overcame him, he rolled her over, their mouths together, their tongues licking, and Caz thought, Oh God! Now!

She knew he had to have an erection that hurt but she left the moment to him. When he suddenly disappeared down her body, though she didn't mind some of that, she felt vaguely cheated.

Valerie acted as though he was fighting to win a personal bet, not yet, not yet, not yet, his tongue, then his lips moving around her, anywhere, everywhere, but mainly below the waist. Whenever he slipped between her legs she would open to him and he would visit her pussy, whip up the beginning of a storm and then slip away up or down her legs, the ultimate frustrating, teasing, flicking tongue.

At another time Caz might have shouted instructions, insisted on direct action, but something about Valerie, this somehow *different* Valerie, made her wait, each re-visit now longer, hotter, more compelling. When he finally, finally, lost his bet and lifted her to slip with a single pulse inside her she felt like punching the fisted air and shouting, 'Yeah!' Instead she simply said, 'Valerie!'

'I do too,' he said. When he came it was more like an explosion than an ejaculation. She didn't stop moving and he had to scream, begging her to be still.

Thirty-Two

Caz hadn't bothered with her usual extra-early alarm, trading the fitness of a four-mile run for another hour in bed with Valerie. Sod's law, of course, took a hand and she woke at five fifteen anyway, ten minutes before the clock would normally have buzzed her awake. She looked at the red matchstick numbers clicking over in the dark, tried to offer herself back to sleep, but realised within a minute that her body was already up. She looked at the light muscles of Valerie's shoulders, thought about it, but stopped herself. She slipped away for a pee then drifted like a ghost through to the lounge.

She went into the kitchen, trickled slow, silent water into the kettle, turned it on with a hand over the switch turning a click into a dull clunk, and all this behind two almost-closed doors. When she made her strong black instant and stirred it, it was with a plastic spoon, no clack, no ting, nothing to intrude into the night. When she crept back into the lounge she unhooked some good earphones, plugged them into the NAD and settled down with Elton John's love songs. She fancied a cry.

The night before, after making love, they had slept the peace of the wicked until some time around nine Caz woke up. She had suggested going out and Valerie had said she was a maniac. They compromised and went to Armando's. Caz considered that an extension of her home.

Now she lay on her floor, thinking the unthinkable, that a man could actually, absolutely, permanently get inside her, that a man could get through to the parallel what-if life in there, the one she controlled, the lover, the girlfriend, the girl looking at dresses, the mother, the wife.

How could she ever explain to a good man like Valerie that she would never go that way? How could she ever explain that she didn't *want* to set free her softer side, she didn't *want* to mellow? Whatever drove her, whatever it was that made her need to be a copper, a *good* copper, so desperately, obsessively, also told her that she needed to think like a man, dominate like a man, *use* like a man. It also told her that a man could briefly set up in love, install his life-factory, then click back from it and step back on the gas. It told her she couldn't, no woman could.

That was why she'd cried last night in the bath. Why she was crying now. Why she was playing 'Love Songs', 'Blue Eyes' on repeat. She felt wretched. She was on a razor-thin walk where either side was a hopeless drop, one side without Valerie, one side without her life. That was why she had always fucked good-looking bastards; there was never anything to lose and there were always plenty more bastards.

Finally she broke away and flicked the player on to 'Little Jeannie'. She stood up, the spiral 'phones cord protesting, and began to sway gently, dancing the night, the darkness away. She danced for the single track, then scrabbled round in the dim light until she found John Lennon's *Shaved Fish*. She went straight into track two, turned the amp volume down, pulled the earphones out and started her press-ups.

At ten presses she took an extra breath, at twenty she ached, at thirty she stopped, her arms locked, holding her weight. The buzzing guitars reminded her of the opening of 'Revolution', her early teens and then the Beatles revival while she was at university. She managed five more pushes before her first collapse but fifteen seconds later she was up again, doing single lifts with arm-locked rests, matching John Lennon's 'Cold Turkey' shouts with her own pain. She was still managing to move at the end of the track, did one more searing lift in the silence following, then crumpled on to the carpet, the 03.01 lit red on the side of her face. When Valerie touched her, she turned over. Her tears could have been sweat but he held her anyway.

'We'll work something out,' he said.

She thought, 'It never works out. Not in the end.'

'You're wrong,' he said. She didn't realise she'd not spoken.

He kissed her forehead.

'Hey!' he said. 'What happens, happens.'

Moira had said that.

Thirty-Three

At half past seven, Caz was parking the MX5 underneath John Street. Valerie had taken the Daimler 250 from her lock-up garage and had made a show of noticing how clean it was. He gave her a light kiss, then touched her face before she walked away. Over breakfast, they had nibbled at toast and touched a lot, but not talked. Valerie had seemed to know instinctively that the wrong word would either have started Caz crying or launched them into a row. He preferred tea in the morning – something Caz had only just discovered – and he ate twice as much toast as her. He was being very, *very* good, a new man, soft but strong. When she'd thought that, Caz remembered a friend who had once said the same thing about *her* man. 'Soft and strong?' Caz had answered, raging with PMT at the time. 'Like shit-paper, you mean?'

The War Room was empty and dark. Once she flickered the lights on it was empty and light. It was too early for the troops and she wandered around, 'accidentally' seeing the bits and pieces scattered about on the various desks; files, odd receipts, doodled scraps of paper, Post-Its. She finished up at Bob Moore's worktop where she took a bit more interest, sitting on the corner of his desk, her arms stretched behind her, flicking her eyes over his work and listening for the door.

There was very little that tweaked her except the note neatly central, ready for the morning. She glanced at the door quickly, then read the note. 'H&R RTA 1.1.93 9. KJ's, DM's, Flood at Brown's. 10-on both to Bognor R'. At least she knew what she was doing this morning.

Caz dropped off the desk and huffed before making for the door, figuring on an early coffee and a walk past the DI's and DCS's offices – there was no harm letting them know that DC Flood was in early. She was wearing her usual uniform, 501s with a leather belt, white tee-top, Hard Rock Café jacket and Asics trainers. She was light on her feet so she would need to cough as she went past.

Caz liked the way she dressed and would be stuffed if Sussex CID ever imposed the same dress code as Hampshire. While she was down there, working with Moira and DS Mason on her last case, she'd noticed the few WDCs were all in skirts. When she had asked about it, Peter Mason had simply said, 'Policy!' as if that explained everything. Then she'd explained about the difficulty of chasing villains while dressed for a dance.

'Try clearing a six-foot wall in a hurry, a skirt up round yer ears!'

Mason had told her he knew about the problems. He thought them funny. If they were likely to meet any fences, he said, they always let the girls go first.

The light was on in Tom MacInnes' office. Blackside's was off so she tapped the DI's door lightly, hoping for a minute to chat. There was no answer. As she turned away, MacInnes was coming towards her, adjusting himself as if he'd just left the bog.

'Flood!' he said, expressive as ever.

'Good morning, sir,' she said. 'I was just wondering if you—'

'Cook-Bullen? All ah know is she's haim and she's OK.'

'Any chance of a quick word, sir?'

MacInnes didn't say anything but went into his room leaving the door open. Caz followed after a sticky second of hesitation, knocking again and cursing herself for her awkwardness. Being a DC and a personal friend of a DI was a protocol bastard she still hadn't figured out.

Caz sat down. MacInnes was opening a drawer. When she coughed and he looked up, it was to see her eyes asking a question about next door. 'DCS Blackside is out this morning,' MacInnes said flatly. 'He's seeing the CC at Lewes, ten o'clock.' He took a half-bottle of whisky from the open drawer. Surely not? Caz thought. 'An don't jump't' any conclusions, Flood,' he said as he saw her face. 'Ah've a sair thrait.'

She sat quietly while the DI filled the bottle cap with a medicinal measure of White & MacKay, tipped it into his throat with his head back, and then gargled noisily for about thirty seconds. He finished, and rocked upright; then his cheeks bloomed as he expressed the liquid forward through his teeth. Then, as he swallowed the whisky, he grinned at Caz and said, 'Shem t'waste it, eh?' Caz smiled, coughed, and with a flash in her eyes said, 'Actually, Tom, *my* throat's a wee bit—'

'Gay suck a mint,' MacInnes said and slammed shut the drawer.

The DI's eyes lit with a brief something that reflected the light in Caz, then he settled down, ready for the start of his day. As he spoke, Caz saw a flash of him; younger, fiery, probably vicious in a street fight, continually getting into trouble with his superiors but catching bad people no matter what. His wife Elizabeth must have been his opposite, round-faced, with wind-redded cheeks and tight-curled red hair. MacInnes had once told her that Lizzie was an islander. She would have been old and wise at twenty. She must've known it would never have lasted. That she tried at all must have meant an awful lot of love once, something to bank against the pain.

The marriage had eventually failed but that didn't mean she had stopped loving him. Suddenly, Caz could see that Tom MacInnes. He would have taken Elizabeth back to the island. He would have shaken hands with the man who would marry her after the divorce. He would have let everything of hers go except a single photograph, moved south into England, and then south again until he was as far away from his biggest failure as a man could get alive. She believed what Tom had already said. He had been celibate ever since.

'The Chief Super may be staying a while longer, ah'm thinking, but yer cannee quote me.'

'Blackside? Are they sticking him for Avocado?'

'No. Thaise things happen. Ah'm thinking it's something behind closed doors, but –' MacInnes sat forward to whisper – 'Ah think he's quite happy t'spend a bit mair time here yet, Flood. His wife's not t'keen t'move an' maybe she widdna at all if he went up to the Yard.'

Christ, Caz thought, is there such a thing as a happy police marriage?

'Ah think as well that Norman'd quite like t'be around to see you through yer first nine months. He's taken a shine t'yer, lass, bit like Ah did. Ah'd reckon the DCS is thinking you might be going places. Same as me, ah'd say, an' he'd like't' mek sure y'start out reet.'

Caz was stunned. 'Blackside wants to look *after* me?'

'Aye, lass.'

'Jesus Christ!'

'And it's none o' that eether. The bloke actually *cares*, Flood.'

'I never said—'

'No, lass.'

'I'm just surprised.'

'You don't know th' man's your problem, Flood. Just the stairies. The DCS has caught a lot of villains. Twelve years ago he took a shotgun off a man'd just wounded him, killed his oppo. Like Bob Moore, Norman's problem is he canna see women really doing a serious job at policing. The difference between him and Moore is he's smart enough to see when he might've got something wrong. He's *interested* in you, Flood.'

Caz didn't know what to say but eventually she managed something, changing the subject back to Claire Cook-Bullen's return and the discomfort she felt but had no grounds for.

'But you won't have it that it's women's intuition?'

'No, sir. Their place was just, well, *odd.* And there was something slightly off, iffy, about Daniel Cook. Billy Tingle said Claire had come back covered in mud and wouldn't talk. Is that right? It's a bit peculiar, to say the least.'

'But not a police matter, Caz.'

'But what if something—'

'Flood, she's haim. She's unharmed. Yer not a social worker.'

'But—'

'You want t'*be* a social worker?'

'No, sir, but I—'

'Feel bad about a running-mate, Flood. Fine, then go an' see her when you're off duty and have a nice cuppa tea an' a chat.'

'Sir,' Caz said.

'Don't get mardy, Flood.'

'No, sir.'

'Gidd. Now what else?'

'The hit-and-runs, sir. I was just wondering if we'd listened to the tapes – the incoming calls . . .'

'Can't you talk to DS Moore?'

'Yes, sir, but I'm here now and I was just thinking. You said that a driver stopped and took a chance on getting nicked. He'd been drinking but he was a good citizen and rang in. You said that when the traffic arrived they told him to piss off out of it, sharpish.'

'Yes.'

'Well, why didn't they think this guy was actually the one?'

'I wasn't there, Flood. Maybe they took a look at the car and it was undamaged. Maybe they were too busy making the girl safe, helping the ambulance crew out.'

'Who got there first, sir? The ambulance or the traffic?'

'I'm not sure but I think the paramedics were just getting out of the ambulance when our lot got to the scene.'

'Isn't that a bit impressive?'

'What?'

'An ambulance beating the patrol car to the scene of an RTA?'

'I hadn't thought about it. Maybe.'

'I was in traffic for a year and a bit, sir. We *always* got there first.'

'So what are you saying, Flood?'

'Nothing, sir, but I wouldn't mind hearing Control's tapes.'

'For what?'

'To hear the accident phoned in. It might be that we had two calls. Might be that the guy at the scene knew the drunk-driver.'

'You don't know the guy was drunk.'

'No, sir, I don't, but it's a pretty reasonable guess. And I know we can only do him for leaving the scene and failing to report.'

'Or her.'

'What?'

'You said, "do him".'

'Oh, did I, sir? I didn't notice. Figure of speech. I'll try to be more politically correct next time.'

MacInnes sagged. 'OK, Flood, I'll listen to the tapes. Speak to you some time this afternoon, how's that?'

'That'll be fine, sir.'

'Know what you're doing this morning yet?'

'Not yet, sir. Haven't seen the DS.'

'What about his desk?'

'What d'you mean, sir?'

'Didn't you tidy it for him, Flood?'

'I don't know what you mean, sir.'

MacInnes picked up a file and opened it. When he looked up, Caz was just thinking about standing.

'You still here, Flood?'

'Sir!' Caz said, standing, leaning back slightly.

'Well *why*, Detective?' the DI said. 'Haven't you got any work?'

'Actually, I was on my way to coffee when—'

'Fine. Well fuck off now, Flood. Can't y'see Ah'm busy?'

Thirty-Four

Caz went out quickly and, quickly too, went down to the canteen. The early uniforms had been gone half an hour and the few nine-to-fives and plainclothes were just arriving. She went to the counter, got a dozen coffees plus the usual handful of sugar packets, then went back upstairs. Anyone late in could have theirs cold, but right now, wasn't she being a good girl?

She got back to the War Room and kicked at the door to be let in. The tall streak-of-nothing shadow had to belong to Billy Tingle, as did the massive grin that threatened dislocation to his jaw.

'You asked?' Caz said.

Billy nodded, his eyeballs rolling.

And she'd said yes, surpri-se!

'Have a coffee,' Caz said.

With Billy as her main line-backer and only one slightly wet shimmy, Caz made it to Greavsie's desk to get rid of the tray. In the scramble that followed her nicking two cups, eight others were grabbed and only one spilled, a better-than-average percentage. She had taken a cup for herself and one for Moira but as she walked towards Bobby Moore he chuckled and said that maybe all he had heard about his

WDC wasn't true after all. 'Cheers, Flood!' he trumped as he took his cup.

Moira looked up, no coffee, then she shouted, 'Billeeee!!'

Billy looked across the room at her mini-pout, then, for a dangerous split second, down at his drink, weighing the options. It was no contest. There were a few chuckles as he took Moira the coffee he'd got specially for her. As he passed Caz, Caz whispered, 'You should've got two, Billy.'

'Tell me about it,' Billy said.

Caz turned to the DS and asked, 'What gives, Sarge?' Moore told her – they were going out in his nice shiny car to see three repair shops at the top of Worthing and then they'd be going on to one he knew was a bit suss in Bognor Regis.

'We can let the plods do most of the work fer starters, Flood, but I've kept these four back because I think at least one of 'em is iffy. There's bin a fair number of motors goin' west that end of the patch. If they're not transporting them out, the cars must be being winged local. Right now we're only interested in the hit-'n'-run. We tell 'em that and we tell 'em we're blind-eyeing anything else for the rest've the week. We get no co-operation, we shit on someone. Stick pandas on the corner until they come round to our way of thinking.'

'You don't want us to look for evidence of ringing?'

''Course I fuckin' do, Flood! We just don't feel their collar until next week, that's all!'

'I noticed the Sierra was a bit shiny yesterday, Sarge, you turned over a new leaf or something?'

'Nope,' Moore said. 'My eldest, Lindsey. She's got a boyfriend works for a car valeting outfit, Bird's? Came round on Sunday and went at the car with all the gear, electric polishers, half a ton've T-cut 'n' turtle-wax. The lad's all right.

The daughter said he needed a couple of grand t' set up on 'is own. I said I'd think about it. He did the car as a freebie t'show me how good he was.'

'And yer going t' give him the money?'

'First time the Albion win three straight games, sure.'

Thirty-Five

The money on the coffee tray was short but that was par for the course. Caz had never known it to be right. She scooped up the coins, now wet with cold coffee, and made a mental note to rinse them the first chance she got. She almost had time now, but she fancied a quick chat with Moira about Billy. She wanted to know how OTT he was when he proposed – all the pathetic details – and had he bought her flowers yet and had she told him about little Albert sixty-four eggs?

But Moira was having none of it. Whether she was on a guilt trip or just wasn't in the mood, Caz wasn't sure. She *was* sure that Moira didn't want a natter – her body language made it clear that now was *not* the time. On the two occasions Caz made a gesture towards a corner, Moira became immediately busy, and more to the point, had to bring Billy into the act. Fine, Caz thought, your business, just let me know when you're in the shit, Mo, and I'll try to be available.

At ten to nine, Sergeant Moore decided it was time to go, and he bawled at Caz to grab 'er 'andbag and come on. Making a point, he sent Caz on ahead, flicking her the Sierra keys and telling her she would be driving. First off, they were going to Mafeking Street in Worthing. He would be talking to KJ's Wrecks and Doc Martin's Auto Hospital while she would be just down the road talking to Brown & Brown, the Car Shop. Caz did her best to be surprised.

Caz went down the back way and emerged into a basement car park still tacky with the morning's breath; the vague smog of lingered car exhausts, stale rain, leaky oil sumps; faint footfalls cut with the crêpe perfume of nervous sweat and tobacco. It was a smell that Caz would know at one part per million, like the smell of hot rivets would call to a shipwright, or rising bread would turn the head of a baker.

Moore's Sierra was tucked away in one corner and she went over, knowing before she got into the car that the ashtray would be full and nothing would quite hide the creeping, clinging staleness of too many cigarettes. When she opened the door, she felt it straight away, smelt it straight away, beneath the layers of deodorant polish, sharp cleansers and a hanging plastic pine. Beneath everything it was still a bookmaker's, an early-morning casino, the buffet on a train packed with too many people each trying too hard not to be doing nothing.

She started the car and backed it out while she waited for DS Moore to come down. Already the smell was fading into normalcy, even as it settled into her, wrapped her up. She would soon have forgotten it. It would be up to others to ask, 'Christ, Caz. Where the hell have you been?'

The electronically controlled up-and-over doors into the basement were still closed but even in the half-light, through the windscreen, Caz could see the sheen of the car's burnished paintwork, the crisped glasswork, the extra shine on the few bits of chrome.

Inside, despite the nicotine, the Sierra smelled of polish

and new car, that indefinable oomph-smell best tasted on August the first. Compared to the outside, though, she thought the interior was only just passable. If she remembered to mention it, she would tell Bob Moore that his prospective son-in-law still had a bit to learn.

Moore came out, banging the yellow bomb-door back with a clang. He looked beefed up, his eyes a little too bright. Caz flashed the Sierra's headlights and he crossed the car park towards her, punch in his stride. She wondered if he'd fallen out with someone.

As he got in he said, 'Some fuckin' motor's turned up on the Downs, burnt out!' He landed in his seat with a thump. 'Some SRi, dark green, nicked Christmas Day. There's no chance of prints but it's got a cracked bumper and a smashed light. Came in five minutes ago. There's a fair chance it'll be the hit-and-run from North Road. If it is, the only way we're ever gonna get the driver is if he walks into the station and confesses!'

Caz shrugged. It happened.

Moore rapped the dashboard. 'So let's get out there, Flood. See if we c'n catch the other fucker before he has the same idea.'

With a buzz, the doors lifted, letting in Brighton, an edge of crisp sun wedged at the entrance. Caz's spirits lifted slightly. As the car broke from the grey underground into the light she pressed the switch for the electric windows, looking for the second lift of fresh air. There was salt, sea, ozone, flighting in the wind. Caz grabbed at the freshness and light, knowing its life was very short. It lasted maybe seven, eight seconds; the time it took for the DS to click in his belt, glance at his watch and growl at his DC.

'Fer fuck's sake, Flood!'

Caz was turning. 'Fer fuck's sake what?'

'The fuckin' winder,' he said.

'What about the winder?'

They were dropping down the hill, still in third gear.

'Shut it, girl! It's fuckin' cold out there!'

Caz buzzed the window closed as she steered the Sierra down the Old Steine, swung it right at the pier, and slicked it along the sea front, throwing aside a light fuzz of rain water. The green-white-grey of the English Channel to her left looked fresh and deadly. Old people muffled against the wind walked slowly between the piers.

The DS wasn't exactly full of the joys of spring, ditto Caz, but she thought she should make an effort, if only so she could say she had tried. As they passed the Brighton Centre she asked if there was any news on the ram-raid or whispers yet on their hit-'n'-run.

'No,' Moore said.

'Is that no as in fuck-all, Sarge? As in definitely nowt?'

'No.'

'Is that no as in no, it's not really a no, or do you really mean yes it's no?'

'MacInnes was right,' Moore said.

'About what?'

'We ain't gonna get on.'

Caz smiled at the road. 'Of course we will, Sergeant.'

'There's the Queen Vic,' he said. 'Hang a right here.'

They turned right at the statue of Queen Victoria and slooped slightly uphill until they reached the A27 where they turned left. They were close to the Goldstone ground, close to the scene of the hit-and-run. Caz asked the DS if he knew exactly where the accident had happened. He told her to stop the car.

'It was here,' he said, a minute later. 'The girl was coming up the hill, darted out. The car was coming from town centre, this side of the road.' He walked another fifty yards towards town, then turned round.

'Looking from here, if she dashed in front of him like she said, he'd've had very little chance of stopping, even if he had been sober. Looks like it was as much the girl's fault as his.'

Caz looked at Moore. 'But that's down to the courts, right?'

He stared back. 'Yes, Flood. We just catch them, let the CPS find a reason t'screw up the case.'

The DS suddenly dropped to his haunches, looking down the road at the white PVC bollards near the crash scene. He looked pensive, deep in thought. Then Caz watched him gesturing with his hands, swerving an imaginary car away from the inevitable, the heel of his hand the rear of the car that had swatted young Jenny Fullerton. His fist suddenly clenched and he looked as though he wanted to punch 'one potato' at his own leg. As he got up he said, 'Stupid fuck!' Caz presumed he was referring to Fullerton.

The skid marks on the road showed that the driver had made a real effort to avoid the girl, brakes to begin with, then a handbrake turn which threatened to roll the car. 'The guy couldn't have been that pissed,' Caz said. She looked again at the skid marks. 'And to react that well, pissed or not, he'd've needed t'be a pretty decent driver. I think Jenny Fullerton was lucky.'

Moore shrugged his shoulders. 'You're not wrong there, Flood.'

They walked back to the Sierra, got in and drove off towards the three Worthing car shops. As they went, the DS told her he would be dealing with the first two outfits while she nipped the half-mile to the third one, Brown's. Caz said he'd already told her.

'Oh, did I?' Moore said. 'Ah well, nothing like bein' sure.'

Mafeking Street was an old red-bricked terrace backing on to the Brighton–Portsmouth railway line. The two car shops were out the back, along a black pot-holed track that ran parallel to a long thin allotment. It was just the sort of place to find a few lock-ups and a couple of Maggie Thatcher's much-vaunted small businesses.

KJ's Wrecks was a small corrugated-metal building at the end of the lane. Caz pulled up, the front wheels turned hard, splashing dark smelly water from a puddle as she stopped. The DS got out, muttering as he stepped on to the wet gravel, and as Caz did the first manoeuvre of a six-point turn, she heard the metal rollers of a sliding door pull back and a loud voice groaning, 'What the fuck'sit now, Moore? Don't y'ever get sick've cummin'ere?'

As Caz edged the Sierra forward, opposite lock full on, she heard the DS say, 'Inside, Kenny.' As he did so, he pointed with two finger-barrelled hands, pistols aimed at the garage. The last person Caz had seen use that gesture was the lieutenant in the opening credits of *Cagney and Lacey*. Nevertheless, it worked on Kenny who walked into the darkness, waving his arms and no doubt talking about police harassment. Moore shouted back to Caz, 'Pick me up at Martin's, Flood! Soon as you like.'

Thirty-Six

Brown & Brown, the Car Shop, may have been a step up from the two shacks in Mafeking Street, but if it was, it was a very short step and with a gammy leg. To get to it, Caz had to park up next to a round-arched tunnel underneath the railway and walk through the half-light past the barriers that had stopped her car. The underpass was gloomy, dripping, wet and isolated; the haunt of flashers or rapists. The kind of place where women go when they have to, but suddenly remember their lack of strength and the awesome power of men.

Halfway through there was a puddle the width of the tunnel, wide enough to force one jumped footfall, deep enough to wet Caz's trainers and splash her 501s. Now she knew why Moore had given her Brown's to talk to! For a second, her face hardened. A sex freak appearing now would have made a huge mistake; Caz was in the mood for a bit of payback and was pumped up enough to dish it out. In the small of her back she could feel the press of the short riding crop that was tucked into her jeans. For reassurance, she put her hand behind her to touch it. Her nostrils flared briefly as she reached the tunnel mouth.

Brown & Brown's was painted green, a huge wooden firetrap heading a wired compound littered with the carcases of accidental cars. The owner's name was White, Caz didn't ask why, and if he was bent he should give it up and go into films. As Caz questioned him and the one mechanic within reach, there wasn't a flicker of nerves, no tremor, no 'here we go again, what the hell do you coppers think you're up to – why don't you get out there and bother somebody else – catch some *real* villains, eh?' They were clean. Bore-ring. The only thing they said worth mentioning was that those two repair shops back've Mafeking Street were the iffiest businesses between Newhaven and Pompey. But then they prob'ly knew that, didn't they? That was why they was bothering hard-working clean garages like theirs . . .

Caz left them after telling them that if anything came up, especially car-ringing or someone needing a covered-up repair . . .

They said they'd ring.

She went back through the tunnel, got wet again, met no strange men and got back in the car. As she sat down and felt her trainers squelch, she wished she had taken the long way round to Brown's. She put the heater on full and the fans on maximum blow, feeling the hot air slowly drying her out, slowly bringing her mood back.

When she jerked back up the lane behind Mafeking Street she saw a couple of men on the allotments, undoing their separate huts, spilling out forks and hoes to tend their rows of cauli and potato. She had a sudden flash of her grandfather and an uncle, two lovely men who, like these two, produced real vegetables from their own soil and their own toil, no crap additives and no three months' storage between harvest and plate. She had almost forgotten what that kind of spud tasted like.

On a whim, she stopped briefly, stepped out and shouted a hello. The nearest guy, dungarees over an old sweater, flat cap, brown sinewy hands, strolled over, a hoe balanced in his hands. As he got closer, Caz saw he had a row of enamel railway badges on his hat.

'Can't keep away, eh?' the man said. 'You after a plot or something?'

'It's a thought,' Caz said.

'You've not much chance, lass. Sorry. The plots go t'relatives first. Only one's come free in eight years and there was two hundred people on the waiting list for that.' He smiled and offered his hand.

'My name's Jack, by the way.'

Shaking his hand, Caz said, 'Kathy Flood, call me Caz.'

Jack smiled again. 'D'yer fancy a few Edwards?'

'King Ed's? Are they ready?'

'They're smaller than they'll be next month, but they're ready.'

'I'd love some!' Caz said. There was only one food better than a fresh old potato and that was a fresh new potato. She was already planning a meal. Did Jack have anything else?

'Might be able to find you a few kidneys an' a small cauli . . .'

Caz was ecstatic. 'That'd be fantastic. How much do I owe you?'

'Owe me? Don't be daft, lass. If you want t'pay me back, come round some time, any afternoon, number thirteen Mafeking Street. Have a cuppa tea with me. I'm on my own now, the company'd be nice.'

Caz liked him. 'I'd love to,' she said.

'Not in the mornin', though,' Jack added thoughtfully. 'I'm

here from quarter after nine until lunchtime most days, so afternoon's best.'

'It might be a few days, Jack. I'm a bobby and we're pretty busy at the moment.'

'I've got lots of time, love.'

'I'm sure,' Caz said. She really liked this guy. 'I'll find some time to get round.'

'Champion!' Jack said. 'I'll just get these spuds.' He turned away as if Caz was meant to follow. She thought about it but before she could act she heard Moore's voice bawling down the lane, '*Flood!*'

'My boss,' she said apologetically, 'I'd better go.'

'I can have that veg ready in a minute . . .'

'On my way back?' Caz offered.

'Good idea,' Jack said.

She got in the Sierra and bumped down the track, feeling faintly pink. She had been quick at Brown & Brown's and hadn't expected Sergeant Moore to be finished quite so soon. When she got to the end of the lane she splashed more black water over his shiny car. When he got in he was not amused. 'What the fuck're you playing at, Flood?'

Caz was tempted to lie but didn't. 'I was buying some veg, Sarge. Off the old guy on the allotment. I didn't think you'd be done yet.'

'Well I was.'

'I'm sorry, Sarge.'

'And I suppose you got nowhere at Brown's?'

'Squeaky clean.'

'Same here, this pair. They've got Cliff Richard in the front office and Mother Theresa doing the books.'

'So where to, Sarge?'

'Bog Regis. Tell you exactly when we get there.'

Caz inched the car round, managing the turn in five locks this time. Moore was distracted, too pissed off to barrack her. As they moved away, he glanced very briefly at the sliding door of K&J's. In her rearview mirror Caz saw it finally close on the last two inches of black.

Jack was ready at the gate and waved a Sainsbury's carrier bag at them, heavy with goods. Caz stopped and lowered Moore's window. Jack leaned in with the bag and she took the vegetables. Moore, leaning back, was even less happy. He glowered.

'Thanks, Jack,' Caz said pointedly. 'This is really appreciated.'

'It's a pleasure,' Jack said sweetly. 'See you soon, I hope.'

He watched as the two of them pulled away, the woman with a little lift in her eyes, the man, dark and brooding.

Bognor Regis was a waste of time. There were three car repair shops to visit; they went to them together and they all looked clean. By half past eleven they were travelling back to Brighton, by twelve o'clock they were at John Street, and by ten past they were parked up, upstairs and doing paperwork, the one thing coppers never tired of.

Bob Moore gave Caz an hour, plus the hour for lunch. He told her that come half past two, the beats and the pandas would be reporting in and she'd have plenty to do. She wasn't thinking of having a social life, was she? No? Good. They'd talk at four o'clock unless something brown collided with a fan. Caz said, 'No probs!', rang Valerie to put him on a possible late, left Moira a message to bell her at home after eight o'clock and then dug out the home number for Claire Cook-Bullen.

When she rang, there was no answer. She counted fourteen rings, put the phone down and tried again. This time she left the phone on low speaker for a minute while she finished off a report. If Claire was there she definitely wasn't in the mood for a chat. The burr-burr, the link across the miles, hooked hypnotically into Caz, one more, three more, three more, then another three, on and on as she worked. Eventually, she had to, Caz broke the spell, then the connection. She had one hour forty-five minutes. She thought, 'Sod it,' grabbed her Goretex and headed for the car park.

Thirty-Seven

She drove the MX5 close to legally, down to the front again and over to Hangleton. The sea was still as filthy as before and old people still muffled their furrows, slow-walking along the promenade, this time towards their half-warmed flats or expectant fish-and-chip lunches.

Tchaikovsky's *Nutcracker* was playing on the car stereo – Tom MacInnes was getting to her – and there was a temptation to stop up somewhere, sod Claire Bullen for now and enjoy her freedom. She passed Victoria's statue and headed for the few scruffy cranes ahead and to her left. The temptation passed.

She headed for the golf course through classic suburbia, passing houses that had been built when the only plastic was Bakelite, when solid was not a rude word and a dollar meant five shillings. When she found the Cooks' close, it was with a sigh.

The yellow Metro was outside the house, which could mean almost anything, but Caz had a strong feeling that despite the unanswered phone, Claire Cook-Bullen would be in. Whether she was 'at home' was another matter. If she was in, she was going to have to speak to Caz. Now she had got here, Caz had decided she wouldn't be ignored.

She knocked rather than use the door bell, waited, then knocked again. When there was no answer to her second knock, she tried the bell and was given a dose of electronic muzak. Third press there was noise from upstairs, the dull clunk of someone finally responding.

Yes!

The last time Caz had called on the Cook-Bullens it had been Daniel Cook's larger figure that had shimmered from the other side of the door's frosted side-panel. This time it was the slighter, shorter, white-clad figure of his wife. Caz waited as latches clacked back, a chain clattered and then the door was slowly pulled open, not the expected crack, but fully, blatantly, revealing Claire Bullen barefoot, in a white shop-assistant's coat, a four-inch brush in her hand, white emulsion on her fingers and in her hair.

'Hello, Caz,' she said, 'I thought you'd have been here earlier.'

Caz followed Claire into the hall, into the kitchen, and then, once Claire had switched on the kettle, back out through the hall, up the stairs and into Claire's bedroom. As they went, Claire told Caz she was redecorating; the room needed it. Did she mind, only it was nearly finished and once she was done she could chat to Caz without a guilty conscience . . .

When they went in, only the slight wetness in places told Caz what had been done, what had been redone. Claire's rewhitened whitened bedroom was receiving yet another coat of white. The distant patterns in the anaglypta were almost completely submerged now, as if Claire's long-term aim was a smooth finish without ever stripping the walls. 'I've bought a new desk,' she said as she splashed white into the last corner.

'Oh?' Caz asked innocently. 'And what colour would that be?'

'I couldn't decide between black and white,' Claire said. She put the brush down on the edge of the tin, 'but in the end I went for white.'

The kettle had boiled once and came quickly back up to speed. As she made tea, Claire seemed almost normal except maybe she spoke a little slower, a little more deliberately. They were both runners so Caz wasn't expecting sugar on the tray or a biscuit tin within reach. Claire filled two mugs and they went through to the lounge to empty them. They sat down, opposite each other in the two armchairs. On an instinct, Caz kept shtum, waiting for Claire to speak first.

After a minute, Claire sat forward, slightly stiffening, rolling her already empty mug in her hand. 'So how's your running, Caz?'

'Just enough to keep fit,' Caz said flatly. 'I was working Saturday, so I missed the Hants Cross-Country league. On Sunday, I jogged round the Stubbington 10K.'

Claire sniffed. 'I think my lot must have been short in the Hampshire because I didn't turn out. I won't be that popular with the team the next time I get to training.'

'So why didn't you run?'

'I couldn't,'Claire said.

'Am I supposed to know what that means?'

'It wasn't convenient.'

'Yeah?'

'I was – with someone.'

Caz raised her eyebrows. 'Ah . . .'

There was a pause then Claire looked at Caz and said,

'Daniel and I haven't discussed it yet.'

'Discussed what?'

'Where I went.'

'And where was that, Claire?'

'I told you.'

'No you didn't,' Caz said sharply. 'You said you were *with* someone. You never said *where* you were.'

'I can't.'

'Why not, Claire? What you say to me is confidential, you know that. We need to clarify what happened to you this weekend.'

Claire raised her voice. Her fingers were white round the mug.

'Nothing happened!'

Caz sat up, letting some of her annoyance show. 'Claire, you had half the county searching for you! Did you know there was another missing person? While we were fucking about trying to find *you*, some poor teenage girl from Shoreham was missing.' Caz was lying now but so what? 'This kid, she's an asthmatic and so far, there's been no trace of her. We had to halve the numbers looking for *her* so we could look for you! And now you say nothing happened? Fer fuck's sake, Claire!'

'Shoreham?'

'That's right, Claire, Shoreham. You know, where you go for your fast three miles in the middle of seven, remember? Remember, Thursday nights, the mud flats, the houseboats, the Adur bridge?'

The blood drained from Claire's face.

'I can't say anything, I really can't. Caz, I—'

'Why the fuck not?'

Claire's colour was returning. 'Are you allowed to swear at me?'

'I'm off duty!' Caz snapped.

'I'm sorry,' Claire said. She had stood up, ready to move back to the kitchen. 'Nothing happened, Caz. I just couldn't ring, that's all.'

'Tell me why, Claire.'

'No,' Claire said. 'You can shout at me as much as you like, but I can't. I can't.' She went to make more tea. When she turned to ask if Caz would like another, Caz had already left.

Thirty-Eight

Everyone knows you can choose your friends but you can't choose your family. Every runner knows that when it comes to running you can only half choose who you leave the gym with. Pick some runner who's two minutes a mile slower than you and someone is going to suffer; go running with a twenty-eight-year-old sub-thirty-minute 10K man and *you* are going to suffer. Forget politics, religion, sexual persuasion and body odours, the first criteria for a running partner is 'How fast do you do your mile reps?'

Caz had run on and off with Claire Bullen because Claire was good. She wasn't as raw, out-of-the-blocks fast as Caz but she had so much stamina that she could cope with everything Caz could invent except eight-hundred-metre repetitions. Even then, the one or two times they had done them, Caz just gave Claire a ten-second start, caught her in the second half and beat her by another five. When they were doing longer stuff, their match came closer. At anything beyond fourteen miles, neither of them ran fast anyway, so they could stay together without a problem. Claire had never talked much. It wasn't a marriage made in heaven but it worked.

But now Caz was so mad at her *ex*-running partner, she burned.

She crunched the gears as she left the close, crunched them again when she turned into the main road. She'd lied through her teeth to Claire about the Walters girl and now, suddenly, perversely, she felt guilty and wound up, seriously worrying, imagining that somehow she had tempted fate and something really *had* happened to her.

And it was all Claire Bullen's fault. She was fucking some no-chin and hadn't come home for a few days. Why not just tell Caz on the QT and let her slip away?

Some tosser in a Montego cut her up. She flashed him and gave the finger automatically, still thinking about Claire. Mrs Fucking-Cook-fucking-Bullen had done the unforgivable. She had given Caz a problem. One Caz didn't know how to attack.

The arsehole in the Montego had slowed down for effect, drifting out into the road to make it difficult to overtake.

She dropped into second gear, screamed up to six thousand revs and went the wrong side of some bollards, her hand flat on the horn as she blasted by. 'I am fucking *annoyed* now, Bullen!' she shouted. She only stopped blasting the horn to put two fingers out through her window. Then she shimmied the car's tail and sailed towards town. She thought about things. This was *not* over.

But first she had to speak to MacInnes.

Thirty-Nine

Caz got back to John Street with half an hour of her official lunch break left. Saint & Greavsie were at their desk, a definite whiff of curry and Carlsberg floating round them but, amazingly, no ciggies.

'Light of my life!' Saint said when she came in.

'And you of mine,' Caz said. 'Anything happening?'

'Nowt much. Coupla notes on Bob Moore's desk for you.'

Caz thanked the DC. Then she asked how come neither of them were smoking.

'We've been converted by Billy T!' Greavsie chipped in. 'If a pillock like 'im can harvest something like Moira Dibben, there's got t'be something in it!'

'And besides,' Saint added, 'you said you weren't available . . .'

'Give up *breathing* for a week, Bob, I'm yours. A deal?'

'Let me think about it,' Saint said.

Caz went to Bob Moore's desk. Her two notes were stuck to a sheet of A4 with '*Flood*' scrawled across its top. Next to that was the note from earlier that morning. Caz glanced to see three bold red ticks alongside the name K&J Autos, single ticks against Martin's and Brown's. She picked up her notes. Both were from Southampton, one from DS Mason at Shirley, the other from a name that hardly rang a bell, Jenny Wilkinson. Curiosity made her call the woman first.

Caz wondered if it would be all right to sit in the DS's chair. She decided to risk it, dialled up the Southampton number and sat back. The other end was picked up second ring, an attitude-trained voice. 'You are through to The Ice House. How can we help you?'

Caz said could she speak to Jenny Wilkinson?

And she was?

'My name is Caz Flood. Ms Wilkinson asked me to call her.'

'I'm Jenny,' the voice said.

'What can I do for you?'

'You don't remember me?'

'Not that I can think of—' Caz paused, then it came back to her. 'Trevor Jones's girlfriend?'

'Trevor's out on bail but I've just heard that the CPS aren't going to proceed. Something about undue pressure when he was picked up.'

'But he was as guilty as sin!' Caz said.

'I know that, you know that, Trevor knew it too. He was expecting to go down, but his brief argued that he'd only said he done all those burglaries because of the murder charge that was hanging over him.'

'Are you sure the Crown Prosecution Service is dropping the case?'

'Yes, but that wasn't why I rang you.'

'So why did you?'

'I'm pregnant,' Jenny said.

'Well, don't look at me!'

'I'm expecting; it's Trevor's kid and now this on top, it's

like everything's suddenly starting to work out. I wanted t'thank you. Trev's got a job working in Dixon's. He said you helped him get it. You wouldn't know him if you met him, he's really trying.'

Caz had forgotten. It had been one phone call to a probation officer in Southampton and one instinctive 'give him a chance' remark. She hadn't forgotten Trevor John Jones, only the common-law connection between him and Jenny Wilkinson.

Caz had met Jones in her first week as a DC. His arrest had been a good one for her, a one-on-one confrontation on what was more or less a building site, just him, her, and her riding crop, with Saint & Greavsie pounding towards them. It was months ago but it felt like years.

'I'm glad,' she said, 'for both of you.'

'Thanks,' the voice said. There was an awkward pause, the word pregnant came to mind. Was there anything else? Caz asked.

'Yes,' Wilkinson said. Caz could almost sense her looking behind her as she spoke. The voice lowered. 'Trevor *knows* something.'

It could only happen to Caz. People like Saint & Greavsie had their half-and-half druggies who fed them titbits in exchange for bad eyesight. The Bob Moores of this world paid out tens and twenties to their snouts, but when Caz got an informant he was sixty miles away; in a place where the women coppers had to wear skirts. She thought, 'Fuck it.' Then she said she'd ring back as soon as she could.

As soon as she'd put the phone down on Jenny Wilkinson, Caz dialled Southampton's Shirley High Street nick and asked for DS Mason. She was put through to the detectives' barn.

Someone there picked up the phone, grunted, 'Flood, d'yer say?' and put her on hold. While she waited she heard, 'Simple!' and someone else bawl back, 'Fuck you, dick'ead!' When Peter came on the phone he said, 'I see you've met our other DS.'

'Nice telephone manner,' Caz said.

Peter didn't laugh. 'We need t'talk,' he said.

Forty

'Flood, I've just heard, is it true?'

'What, that Jimmy Case is retiring?'

'About Moira.'

'What about Moira?'

'I heard she's—'

'Brown?'

'No.'

'Decorating her dining room?'

'No.

'I give in, Peter. Now you know why I never watch quiz shows.'

'She's pregnant, Caz!'

'Get away!'

'I'm serious. Didn't you know?'

'Know what, Peter? I'm Moira's best friend. Don't you think she'd've told me if she was up the spout? Where d'you get such an idea?'

'I heard.'

'And you just believed what you heard. Why didn't you just ask me?'

'What d'you think I'm doing now, Flood?'

'How's panicking sound?'

'So it's not true, then?'

'Put it this way, Peter. Moira tells me everything, and I mean *everything*. If she was pregnant she would've told me.'

'Well, what's this about her having to get married?'

'What the fuck're you on about? She's getting engaged to Billy but that's because she *wants* to not because she has to. I don't know where you're getting your information from, Peter, but I hope you're not paying for it.'

'I heard she'd bin to a chemist . . .'

'Oh yeah? Ever heard of aspirin? Toothbrushes? Condoms? You ever heard of thrush, Peter?'

'So it's not true?'

'I've already told you, Pierre. If Moira was pregnant, she'd've told me before anyone else, and that's *anyone* else. Fret you not.'

'Jesus!' Caz could see his shirt collar undone. The grey in his face slowly giving way.

'Peter?'

'What?'

'You coming to the christening?'

That end, there was a short corked sound, a gulp maybe, someone swallowing their false teeth, the pop of a brain haemorrhage, a heart valve jamming shut. This end, Caz grinned smugly.

'Jesus, Flood, you're an evil bastard.'

'Yer think so?' Caz said, 'How kind of you to say.'

'More than evil.'

'Does that mean a favour's not likely?'

'A what?'

'I need a favour.'

'Are you serious?'

'Perfectly, Peter. Look, I've got some street intelligence. The source is Southampton. I don't particularly want to come over just for that and I thought we might go halves on whatever it is.'

'A snout.'

'An intelligence source in the community, yes.'

'How much?'

'I should think free.'

'Can we afford free?'

'Yes. D'you think it'll be a boy or a girl?'

The DS promised not to go away. Caz rang Jenny Wilkinson and told her that a mate would be calling on her behalf. Jenny seemed to think that Trevor would want to talk direct to Caz but Caz explained there was a big operation going on in Brighton and she couldn't make it over.

Jenny still wasn't sure. 'I don't know if Trevor'll like it, but OK. Get the bloke t'ring me here. I'll talk to him.'

'You're an angel, Jenny. Give my love to Trevor. And you can tell him that if he lets you and that baby down, I'll come visiting.'

'*And thank you for calling The Ice House*,' the voice repaired.

'Company?'

'That's correct, madam. Nothing too hot, nothing too big.'

'Good luck, Jenny.'

When she rang Peter to give him the telephone number, the friendly DS answered. Caz told him she was the GUI clinic ringing with Mason's results. Peter obviously didn't have a sense of humour. When he came back on the line he accused Caz of ruining his sex life. Caz thought that was fine. He'd have more time for policing. 'Just remember, Peter. This is my snout. He's free but don't hurt him.'

'As if . . .' Peter said.

Forty-One

When Caz put the phone down she was quite proud of herself. She had smoked Peter Mason and as far as she could remember she had told not a single lie. She should've been a politician. If she'd been a little less intelligent she might've been.

She tossed a coin between low blood sugar and something from the canteen, lost, so went downstairs and got the last Cornish pasty, to go with a can of Diet Coke. By the time she got back to the DS's desk his bulk was filling the chair. As she walked in he sulked out loud.

'Why aren't you fuckin fat, Flood?'

Caz told him, 'High muscle-to-weight ratio, high metabolism.'

'Jam, more like.'

'Maybe it's the exercise,' she said.

There was little or nothing in from either the section cars or the area back-ups. It was beginning to look like the hit-and-run car was locked away in a garage or languishing in a quarry pond somewhere. Bob Moore didn't look any too pleased and he was even less pleased as he told Caz that the ram-raid investigation was going nowhere. A known family on Brighton's north side had been favourites for that one but at least two of them had good alibis, namely that they'd smacked someone in a pub in Hove and had spent from ten till breakfast banged up!

'I don't know of any other regulars. It was New Year's Eve, surely no one's going t'travel a long way for a blag, not New Year's Eve?'

'It was at half two, wasn't it?'

Moore corrected her. 'Quarter past.'

'Well, maybe it was an idiot job. Gang've lads going out t'do damage for the sake've it. They get stoked up with Stella and then go out and smash up a shop.'

'No, this is a gang,' Moore said. 'They were pros. A proper driver.'

'Did they get much, Sarge?'

'Coupla videos, coupla camcorders. They were disturbed and legged it before getting all that much.'

'They were caught at it? Did we get a statement from whoever?'

'No. If you watch the video you can see that someone's challenged them. They take a look at some citizen, try to decide whether to fill him in or not. The other option is run. They stop about a second 'n' a half, then they get out of there quick with the camcorders.'

'This passer-by,' Caz asked, 'is he on the video?'

'Nope.'

'Have we made an appeal?'

'The *Argus* ran a short on it but it's not exactly *Crimewatch*, is it?'

'So what now, Sarge?'

'We keep an eye on all the known handlers, punters buying as-new videos. We might get lucky. In fact' – Moore suddenly sat up, something to do – 'we can do the rounds of the second-hand shops this afternoon. Nothing much looks like happening on the Goldstone Road accident.'

'You want me, Sarge?'

'No, Flood. I thought you could stay here and make everyone tea.'

Caz decided. This was wry humour, yes? 'You want me . . .'

'Like a bleeding pile, Detective. Let's go.'

Forty-Two

Brighton is Little-London-by-the-Sea. It has character. It has seaside landladies, a shingle beach and one and a half piers. Little London has the Pavilion, the Grand, the Metropole, the Lanes. It also has a pub called The Queen's Head with a *man's* head on the sign that hangs outside. The Lanes has a few interesting shops and a tourist price-tag.

But walk away from the sea, cross North Street and walk along Bond Street. (The Queen's Head will be to your right at the bottom of North Street, just the other side of the Steine.) This is definitely *not* the Lanes. It's an alternative. For electronic POS tills substitute bum-bags slung on the belly or Indian-weave satchels full of change. For crystal glass substitute crystals. Find second-hand bookshops, vegetarian food, pyramids to sharpen old razor-blades, psychics, masseurs, recycled clothes, tarot cards, Forbidden Planet. The streets are one-way and narrow. The parking is hopeless and for half the week the area is cluttered with market stalls. In a square mile is everything from an enamel painted thimble to a line of coke. There are few thirty-day citizens here. Instead they have people.

But better-off people? Caz wondered. She had done all that, had her hair black, green, then braided; worn beads on her head and round her neck; scuffed round Turkey with dirty feet and sandals for a year; did Greece, Europe by train. Then she'd stopped.

Now she was a copper, just about as straight and 'citizen' as you could get, but Caz still liked the smell of anarchy, of nonconformity. When she thought of herself, her character, as Jekyll and Hyde, her only problem was she didn't know which half was the bad side.

She had done the hippy sod-work-get-a-life thing. She'd enjoyed it, but in the end it didn't seem enough. When she met the older drop-outs, guys with greying hair and John Lennon glasses desperate to screw her, they always seemed to be *explaining* their way of life, apologising to Caz for her failure to understand, justifying their not being citizens. By the end she'd decided that the life wasn't a *chosen* alternative, it was just something that these guys had tried when they were younger and had never stopped. They were as much in a rut as the suits that commuted into London Victoria every day. Those that stayed, it seemed to Caz, stayed because they couldn't do the other thing, not so much didn't *want* to do the other thing.

As far as she was concerned, Caz had never expected it to last and was back in England twenty-six months after she had flown out. She temped in an office and worked behind a bar for three months just to get the feel of things again and put a few quid in the bank. Then she had joined the force.

She was on the other side now, the filth, the law, a pig travelling with a fat sergeant. Caz knew that half this lot would instantly clock both of them as CID and would presume her as the type to pull one of them for possession or to check out the cassette tapes they were selling in case they were copyright rip-offs from Singapore. They didn't know Caz. They wouldn't know that really, she didn't give a toss.

The DS was feeling foul. 'Fuckin' glad I'm not that little Dutch boy.'

'Sergeant?'

'You know, put his finger in a dyke.'

'Very funny, Sarge.'

'Are you gonna park, Flood, or just drive round all day looking at the queers and loons? Fuckin' UFO landed'ere, turn round and piss off back t'Mars . . .'

'Done a lot of community policing, have you, Sarge?'

'Just park, Flood.'

But there was no parking. In the end they pulled up half on to the kerb outside a nearly-new shop and Bob Moore went in, leaving Caz to go off and find somewhere. He said she'd catch him up easy enough.

Caz drove away as the DS went into the shop. Eventually she found somewhere to squeeze in the Sierra and then jogged the half-mile or so back to find him. She went in two shops he'd already been to and left, then found him in a third that called itself a recycling centre. The owner was nearer fifty than forty, wore a floppy khaki jumper, bags and sandals. He didn't do electronic stuff, he said, too materialistic.

'Keep it that way,' Moore said.

The next place was a few shop doorways away, past an antiquarian bookshop and a vegetarian café. It called itself Kee's Amazing Mart, a title a little more American than they expected but a second-hand shop for all that. Before they went in Moore paused.

'Fairly regular fence, Flood, but only one- and two-offs, never anything major. Done us a couple of favours in the past and so far's never been down. Let me deal with him, right?'

They went in to the sound of a blatting bell, loud enough to make a deaf man wince. There was one customer, a lanky teenager with a red baseball cap reversed on his head. 'Police!' Moore said. The kid gulped.

The kid muttered something like, 'Back later, Mr Kee,' to the man behind the counter, and quickly exited right. Caz took in Kee, seedy, a caricature of the dirty old man. He was almost bald, with a sweep of Bobby Charlton hair; his shirt might have been white once and his long grey cardigan sagged with the weight of keys, cigarettes and a lighter. As he came round the counter, he stooped and undid his half-gloved hands to make a pathetic gesture of welcome towards the DS. The fingers protruding from the gloves had black nails. Yellowed teeth completed the ensemble. 'Mister Moore . . .'

The sergeant ignored the hand and it was very slowly lowered. Kee put his hands together and like something straight out of Dickens, twisted and untwisted his grubby fingers, waiting for the sergeant to speak. The two or three seconds he waited seemed like forever and his head slowly tilted, first inquisitive, then frightened. Moore held the silence for another few seconds then he said, 'Book him, Flood!'

'But Mister Moore . . .'

'What?' Moore said.

Kee offered a sickly yellow smile. 'I haven't done anything, have I?'

'Why are you so nervous, then? You got a coupla kids out back?'

'That's not fair, Mister Moore.'

'Fuck fair,' Moore snapped. 'You taking me out back?'

'What for?'

'We wantta take a look at yer video collection.'

'You know I don't do the films any more, Sergeant.'

'Not the films, machines. I wanna see yer *players.*'

'I don't have very many new ones, Mister Moore. What is it that you're looking for, exactly?'

Moore turned to Caz. 'It's me that's the copper, yeah?'

'I think so, Sarge.'

The shopkeeper was bowing even lower now, finally getting the message. 'I'm sorry, Mister Moore. It's through here.'

'Right!' Moore said brightly. To Caz he said, 'Watch the shop, Flood.'

Caz looked around her as Moore and Kee went out the back through a glass-wired door. Kee was trying to say something about being clean for years. The sergeant was bundling him out of it and saying 'Yeah, yeah, we know, we know . . .' Almost as soon as the door closed behind them, Caz heard a crash and a faint hissed 'Yes!' She hoped to hell that was the only noise she was going to hear – another one and she was going to have to go through.

She suddenly became interested in the old records, LPs and 45s, stacked along the glass counter. The one on the end had a cherub-faced kid in a kilt and a toothy smile, standing with a silver loch behind him and no doubt his mummy the other side of the camera. Caz was so tense she actually picked the cover up, the vinyl immediately slipping out and flipping like a frisbee to the floor. There was another bang. Caz flinched, but this time it was just the door slapping back. Moore and Kee came through as a couple. Moore was saying, 'Excellent! Excellent! Show me!' Kee said, 'They're by the till, Mister Moore.'

'Flood!' Moore said. 'Looks like we've found the cameras.'

Kee nodded limply to Caz as if he was glad to see her there.

He passed some pieces of pink paper to the sergeant. 'Here you are, Mister Moore,' he said, a flutter held back, 'like I told you, completely legal.'

Caz could feel sweat in the small of her back.

Forty-Three

Kee had bought two Sony video-cams for £125 each, expecting to move them for twice that. They weren't going to get him for receiving this time because he had two handwritten receipts from the shop, cash sales in October. 'Unwanted birthday presents, apparently,' he said, 'quite a coincidence getting two in one day.'

'Off, I am very pissed,' Moore said as they walked back to the car, one camera each in a box under the arm. 'It's not even worth trying to book him for this one. A good brief would eat us alive. CPS won't touch it.'

'So where'd they get the receipt book? Do we need t'talk to the staff?'

'Been done,' Moore said. 'They grabbed the receipt book when they hit the shop.'

'Shit. So how do we pin receiving on someone like Kee?'

'With great difficulty, Flood.'

They went back to the station.

It was dark as they pulled into the underground car park. The bays were softly lit with yellow light. DS Moore was still sulking and Caz gently prodded, looking for the problem. He was still pissed off. Why?

'So you're my confessor now, Flood?'

'No, Sarge. It's just that you haven't taken the piss for an hour or so and I was beginning t'think that maybe you were sickening for something.'

'Sick *of* something, more like.'

'What, the job?'

'And why not? We catch villains and the CPS kisses them goodbye. Half the fuckers out there hate us, the other half think we're useless.'

'So what's new?'

'The year, Flood. I go on a course, come back full of it. Two days later I'm knee deep in piss and crap again, chasing no-hoper cases and having t'deal with arseholes like Kee.'

'We get 'em in the end, Sarge.'

'That makes you feel better, does it? I'm not MacInnes but I want to put villains away. When I started, the public wanted that too. Now I'm not so sure.' He clicked the door open, then sat back a second.

'I think we might get the hit-and-run driver,' Caz said.

Moore moved to get out of the car. 'Oh yeah? Why's that then?'

'Just a feeling, Sarge.'

He was out of the car, leaning back in before he slammed the door. 'This is the famous Flood, is it, or you goin't' say why?'

'Not yet, Sarge. For now it's just a feeling.'

'God help us!' Moore said as the door closed.

It was now almost half past five. Caz got out of the car and made a point of locking up carefully, letting the DS get far enough ahead so she didn't have to chase after him or go up the stairs with him. When she got upstairs, she walked the long way round, clocking that the chief super was still not there but that the DI was. She stopped outside the door and waited long enough to hear nothing before tapping the glass gently, a girl's knock.

'In!'

She pushed open the door and tipped her head inside, 'Would you have five mins, sir?'

MacInnes looked tired. 'Tek a seat, hen.'

She went in.

Forty-Four

'So where d'you want to start, Detective?' the DI said. He wasn't looking at Caz but bent to the side, opening his bottom drawer.

'The tape, sir? Any joy?'

'Anything else?' He was pouring a smut of Glenfiddich for Caz, twice as much for himself.

'I'd like to talk about a couple of problems, sir; my misper, Claire Bullen, and a possible snout.'

'A snout?'

'Yes, sir, but he's in Southampton so I'm not sure what—'

MacInnes passed Caz a plastic cup. 'Do I know him?'

'Trevor Jones, sir.'

'Trevor Jones? The burglar from October?'

'Yes, sir. He's working, his girlfriend's pregnant. He's out on bail and I heard this morning that the CPS aren't proceeding on the burglaries.'

'You think this toerag is going t'be any good?'

'I won't know that for sure, until I meet up with him, but I know him and I know his missus. I think he's serious about trying to go straight.'

'But he's in Southampton?'

'Yes.'

'How've you left it?'

'I asked DS Mason to go have a chat with Jones's girlfriend, Jenny Wilkinson. He was going to come back to me this afternoon.'

'And has he?'

'I haven't been to my desk yet, sir. Thought I'd catch you before you sloped off.'

'I don't slope off, Flood.'

'Before you left, sir.'

MacInnes took a good swallow of his Glenfiddich, waited a second to enjoy it, then sat forward, his elbows on the desk.

'Well, Caz,' he glanced up at the clock, 'like as not an informant in Southampton is going to provide intelligence for the city. It might piss you off, but the way I see it, you'll have t'pass him over to Mason or one of his mates.'

'I guessed that, sir. It's just that Jones is my first real snout.'

'It's called life, Caz, but at least they'll owe you one. Never hurts to put markers in the bank. Never know when another copper might bail you out. We all need friends.'

'Can I ask a bit of advice about my misper, sir? I think she's holding out on me. She was pretty strange this morning. I'm not very happy.'

'So what d'you want?'

'Well, I'd like to lean on her a bit, sir; threaten her with wasting police time, something like that. Thing is, if she rings here . . .'

'What exactly d'you think's going on, Caz?'

'No idea, sir. I just know she's being evasive. She was gone, what, nearly three days, and when she came back she was a mess, covered in some kind of crap. Julie Jones said she was out of it and they sedated her. She won't talk to her husband, told me she was with someone . . .'

'So what's the big deal?'

'Well, sir, if it was just a fella, she'd whisper it t'me and that would be it. I don't understand her attitude. Something isn't right.'

'How about *we* call on her, give a bit of a push?'

'When, sir?'

'How does now sound, Flood?'

'Time t'check my desk?'

'Ten minutes, off y'go.'

When Caz got back to the War Room, Bob Moore was waiting. He was bawling her out before the doors had stopped flapping.

'Where the fuck've you been, Flood?'

'What? The bog. Speaking to the DI. Where's the fire?'

'Yer working with *me*, Flood!'

'Yes, Sarge. And I thought we'd finished for the day. You shot off. I was just going to bring you your keys and get away.'

He held out some Post-It notes. 'You've got messages.'

Peter Mason wanted her to ring urgently, he'd be in until five thirty, Mo would ring between eight and nine, Valerie had left a message saying he wouldn't be over tonight – too much catching up at work – would she give him a bell some time? 'Exciting times, eh?' Moore said.

Caz looked aghast. 'You reading my *mail*, Sarge?'

He held out his hand.

Caz leaned to drop the car keys into Moore's palm, then turned away with a little puff. She picked up a telephone from the next desk and punched the number for Shirley. It was ten to six. If she knew Peter Mason, he had already slipped off home. Five rings. 'Hampshire Police?'

'DS Mason, please.'

'Comes on duty at eight thirty,' a voice said, bored. 'Can I take a message?'

'Doesn't matter,' Caz said. She hated being right.

Forty-Five

There was no way Tom MacInnes was going to squeeze himself into Caz's MX5, not when they could use his Scorpio. Bob Moore's head went by the door as he told her.

'How are you and the DS getting on?' he said as he grabbed a coat.

'Yes,' she said.

They went down the back way, treading in Moore's echo. As they came through the door to the car park, he was reversing his Sierra out too quickly. He flipped the wheel one-handed as he braked, slammed a gear and squealed the tyres as he shot forward, eyes staring down a tunnel. The up-and-over doors were already open and he dipped the car's nose as he turned out of the entrance, his head flicking a perfunctory left-right as if he actually cared if there was traffic coming. Caz could feel the sergeant's anger but said nothing. There was no way the DI would comment. As she got in to the DI's car she joked, 'Right, sir, is it Moore-style or just very fast?'

'Very fast is fine,' MacInnes said, going with the joke. The DI belted himself in and Caz started the car. Then he added, 'Don't worry about Sar'nt Moore, Caz, good driver, done all the courses.'

Caz backed out carefully. There was nothing to say.

The evening traffic was evening traffic and the normal ten-minute drive to Hangleton was quick at half an hour. When they pulled up outside the Cook-Bullen house, both cars were there. They got out, made a show of slamming their doors and strode purposefully up the front path. MacInnes knocked, rang the bell and knocked again, all within fifteen seconds. A loud TV in the lounge was turned down, a door flopped open and then the hall light came on. Daniel Cook came to the door. He seemed surprised to see them.

'Police!' MacInnes said brusquely. 'We need to speak to Mrs Cook.'

'It's Cook-Bullen, actually,' the husband said. 'She's upstairs.'

'Can you call her, please,' MacInnes said. They stepped inside. 'Matter of some importance, yes?'

'Oh, right,' Cook said. He waved them into the lounge. 'If you'll just take a seat, I'll go upstairs and—'

''Fraid DC Flood'll have t'go with you, sir.'

'What?'

'The detective constable, sir. I'm sure y'understand . . .'

'No, I do *not*,' Cook responded, trying for some height. He was about to say something very clichéd like, *Look here, Officer, what's this all about?* but MacInnes pre-bullied him, snapping out again, 'Sorry, sir. Matter of some *urgency*, as I said!'

Daniel Cook's shoulders noticeably sagged. He turned to go up the stairs calling out, 'Darling!' The DI gestured to Caz to follow closely and she went with it, bumping into the back of the man as he went up.

Then Claire Cook-Bullen appeared at the top of the stairs.

She wasn't in her decorator's coat but there was fresh white paint on her hands. 'Ah, Claire!' Dan Cook said. He stopped, looking up. 'It's the—'

'I can see who it is, Claire said.

Forty-Six

'I'll put a kettle on,' Claire Bullen said. Without waiting, she went through to the kitchen. MacInnes nodded and Caz followed her. As soon as she got into the kitchen, Claire turned on her.

'You didn't have to do this, Caz.'

'Yes, I did, Claire.'

'Why?'

'You know why.'

Claire worked automatically, filling an upright kettle from a jug of filtered water, clipping out four mugs from a cabinet, uncapping a caddy on the side. 'What do you expect of me?' she said.

'The truth,' Caz said.

His name, Claire said, was Tim Hacht. He was a nice man, a teacher, a little older than her. No, he wasn't married and no, it wasn't just a bit on the side. Yes, she said, he was a runner. No, he wasn't with Worthing. It wasn't just a bit on the side. He loved her.

'But Daniel must never know,' Claire begged. 'He can't know.'

'I don't understand,' Caz said as the mugs were filled. 'This place, you and Daniel . . . Why don't you just leave?'

'I can't. Not yet. Danny needs me.'

Claire turned with a tray neatly set, and a smile in the middle of her put-back-together face. 'Bollocks,' Caz said. This was a cold house, a house devoid of love. If Claire insisted on staying, it wasn't because she cared for Daniel Cook.

'You're lying through your teeth,' she said.

Claire ignored the provocation and stepped forward, using the tray as a wedge. 'Shall we go into the lounge?' she asked blandly. Caz was forced to move out of the way to avoid a collision but as Claire swept past her she said, 'I am *not* letting this go.'

When the women came into the lounge, Dan Cook and MacInnes were a couple of paragraphs deep into an awkward small-talking charade, trying to be men, trying to be neutral and not unfriendly. Cook got up awkwardly to clear a coffee table for the tray. Claire beamed at the DI. 'And how do you like your tea – er . . . ?'

'White without,' the DI said. 'I'm Detective Inspector MacInnes.'

Claire put down the tray, wiped her hands down a nonexistent apron and reached out to the DI. 'I was just saying to DC Flood, I am so warmed by your concern for my welfare. You do your profession proud.'

'It's our job, Mrs Cook.'

'Cook-Bullen.'

'Our job, Mrs Cook-Bullen.'

'However I can help . . .' Claire said. She looked at her husband, slicked a smile like a panther and went to him, sitting on the arm of his chair. 'Now tell me again, Inspector. What precisely is it you wish to know?'

* * *

Caz sat down as MacInnes began to speak.

'Mrs Cook—' Claire went to interrupt '—Mrs Cook-Bullen. You left your home some time between six p.m. and six thirty p.m. on Thursday last and returned home, in a somewhat distressed and dishevelled state, on Sunday morning. Can you confirm this is correct?'

'Perfectly, Inspector.'

'I require you to account for your whereabouts between the hours of six on Thursday and the middle of Sunday morning. Are you prepared to do that? Do you wish your husband to be present and do you wish to make a statement here or at John Street police station?'

'I keep nothing from my husband, Inspector. Why should I? And I have no desire to go to the police station.'

'Then you'll give us your statement here?'

Claire picked up her mug, 'Whatever gave you that idea, Inspector?'

If MacInnes changed it was in a flicker. Rather than sit up or bristle he sat forward and spoke slowly, softly. He sounded like Robbie Burns comparing a lassie to a red flower. To Caz he felt like someone about to drown a puppy. 'Mrs Cook-Bullen . . .' he began.

If they couldn't get Claire for wasting police time, they could have a good run at Daniel Bullen. If they couldn't finally convict either of them of an offence, nevertheless, their lives would be opened up in court. Of course, the inspector realised, all families had matters they wished to keep private. That was why he was speaking to them now, informally, to protect that privacy. 'Please, Mrs Cook-Bullen,' he said softly, smiling with his eyes, 'don't make this matter public.'

Claire shifted only slightly. She glanced at her husband, then back at MacInnes. 'I'm afraid,' she said with a breath, 'that this whole unfortunate thing has arisen out of a misunderstanding.'

Forty-Seven

In basic training they had told Probationer Constable Kathrine G. Flood about lots of things: about the difference between bravery and stupidity, for example; about the line between assertiveness and aggression, or about the fuzzy movable feast that was the border representing 'reasonable force'.

The same people had read a Desmond Morris book or two – maybe even a first-year psychology text on body language – and passed on its half-truths and simplifications, only slightly second-hand and only *slightly* abridged, to thirty-six very keen, *very* impressionable young recruits. Anyone foolish enough to briefly brush his nose while being interviewed by any one of *these* young coppers was in for a shock; and heaven forbid that they should avoid eye contact or place a hand in front of their mouth! Listen to the words but watch the body, the instructor had said, the body cannot lie. Absolutely, Caz had thought at the time; and let's not worry about psychopaths, sociopaths, actors, poker-players, magicians, con men and every other plonker that's ever read a thing about body language.

Daniel Cook and Claire Cook-Bullen hadn't read the books or played much poker. When either of them spoke, they spoke the truth. But Caz was watching the partner each time the other one lied.

'That row, that afternoon, well, it was a bit worse than normal. I'm afraid I lost my temper. I swore rather a lot at Claire and when she said she was going out running whether I liked it or not, I told her that I would be going out whether she liked it or not.'

'So I didn't ring, you see. I knew Daniel wouldn't be in . . .'

'I did go out, for a while, to the local pub. I had a bit to drink, I wasn't drunk but I'd had too much to drive. I decided to walk home. Claire wasn't here when I got back. Gradually I got myself more and more worried until eventually I rang the police station.'

'I'd jogged down to Southwick, I do sometimes, then I'd jogged out on this particular route I have. I was upset and not really thinking. Sometimes running helps me sort myself out. I was not pushing it very much, something around eight-minute miling. What I usually did was to do a fast three miles round the island at Shoreham.'

Dan Cook butted in, speaking directly at MacInnes.

'Claire liked a short, sharp run on Thursdays, then a couple of shandies with some of the other runners, ladies, in the bar at the recreation centre.' He smiled at Claire.

'I think it might have been because of the row, I don't know for sure, but I had a turn, as they say, while I was running on the island. I felt bad and had to stop. I went to one of the houseboats.'

'A friend of mine's . . .' Daniel said.

'Danny plays for Kingfisher Athletic. One of his team-mates has a houseboat on the Adur at Shoreham. I really didn't feel very well so I went there. He gave me a cup of tea and let me lie down until I felt better.'

'Tim Hacht,' Daniel said, 'central midfielder.'

'I must've fallen asleep,' Claire continued. 'I woke up about eleven o'clock. Tim had already had a few. I was feeling better so I had a few too. I was angry at Danny so I just got drunk. Then it was late so I crashed out at Tim's. He had a spare bunk and I slept in that.'

'That deals with Thursday night,' MacInnes said.

'I didn't wake until very late on Friday morning,' Claire replied. 'I had a terrible headache and I just felt like I wanted to die. Tim wasn't there. I waited for a little while for him to come back and while I was waiting I had a couple of gins. When he came back, he said he'd rung Danny and squared everything up with him.

'That was the misunderstanding. I'm afraid I was a little bit drunk again. Tim had come back to say that I should ring Danny but I thought he had already done it. Maybe it was wishful thinking on my part, I don't know. When I didn't rush out to use the phone, I guess Tim thought I was still unhappy.'

Dan Cook smiled. 'D'you see, Inspector? Just a silly mistake . . .'

'What about Saturday afternoon? What about Saturday night?'

'I always go out on the South Downs Way first weekend of the New Year,' Cook came back quickly. 'Rain or shine.'

'That wouldn't stop Claire phoning or coming home.'

'I wouldn't have been there, Inspector.'

'But you were. DC Flood telephoned you Saturday evening.'

'I know I *was* there; but Claire would have presumed I'd be away. Every New Year, the first weekend, we go out on the Downs, hike, stop in a hotel, hike back on the Sunday.'

'Mrs Cook-Bullen. You said you thought everything had been squared up with your husband. Didn't that mean either you were expected to go home or that he would come and pick you up?'

'No.'

'Why not?'

Claire smiled. If there was a hint of triumph in the smile it was very quickly covered up. 'We had been arguing over Christmas. One of the things we had been rowing about was the New Year walk. I had told Daniel that I didn't want to do it any more. He thought that I had changed since I became serious about my running.'

MacInnes remained deadpan. 'Now let me just check, Mr and Mrs Cook-Bullen. You are saying that Mrs Cook-Bullen went for a run, became unwell and called at the residence of a mutual friend who was, fortuitously, close by. Mrs Cook-Bullen then did not ring home, first because she was unwell and angry, later because she was intoxicated, later still because she thought Mr Cook-Bullen would not be at home. The following day, due to a misunderstanding, she thought Mr Cook-Bullen knew where she was but he was going away so there was no rush for her to get home.'

'Yes,' Claire said.

'Exactly,' Daniel said.

'And the mud? Mrs Cook-Bullen's distressed state?'

'On the Sunday morning, I had breakfast with Mr Hacht then we went for a run. There's a long one due north, up the side of the river on the bank. There's an old footbridge where you can cross. Tim was going to run me as far as my home and then find his own way back. I think some of the alcohol was still floating around my system. We were near where the A27 crosses, where the big bridge is. I stumbled and fell off the bank into the mud. It was quite a drop, I got very muddy and I was a bit shocked. Tim brought me home. I was a bit surprised to find Daniel here and, I don't know, but all the weekend came together in one lump and I broke down. That must have been when Daniel phoned the doctor and the police.'

'And we can talk to this Mr Hacht?'

'Of course,'Claire said.

Caz had seen a full DCS Blackside big-man blow-up; she had seen both Saint and Greavsie lay on the good, bad and ugly routine. What she had never seen was MacInnes when he went for the throat. He sat there almost unmoved for fifteen, maybe twenty seconds. Then he looked up, fixed Dan's eyes and smiled. 'Mr and Mrs Cook,' he said, very, very softly, 'you are both lying, and very badly.'

Blackside's bluster worked on low-lifes and on coppers like Bob Saint and Jim Greaves; he probably thought of them as one anyway. But this was the era of PACE, the Police and Criminal Evidence Act – a raised voice these days could get a villain off. Where Blackside was a sledgehammer, MacInnes was a stiletto, a hatpin, needle-sharp, even more deadly, but more importantly, fit for public consumption. Videos and tape machines didn't record low menace.

The DI was now absolutely still, absolutely silent. Caz suddenly thought about something a salesman had once told her. 'Give them the price and shut up – first to speak loses.' DI MacInnes knew what Caz knew; that they had nothing but instinct to go on, nothing but their personal annoyance at the Cook-Bullens to use against them as a weapon. If the Cook-Bullens kept their cool, whatever it was they were sitting on could remain covered up. Caz and the DI could cajole and bully, but only gently. Even then, it was only a matter of time before an injunction would land on the DI's desk

Caz still had a lot to learn; she had a fair way to go before she could instil with just a look the kind of fear that the DI threw into Claire and Daniel. Their reaction was quiet, then white shock; then a competition as to who would speak first. Dan Cook won by a split second, more bullshit. 'My wife and I have been perfectly frank with you, Inspector.'

'Perfectly honest,' Claire Bullen said. They were scared, under pressure, but neither Daniel or Claire was actually stupid; stonewall dumb insolence would work.

'*Mister* Cook,' the DI said wearily, 'when you first contacted John Street police station you said that your wife went for a long run every Sunday, Tuesday and Thursday night. You told the responding officer that Mrs Cook-Bullen had gone out for a twelve-mile run that evening. Is that correct?'

'Yes, but I—'

'And when Detective Constable Flood came to see you here, you repeated that statement. Is that correct?'

'Yes, but—'

'Were you lying then, Mr Cook, or are you lying now?'

Cook stumbled slightly but kept up the charade. 'It was . . . it was just a shorthand. I knew Claire was out for four hours or so. It didn't seem necessary to explain that she went for a drink with her friends and all that.'

'No? But if we had had reason to suspect foul play, we would have been looking for Claire on a much longer, much different route. You would have sent our officers in completely the wrong direction.'

'I was stressed – a bit confused. I didn't intend—'

'I'm not interested in what you *intended*, Mr Cook, I only know what you *did*. You wasted police time and you may have aggravated the predicament of at least one member of the public. I intend to discuss this matter with my superiors with a view to bringing charges against you, if at all possible.' He shifted, a note to Caz that they might as well go. Cook nodded sagely, almost patronising.

'Inspector, I understand your situation and I know you are only doing your job. I cannot help the fact that what we have told you doesn't appear neat enough an explanation, but that is how the truth often is; messy. I hope you do not feel so aggrieved that you attempt a prosecution in this case, but, if you do, I'll see you in court.'

MacInnes stood up, his face fixed, holding his anger in. He still sounded like an English textbook so Caz decided he wasn't yet really mad. Daniel Cook smelt victory. He stood and offered his hand, smugly. 'In court then?' he said with a smile.

MacInnes smiled back, 'Oh, Ah think mebbee yu'll see us 'fore that, *Mister* Cook . . .'

Caz was standing now. Cook was obviously amused by MacInnes's accent finally surfacing. You poor sod, Caz thought, the accent isn't funny. 'That it, sir?' she said.

'Aye, Flood. Let's get us aweh fr'm here.'

'Sir!' Caz said. She opened her bag. Claire looked up from the arm of the chair. Caz fumbled for a few more seconds, camping up on the woman's handbag joke. Eventually she said, 'Ah!'

MacInnes didn't know what was happening but sniffed blood, the first counterattack. As Caz looked up she saw him lock eyes with Daniel Cook.

'Ah, here it is!' Caz said joyfully. She pulled out the white cotton sweatband and held it up. There was a moment before she spoke. 'Bet you never thought this would turn up again, eh, Mrs Bullen?'

'No,' Claire said as she took it. Even as she whispered she dropped the band into the chair. She looked like someone had punched her under the heart. 'I, um – thank you, Caz.'

Caz said nothing. They could have stayed and tried again but MacInnes made the decision for them. 'Wu'll see oorsel's oot,' he said. He went into the hall first. Behind, Caz nodded, 'Mr and Mrs Cook.'

Forty-Eight

Caz and the DI drove away in silence. The black of the evening was wrapped around them, headlights flashing past on the main road as they waited to join the flow. Both were thinking hard. It was five minutes before Tom MacInnes spoke. 'Well, Caz?'

'Well what, sir?'

'What d'you think?'

Sometimes a question like this from the DI was an on-the-job test. This one felt as if the DI was lost, looking for help. Caz felt vaguely worried for him. 'That was her headband,' she said flatly.

'And?'

'The one we found near the chain bridge.'

'I know that, Flood.'

'Claire wasn't surprised when I gave it to her, she was shocked. It wasn't just that we'd found a way through their bullshit. Seeing the headband frightened her. Something's really—'

'Odd.'

'You can say that again, sir!'

'Odd,' MacInnes repeated, 'but *what's* odd, Flood?'

'Daniel Cook's attitude?'

'He was playing with me; trying t'make me mad.'

'But why? For Claire's sake, d'you think? Was he saying something to her?'

'That's ma guess.'

Saying what?'

'Ah'm strong. Ah c'n deal with stupit coppers. Din't ferget that yu've seen me in action, wife.'

'You think so?'

'That wassnee an interview, Caz. The bastard was playin' a gemm. What I canna see at all is *what* gemm. I can't see why.'

'If it's a game, then they were both playing with us, Tom. While we were making tea, Claire Bullen told me about Tim Hacht. She said that no matter what, Daniel mustn't find out. Then we came into the lounge. I was quite prepared to sit on it, but as soon as you started talking, Hacht's name was flying round the room like it wasn't a problem.'

They were leaving the Old Steine, turning up towards the nick.

'Yu've time for a drink in the Grapes, Caz?'

'One.'

'A double then.'

'Why not?' Caz said.

MacInnes came back from the bar with two big Bell's, one with Canadian Dry. 'OK, Caz, say Daniel Cook knows his wife is having an affair. She's seeing this Hacht bloke, she runs off with him, wants t'be with him for the New Year. She comes back on the Sunday to tell her husband it's all over. Cook maybe is prepared to let that happen but he can't admit it publicly; he can't let us know, can't face the humiliation.'

'So why straight away raise the guy's name? Why say we can go t'see him? Why would they say it's OK for us to go and see him?'

'I don't know. P'raps Dan Cook's got something over his wife and can get her to do what he wants.'

'It's not violence, Tom.'

'You sure?'

'I'd know. I know Claire too well.'

'So what then?'

'What d'you mean, what? *I* didn't say Daniel was coercing her, you did, boss. We don't even know if he is trying to save face.'

'Well, if it's not that, Flood, what the hell is it?'

Caz pointed. 'Another one of them?' MacInnes nodded and she stood up. 'Claire Bullen is frightened is my best bet, Tom. When I gave her that headband she looked sick enough to faint.'

She moved as if to go to the bar, then turned back. 'What I find strange is that she doesn't seem scared of her husband. He controls her, I think he controls her, but she's not scared, not of him.'

She went to get the drinks. While she was there she figured it was best to let this one lie fallow for a while, let the truth float upwards. As she paid for the Bell's she wondered about Tim Hacht. Thirty-five-ish and a fair runner? It didn't ring a bell with her. The Cook-Bullens had said he was a footballer; soccer players didn't usually run twenty miles – long distance shortened their hams and quads and they ended up getting injured when they played. Something about all this was crap, but what? Where to start? As she turned round she thought, 'Hacht.' She knew they had to try the midfield maestro.

'So who's going to visit Ossie Ardiles?' MacInnes said as she sat down. 'No one's getting paid f'this; you daft enough?'

'Is that your way of saying you're not, sir?'

'Oh, *Ah'm* daft enough, Flood. But *Ah* thought y'had a man t'go home t'.'

Forty-Nine

'We going straight away, sir? Or we gonna get pissed first?'

'Don't be a prat, Flood.'

'Just a little joke, boss. D'you get anywhere with that tape from Control?'

'Yes.'

'Y'gonna tell me?'

'There was a telephone call at 2.47, a woman. She said, "I want to report a road traffic accident. There's a girl injured on the main road near the Goldstone Ground." '

'You said a woman.'

'That's right. It was a female voice, not that young. She called in the RTA just after half two. She was quite distressed. It sounded like she was fighting hard to stay on top of it.'

'I thought it was a bloke had rung in, Tom. Didn't you say that it was a guy who was a bit over the limit that had rung in? You said the traffic that turned up told him t'piss off out of it quick.'

'Did I?'

'Yes, sir.'

'I'd forgotten. I played the tape. Soon's I heard the RTA phoned in I stopped listening. You saying there were two calls in, Flood?'

'I heard it was a bloke rang in. If you're saying it was a woman, Tom, then there must've been two calls.'

'Or we got it wrong,' MacInnes said slowly.

Caz glanced up at her friend. 'You feeling all right, Tom?'

'Aye, lass. Just a bit knacked.'

He swigged his drink and put down his glass. 'I'm thinkin' mebee I should take my holidays next time they come round.' He laughed. 'I'm beginning t'feel my age, lass. Yu'll be looking after me soon.'

'Sure,' Caz said. 'Do we know who was in the Traffic?'

'Dave Shott.'

'Oh, I know Buck,' she said brightly. 'He's a good bloke. Mates with Bob Reid and Bob Moore, isn't he?'

'If y'say so, Flood. Anythin' y'don't know?'

Caz let out a little laugh. 'Yeah, but I'm working on it, sir!'

The DI looked at his glass. 'Wouldn't mind another one of those.'

'You'll have t'wait till you get home,' Caz said seriously. 'Duty calls. We're off to Shoreham now.'

MacInnes shrugged. 'Ah'll have t'buy you a pair've jackboots fer yer birthday, Flood.'

'Oh, Tom!' Caz said. She fluttered her eyes. 'I didn't know you were into that sort of thing.'

'What?' MacInnes said.

Caz looked at him. He really *didn't* understand.

'Buying presents,' she said.

MacInnes had the decency to let Caz pick up her MX5 before they left for their third hour of unpaid overtime. He parked on the hill until she burred past him, then flashed his lights and followed her down to and along the front. When Caz reached the turning into Inkerman Terrace she blipped her hazard lights then indicated right. The DI waited on the seafront while she popped the sports car into a slot and then jogged back to him. He had his window wound down. As she got in the car he said, 'Find it hot in here, Flood?'

Caz didn't. 'It is a bit,' she said.

The DI pulled back into the traffic and headed for Shoreham.

'D'you remember, Tom, when you first told me about Claire Bullen not coming home? Dan Cook rang? He said that Claire had gone out for a twelve-mile run.'

'We've been through that.'

'I know, Tom. Sorry. It's just that while I was driving my car over, something occurred to me. Dan Cook changed his story about Claire's Thursday runs; he'd said they were long ones, twelve-milers, then he just casually started talking about her doing fast work.'

'If you say so, Caz.'

'Well, doesn't that strike you as odd? He's been pretty confident and devious up to now. Do you think he just made a mistake?'

'Do you?'

'I think Claire told him that I knew she ran short stuff every Thursday. She knew that I had to know so she told him. He casually changed his version of Thursday nights and, one way or another, got rid of a massive lie.'

'Which means what, exactly?'

'That Claire Cook-Bullen is somehow colluding with Daniel Cook. Whatever is going on, she's participating.'

They stopped at some lights. 'Well, we already knew they were both lying, Caz, where does this news get us?'

Caz waved her hands. 'Further up the garden path?'

Fifty

The tide was out when the Scorpio crossed the Adur chain bridge. First left was the road that looped through a slightly dowdy fifties- and sixties-built housing estate, running out towards the sea and back round the island. To their left, the first swathe of houses looked to be below sea level, backed by a high sea wall. Curiously, above this embankment, they could see the tide-discarded huddle of houseboats, fading personalities, dark green from hanging neon.

'We didn't ask Hacht's address,' MacInnes said.

'Do houseboats have addresses?' Caz answered.

MacInnes drove slowly, then turned left down a narrow track towards the water, breaking out into a rough car park closed at one end by the sea bank. He burred the car slowly along the base of the embankment as his DC leaned from the window looking for Hacht's place. Caz was holding a heavy metal search torch, its beam wobbling off into the distance. Every thirty feet or so were rickety-looking wooden stairways, most edged with white lines and stamped, 'Private Steps. Do Not Enter'. At the top of the steps were anarchic hand-painted signs, owners' names or the names of boats, etched in differing scripts on a range of mishmashed posters.

There was no 'Dunroamin' and no 'Hacht'.

'Were we really that stupid?' Tom said.

'Yup!' Caz said. She got out and crunched across wet gravel. They had agreed she would try the third houseboat, a grey converted motor-torpedo launch still with sharks' teeth gaping on its prow. While Tom waited, Caz went carefully up some distinctly bendy steps towards it, reaching the top, a towpath. In either direction, faintly lit by low-watted lights tacked to telegraph poles, the line of homes stretched both ways, each one loosely attached to the land, telephones, electricity, rates, the postman. In the half-darkness it was impossible to be sure, but the oddball flotilla looked distinctly shabby, more junkyard than Greenwich Village, but wonderfully independent for all that. No doubt about it, given the slightest help, Caz could quite fancy being one of the neighbours.

There was no one home on the MTB, but next door there was a pale gold light and a smell of chilli looping up from below decks. Caz clacked at a brass bell, watching the sound drift across the mud. The curtains cracked, a long face, then the door opened, a man, thirty and counting, short sandy-red hair, fantastic eyes. Steve McQueen.

'Well, hello me hearty. Be you a pirate?' A voice like honey.

'Not that I know of,' Caz said. 'Looking for a chap called Tim Hacht. Wondered if . . .'

'Next door but one,' the guy said softly. 'Beached.'

'He is?'

'The name of the boat. Blue and yellow, red deckhouse.'

'Appreciated,' Caz said. She paused.

'No, you don't know me,' the guy said, 'which is a shame.'

Caz blipped him a tiny cheek-lift smile. I like you.

'D'you like red wine?' the man said.

'And chilli,' Caz said, 'but I'm with my – dad – in the car – I, er . . .'

'Fred Kermy,' the guy said, almost off-hand. He appeared ready to pull the door closed. 'If you're passing again, and you care to visit with us, you'll be welcome.'

'American?' Caz said. There was no accent.

'Well spotted,' Fred said. 'I'm ex of Oklahoma but I've been ex for longer than I was Oke.' His face was green-grey in the light but Caz saw his goodbye smile as the door clubbed closed.

'Caz Flood,' she said, finishing as the door went flush.

She felt slightly foolish, wondering if Fred had heard. Then the door opened an inch and a fist protruded, a long thumb pointing up. He'd heard. Caz was grinning as she went back to the DI's car.

'Hi, boss!' she said through the open door. 'You coming in with me or staying in there and getting cold?'

'What d'you reckon?' MacInnes said.

'As long as you're here as back-up, Tom, I'd just as soon try Hacht on my own. But keep the engine running and the lights on. I'd like to make sure he knows you're here.'

MacInnes laid his head back. 'No more than ten minutes, Caz.'

'Absolutely!'Caz said. 'Some time tonight I wanna go get a life!'

Tom's eyes were already closed. Caz walked off into the gloom.

Hacht's boat was yellow, blue and red, just like the ginger-haired American had described it, but the red was faded and peeling and the yellow was puce, even allowing for the cast of the neon that swung nearby. Caz could smell onions, something frying. All of a sudden she was starving. Lunch had been a joke, the day had been long, and now she realised with a jolt that her blood sugar was at falling-over level. She actually heard her stomach as it rumbled.

The boat was a sort-of barge but Caz wasn't that sure; boats, ships, yachts and knots were her fourth-biggest blind spot, after antique furniture, British history and the hits of Cliff Richard.

She vaguely recalled a narrow-boat trip on the Nottingham-Trent canal that had coincided with her first period. This barge was probably bigger, heavier and longer than her holiday accommodation had been then, so maybe it was seagoing, like one of those big barges you used to see on the Thames when the UK still had an economy.

Remembering a vision of herself in white ankle socks, she climbed down onto the deck, found a door and put a hand up to the faint illuminated plastic of a door bell. 'How civilised,' she thought, until a distant electronic box played 'Colonel Bogey'. Inside there was a heavy thud, like a drunk falling out of bed. 'A minute!' someone shouted, then the door opened, onions escaping across the river.

She thought she would faint. 'Tim Hacht?' she asked.

He was her height, not actually ugly but with piggy little eyes.

''Oo wants to know?' he said.

Caz waved her warrant card and smiled. 'I'm Detective Constable Flood. Claire Bullen gave us your name. Mind if I come in?'

Fifty-One

'You on your own?' Hacht said, stretching to look past Caz. She tried to look inside, but he neatly blocked her view.

'I'm with my detective inspector. He's in the car.'

'What car?'

'If you come out of your shell, you'll be able to see it,' Caz said. 'He's just down there.' She pointed. 'See the lights? Hear the music?'

MacInnes was playing George Gershwin, at least Caz thought it was Gershwin. A couple of months ago, she wouldn't have had a clue, but the DI was insisting on gradually educating her. This was one of his 'cut-glass, good whisky, let's talk' composers.

'*An American in Paris*,' Hacht said.

'Is it?' Caz thought. Then she remembered *Rhapsody in Blue* and said she preferred that. Smooth, eh? Three months of this and she'd be an intellectual.

'I agree,' Hacht said as he pulled the door wider. 'Do you like his Piano Concerto in F?'

Oh shit, was that the one that had the really sad bit in? She tried anyway. 'I find the range of moods a little off-putting, don't you?'

'Well, that's Gershwin for you,' Hacht said. He bowed her in.

As she stepped past Hacht, Caz felt a slight prickle of disquiet. The fact that he managed *not* to touch her in the narrow doorway made her feel worse than if he had allowed some contact. She was so used to the average touchy male that she rode that sort of thing unconsciously. It was perverse that his politeness should disturb her.

But the instant she walked into the cabin, his home, Caz felt its warmth; not just the heat or the brownly warm smell of the food but the rustic closeness of the long thin enclosure, the thick curtains, the heaviness of polished wood floor, the deep secure scarlets and greys of the upholstery. It felt like a cocoon, a womb; the kind of place that would feel even better when it was raining outside. It made her think of red hospital blankets, kind nurses and scalding mugs of Oxo.

'I need to do something about my food,' he said, waving a hand for her to sit down. 'Can I offer you a drink or something.'

'A fillet steak?' she suggested, fantasising.

'I can manage a glass of red wine.'

Caz was thinking no, but she said yes, please. Hacht passed her two glasses, both gleaming, and a dark bottle, the label towards her.

'Oh,' Caz said, 'Faustino V. Very nice! Bit special for Monday night!'

'I was expecting a guest,' Hacht said.

'And she's late?' Caz thought out loud. Hacht said nothing, turning instead to his tiny stove and iron cast skillet. She was in pain. 'That smells gorgeous!' she said.

'Shame you're not stopping, then, isn't it?' Hacht said to

the pan. Then he looked up. 'I don't suppose you could flop a little of that Rioja in here, could you?'

Caz could but it seemed a bit of a waste. 'Are you sure?'

'It's all I've got,' Hacht said, 'and this has to have wine.'

Caz had only just filled her glass and barely had time to sniff and sip at it. She got up, sighing quietly, and moved to the kitchen alcove, squeezing past the cook to pour. She looked down at the sizzling pan, onions, mushrooms, butter . . . A lick of blue Calor flame appeared briefly as Tim Hacht circled the pan above it. The smell and the close heat almost overwhelmed her. Nearby was a spray of bread sticks. 'May I?' she said and took two sticks, crunching into one straight away. She went back to the lounge and her wine.

'If I'd known . . .' Tim said.

'Don't worry about it,' she said from her seat in the lounge.

Caz knew it was a bad habit, but she often thought she could read people by their furniture and their bookshelves. She vaguely recalled hearing somewhere about people in the US buying their books colour-balanced and by the yard. She didn't know if the suppliers also sold a mood or an image. 'Does sir require "educated eclectic" or would he prefer "recognisably academic". We have a particularly good line in "obscurely erotic" and perhaps madam might require a half-shelf of feminism . . .'

The shape of Tim Hacht's furniture had been forced on the owner by the boat's design. There were two narrow fitted bookcases crushed into corners and high up along the length of the cabin, half hidden, a shelf carried yards of paperback poetry. The wine was lovely. As she drank she saw some serious psychology, Milgram, Maddi, Skinner, Freud; a hardback copy of Brian Keenan's *An Evil Cradling*, a lot of stuff on Korea.

The compactness, the built-in cosiness of the boat, had been exaggerated by the choice of rich velvets to create this all-enveloping cell. The whole effect was as far from the clinical white of Claire Bullen's box room as a designer or a lover could get. Caz tried to imagine Claire and Tim. It wasn't easy.

Fifty-Two

There was a sudden flare and sizzle from the galley kitchen. Caz looked up. Tim Hacht was grinning, food steam haloed around him. 'So,' he said, a pleasant at-home smile, 'what's Claire told you?'

'She gave us your name,' Caz repeated. 'She said that you might be able to shed some light on the events of this weekend.'

'What d'you want to know?'

'Well, first off, Mr Hacht, would you clarify your relationship with Claire?'

'Relationship?'

'Do you have an intimate relationship with Mrs Cook-Bullen?'

'What does Claire say?'

'I'm not asking Claire.'

Tim Hacht ducked his head to pull something from the oven. As he came up he spoke again. 'We've been intimate, yes.'

'You're having an affair with Claire Cook-Bullen?'

'We've been intimate. I told you.'

Hacht was looking at his cooking. Caz stood up; partly to see what he was up to, partly to re-align their respective heights. 'And is this affair continuing, Mr Hacht?'

'I don't know,' he said.

Tim was forking thin slivers of meat on to an octagonal plate. It looked like veal stained with marinade. Caz poured herself a second glass of wine as he spooned the mushroom-lumped sauce over the meat. He turned to her with the plate on a tray. Next to the plate was a small bowl of crisp salad. As he walked through, she asked him to run through the weekend's events again, just for her. He said he would be happy to; just as soon as he had eaten.

Caz's ten minutes were up already. She thought about going to speak to the DI but didn't want to break out into the night's cold. MacInnes might get himself wound up, he might not. She decided to risk it. If he did choose to come knocking, Caz would protest; then she could be nice to his Mr Nasty. Tim Hacht seemed intent on his meat but, for show, Caz pulled out her two-way radio and called the station. Over the static she confirmed she was DC Flood, and yes, she was still down at the houseboats with DI MacInnes. If Hacht listened at all he never showed it. She noticed he hadn't touched his salad. The meat was all gone bar a single bite.

He dabbed his lips with a napkin. 'I work for the county council, the new offices at Lewes. Claire works there too, in the legal department. I work on the engineering side, in the highways division. Claire and I have known each other for five years and we have been friends for most of that time. I have already told you that we've been intimate but I would not say that we're having or have had an affair.'

'Tell me about this weekend,' Caz said.

'Claire must have told you she runs on the island quite often. She jogs here from Southwick Sports Centre and she runs round the loop. She cuts through the car park. If she sees my light on, sometimes she stops for a rest. We'll maybe have a coffee, then she jogs back to the sports centre. Occasionally, I give her a lift there.'

'So this weekend?'

'I'm getting to that. Her husband is an arsehole. As it happens we play for the same football team, Kingfisher AFC, but I can't stand the creep. Claire and him had had a huge argument in the afternoon and when she turned up here, she was quite upset. I offered her a cup of tea, which she had, but then she asked for something stronger. In the end we got fairly badly pissed together. It was New Year's Eve; I was on my own and so was she. We took care of each other.'

'Did you sleep together?'

'As it happens, yes, but not in the way you're thinking. We slept in the same bed but we didn't have sex. Neither of us was interested and we were both very drunk.'

'What happened the next day?'

'I got up about eleven and went for a walk. I rang Claire's husband to say she was at my boat. He knew where I lived. About six months ago, Claire turned an ankle somewhere on the island and I helped her out. She was hobbling past and I brought her in here, sat her down and rang her old man. He came and picked her up.

'I told him Claire was with me and he said he didn't care. He said he was off on some walk he did every year. I told him I didn't think Claire would be doing anything strenuous for a couple of days and he went apeshit, calling her everything under the sun. I just waited for him to finish, then I asked him what did he want me to say to her. He said, tell her nothing has changed, they were still squared up.'

'And Saturday, Sunday?'

'The Friday we just got pissed again; we'd never really

sobered up from the Thursday night. It was much the same on the Saturday. I lent Claire some of my clothes and we got out for a couple of hours, but mostly we just stayed on the boat, ate, drank, and fooled around.

'On the Sunday, I ran with her up the river and that was when she fell in – not into the river, the tide was out – into all that mud. She was a real mess, hair, face, clothes, the lot, covered in mud. It could have been serious but she looked so silly, for five minutes I couldn't stop laughing.'

'And then you went to her house?'

'Yes.'

'You really love Claire, don't you, Tim?'

'What?'

'I said you really love Claire.'

Hacht picked up a sprig of raw cauliflower from the bowl. 'What are you talking about?'

'You and Claire, Tim. I'm talking about you and Claire.'

'We're just friends. I told you.'

'So why are you lying for her?'

'I'm not,' Hacht said, biting into the vegetable. 'I've told you exactly what happened.'

'I know,' Caz said with mock friendliness. She paused, then sighed. 'It's just that your exactly isn't exactly what Claire said . . . exactly.'

'Well, someone is getting confused then,' Hacht said, 'but it isn't me. I know what I'm saying.' He picked up a carrot stick; a trophy in front of her. 'I know what I'm saying,' he crunched, then fixed her eyes with his, '*exactly*, Detective.'

Caz was too tired for this. 'In that case, I'll be off, but I'm pretty certain we'll be speaking again. Where can I find you?'

'I'm at work from eight thirty to five thirty. Most nights

I'm here. Wednesday nights I train with the football club at Whitemoor Grange.'

Caz offered her hand. 'I hope it's worth it.'

'It is,' Tim said. 'You can bank on that.'

Fifty-Three

When Caz got back to the DI's Scorpio, the DI had the driver's seat tilted back and was dozing, his hands together on his head, fingers intertwined. The Gershwin tape was still playing. As she opened the door, he lowered his hands; the message, 'My eyes were closed but I was not asleep, Flood.'

Caz clicked in her seat belt. 'Ah, the Piano Concerto in F!'

'Ah'm glad I didnee hold ma breath,' MacInnes said.

The car was more than warm. They drove off, oozing away, MacInnes turning left to continue all the way round the loop, out of curiosity, he said. As they left the few dangling lights from the houseboats, he asked how it had gone. She said, 'Tricky.'

'What d'you mean?' the DI said.

'Hacht came out with a story not that much different from the one we already got from Claire and Daniel Cook-Bullen, but it *was* different, Tom, different enough for me to wonder whether they've all been talking, whether things have been arranged.'

'And if things *have* been arranged?'

'Then we should lean on them all some more, sir.'

'For why, Caz? What exactly is it you need to know?'

'They're lying to us, Tom. I'd just like to know why. Why

would a husband, wife and boyfriend consort like this? It makes no sense.'

They were almost back to the road. 'Mebbee, mebbee not, Caz, but hang on a minute, this is not exactly a major enquiry. Claire Bullen went off for a few days, then she came back. We've been talking to them because we're annoyed, because you don't feel right, for that as much as we're directly suspicious about anything. Far as Ah c'n see, they've done nothing wrong.'

'Not even they've wasted police time?' Caz asked as they pulled up on to the road.

'I doubt it!' MacInnes said. 'Even if it got past the chief super, the CPS would never go with it. We don't know what's been going on. We don't know if *anything's* been going on, but yer cannit investigate people jus' because they seem a wee bit funny.'

'Well, it's still damn odd, Tom. Claire said she fell in the Adur, right? She got covered in mud. Tim Hacht said he lent her clothes on the Saturday. If she came home covered in mud, was she in his clothes or her own? If she *was* in his gear, what did she do with her own stuff? Did she carry it with her, leave it at the boat, what?'

'Did you ask Hacht?'

'I didn't think of it.'

'And we didn't ask Claire Bullen about her clothes either.'

'No, we didn't!' Caz hissed out suddenly. 'And we didn't ask her about the gear she always left at the sports centre. She dumped her change of clothes there after jogging down. If those clothes are not still there, when did she pick them up?'

They were approaching Hove, passing the dark derricks on

the sea line. MacInnes had decided to give it up as a bad job. 'This is going to go nowhere, Caz. It may annoy you, it sure annoys me, but yer cannee waste any more time on it. Why some fella chooses t'talk with his wife's boyfriend doesn't interest us. Best we drop it, Ah think, before we drive oursel's scatty.'

They turned into Inkerman Terrace, the end of an over-long day. Caz felt uncomfortable without precisely being able to say why. She was about to go to her empty flat, Tom MacInnes was about to go to his. Then she remembered how hungry she was. 'Fancy a quick bite at my place?' she said.

'On one condition,' the DI said.

'Name it.'

'We drop the Cook-Bullens fer the night.'

Caz sagged. 'OK, boss, just one more question and I'll shut up. Claire Bullen doesn't sleep with Daniel Cook. They have separate bedrooms, separate lives. Claire Bullen likes to paint her bedroom white about once a week. She hates her life and if she doesn't loathe her husband, I'm not a DC. She's got a lover, so why does she stay with Dan Cook? I can't understand why she doesn't just get out.'

'Was that a question?' MacInnes said.

'No, but tell me the answer anyway.'

MacInnes groaned and sat forward, pulling himself towards the steering wheel. He didn't look at Caz but at a couple walking slowly down the street towards them. 'The woman has, you say, great motivation to leave her husband. If she stays, then she must have an opposite emotion, another drive, one strong enough to override that motivation, something powerful.'

'Like what, Tom? Fear?'

'Pity, mebee,' Tom said. 'Or greed.' He shrugged. 'Shame, perhaps?'

'I can't see it,' Caz muttered. 'Claire doesn't pity Daniel Cook. These days I don't see shame and I don't really see fear, although I do wonder about control. And I can't see greed, either.'

MacInnes clicked his door open, cold licked in. 'Yer can't see *why* greed, y'mean, Caz.'

'You're right there, Detective Inspector!' Caz said loudly, breaking loose from the car. She slammed the door and MacInnes locked up. 'There's lots've things this young DC doesn't know, including "why greed".' They crossed the road and stepped out up the street. Caz was going to have the last word. 'There's lots I don't know, but I sure as hell know when someone's taking the piss!'

Fifty-Four

The DI didn't stay long; just long enough to gobble down a tuna, cream and pasta mix-up Caz had dashed off, one glass of Chianti and another of his more favoured Scotch. He sounded world-weary and Caz got the impression he was off home to down some more whisky. Their plates were empty, smeared with fawn traces of their meal, and she thought about his sombre, book-dark flat. She had the urge to reach out and touch his thin-knuckled hands.

'You take care now, Flood,' he said as she closed her door.

Val's phone rang a dozen times before she rang off; Moira's rang at least ten before her breathless voice said, 'Yeah?'

'Caz.'

'Oh,' Moira said, profoundly disappointed.

'Oh, thank *you*, Moira!'

'We were in . . .' There was a moment's break. 'Billy's over.'

'Nice for you,' Caz said. 'That right congratulations are in order?'

'Last night. Billy asked me and I said yes. We said we'd get married early next year.'

'Next year? But—'

'Unless, of course, something happens to change that.'

'Like pregnancy,' Caz said

'Well, it's not impossible, Caz. Even when you take precautions, accidents can still happen, can't they?'

'So everything's all right?'

'Great!' Moira said.

'How's your misper going?'

'Walters?'

'Have you got more than one?'

'Sorry, Caz. We haven't got too far but they've upped the concern a touch. We've found most of her mates and they all reckon she didn't have a boyfriend. Her best mate is a girl called Sharon Clark; she reckons that Pixie didn't do it; she was a virgin.'

Caz wasn't sure she'd heard right. 'Did you say Pixie?'

'Yeah. Her real name's Petula but she's called Pixie.'

'Why Pixie?'

'I thought, why Petula,' Moira snapped back. There was a double-distant 'Mo-Mo?' Moira spoke again. 'Look, Caz, it's late . . .'

'Yer right,' Caz said, apology in her voice, 'you go back to bed, Mo.'

'See you at the nick, Detective.'

The line clunked dead then burred with the distance between them. Caz tried Valerie again. She put the phone down when it had rung thirty times. There was a glass of red left. She drank that. Then she sat down with one of her piggies and stared at *News at Ten*.

Fifty-Five

Caz's Tuesday opened in darkness with the repeating bree-bree-bree of her electric alarm clock. If she left it to buzz for ten more minutes it would be five o'clock. She woke alone. Last night, when Valerie had eventually rung her, 'just to say hello', she had asked him to come over but he hadn't made the effort. 'I can't, baby,' he'd said. 'I treated myself to a meal and a bottle of wine, can't drive.' After they had small-talked for two minutes, they'd said good night. It was only later that she thought, 'What's wrong with a taxi, arsehole?'

She had decided on a long, smooth run, and mixing business and fitness, she was going to Shoreham. There and back was about eleven miles, all flat; with the three-mile loop around the island, she'd be doing a fourteen, too much for a work-day morning, even for some distance nut like Claire Bullen. She would need to drive out a few miles to chop it down to an easy eight.

When she came out of the loo she was wearing skin-tight dark blue Lycra bottoms flecked with reflective silver, a white Helly Hansen top, a dayglo yellow safety waistcoat and white Asics shoes with little reflective patches of silver built into the heels. She knew from experience, coming across runners when *she* was driving, that the bobbing lights, her lifting heels, would be the first things a driver saw.

Thinking again, Miss Safe Jogger 1993, she went into the lounge and grabbed a pair of white gloves. If anyone managed to hit her on this run now it would be no accident. Lit by a car's headlights, she would be as bright as Regent Street the week before Christmas.

It was shit outside, but this was Brighton in January, at ten past five in the morning, so shit wasn't exactly optional. As she came out of the house she shuddered. She walked down the street towards the sea front and her car, neon-buzzed mist in her face and her ears tingling. Beyond the promenade, little but moonlight opened up the sea with only a shifting darkness marking the waves. She could feel her breath change, heavy and salten as it drifted from her.

She got into the Mazda, started up and reversed into the main but empty road. As she flicked on the car's headlights, their bug eyes popped, spoiling the line of the bonnet. She set off, cruising past a saw-toothed horizon of beach huts to her left, then, to her right, quiet bedsits, a few lights . . . Then failed holiday apartments now let to DHSS clients, the only place they could go, cold and miserable. Briefly, she wondered about the dispossessed, the single mothers somewhere inside, huddling in the half-darkness, listening to drips, their children crying.

In her time, Caz had done the odd favour for the homeless and the battered; had offered a hand, turned a blind eye; but somewhere along the line she had drifted back from them, to a long arm's length, preferring instead to catch villains to salve her conscience. It wasn't that she didn't care, but sometimes she had felt as if she was trying to empty a slowly filling lake with a teaspoon.

What made it all worse was knowing that these buildings were money machines; that somewhere, other human beings slept warm and comfortable, with the DHSS busily feeding them names and money.

Not political enough, Caz had been convinced for a long time that there was nothing she could do. She hated feeling powerless. She drove on for another cocooned half-mile, trying not to think, but the thoughts still insisted on intruding. She wondered, where did these landlords socialise? Was it in the same circles as the captains of industry, as chief constables? Then she asked herself, 'Does it matter?' Then again, '*Did* they step over the homeless as they left the opera?'

This was supposed to be a smooth, easy run, but her mental state made her feel like hammering herself with push and rest, push and rest. A mile later, Queen Victoria's statue was behind her and she'd forgotten the disenfranchised, the underclass, pulling to the surface instead those things she felt she could, the CPS notwithstanding, do something about. She stopped, parked up, and got out of the car, a simmering annoyance with Claire Bullen now energising her. As she set off, she once again wondered what it was all about. She wondered what could have happened, what chain of events there could have been to explain Claire's behaviour.

She pushed a little harder as she skirted Southwick, thinking about Daniel Cook. Approaching the Adur bridge, she first cursed her original offer to help him, then cursed him. Somewhere inside her head, she was making an unwritten contract to repay all debts owed. It had occurred to her that Claire's disappearance might, in the end, have an odd but innocent explanation, but as she reached the bridge, her guts told her that it wouldn't.

It was still a long way from being day and the quarter-light being thrown weakly out by shop signs, garages and occasional streetlamps barely reached down as far as the ebbed river, the grey-green mud. As she jogged down from the bridge, the houseboats loomed, half-silhouettes, their colours just different shades of dark grey. A tiny light bloomed on board the boat where she'd met the thin American, the man with the fabulous eyes.

She was moving at her most efficient now, with maybe eighty-five per cent effort, something around six-minutes-fifteen miling. One car passed her as she turned on to the island loop, lighting her up and then throwing her into near-darkness. She recognised the island as a classic trap; built up and open, but silent, unhearing, unheard; the sort of place where a sudden attack, even a sustained one, might first not sound and second, worse, not be heard. It occurred to her that maybe the route was a little bit dangerous, both from cars not expecting her and night wanderers, creeps that might be expectant, waiting, not for her, not particularly, but still waiting, like a clam waits, like a Moray eel waits; until something comes fatally close and with a snap is gone, never existed.

Again, she suddenly felt angry at the Cook-Bullen-Hacht triad. They pissed around with their silly little games while Pixie Walters was still missing. She had last been known somewhere near here; had passed near here; had maybe gone missing near here. Caz was able to imagine Pet Walters dead. No matter how hard she ran, that thought was not going to go away.

Fifty-Six

She passed a row of shops, back-lit over their counters, a newsagent, a hairdresser, a launderette. Just afterwards, there was a puddled lane, the exit from the riverfront car park. It was maybe not the most sensible idea, but she turned down there, a sudden urge to see the houseboats overriding her thinly veneered fears of the dark and unknown.

She broke out into the car park, into a black well between the feeble leaking light from the estate and the barely sufficient towpath lights up on the sea wall. The darkness was peculiar, as if it had drifted in whole from somewhere even darker and settled there, against the sea, against the back gardens. Above, one or two of the boats were warm with amber, either early risers or arms against the night.

Ahead of her, like grey stripes, were the parallel wooden steps, every one, it seemed, roughly painted 'PRIVATE', one without a final 'e'. It was perverse, but Caz moved along the bank until she found some steps that were not so rudely signed. Feeling like a thief, she crept up, sensing the wood's bend, the wet, the night, the sea. At the top she stopped, ear-pricked and guilty, before turning seaward and jogging again. She hadn't noticed the other night, but the moorings were numbered, just like 'real' homes. She wondered briefly what the street name was, or were they just 'the houseboats'? As she passed the thin American's she noticed no light.

Caz wasn't sure why she was here, but now she was, she jogged slowly, a drop to her right, the cluttered front-back gardens of the boats to her left, almost every one with peculiar sculptures of scrap, of wood, of clutter with nowhere to go. Each garden had some sort of rickety bridge crossing from the towpath on to the boat, some with gates, some with doors, most, again, roughly painted 'PRIVATE'.

As she passed Tim Hacht's multicoloured barge, a soft orange light blupped alive in the wheelhouse, outlining his upper body. She glanced up as a second light, this more yellow, revealed his face. He was staring through the glass, apparently not seeing her. Then it occurred to her that the wheelhouse windows would be mirrors, bright-lit inside against the darker outside. Convinced, she stopped and waved her hand. There was absolutely no response from the face. Caz found it disquieting. She turned and ran towards the sea. As she escaped, she thought about the riding crop she had left in her lounge. Sometimes she was such a prat.

She picked up the pace between hanging lights, sufficient to give herself some feeling of power but not so fast that she took the risk of stumbling. To her left, the houseboats were becoming more spaced out and the lights ended. Ahead of Caz was tufted mud, the open sea and an almost complete dark, save for the drifting glow of bathrooms and kitchens, the rear of the estate houses. Caz stopped dead. She felt vulnerable and close to fearful. She did *not* like this; was *very* annoyed at herself. She came back fast, her feet slapping the path, a dog barking, another light clicking on. As soon as she found herself above the car park, she went down the first set of steps.

She crossed the car park's dark well as quickly as safety allowed, breaking out again into the quiet estate street. Behind her, she left the gorge-inducing sensation of vulnerability that no woman should ever be made to feel. Already it was fading. Ahead in time was the relative safety of the main road, lights, traffic. She turned quickly, heading for that, cursing her stupidity, her obstinacy, her total brain-dead bullshit ideas about 'taking back the night'. No matter how brave, how bright, how fast she was, she was still a woman. The night was made for animals. She was not an animal. She'd rather catch bullets in her teeth.

She ran steadily, then hard across the bridge, then steadily again through Southwick, taking care underfoot. Her earlier fear had slipped from her, transferred now, transmuted into concern for Petula Walters. She thought about her, where she was, who she was. An image, a feeling swept up into her head; that Pixie needed her, that she was waiting, holding out.

It was still near freezing and Caz's breath turned to clouded salt as she steamed towards Brighton. Despite the cold she was wrapped in a veil of warmth, her own body heat running with her. She thought about Tim Hacht. His light had been off when she came back down the path. She thought about Fred, the tall American. Maybe her passing-by had disturbed him; his light was on. She thought again about Pixie Walters.

'Hang in there, mate!' she said loudly as she ran. It was something somewhere between a prayer and a commitment. To a passer-by the prayer would look like the puff of just another breath.

Fifty-Seven

Caz was at the bottom of Inkerman Terrace and locking up her green MX5 as distant clocks chimed six o'clock. In the end, she had run about six miles but, instead of her usual sense of well-being, she felt low and sad. Once inside her front door she slapped her own face to knock herself back into shape and stumped up the stairs to the flat. In the flat she turned to the stereo, loaded it with noise and played it too loud.

She was at John Street by seven, preferring to be in and doing something than sitting at home brooding. The flush of fear she had felt on the towpath was still unsettling her, like water rushing in through a fault and liquidising sand. She felt bad about Petula Walters. Today, she'd find out if they'd let her get involved.

Tom MacInnes came in just after half past seven. By then, Caz was on her second coffee. She had listened for his arrival, expecting him to be in maybe twenty minutes, half an hour before Bob Moore. As soon as he had sat down, she was knocking at his door.

'Yes, Flood!'

Caz went in. 'You knew it was me, sir?'

He grunted. 'Who else is this stupid, Flood?'

While MacInnes had his gargle and popped a Trebor extra-strong mint, Caz explained how she felt, that she would like to get involved with the Walters case. 'Don't tell the DS, sir, but I just feel I have to be involved. I can't really explain why. I just want to help.'

MacInnes was already putting the bottle away. He spoke to the drawer. 'Jesus, Flood! If I told Bob Moore that, he'd probably give up swearing.'

'Can I get involved, sir?'

'I don't mind, now the Cook-Bullen thing is squared away, but you'll have to ask your DS, see what he says.'

'Of course, sir.'

MacInnes stopped for a moment as if trying to think of something to say, then he sat forward. 'So what're you on today, lass?'

'More legwork on the ram-raid, I guess, sir, and I've got to get hold of DS Mason over in Hampshire. Remember my snout? Mason's been talking to him. He tried to get hold of me yesterday but we kept missing each other.'

'D'you want t'give him a ring now? Use my phone?'

'Too early, sir. Pete Mason's an IAN, an ESSO worker – in at nine, every Saturday and Sunday off.'

'Not in CID!'

'Well, no, sir, not really, but he's been having a crack at saving his marriage, the last month or so, so he tends not to be around.'

'And you're going to give him this snout?'

'Like you said, sir. I can't do anything else.'

'So that's it?'

'For now, sir, but if you can give me good reason to get back at the Cook-Bullens, I'll pay. I still can't figure it all out, but something has to have happened, something.'

'Don't harass them, Caz.'

'Sir!'

'Don't even think about it.'

'I won't.'

'Be warned, Flood!'

'Warning taken, sir!'

'Good, Flood. Now off you go. Show off, be at your desk when your DS turns in.'

Caz got up to leave. As she did so, she remembered the tapes. Had the DI listened to them again?

'When, Flood? Fer Chrissakes, you leapt on me the moment I got in!' He rummaged in another drawer. 'Ah'm s'pposed t'hand this back this morning. You piss off now, Ah'll have another listen. If there's anything else of interest, Ah'll give your DS a shout.'

Caz hesitated. A vague 'not such a good idea' notion was floating around in her head. It was bare-feet-on-hot-coals time. Stand still and you get burned.

'I was wondering, boss. If there'd be any chance of listening to the tape myself? I'm not on officially until eight thirty and I'd really . . . it would be useful . . .'

MacInnes sucked air. 'God, Flood, that was pretty poor.' He stood and told her to follow him. He was waving the tape as he went out of the door. 'Interview Room One!' he snapped.

The phone call to Control had been timed at 02:46:52. It had been very short. 'Road Traffic Accident, A27, near Goldstone Ground!' The duty sergeant had asked a question; could the caller please clarify and give her name? This time the script wobbled. 'I'm to say RTA at the football ground, a person injured.' The woman had rung off before she cracked up completely. The call was traced to a BT Kiosk in Preston Road, the A23 out of town.

They let the recordings run. There were two other unconnected calls, the second timed at 3.03. There was no male witness, no second phone call. MacInnes finally stopped the tape.

'A woman caller, that's pretty clear, Caz.'

Caz bristled. 'It wasn't me said it was a bloke, boss!'

'Point taken.'

'So where did we get the idea?'

'It'll be checked, Flood.'

'How about the ambulance service? We contact them?'

'Two fifty-one, according to the log.'

'But they got there before our boys . . .'

MacInnes picked up the phone and punched some numbers. When he got through and explained his position, the voice at the other end was one of protest. Did he really want them to go through the old tapes? Yes, MacInnes said, fairly urgent police business. They said it would take a couple of hours.

'Nowt we c'n do till then, Flood. Suggest y'get off t'work. Soon as Ah've got anything, we'll chat.'

There was nothing for Caz to do except say,'Yes, sir!' and go.

Fifty-Eight

Bob Moore was in just after eight, twenty-five minutes before official turn-in, about fifteen minutes before his average. When he came through the door, Caz was on the phone to Southampton, trying to get hold of DS Mason. She was about fifty minutes too optimistic. A young-sounding DC called Bob Goddard answered. He promised to get Pete Mason to ring the moment he came in.

'Unless I'm out on a shout, of course . . . You know how it is.'

Moore was in a foul mood. He had been to see Jenny Fullerton's hysterical mate and, apparently, screaming was the most intellectual thing she did. 'A complete div!' he spat as he sat down. 'When I asked her about the accident, first thing she said was, "What accident?" '

Caz was just a little bit surprised. Jenny Fullerton had been full of spunk and was not at all thick. Usually, 'birds of a feather' was a good rule of thumb. She might have thought some more about it but the DS pre-empted her, throwing her with a question about the other hit-and-run. Had she been to see the Barclays Bank crowd or what? No, she said, she'd thought the other investigation was dead.

'That's *my* job, Flood!'

'What is, Sarge?'

He looked dark. 'I decide what we push and what we dump.'

Caz apologised. She was thinking, 'Actually, that's down to the DI.'

'Yeah, right!' Moore said. 'But yer right. You might's well leave it fer now. I'll be speaking to the DI shortly, tell him it's a dead one.'

'Yes, Sarge,' Caz said, then on a whim she asked, 'Coffee?'

When she got back from the canteen, Bob Moore had gone through. She put a 'Sussex Police' coaster over the steaming cup to keep the liquid warm. It was still too early, but for something to do she rang Peter Mason again. Again, she got Goddard. 'No, he's still not in,' he said – then, almost as quickly, 'I tell a lie. He's here now!' She heard the distant shout of 'Simple!' and some sort of reply. That was the second time she had heard Mason called that. He wasn't, particularly. Idly, she wondered how he'd got the nickname.

There was a clunk. 'That Caz Flood?'

'Good morning, Peter.'

'I tried to get hold of you yesterday. Your snout's come up trumps.'

'How exactly?'

'You had a ram-raid, early hours of New Year's Day, electrical shop in the middle of Brighton, right? Clever Trevor says he knows who knocked the shop over. The gang wanted him in on it as a driver but he said no, he was trying to be a citizen.'

'His girlfriend is expecting,' Caz said.

'Yeah, I met her; very tasty. Anyway, this gang were

threatening to get heavy with your snout. He decided it might be better for him if they went down for a while.'

'We've got some names, is that what you're trying to tell me?'

'Better than that!' Peter crowed. 'We got names, addresses and a pretty good idea where the stuff is stashed away.'

'And now you're going to tell me what *my snout* said, right, Peter?'

'Sort of, Flood.'

'Don't fuck about, Pete. I did you a favour, remember?'

The phone voice went slightly camp. 'Oooohh, PM Touchy!'

She waited, clenching her teeth.

'You got a pen, paper, Flood?'

'Fuck off, Sergeant.'

'Are you ready?'

She sucked air. 'Yes, *Sergeant*. I am ready. I am *all* ears. I am hanging on your every word.'

'That's better, Flood. Can I come over, share the arrest?'

'What happens if I say no?'

'I come over anyway.'

Shit! Caz looked up at the ceiling and sighed, the phone in her lap. She took a big, slow breath. When she spoke she wore a wide, totally false smile.

'Hello, is that Detective Sergeant Mason? I wonder, Sarge, we're a bit short-handed over here. D'you think you and a couple of your lads could get over to Brighton, help us out?'

'Oh, I don't know,' Mason said, 'things're a bit tight over here . . .'

'Puh-lease . . .'

'OK, Caz,' Mason said, suddenly more reasonable. 'I'll be there before eleven o'clock. How's that?'

'I really appreciate your help, Sergeant.' She sounded warm.

'Now that's *much* better, Flood.'

Caz put the phone down and waited to tell Bob Moore the good news.

Fifty-Nine

When Bob Moore came back from seeing the DI, Caz told him that DS Mason was on his way over from Southampton with information on the ram-raid gang. She had expected him to be miffed, a little pissed off. She hadn't expected him to go wild, his face a deep, dark red as he screamed at her.

'What the fuck's going on, Flood? Who the fuckin' hell do you think you are? You're a DC and you're on probation! What the *fuck* are you doing bringing in people from outside?' His eyes were bulging.

'I didn't bring *anyone* in, Sarge. DS Mason invited himself over. I got a phone call from a snout in Southampton, Mason went to see him for me. We missed each other yesterday afternoon. I rang this morning and he said he knew the ram-raid gang and he wanted to be in on the arrest. He didn't give me an option; that was it.'

Moore grunted under his breath, 'Fucking women, Jesus!'

Caz felt slightly less off-balance. 'He's been over before, Sarge, on the rapes case we had. He was working with Bob Reid and me. The DCS dragged him over. He did a good job.'

'I don't want some tosspot Hampshire twat with big feet trampling all over one of *my* cases!'

'I don't think it'll be like that, Sarge. Mason won't have

been in the job as long as you; he'll give way. I think he just wants in because his snout has come up with a good arrest.'

'I won't forget this, Flood!'

'What's there to forget, Sarge?'

Moore glowered. For a second she thought he was going to hit her. Then he burst past her and slapped out of the room.

'Fucking *hell*!' someone said behind her.

There was little Caz could do except duck her head and do some work. She thought of Barclays and rang the bank. A woman's voice answered and she asked to speak to the manager.

'Is it about an overdraft?'

'Detective Constable Flood.'

There was no reply, just a click and a short silence. Then a soft voice said, 'I am Mr Peak, deputy manager, how can I help you?'

Caz explained. She needed to re-interview the witnesses to Roland Prout's accident. Could she do that there?

'I'm afraid not, Officer. We gave them all three days off to get over the shock.'

'Doesn't that leave you a bit short-staffed?'

'Yes, but it's better than have them make lots of mistakes.'

Caz asked for the addresses. Peak said it would be no problem. He had them to hand and could fax them all over within ten minutes. She told him great. Then she had an idea.

'Could you just give me the first one on the list, Mr Peak?'

'Surely,' Peak said. 'One moment . . .'

She heard papers, his breath in the phone.

'Ah, yes!' he said. 'Right! The first one, you said?'

'Just one.'

'Right! Here we are. May Williams, Worthing.'
'Smashing,' Caz said. 'And the address?'

She wrote it down, scribbled out a copy for the DS and got out of there quick. As she left, she asked one of the DCs to let Bob Moore know she had gone to speak to a hit-and-run witness.
'I'll be back in an hour,' she said.

Sixty

Caz used the MX5 but was too unsettled to take in the sea's flash or the slow plod of the winter promenaders. She touched along at about forty miles an hour, covering much the same route she had followed when she'd accompanied the DS to the car repair shops. If she'd been less uptight she would have made the connection between the Mafeking in Mafeking Street and today's address, Cairo House. It came to her about the same time as she reached the A27. Now she realised where she was going, she thought, if there was time she'd drop in on the old chap on the allotment. Anything to keep out of John Street.

May Williams had been so traumatised by the New Year events, she'd gone off for a two-day jolly with her boyfriend. At least that was the information supplied by the next-door neighbour, a Hilda Ogden type with a scarf wrapped round her curlers and a stereotypical drooping fag Blu-Tacked to her face.

'Shall I tell 'er you was looking f'er?' the fag said.

'No, not important,' Caz decided. 'I was just passing . . .'

She got back in the Mazda and drove a few streets further until she found Mafeking Street and the rough lane out back.

She parked in the main drag to spare the sports car's suspension and walked the hundred-plus yards towards the garages.

'Come to scrounge more taiters have yer?' Jack said a few minutes later. She had called the old fella over to the gate after watching him work at his patch for a few minutes. He had been unhurried. She envied him his peace.

'Just passing, Jack,' she said. 'How long have you been here?'

'Twenty minutes,' Jack said. 'Yer c'n set yer watch by me. I told yer last time. I get here quarter past nine every day, never early, never late.'

'Oh, yes, you said. I'd forgotten.'

The railwayman laughed. 'I don't believe that for a single minute, young lady. Still, now that yer here, what can I do for yer?'

Caz smiled apologetically. 'Nothing, really. I really was just passing. Just thought I'd say hello.'

Jack shrugged. 'OK. D'yer fancy a cuppa tea. I bring a flask down; it's in the shed.'

'Why not?' Caz said.

'Grand!' The old man said. He was grinning as he led the way to the hut. Inside, he said, 'I hope yer don't mind sterry . . .'

Caz sat on a bench of boxes, an old army blanket beneath her. She sipped the tea, very strong and with a childhood-evoking whiff of the sterilised milk. 'So how's it with you?' she asked pleasantly.

'Oh, fine,' Jack said affably. 'More's the point, how're you? You got that car fixed yet?'

Caz was a bit off-base. 'What car?'

'Yer red Sierra. Din't you have it fixed at one of them spray shops at end of lane?'

'I drive a sports car, Jack. A little thing.' Then she stopped. 'But you wouldn't know that, would you? When we first met, I was in the Sierra.'

'That's right. But I saw you ont Saturday, din't I? The car were a bit knocked about. Fixed it quick enough though. I thought that were the problem. When you came back with that fat chap I thought you'd come t'complain. Rush job gone wrong, you know. It's all right then? They did a good job?'

Caz heard herself say, 'Yeah, fine, Jack.' She was thinking, some argument going on in her head. A red Sierra, so what? How many red Sierras were there in Brighton? A thousand? Five hundred? One? One in particular? She broke out her radio.

'Yes, that is correct,' she told Control after a brief exchange. 'Worthing. And this is DC Flood. Could you tell DS Moore I'm at K&J Autos following up a lead.'

'Thanks for the tea, Jack,' she said, giving him a real smile. Jack dropped his eyes like a shy young man. 'Got t'get back t'work. You know, Jack, duty calls.'

'Come round again, eh?' Jack said quietly, 'in an afternoon?'

Caz smiled again.

'It's a promise.'

Sixty-One

Caz turned left as she came out of the allotment, towards the road, towards her car, *away* from K&J's Autos. When she got to the Mazda, she slipped quickly inside, started up and drove away.

She drove about a mile, away, to anywhere, to nowhere in particular while she tried to work things out. She was trying to put together all the little things, trivial things, the weight of circumstance, evidence. She was heading for Arundel on the A27 when she hissed, 'Fuck it!' and swung the Mazda across the road, into a hotel car park and back out again, leaving rubber, smoke and a shocked cyclist in her wake as she headed back towards Worthing.

She turned off the main road, passed by Mafeking Street, and turned on to the track. As she bumped down it, old Jack tending his simple field, she prayed. But when she got to the lane's dead-end, the red Sierra was there; Bob Moore's Sierra. Mud flayed its wheel arches but the spray only heightened the gleam of the red paintwork. Now she was looking for it, she could see the fresh red. Despite the T-Cut, the half a ton of Turtle Wax, she could see the new wing, the extra shine of brand-new glass, the cracks papered over. The guilt.

Not so long ago, Moira Dibben had been forced to make a no-win decision; whether to point the finger at another copper, whether to bite her tongue. She had stayed silent and Caz had run with her. Now Caz was in the same boat. Her insult wasn't as personal but, if anything, her predicament was worse.

The hit-and-run driver had been seriously good. Police-trained was that good. The car was a red Sierra. If it had been fixed, it would be shiny. The woman who'd rung in, obviously on orders, had said, first, 'Road Traffic Accident' then, 'I'm to say RTA at the Goldstone ground.' Who says 'RTA'? She was an ambulanceman's wife, a fireman's wife, a policeman's wife . . .

And the DS had been so keen to be on the case; this along with the ram-raid. He had taken Caz to the repair shop but sent her on to the third one, already knowing where the work had been done. And the interview with Fullerton – the lid had been put on that too quickly; and Jenny's mate was 'useless' – at least according to Bob Moore.

Even the timing of the calls now made sense. An over-the-limit copper going home hits a kid. If he stops, he's dead; out of the force. But if he's decent – he had almost managed to miss her and it was at least half her fault – he stops off at a kiosk and rings, not the police, they might suss his voice – he calls out the ambulance service, gets the paramedics there quickly. Then his wife, dragged out of bed, in sudden shock, just manages to phone the police from a call-box half a mile from her home. And the DS, in her car, drives up to the accident unmarked, undamaged, just to see that the kid is all right. And Buck Shott, in Traffic, knows Bob Moore; tells him to fuck off home. This bump is nothing to do with the DS. He says,

'Best just get out of it quick, Bob, no point in hanging around to get breathalysed . . .'

It was all feasible, but only feasible. Caz hadn't been sure. One thing that had thrown her was the car – it was travelling *out* of Brighton at gone half past two in the morning. Moore lived centrally, just off the A23, so where was he going? And the girls had said the Sierra was racing a bigger car – that wasn't in character.

So there were still doubts. But then Caz had called in and the DS had rushed out – straight to K&J's Autos. Now she knew for sure. She tooted the Mazda's horn. Fifteen seconds later, Moore came to the crack in the door, darkness, the silver-blue flash of welding behind him. He looked grey. Caz still hadn't decided what to do.

Sixty-Two

Moore strode to her car. For all his greyness he looked strong. He put his hand on the top of her windscreen and looked straight into her eyes. 'We're needed at the nick, Flood. Now!'

'Sarge?'

'We've got a body. On the oyster beds at Shoreham.'

Caz had made herself uncontactable. 'But I – I didn't . . .'

He leaned towards her, taking her light. When she looked into his face again, she knew for sure. They both knew they had unfinished business, but it would have to wait. Moore growled but there was an odd note in his voice, sadness, compassion even. 'Next time, Flood. Leave yer fuckin' radio on!' With that he went to his car.

Moore started his Sierra but when he went to leave, he couldn't squeeze past Caz's Mazda. He stopped, grey-white exhaust fumes trailing along the car. Caz could see his anger, white-fisted on the steering wheel.

She sat up and pushed the MX5 into first gear, ludicrously feeling guilty and not having a clue why. As she bundled down the wet track, she could feel his dark face, his eyes burning into the back of her head. When she got to the road she shot off quickly, putting distance between their cars.

* * *

They got to John Street within a minute of each other, just enough time for Caz to have got out of the car and be walking across the car park as Moore spun quickly down the ramp in his Sierra. He stopped when he saw her, his dipped lights on as she crossed in front of him. When she had passed, she heard the car shoot forward and park with a squeal. She ran up the back stairs.

The riot was just at stage two, people being called in, people being called out. Doug Simpson, the Community Crime Prevention DI, was trying to persuade two councillors on an awareness visit that they would have to leave immediately. George Lindsell had just stuck his head out of the sergeants' office and bawled at Billy Tingle. Bob Reid went past carrying a computer monitor, a whiff of nervous sweat.

'The fuck you been, Flood?'

Caz turned to say, 'Interview', but Reid was gone, disappearing into the Major Incident room. Caz felt left out. Was it Pixie Walters? She desperately wanted to go and ask Tom MacInnes what had happened, but she knew she couldn't. Instead, she went into the noise and apparent chaos of the CID room. It looked like headless chicken time but Caz knew it wasn't. In half an hour they'd have their first briefing and by lunchtime there would be thirty pairs of feet on house-to-house, one pair most likely hers. There was a buzz. There was nothing like a G28 – a sudden death – to galvanise a nick.

Moira was on the far side of a group of DCs and uniforms moving bits and pieces around to set up the MI room. Caz shouted across. Moira lifted a keyboard with shrugged shoulders, what can I do?

'Is it Pixie?' Caz mouthed.

'No one knows yet!' Moira barked back.

Caz elbowed towards her. 'It was on the mud flats, yes?'

'The old oyster beds.' Moira said. She was still lumping things into her arms like a contestant on *Crackerjack*. 'I heard it was a woman. Found naked. Signs of sexual activity. Someone reckons she was older. Doesn't sound like it was the Walters kid.'

'Thank God,' Caz said.

'It's still a dead 'un!' a PC said as he humped past.

Caz floundered. 'Yeah, I—' She felt odd. 'I was just worried—'

Then Moore's voice thundered down the room. '*Flood! Get yerself down here! Now!*'

She felt herself jerk with shock, maybe even blanch. Then it all came back together and she bawled back, 'Yes, Sergeant!'

As she strode out towards him, Moore said, 'Your fancy DS from Southampton has turned up. He's in with the DI. Get yer skates on!'

She was close now. 'D'you know anything about the G28, Sarge?'

'I know absolutely fuck all, Flood. But according to Bob Allen, it's definitely murder.'

'Why's that, Sarge?'

Moore bristled. 'What am I – the fuckin' *Nine O'Clock News*?'

She brushed past him. 'You said the DI's office?'

'That's right, Detective. Now run along.'

She went quickly. Behind her there was a crash of equipment. Moore bawled again. 'PC Dibben!'

Caz was glad when she had turned a couple of corners and the noise had faded away.

Sixty-Three

The general level of noise throbbed through the nick, like a huge ship's diesels, distant, powerful, unstoppable. The first time Caz knocked the DI's door she wasn't heard. The second time she almost broke the glass.

'In!' MacInnes shouted.

She opened the door to see Peter Mason's back, suddenly recalling the last time he'd been in this office and she'd been one stupid remark away from being a civilian. He turned round and smiled.

MacInnes was being particularly terse. 'DS Mason, Hampshire. Info for you and DS Moore concerning the ram-raid New Year's morning. Looks like the McLintocks. Bit surprising; their usual MO is burglary and pub punch-ups.'

'Are we picking them up straight away, sir?'

'No. Sergeant Mason's snout – your snout – has told us where the stuff was stashed away. There may be other items there. We find the stolen goods, log them and photograph them, then we pick up Tommy and his boys. If we do it the other way, someone might get to the gear first.'

'OK, sir, so where's the stuff?'

Mason turned round and grinned as MacInnes said, 'That's

a wee surprise, Flood. The DS will take y'there.'

'Pictures, sir?'

'Nick Morton is at the mud flats right now. We've arranged for a PC to bring back the film. Nick'll stay there and wait for you.'

'So three of us?'

'For the gear, yes. Bob Moore is taking three lads to keep an eye on the McLintocks. Soon as the gear's been picked up, you, Nick and the DS can get over there, help out with the arrests.'

Caz felt slightly fragile, her emotions and her brain in conflict. She was desperate to know that the body wasn't Pixie Walters.

'Could I just ask about the woman on the oyster beds, sir? Could it be the Walters girl?'

'She's unknown but at least thirty.'

'Thank you, sir.'

'Speak t'you later, Flood.'

It sounded like he meant this evening.

'Yes, sir! Thank you, sir!'

The DI visibly softened. He glanced at Peter Mason then back at Caz. 'Good t'see you two have made up.'

Caz turned and left the DI's office, Peter Mason a sentence and a few seconds behind.

'We've got to take a van,' Mason said, dangling some keys. 'And there's absolutely *no* way I'm driving.'

'Thank you, Simple,' Caz said. He dropped the keys in her hand.

The van was a heap of shit, black with a little Sussex star on the side. It was a monument to the cuts, a year past its sell-by date. When Caz started the engine, there was a huge backfire which made both of them duck. Someone shouted abuse from the far end of the car park. They drove out, down Williams Street, then Edward Street and on to the Old Steine.

'Along the seafront,' Mason said, pointing a finger. 'I've been told to head for Portslade-on-Sea and go straight through it to' – he looked at a piece of paper – 'towards Shoreham.'

'So where exactly was the body found?'

'Your DI told me a couple of hundred yards upstream from where the main road crosses the river.'

'The chain bridge,' Caz said automatically.

'The what?'

The chain bridge. It isn't any more, there's a new one been built, but people still call it that.'

'Is that Brighton logic?'

'No, Sergeant, it's called popular reinforcement of oral history.'

'It's called habit, Flood.'

They passed along the front and went by her own street. The DS briefly nodded as they passed. 'Your place . . .'

Caz looked and grunted something back. The last time they had been in that street together, they were on the tail-end of a case. It had been blood-and-teeth time, armed officers trying to subdue a serial rapist; a freaked-out giant with Caz next on his list. It was not that long ago, but it felt like another life.

'It ever worry you?' Mason said.

'Only when I think of it,' Caz said to the windscreen.

Sixty-Four

The van clackered and flacked, the big steering wheel in Caz's hands jagging from ten-to-two to five-to-three in her hands and buzzing like a slightly manic vibrator. Caz was suffering a peculiar kind of *déjà vu*; cases, people, places were intertwining, repeating, coming back, each time with a different slant. It was like that strange no man's land between morning dreams and consciousness where the mind reruns the better bits of the imagination but each time with a different perspective, an edited script.

Some guy at uni – he hadn't lasted long – had once said to her that coincidences and intuitions were God's clues to his existence, his free gift, his leaked-to-the-person confession that he really was there. 'Any more direct and you would *know*,' he had said. 'But you can't know; you must *believe.* So he gives us all the information, but in little titbits. He never makes it concrete. He knows that absolute proof would create a world of fawning zombies. Faith creates a drive.'

The same guy had believed in flying saucers and razor-blades that sharpened under pyramids. A shame really. From what she remembered he'd had a great body, but his face was always red and raw from scraping away hair with blunt steel. What *was* his name?

* * *

Caz found herself approaching the Adur bridge. She came alive with a flash and shook her head, suddenly aware that she had come here on autopilot with absolutely no idea how she had done it. It was, as it always was, a frightening, disturbing realisation. If a child had stepped out in front of the car, would she have reacted, would she have stopped? Or would some timid, pink-cheeked WPC have had that awful job, the very worst job a copper ever had to do, 'Mrs Evans. May we come in. I'm afraid it's bad news . . .'

She bit the inside of her cheek until she tasted blood. The van was stationary with the right indicator flashing. In her head she was shouting at herself, 'Yes! Yes! Get on top!' searching for adrenaline, searching for control. Someone tooted from behind and she glared into her mirror. 'Fuck!' she said. 'Off!' She wanted to drop down out of the van and book the wanker for winding her up.

'There's a gap, Flood!' Mason said.

'I know,' she replied as she pulled away. Then the van threatened to stall, picked up and bucked once before it settled. She had got mad now. 'What a heap of Friday afternoon *crap* this van is!' she said.

Mason pointed. 'Park up over there, Detective!'

Caz was spitty. 'My name is Caz, Peter.'

He looked at her and grinned. 'Oh, I love it when you get angry . . .'

'Fuck off!'

'And don't hit that area car!'

The van was the sixth police vehicle on the gravelled area. There were a couple of section cars, a seven-series Traffic BM, and two CID unmarkeds. The Scorpio was DCS

Blackside's. Across the river by the Outdoor Sports Centre were two more blue 'n' whites. Down in the river basin there were half a dozen people and yellow stakes marking out where the body lay. It was low tide but they couldn't hang about.

The blokes on the mud flats were all wearing waders, except for the DCS. He was in green wellington boots and somehow managing to find more solid mud than those who floundered around him in their rubbers. He was huge. Caz could see him standing close to Nick Morton as Nick took pictures. A striped screen three-quarters hid the body, protruding blue feet side-flopping in the mud, the muscles no longer attending, and rigor still to arrive. 'Poor sod,' the DS said.

As they got slowly out of the van, a white minibus pulled in on the other side of the river. Half a dozen, seven coppers piled out, all in yellow waders. They walked awkwardly, like penguins. After a brief word from their sponsor they began climbing down the bank. The second policeman, tall and thin, slipped as he met the river floor and slid a dozen feet, turning over as he tried to stop, streaking the river with his face, his face with the river's mud.

'If that's not Billy Tingle, I'm a Russian shotputter,' Caz said.

Remembering the situation's other elements, she was trying not to laugh, but then 'Billy' tipped over again as he tried to get up. Even from here they could hear the jeers and cries of 'Wanker!' from the rest of the lads. Then she noticed the shorter, rounder shape, the only one not laughing; a woman's hipped shape. Was it Moira? She couldn't get a clear look amongst the flapping heads and the slapping thighs. Then a single black shout from Blackside cut them all dead. The laughter stopped and the seven waddled towards the DCS. Now she could see Moira and see that the mud-streaked PC was Billy.

Mason had walked the few yards towards the edge of the gravel and stopped. He had his hands on his hips. 'I can't see them getting much evidence down there,' he said dismissively. 'The tide will have washed anything away.'

'They have to look, Sarge. They can't *not* do it.'

The DS turned round with a shrug of his shoulders, the way only a copper can turn away from death, a copper who has seen a few too many bodies, one who understands the difference between concern and watching the show for the sake of it.

'You seen a lot of G28s, Flood?'

'Lost count, Sarge. I spent a year in Traffic, that was bad enough. Turned up on two murders just a couple of months ago and had a guy top himself in front of me.'

'You sleep all right?'

'Like a baby.'

'What's the worst you ever had?'

'I don't want to talk about it.'

He shrugged again. 'Worse one I ever 'ad started out as a funny, when I was a DC.' Caz glanced away but he had started so he was going to finish. 'We were keeping tabs on a couple of burglars, young blokes, obbing them from unmarked cars. This was, what, must be three years ago.'

'Oh, really?' Caz said, still looking at the river.

'These two lads break into a big house. Obviously they're doing a job. My DI gives them a minute, then sends us in. We're just going to go in and pick 'em up when they come out of the house screaming. They were hard lads but when they clocked us they just put out their hands for us to cuff 'em.'

Caz was vaguely curious. 'So what was in the house?'

'A very old dear lived downstairs, son lived upstairs. Turned out, one day the son goes upstairs to the bog, has a wank and dies just sat there. The old dear is locked in downstairs – the son did everything – and goes weird living on cat food, not changing herself, all that, but the son is upstairs.'

'Is this going to be disgusting?'

'I told you. It's the worse thing I ever saw.'

'Worst.'

'That's what I said.'

'No, Sarge. You said worse.'

'Most bodies blow up but this one didn't. This guy just sat there for weeks and kind've melted. It was like cheese dripping off a pizza. When these two burglars went upstairs and got a sight of it they nearly died. They came out so fast we thought they were being chased. One of 'em, the black one, went straight. Now he's heavy into one of those hallelujah churches.'

'What happened to the other one?'

'Can't remember. I got pictures of this bloke, you know, the wanker. Next time I'm over, I'll bring 'em, yeah?'

'I don't think so, Sarge.'

'Don't you like pizza, then?'

Sixty-Five

They saw Nick Morton finally break away from the centre of the river scene with what looked like a salute followed by a practised jerk to put his camera bag comfortably on his shoulders. He made for the bank, taking extra care. Behind him, Blackside was gesturing at the troops with short, sharp jabs of his arm. Then he looked up, their way, as if suddenly sensing the presence of Caz and DS Mason. He raised one finger, enough to say, I know you're there.

'Nick already knows where to come,' Mason said. 'It's over 'ere.'

'Over where?' Caz said.

Mason ignored her and grunted past, heading for the bridge. Caz stopped, looked down at the DCS and then at the back of the DS.

'The gear's here?' she shouted, scampering after him. 'Where?'

Mason reached the bridge and ducked underneath the edge of concrete. When Caz caught up with him, he was standing where she had stood with the streetwise lads. He flicked at the big brass lock.

'We'll need a key,' Caz said.

Mason held up his hand. 'Like this, you mean?'

'Yes, Peter,' Caz said. 'Just like that.'

Peter keyed the heavy lock, broke it open and passed it to Caz. It was so heavy Caz's accepting hand dropped with the surprise weight. The trapdoor was still closed, years of vandalism in the misalignment of latch and groove.

'Want a screwdriver?' Caz said helpfully.

Mason grunted. 'No thanks, love. I'm fixing my car . . .' She groaned.

He produced a Swiss Army knife as big as a healthy erection and with a well-oiled shlupp! produced a curly bit to prise open the door.

'You do horse hooves as well, Sarge?'

'I can do' – Mason grunted and held the weight of the door, then flapped it downwards with a scrunk of metal on metal – 'anything!' They were in. He disappeared straight away, a torch in his right hand, his next sentence echoing and comic, 'You know where to C-Come, come to Comet! Get in here, take a look, Flood!'

Caz ducked underneath Mason and then up his body to squeeze her head through the hole. Peter could have moved but that would have been only half the fun. They were face to face, a lump between them. 'Tell me that's the knife,' Caz said.

'Sorr-rree . . .' Peter said. He had the knife in the hand he was waving at their haul of treasure. 'You ever shop at Argos?' he said.

Maybe the two videos from the ram-raid were in there somewhere, it was difficult to tell, but there was enough boxed electronics squeezed into the bridge's box-girdered first span to start up a nice little shop, even a modest warehouse. Virtually all the names were Far Eastern. Even at a glance she could see Sony, Hitachi, Samsung and Kenwood. At recommended retail prices there was twenty, maybe thirty thousand pounds' worth of kit here. More to the point, it wouldn't all go in the van. 'This won't all fit—'

Mason finished for her, 'in the van.'

Nick Morton's 1100 Escort arrived with a toot and a swirl of pebbles. The DS squeezed his head out to shout, 'Over here, Nick!' He turned to Caz. 'Swing yerself up inside, Flood. Nick'll probably want a hand when he starts flashing.'

Caz couldn't see the DS's face but to his waist she said, 'Give it a rest, Peter.' Then she added, 'And leave the fuckin' door open.'

She swung up inside, the smell of steel, cardboard. 'Hey!' she shouted down. 'It's as dry as a bone up here!'

Mason's head appeared through the hatch like a jack-in-the-box. 'What was that?' he said with a silly voice. He grinned maniacally, then his head disappeared. Caz was looking at the boxes, at what looked like the proceeds of more than one robbery. She heard Nick Morton say something obscure, then Mason laugh something back to him. Then the lights went out with a clang as the trapdoor slammed shut. For a split second Caz did not react. From outside she heard Peter's voice shouting, some sort of crass remark, some little-boy nah nah nah-nah nah but it was blunted, no words, just the buzz of a broken loudspeaker. Then the horror hit her, she couldn't hear, she couldn't see. Absolute darkness. Absolute darkness. Not a crack of light, not a razor's edge, not even a leak from the day. A childhood terror rushed over her. She froze, asthmatic, tetanoid, locked up, too solidly frightened even to cry out.

The men probably left her like that for a minute. Caz had absolutely no idea of how long. When they cranked open the square of metal to flash in air and light, they couldn't see her, rolled as she was into a defensive, autistic ball. She didn't move until Peter had climbed up, climbed in, touched her and said sorry. His voice echoed, 'Fer fuck's sake, Flood. Get a grip! It was only a little joke.'

Caz untensed enough to look at him. All sorts of thoughts were flashing through his head, including disciplinary charges. Beyond him she saw the light, outside. She hissed at him, 'You stupid, stupid bastard!' and pushed past. Behind her, she heard him bluster another apology. She could have killed him. Not because he had frightened her, but because he had seen her weak. When she dropped to the ground, her legs felt like someone else's. Her stare was enough to dumb Nick. She rushed away, crouched like a soldier leaving a helicopter, standing to her full height only when she was yards from the bridge. As the men watched she suddenly slammed the pad of her rolled hand against the van's side and turned to look at them. She did not look pretty.

Sixty-Six

She told them about it later, why she was so scared, after Nick had taken his photographs and they had removed the first vanful of hot electronics from the bridge. 'I'm sorry,' she said to Peter. 'It was a joke, I know. You just picked the wrong copper.'

Like when she had pot-holed, she had forced herself to go back in there; but only with Mason's torch. As she had climbed in, she had given the DS one definite look. He wasn't going to play any more games. Had he, if she had ever got out, Caz would have killed him.

They had three-quarters emptied the steel vault. Caz had shuffled stereos and videos to the trapdoor, Mason had lifted them down and ferried them to the open air. With Nick Morton lugging the boxes as far as the van, they'd formed an overstretched, undermanned and too laid-back human chain. If the goods had been fire buckets, the ranch house would have burned to the ground long ago.

They were taking a breather. Nick had lit a cigarette. Mason had pulled out a cigar, looked at Caz and then put it away.

'When I was a kid, my parents split up, and my mum eventually set up house with a chap called Graham. I never really got on with him but we managed. When I was about ten, eleven, I was going through a stroppy period, period no doubt being the operative word. I'd never got used to not being with my real dad and this particular day I was being even more than usually obnoxious with the stepdad. My mum had gone out; we were living in Wembley and she'd had to go to Birmingham. I'd wanted to go out with one of my mates and Graham wouldn't let me.

'I never gave in in those days and we were having a flaming row. I called him something, I think, or I took a swing at him, I don't remember exactly. He was going to hit me, but at the last second, he didn't. He stopped himself and just grabbed my arms. I couldn't do anything so I spat at him, right in his face. It was really hateful, but he said nothing. We were in our front room. He picked me up. He didn't say a word. He just carried me out and locked me in the cellar.

'I screamed my head off at him for a while, just abuse. I wasn't particularly scared, but I was bloody mad. The cellar was at the back of the house and I was making a hell of a racket, so Graham went through to the front room, closed the door and stuck some music on.

'I got tired of screaming and shouting eventually, and I just sat down to wait until Graham came back and let me out. I was a bit scared but I wasn't totally freaked out. I've never *liked* the dark; but it was just gradually, as the time went on, that I started to get more and more frightened.

'But Graham didn't come back. My mum had been in a car crash on the A40 on a notorious piece of three-lane between Oxford and Stratford. She'd been very badly hurt. Graham rang where she was supposed to be because she hadn't rung him. She wasn't there, of course. Eventually he rang the police and they found out she'd been rushed to a hospital in Oxford. With the shock and everything, Graham just rushed to get to her. She was dead when he got there.

'I didn't know all this then and I didn't have much idea of the passage of time. They'd let Graham go into a side room to compose himself. He was in there for a long while. They wouldn't let him see the body and he left. He went to an off-licence, bought a bottle of whisky and drank it, sitting on a park bench in the middle of nowhere. He must have fallen asleep. When he woke up, it was morning. It took him ages to find his car; then he remembered me.

'He told me everything, weeks after the funeral. He rushed back to Wembley and to the house. He found me at the bottom of the cellar steps rolled up into a ball, locked solid, he said. He had to carry me out, but even when I was upstairs I wouldn't open up. He called a neighbour round, told her about Mum. This woman, the neighbour, thought I was like that, in a ball, because I'd just heard my mother had died. In the end they called a doctor out, gave me some sort of jab. When I woke up, I wasn't in a ball any more.'

'Fer fuck's sake!' Peter said.

Sixty-Seven

Nick and Peter decided to squeeze the remainder of the boxes into Nick's Escort. Nick managed to rig up a light from his kit, clipped to a girder's edge and running off a bank of rechargeable ni-cads. Caz climbed back into the bridge. She was cool now. She was thinking about the days after her mother died, not as a narrative, but in peculiar flashes, like sentences dug up randomly from a buried pile. The boys were being sweet now, honestly concerned about her rather than covering their backs. Each time they came to the hatch it was with a smile, a little verbal pat on the head.

Caz didn't tell them how cold and absolute the break with Graham Pott had been. She knew with the intelligence that hindsight brings that even the act of locking her up had been reasonable. Her mood swings in those days had been so extreme – she felt so helpless – that she could only be ring-fenced while the storm lasted. She was so bad, there was a time when it looked like her mum and Graham were going to get outside help. That was still on the cards the day her mother's Mini ran out of road. Caz had been unable to control events. What she could not deal with then and thereafter was that impotence, the need to wait. Add darkness to her dilemma and she was jelly.

They got all but four boxes into the Escort, its tailgate high in the air, a strap across the most vulnerable boxes. The DS had already decided to leave a few bits and pieces in the bridge. They would arrange for discreet surveillance and pick up anyone who arrived with a key. Caz was forced to make the point that a discreet ob of the bridge wouldn't exactly be easy. If they parked a van on the waste ground and it looked unattended, someone would have the wheels off by midnight, first day it was there.

'You're right!' Mason said. 'Someone will have to sleep inside with the boxes. Only way we can be certain of catching our villains red-handed.' He looked at her as if she was about to volunteer. If he really thought that, he was stupid as well as sick.

'I'd rather sleep with you,' Caz said.

Mason grinned. 'Seems a good deal. D'you snore, Flood?'

Caz left it. At least they were back to some semblance of normality. Now they had all this gear, they were going to the nick. They'd have to sign it off and use one of the cars to get over to Bob Moore's stake-out. It never paid to mix jobs, Peter said. While they locked up the trapdoor and ducked out from underneath the bridge, he told them about the time when his unmarked car, full of goodies from a number of burglaries, had been turned over while he was knocking on the villain's front door.

'This prat nicked the kit, then we found it, then someone nicked it again from the CID car, all in twenty-four hours. And the bastard got off as well, lack of evidence!'

Nick Morton laughed. 'I love reminiscing.'

'So do I,' Peter said, 'but I wouldn't exactly call that fuck-up one of my fondest memories. I thought I was going back into uniform.'

Caz climbed up into the van with the DS while Nick got into his overladen Escort. She said nothing. Most of her memories were still dressed in dark blue. She'd had some fun, got a few commendations, some good collars, but she was a detective now. Being a detective was so important to her. She had often thought that if she ever did screw up badly enough to have to leave the CID, she'd go the whole hog and leave the force at the same time.

Mason started the van, then tooted at Nick Morton to lead the way out of the car park. The Escort was painfully low on its suspension and looked like it might not make it off the rough ground.

'Knowing our bloody luck,' Mason chuckled as they lurched after the straining 1100, 'Nick'll get stopped by some eager-beaver blues 'n' twos tosser and get booked fer carrying a dangerous load!'

Caz responded with a classic plonker's jobsworth voice. 'Just doing our job, sir. Have you any idea what the stopping distance is for an overloaded car?'

'I'm sorry, Officer. No, I don't.'

'Do you have your driving licence with you, sir?'

'I'm afraid not, Officer. But I've got my warrant card. Will that do?'

'Boom boom!' they said together.

Sixty-Eight

They went in DS Mason's car and found Bob Moore's parked up in one of the terraces just off the Lewes Road, halfway between London Road and Moulescomb railway stations, close to Brighton Poly. When they pulled up, Moore pointedly looked at his watch. Mason just shrugged while Caz and Nick Morton looked the other way.

Mason went over for a quick chat, nodded a couple of times, flicked his head rather than pointed. When he came back he said, 'There's three of 'em inside for sure. We don't know if the fourth one's in the house or not. It's Epsom Terrace, number forty-five. Moore says the McLintocks are a bit of a handful, that right?'

'I've never had to tangle with them,' Caz said, 'but from what I've heard, the whole family are head-bangers.'

'I'll look after the car, then . . . ?' Nick offered.

'No chance,' Mason said. 'DS Moore and his crowd have got the gardens and the cemetery all tight. They expect the McLintocks to leg it out the back way – that's what they usually do. We're the front door. We just go up and knock, make it obvious who we are.'

Caz shifted in her seat. 'If I'd known I was going to get a chair in my face, I wouldn't have bothered making up this morning.'

'Very funny, Flood. We knock the door in – ' he glanced at his watch, 'three and a half minutes.'

'Synchronise watches, all that stuff, ay, Sarge?' Morton said.

Mason swung round. 'You can tell the time then, can you?'

'Night school,' Nick said.

The DS started his Saab. It caught quicker and sounded a whole lot smoother than the Talbot van they'd driven earlier.

'Right!' he said. 'We just roll slowly round the corner . . .'

Number forty-five Epsom Terrace was a third of the way down a long, straight row of red-brick and pebble-dashed buildings, every fourth one adjoining a narrow arched alleyway leading into the back courtyards. The McLintocks' house had been plastered with pebble dash about ten years before. What was once white and pink granite chips was now a dull grey. The windows had been replaced with white PVC double-glazing and the front door, also PVC, had mock-stained glass in its top light, a football shield with CELTIC! splashed in a semicircle above it. Above the door was an Astra satellite dish.

There was no time to comment on the décor as Pete Mason first rang the bell then tried to clatter on the aluminium letter box. They had wanted to make a dramatic racket but three inches of plastic and brush-pile insulation turned their rude bang-bang into a delicate phutt-phutt. Pissed off, Mason leaned on the bell but 'Clair de Lune' buzzing away inside hardly made their little squad sound like the Special Patrol Group.

'Margritt?' a woman's voice squawked, raw, low Glasgow coming through from the back. 'Liff yer finger offa that fickin' bell!'

The door opened, a little shlupp! of unsticking. A crone face, but wild-eyed – Mother Teresa on something. 'The fickin' hell are youse?'

Mason said, 'Mrs Mary McLintock? Police. Are your boys in?'

'Fuck yew!' the woman said. 'Where's yer werrant?'

'We don't need a warrant, Mrs McLintock. We want to talk to your boys, and that's now! Are you going to let us in or do we have to book you for obstruction?'

The old woman had her foot against the bottom of the door, her hand loosely on the handle. She obviously knew that this was the best way to hold the pass. Brute force five foot up would barely make a determinedly wedged foot slip backwards. McLintock may have looked frail, but Caz could imagine her putting up a hell of a fight.

Mason shouted into the house, 'Sammy, Billy, Terry, Frank. This is the police. Don't fuck us about!'

'They're not in,' Ma McLintock said. As she spoke there were a few thuds somewhere deeper in the house. She grinned and stepped back from the door, 'Well, not any mair they're not!'

Caz and the DS burst past. Caz heard Nick Morton say something to the old woman and shepherd her into the front parlour, out of the way. Crafty bastard, she thought as she broke into the kitchen, just in time to see an arse dropping into the garden – he looks after the old dear, head down while we have to collar three or four mad Glaswegians.

Caz leapt up on the fitted kitchen worktop and followed the bum through the open window. She didn't know which McLintock it was but he was big and he had a nifty little rounders bat in a thick fist.

'The door!' Pete Mason was shouting as she dropped into the garden; later she worked out he meant, 'I'm unlocking it.' She hit the garden, a bit of wet grass, dog shit, just as McLintock Four reached the back gate, threw it open, changed his mind and turned.

Mason was shouting. He couldn't get out of the door.

'Oh, fuck!' Caz said.

Sixty-Nine

The nearest thing to Caz was a garden rake. She grabbed it just as Frank McLintock turned round to discover he was being chased by a woman four inches shorter and six stone lighter than him. The grin that spread across his face was disgusting. If this had been a dark alley and one-on-one, Caz would be running already.

McLintock was in vest and jeans, no shoes. He had the lot, scars, broken nose, shaved head, like a very bad photofit of a bank-blagger. Caz was terrified. She was thinking, 'Jesus! This lump could pick me up, eat me and spit out the bits before the DS is through the window.' She decided to attack, throw in a bit of verbal to give him time to think. She was holding the rake diagonally across her chest.

'Only a pissy little bird, Frankie,' she said. 'That what you're thinking? You fancy your chances, do yer?'

She spun the rake so the prongs were forward. Did he fancy his chances? Who was she kidding? And where the fuck was Mason?

'Come on, Frank. What are you, a poof?'

''Oo said I was a poof?' Frank asked. He hadn't lifted the bat but Caz thought if she stayed still much longer, he'd see her shaking. Then she heard Mason grunting, coming through the window.

'Fuckin' tart!' McLintock said, and took off, over the fence.

Here we go again, Caz thought. She had been hoping Frank would run. All she had to do now was keep pace until he knackered himself out. A few fences, all that adrenaline and six coppers after his collar . . .

'Not worth it, Frank!' she shouted and followed after one quick peek over the fence to make sure he wasn't waiting on the other side.

Some blokes hit women, some hit women coppers. Caz didn't try to catch Frank McLintock, just keep pace with him. She could hear feet the other side of a wall, then she heard Pete Mason's shout, a half-explanation from his perch. Someone else shouted, 'The front way!'

McLintock was a garden ahead. Each time Caz topped a fence he would be just clambering out of the garden into the next one. She could catch him easily but then she'd have to try to cuff him. She still had the rake. There was no way she was going to go up against a brick shithouse like Frank McLintock without something extra.

She reached another fence, bobbed up, saw he was still running, threw the rake over and then followed it. The weapon felt good but she knew that if she used it, she'd be on a disciplinary charge and McLintock would sue. Just the same, she knew she would use it. Her motto was 'Be safe. Keep your face and worry about the flak later.'

Frank was climbing the next fence and Caz was up on the one behind when they both saw Terry McLintock coming back their way, two hairy coppers a couple of gardens behind. Caz had dropped into the garden almost as she realised what was happening. When Frank dropped back and turned to face her, she swallowed. Terry was just behind, the wood of the fence swaying as he clambered up. He was on the top when he saw Caz and grinned. 'Well, what have we here?'

'Evening up the odds, are we, boys?' Caz said quickly. 'Is that it, or do you want to wait for a couple more brothers?'

The basic rule is that rules only work at training school. The best thing for Caz now, if she was worried about her looks, was to leg it back over the fence or try and get down the alleyway between the houses. She looked at the guy on the fence, the one on the ground. She desperately wanted to run but she knew she wouldn't, couldn't. She wasn't a Nick Morton. She was just as scared as him but she couldn't walk away.

There were coppers less than a minute away in both directions, but if these guys wanted to, they could hurt her very badly before they arrived. Terry dropped down, a bully's leer, a rapist's.

'Hello, darling,' he said.

'Thought you were going to sit on the fence all day,' Caz said. 'Which one are you?'

'I'm Terry. My friends call me Porky.'

'Why's that?' Caz asked. She couldn't hear the lads coming.

Frank broke in, ''Cos he fucks pigs!' They both laughed.

'*Fucking hilarious!*' Bob Moore said.

Seventy

Moore came straight out of the alleyway, on his own, no truncheon drawn. He slammed into Terry McLintock and the pair bundled Frank to the ground. Moore rose first, an aikido lock on Terry. He kicked Frank once behind the ear. Then he half stood, his foot still there, blood seeping on to shiny black shoe leather. He shouted, blood somewhere, 'Flood, cuff the twat!' Terry McLintock was squirming, screaming that his arm was breaking. Moore hissed in his ear, 'I'm *trying* to fuckin' break it, you dull cunt!' Then he shouted, 'Flood!' again. Maybe five, six seconds had passed.

Caz reacted. 'Sarge!' she said as she bundled in, clipping Terry's loose wrist. Moore grabbed the other cuff, pulling it towards the locked arm. 'Get mine!' Moore shouted again, nodding at his waist. 'On the other moron before he works out he can get up!'

'Sarge!' Caz responded, feeling chided. Moore lifted an arm to show the handcuffs on his belt. Terry roared in pain. She took the cuffs and got one on to Frank McLintock's wrist before he grunted and tried to lurch to his feet. Caz threw her weight on to his head, grabbed for the other arm and clicked the plastic clamp round his wrist as he fell forward. Bodies were coming over the fence both sides now, dropping around them. 'Who's trod in dog shit?' someone said.

The policemen came out through the alley into Epsom Terrace. Caz was trying to scuff the dog doo from the soles of her trainers. The waffled tread that normally helped her now annoyed her, the Indi-rubber ripples clogged with crap. Caz looked behind her again at her turned-up foot. Why *did* dog mess stink so much?

The locals, almost all Asian, were gradually emerging to see the reason for all the fuss; a couple of handsomely brown teenage lads in smart school uniforms, one or two older men, slow-moving and dignified in traditional baggy silken pants. Shy wives hid inside, behind lace curtains and their own veils, their eyes wide and brown. Pete Mason wandered up to the oldest man and bowed politely. A teenager jogged over to interpret, his school tie flapping.

'Please apologise for us,' Peter said.

The boy nodded and spoke to his elder, nodding slightly. The old man, his beard almost white, jabbered something back, the tone resignation, sadness. What he said included the word 'McLintock'.

'Thank you,' the schoolboy said. 'They are the only white family left in the street and the only ones who ever bring trouble to it.' Peter spread his hands, apologising for his own race.

The boy smiled. Caz had come close. The boy noticed but remained polite. 'Er, would the – lady – like some soapy water, a brush?'

Caz went slightly pink. 'Thank *you*,' Peter said.

Sammy McLintock was cuffed to a car bumper in the wide alley behind the terrace. He was *very* unhappy. He was even less happy when he realised that Terry and Frank had been collared. There was an argument about whether the fourth brother, Billy, had come out through the back and slipped the net or hadn't been in there at all. When Nick Morton came out of number forty-five with a nose bleed and a handkerchief to his bloody mouth, they got their answer.

'Fucker was still in bed!' Nick spluttered through gooey loose teeth. 'Came rushing out while you lot were in the gardens.'

'Billy do that?' someone asked, nodding at his face.

'No, he bloody didn't,' Nick said. There were tears in his eyes. 'His bloody mother did!'

'You want her arrested?' Moore said.

'I'd rather leave it, Sarge, if it's all right with you . . .'

'Should've left her with Flood,' Moore said, 'but then you probably couldn't jump the garden fences . . .'

Sergeant Moore turned to walk towards the cars. There was a sullen McLintock in the back of each one. 'Not bad, Flood,' he said as he turned away. 'See you at the nick.' He looked again at Nick Morton and shook his head.

Morton spat a blob of blood. 'I'm a *photographer*, for fuck's sake!'

Peter Mason waved them back to the Saab. 'Well, don't bleed in my motor, Lord Snowdon,' he said. Caz got in the front. As she belted up he realised out loud, 'Billy could be on his way to the bridge now. We'll have to cover it.'

He was reaching for his radio.

'No,' Caz said. 'If we stick a car there, he won't go near.'

'You're right,' Mason said.

'But if he goes there, and we catch him inside . . .'

'OK.'

'Better drop Nick off at John Street first, Sarge . . .'

'Better had, Flood.'

'Oh fuck!' Nick said from the back seat.

When Caz turned round he had two teeth and a pool of dark blood in his hanky. She offered him a falsely sympathetic smile.

'Can't trust anyone these days, can yer, Nick?'

Seventy-One

They drove quickly into Brighton, with Caz calling out the best rights and lefts to avoid the worst traffic lights and bottlenecks, Nick Morton moaning in the back seat. Most of what he was saying was depressing mumble. The only time he raised the energy to speak clearly was when he decided to explain that, actually, it wasn't that Mary McLintock had whacked him, but that she'd tripped him with her walking stick when Billy McLintock came down the stairs. It was when he hit their cast-iron fire grate that he smacked in his teeth.

Pete Mason parked the Saab out front and stayed with it to ward off traffic wardens with a large crucifix. Nick Morton shuffled slowly inside to call out the police surgeon and Caz nipped in sharply to scribble out a message for Bob Moore. Someone tried to tell her there were messages, but she shouted back that she had a villain to catch and they'd have to wait. She was back in the car and moving down towards the Steine within five minutes of their arrival.

'It's calmed down a bit inside,' Caz said. 'They must've got themselves sorted on the G28.'

Peter seemed surprised. 'Don't you fancy getting involved, then?'

'I'm involved already,' Caz said. 'I just don't know exactly how.'

They hadn't worked out a sensible plan, nor cleared it with the DI. All they had decided was that Billy McLintock or his proxy would have to get to the bridge pretty quick to shift the evidence.

'We can just pull in close to the bridge, out of sight of the road,' Caz suggested, 'clock the hatch from the car. Anyone comes along, it's just a bit of back-seat bonking.'

Mason raised his eyebrows. 'Is this some kind of an offer?'

'Don't flatter yourself, *Sergeant*.'

They pulled off the Brighton road and bounced down on to the rough parking area that overlooked the oyster beds. Peter Mason responded first, muttering out loud, 'Shit and bollocks!'

Maybe it was the excitement of the earlier find, followed by the adrenaline of the three arrests, but Caz and the DS really should not have been surprised by the uniformed PC waiting for them in the car park, or the blue and yellow police tape pegged out along the river bank. The dead woman on the river bed had changed everything. Even if her body had finally come to rest some one hundred and fifty yards from where the PC now stood, murder rules, the denial of access to a morbid public, had red-flagged the area. With the car park fenced off like this, and a bored uniform strolling up and down, there was no way Billy McLintock would come to the stash.

'It wasn't taped off this morning,' Mason said, as if stating the fact might make the blue and yellow vinyl suddenly disappear. 'I didn't think they'd tape off this far out.'

'Nor me,' Caz said. 'Any ideas?'

The PC was walking towards them, slowly, with a 'Bill' lollop. Caz recognised his face but couldn't add the name.

'Know him?' Mason said.

Caz thought hard. 'Not really. Try John.' It was one of those faces.

The DS smiled as the constable ambled up to the car. 'Afternoon, John.' Only coppers ever walked like that.

'Good afternoon, sir. Would you mind telling me what business you have in this area?'

'It's not illegal, is it, parking here?'

'No, sir, it's not, but I'm afraid you can't park here today. There's been a serious incident nearby . . .'

Mason pulled out his warrant card. 'DS Mason, Hampshire. And this is one of your own, DC Flood, John Street.'

'Oh,' the PC said. He tilted his lapel to his mouth and called in.

'They're expecting you in, Sergeant. You and DC Flood.'

Caz leaned across. 'We left a message, DS Moore . . .'

'Hang on a minute, Flood,' Peter grunted. He got out of the car and gestured the PC away. They spoke with dipped heads for about a minute, then he came back to the car.

'I've explained the situation to John, you were right about the name anyway. We'll do it the other way round. High-profile police presence for now, frighten Billy away. We'll go back to the nick and see if we can work something out with Moore and the DI.'

'This is all bullshit,' Caz said. 'The tide's coming in. What's Joe Public going to walk on now, water?'

'John says DCS Blackside's got the case and he's by the book.'

'Only all of the time,' Caz said.

'Well, if that's how it is, we'll have to talk to him.'

'I should care,' Caz mumbled. She put her head back in the seat and kept her eyes closed all the way to John Street.

Seventy-Two

As they came up the back stairs from John Street's car park, Peter and Caz both realised they were starving. They considered diving into the dregs of a canteen lunch but thought better of it. If Moore or MacInnes stumbled on them filling their faces, there'd be shit flying everywhere. They made do with a packet of crisps and a Mars bar each and grabbed a sludgy coffee from a machine on the third floor.

Caz took them to the CID room, logged in and then went to see the DS. Someone shouted, did she realise she'd got a desk at last?

Bob Reid was in with Sergeant Moore in the new sergeants' office. CID had been threatening the segregation for ages and now it had finally happened. New desks all round, more space for the DCs.

'Where've you been, Flood, and where's Mason?'

'Didn't you get my message, Sarge?'

Moore just stared.

'We went down to where the electronic stuff had been stashed, Sarge. In the bridge. We figured that Billy McLintock might try to shift it before we found out where it was.'

'But we've already found out, Flood.'

'Billy doesn't know that, Sarge.'

'The place is cordoned off.'

'Yeah, I know. It hadn't occurred to me or DS Mason.'

'There's a stack of paperwork.'

'There always is.'

'Go sort it, then.'

'Yes, Sarge.' She went to leave.

'And there was no rake.'

'Yes, Sarge.'

She went through to the CID room and to the corner where her new desk had been squeezed in between Greavsie's and the computer room. There would have been a lot more room if half this floor hadn't been hived off to the Child Protection Unit, and she could have sat down if Peter Mason hadn't been laid back in her brand-new chair, grinning like someone had a hold of his dick.

Peter had a few Post-Its stuck to his bald head. Caz took no notice and went to get a batch of arrest forms. When she came back, he unpeeled the notes and passed them over.

'You're a popular girl,' he cracked.

'You wouldn't know, would you?' Caz said.

'I guess not,' he said sadly. 'But then' – he groaned to his feet to stretch – 'I haven't got tits.'

Caz ignored the remark and the yellow notes, not wanting their distractions until the arrest was written up. Pete Mason had moved but things were still a bit tight. When she muttered, he said, 'Not a lot of room, is there?'

'There was before we had Child Protection.'

'I saw it,' Peter said. 'Thought it was the CID room. They've got enough bodies to run a murder.'

'Sometimes that's just what they might be doing,' Caz said.

'I know that,' Peter said, 'but we used t'manage without.'

'Not any longer, mate.'

Child Protection units seemed to have come from nowhere and they still grew. It bemused Caz, but there was no arguing with their appropriations. Good, bad and value-for-money never came into it once media politics had raised its head. Caz had nothing against protecting kids, it was just the size of the unit – half as big as the rest of CID now – that freaked her.

'You remember before we had CPUs, Peter?'

'We didn't get the cases.'

'We do now,' Caz said.

'So you think all those kids were being abused then?'

Caz picked up the first form. 'How should I know?'

Even in the few years that Caz had been a copper, everything had changed. There were rumours now that Michael Howard was going to scrap some higher ranks, take most inspectors off overtime, bring in fixed-term contracts, more civilians, crap like that. There was even a whisper that the split between CID and uniform might one day disappear. She didn't believe it, but if it happened she'd be gone. She'd go private or something, emigrate to Florida and join up there.

The other rumour taking hold was that they were going to get rid of the right to silence, stop those alibi surprises in court. That had to be good. She believed in civil liberties, they were fine, but only after the streets were safe. She had seen too many smirking bastards walk away from court to care too much about their rights. She turned back to the forms. What was one more rainforest?

'God, I hate paperwork!' she hissed.

Seventy-Three

1. There was no rake.
2. Frank McLintock was offered ample opportunity to surrender quietly but refused. After a moment's confrontation he addressed the officer as 'You fucking tart,' and attempted to abscond.
3. DC Flood pursued the fleeing suspect, catching him and a second suspect, now known to be Terence McLintock, in the rear garden of number twenty-five Epsom Terrace, the residence of one Mr A. Patel, who was not at home at the time.
4. Both the aforementioned Frank McLintock and Terence McLintock behaved in an overtly threatening manner to DC Flood. As they moved towards DC Flood, Detective Sergeant Robert Moore came to offer her assistance, overcoming Terence (McLintock) and applying handcuffs with the assistance of DC Flood. Mr Frank McLintock was momentarily stunned by a fall sustained during the arrest but was still highly aggressive and attempted to rise and strike at the two officers present. DC Flood briefly struggled with McLintock (Frank) and succeeded in applying handcuffs.
5. At this point, DC Broadkins (4848), PC Ireland (956)

arrived, followed closely by DS Peter Mason (2145) of Hampshire Police. The suspects at this point offered no further resistance.

'You deserve an A for BBB,' Mason said, looking over Caz's shoulder.

'What would you know about it?' Caz retorted, 'You were still trying to squeeze through the McLintocks' kitchen window when we collared the boys!'

'I was right behind you, Flood.'

'What, like Nick, you mean?'

'Hey, come on!'

'Yeah, all right, you weren't that bad. You just cleared your fences like a man that runs forty-plus for 10K.'

'My PB is thirty-nine-oh-three, Flood.' He looked again at the arrest form, one down, fourteen to go. 'And that's still Bullshit Baffling Brains.'

It was four o'clock by the time the paperwork was finished, and that was rushing things. This was a criminal arrest; an average *traffic* arrest, not a big-deal one, required a manila folder with anything from a dozen to forty items packed inside. There were Doctor's Costs, Photographer's Costs, G34B minute sheets, P21s, maybe HORT-5 copies, copies of lab forms, copies of any letters and forms sent to defendants for signature, a form P2 (or P2A /B), maybe a Tl Accident Card, the original sketch plan of the accident scene, hand-written witness statements (if these are not easily legible, typed copies to be inserted at this point, hand-written statements to be attached after item 10).

Then there was the T28 – white copy in the folder, green copy endorsed when lab result received, forwarded immediately to ADP (enter date forwarded); Item 7, second copy of HORT-5, Doctor's Certificate; Item 8, second copy of HOLAB 1/8, Analyst's Certificate; Item 9, copy of voluntary statement made by defendant – note, if handwriting is not easily legible, insert typed copy at this point; Item 10, further miscellaneous documentary exhibits, if any; Item 11, file copy of form CYP 11; Item(s) 12 to follow – further miscellaneous documents, e.g. T7(NIP), P22, V23, Accounts, Letters & Replies.

The folder's cover only took ten or so minutes. HQ Ref, T3 Ref, Station, OIC, Court, Mag/JUV?, Hearing Date? List all accused defendants, anticipated pleas, representing solicitor . . .

Leave the other twenty lines for Bench Office/Prosecutor use; not your problem, Flood. Now get out there and catch some villains!

She saw Bob Moore just the once as his head appeared at the door and he barked an order at some DC. Peter Mason had finished his reports and had got on the phone to his wife. The argument was brief and a short-lived despair went quickly across his face. He put the phone down. While Caz was finishing off, he was lining up her Post-It notes, a running commentary. Valerie; Valerie; Claire Cook-Bullen; Mariella Finch; Valerie again; Moira DB; another one from Claire Cook-Bullen. What you doin', Flood, starting a netball team?'

She slapped the back of his hand. 'Gerroff my messages! Valerie's my bloke, Mariella's some fancy woman he met on a plane, and Claire Bullen is a runner from Worthing AC. I presume you remember Moira?'

He was neutral. 'What we going t'do about Billy McLintock?'

Caz glanced up to check that nobody was taking too much notice. 'I've a feeling the DS might be a pain. What if you went through and updated DI MacInnes? Maybe you could suggest we took away the barriers and stuck a discreet ob on the gang's hideaway.'

'What about Moore?'

'I don't know,' Caz said. 'I'll play it by ear.'

Seventy-Four

Peter went off to find the DI and Caz took the moment for a couple of personals, first off, Valerie, just across the road at the American Express building. She got his secretary. He had just 'stepped out', pseudo-speak for 'in the toilet'. Caz said she'd try again in a couple of minutes. Next she tried Mariella Finch. She got another secretary, a voice from somewhere between Brentwood and Basildon. 'She should be backinna minnit. Fink she's nipped out to the bog.'

Claire Cook-Bullen had left her home number, the 'nothing' that had happened on the weekend was still enough to keep her from work. The phone rang for quite a while. Caz was just about to call strike three when Claire answered, 'Yes?'

'Caz Flood,' she said.

'Can we meet?' Softly.

'Your house?'

'No.' A little stronger. 'Daniel plays football Tuesdays, I was going to go for a run. First time since. D'you want to meet me somewhere?'

'Where?'

'I just want to run a steady six or so. Wherever you like.'

'OK,' Caz said. 'How about my place, say, seven o'clock? I'll ring to confirm about six.'

'No!' Claire snapped, far too quickly. 'I'll be out. Look, I'll come to your place, some time after a quarter to seven. I'll wait till half past. If you haven't arrived by then, we'll make another date.'

'You'll need my address,' Caz said.

Valerie was back from his pee. 'Can I see you tonight?' he said.

'Latish,' Caz said. 'I should be at the flat about eight fifteen.'

'You'll want to bath, all that bollocks?'

'I'm going for a run at seven, yeah.'

'Want me to come round earlier, start something cooking?'

'Why not?' Caz said.

'Something's come up at work,' Valerie said slowly, choosing his words. 'I think we should talk about it.'

'Can't you tell me now?'

'It'll keep,' he said. 'Anyway, how are you?'

'I'm very busy, Val . . .'

Someone spoke in his office. He came back. 'Yeah, OK.'

'Thanks for calling, Val.'

He put the phone down.

Mariella answered when Caz tried the number again, getting to the phone before the PA from hell. 'Mariella Finch!'

'Mariella? It's Caz Flood, Valerie's friend. You rang?'

'Oh, hi, Caz! How's Valerie?'

'Discontent,' Caz said.

'I should know why?'

'I don't see why not,' Caz said, a mock moan in her voice.

'I think he wants me to work nine-to-five and have his tea ready for him when he comes home. Either that, or stop home and get fat.'

'I think, men, they are all like this, but then, the little woman, soon she is not enough.'

'You're doing it again,' Caz said.

'What I am doing?'

'Talking like your dad.'

'I am sorry. It is only sometimes.'

'Hey, it's not a problem,' Caz said lightly. 'I think it's cute.'

There was a short silence at the other end. 'Thank you,' Mariella eventually said. 'I ring – I *rang* – to see if you are able to come to dinner with my husband, myself. This weekend, Saturday, we are having friends.'

'Have you asked Valerie?'

'Of course not! I would not.'

'I'm a policewoman, Mariella. We are always getting last-minute jobs. I'd love to come. I will if I can.'

'And Valerie?'

'Of course and Valerie.'

'Then I can tell you the story about the bridge, Medway.'

'I have one for you, too,' Caz said. 'We found a haul of stolen goods today, inside a bridge.'

Mariella laughed. 'But not furniture, television, a family . . .'

'What?'

'You come Saturday, you bring your man. I tell you then, OK?'

'It's a date,' Caz said.

Seventy-Five

Caz went through to see Bob Moore, the wodge of forms for the McLintock arrests thick in her hand. He was on his own, standing at the window, staring down into the road.

'Sarge? You want to check this?'

He turned round. 'Is it all correct?'

'Yes.'

'Then I don't need to check it, do I?'

'I did appreciate it, Bob, the way you handled those boys.'

'How much?'

'What?'

'You said you appreciated me saving you from a kicking, Flood. Or worse. How *much* do you appreciate it?'

'I'm not sure I—'

'What are you going to do about Jenny Fullerton?'

'I've been trying not to think about it, and we've been too busy. I haven't decided, not yet. With the G28 and picking up the McLintocks . . .'

He sat down heavily. 'Look, Flood, don't fuck me about. If you're going to the DI, the DCS, just do it, don't keep me in suspense.'

'I wouldn't do that.'

'Seems that way to me, Flood.'

Caz looked behind her, into the open doorway. There was no one there. She closed the door. 'Bob, can we talk?'

'Bob Reid's floating about, but . . .'

She sat down. 'Tell me what happened.'

There was a tap on the door. 'What?' Moore shouted.

A head came round. 'DI would like a word, Sarge. He wants to see DC Flood too. Says can you both get round for half past?'

The head pulled back quickly, the door clumping gently.

Moore looked pale. 'I thought you said you hadn't decided yet?'

'I haven't!' Caz said quickly. 'The DI must want us for something else. I think DS Mason is in there with him.'

There was a can of Coke on the filing cabinet near him. He stood up and grabbed it. When he opened it, grey-brown spray sprang out. Moore cursed, 'Shit!' Without thinking, Caz pulled out some tissues and offered them across. 'Thanks,' Moore said, dabbing at his shirt, the cabinet top, one of the drawers. 'I suppose you think I was out driving, pissed up and irresponsible. That about it, Flood?'

'I've no idea, Sergeant.'

He came back to his chair. 'Well, I wasn't.'

Caz waited. He sat down, took a mouthful of his Coca-Cola.

'I stayed in that night. Lyndsey had her boyfriend round for a meal with me and Joan; you've met Joan?' Caz nodded. 'We saw the New Year in, then about one o'clock, I took them to one of Lyndsey's friends, some party. We'd had a couple of bottles of wine between the four of us and I'd had a little first-footer just after twelve. When I dropped the kids off, someone gave me a brandy. I drank it without thinking. I'm a big bloke, Flood. I wasn't pissed. But I knew I'd fail a breath test.'

'You drove home?'

'Carefully. I didn't want to take any risks even though the chances were, if I got stopped, they'd wave me on, a DS from Central.'

'But you hit this kid heading out of town.'

'I know. I'm getting to that.' He glanced up at an image passing the frosted window.

'I saw the ram-raid. I was coming down through the town centre. The McLintocks had just backed the Range Rover through the window of the video shop. The toerags were still inside. I just didn't think. I pulled over and went to catch the bastards. There was broken glass everywhere. They all had balas on but I had the feeling at least one of them knew I was plainclothes. They saw me, thought about it for a few seconds, then they came out mob-handed. Two of them had these little baseball bats.'

'Rounders bats,' Caz said.

'I didn't try taking them on there and then, and they obviously thought better of actually having a go at me. The alarm had been set off. They'd've known there'd be cars on the way.

'They got away in the Range Rover. I should've just left it but I didn't. I went after them in my car. Billy McLintock must have been driving; the bastard was doing sixty through town and eighty on the top road. I just stayed in touch with them, hoping they'd roll it at a roundabout or flash by a patrol car. But there's never a policeman around when you want one, is there, Flood?'

She caught his eyes, close to tears; a man talking about his life; about thirty years down the drain.

'The Fullerton girl just stepped out. I tried to avoid her, I almost did. She only got a little tap with my back end, there wasn't even a mark. I did the wing in spinning the car to try to miss her. I could see she wasn't badly hurt. She was sat there, wide awake, shouting at her mate. I've never had such an awful decision. I knew if I helped her, I'd be breathalysed, fail and be out of the force. I thought about it for maybe five seconds and I got out of there. It was wrong, I know it was, but it wasn't just me, there was Lyndsey talking about getting married, Joan still getting over her illness, everything. I rang for an ambulance about a mile down the road, went back to the house, took Joan's car and made her phone 999 from a BTK. I went back to the scene. Got there as Buck Shott turned up. He sussed I'd been drinking and told me to fuck off straight away.'

'You went to K&J's on the Saturday?'

'Yes. Ken owed me a big one. I kept one of his kids out of nick a few months ago.'

Caz decided to explain. 'The old guy I met, from the allotment. First time I saw him, he said, "Can't keep away, eh?" I thought he meant he'd seen us arrive at the garage. Then I found out he got there every day between quarter past and twenty past. We were already there by then.'

'Well, there's no more guesswork now, is there?'

'No, Sarge.'

'So what are you going to do?'

'What would you do if it was me, Bob?'

'You've done five years. I'd probably turn you in.'

'I said, I'm still thinking about it.'

'The DI said half past,' Moore said. 'We'd better go

through.' He stood up, about half his strength there. 'One more favour, Flood?'

Caz stood up. What was the favour?

'Tell me first,' Moore said.

'OK,' she said.

They went through to MacInnes.

Seventy-Six

'Come in, Bob!' Tom MacInnes said. His door was wide open and Peter Mason was sitting in a chair to the side. 'Trying to sort out how to deal with the McLintock boys without trampling all over evidence.'

'Not sure I'm with you, Tom. We've got three of them and we'll get Billy soon enough.'

'Like to catch one of them with the stuff, Bob. Maybe Billy, if he goes back to get it.'

'He won't go near a police cordon.'

'Ah know that, Bob. Ah've had a chat with the DCS. We think the body came *down* the river. Soon as we have some surveillance set up, we'll pull the uniforms out, give your villain plenty of room.'

'And we do what, exactly?'

'Wait for him t'come. Grab him the moment he goes inside.'

Peter Mason sat forward. 'Problem is, Bob, there's nowhere for us to hide an ob van. If McLintock is sensible and clocks the place for a while, he'll see anything we stick there.'

'Unless it's invisible,' Caz said. 'How about a courting couple? We could get away with steamy windows for a while.'

'We thought of that.' MacInnes said. 'You just volunteered, Flood. Even so we'll have to rotate the cars.'

'Meaning what?' Moore said.

The DI nodded to Mason who grabbed a pad of paper off the desk. 'What's been proposed, Bob, is we use three cars, two male, two female detectives, swap in and out every half-hour or so, a couple in the car park, the other two officers close by as back-up.'

MacInnes continued, 'We bring a car in every so often. The other car then leaves. By using the third car we make it less likely that McLintock is going to suss anything.'

Caz coughed. 'There are kids there most nights, boss. Do we think McLintock'd be that open, unload a load of hot stuff in front of them?'

'Probably not, Flood. What're you trying to say?'

'Why not leave the place covered by a uniform until eleven o'clock, midnight, say, then make a big show of pulling out. If the teams are in place round about the same time, there shouldn't be a problem.'

'And what do they do from now until then?'

'Well, a few hours off wouldn't hurt, sir.'

MacInnes looked at DS Moore. 'Bob?'

'Fine to me.'

'Right!' MacInnes said. 'That's it then. We've got PC Tingle and WPC Dibben already – they volunteered. Apparently, Billy Tingle is after the overtime. DS Mason here says he might as well stop over, so you're spare, Bob. But I presume you'll want to be around?'

'I want McLintock, put it that way.'

'OK. I'll leave the rest of the sorting-out to you.'

Bob Moore went to leave. 'My office,' he said to the room.

The others began to follow. MacInnes nodded to Caz.

'A word with DC Flood, please, Bob. She'll be along shortly.'

As soon as they were gone, MacInnes spoke softly. 'You want to know about the G28?'

'Of course, sir.'

'Cause of death was drowning. As of so far, we can't say it wasn't an accident. No clothes were found upstream but it'll need a more thorough search tomorrow. We still don't know who she was. All we've got is her age, thirty to forty, and she'd had sex not long before she went in the water. If there was a rape, it wasn't violent. There were a few slight marks, wrists and ankles, but they were faint. Something had slightly damaged the woman's oxters but the doc's not prepared to say what they are.'

'Damaged *what*?'

'Ah'm not with you, lass.'

'You said the doctor had seen some damage.'

'Aye, sort've burn marks, her armpits.'

'Armpits!'

'Aye, what's wrong with you, lass?'

'I suppose a tramp could've nicked the clothes, Tom. It *could* turn out to be a suicide.'

'A woman tramp?'

'It was just a thought.'

MacInnes was rummaging through his drawer. Another gargle, Caz presumed. 'We had a chat with two experts about the river. One of them thought she could have gone up the river on the tide and then down again. We blew that out, she hadn't been dead long enough. The other one thought she could've fallen in or jumped in, four, maybe five miles further up.'

'Oh, great! So we've got what, six, seven miles, both banks and her clothes could be anywhere?'

'That's about the size of it, lass.'

'But it's not murder?'

'Doesn't look like it, but it's funny. The marks are a bit funny. Like your mate Claire Bullen was funny. That's what I wanted to talk to you about.'

'She rang me today. I've arranged to meet her tonight at my flat. We're going for a run and a chat.'

'Be careful, Caz.'

Caz was surprised, 'What d'you mean, be careful? I'm going out with a running mate.'

'You're a copper, you don't have mates, Caz. Caution her. Make it a joke, but caution her. Don't let some arsehole of a lawyer screw up any case we might have through some PACE loophole.'

'D'you think there'll *be* a case, Tom?'

'I haven't a clue, lass. I just know that both that madam and her old man lied to us. They lied to us from the moment we sat down and they never stopped their lying.'

Seventy-Seven

It was rare for Caz to be an OAF, off at five, but for once, she was. If she hadn't been starting back to work at half past eleven, she might have thought it was her lucky day.

DS Moore had figured on a midnight start for the surveillance. When he had talked about meeting up, Caz had suggested the rough car park below the houseboats. It was a half-mile drive from Billy McLintock's Aladdin's cave, maybe two hundred metres as the crow flew from the cordon area. Moore agreed. Peter Mason was going to be spare for the next six hours. Out of the goodness of her heart, Caz suggested her place. When she telephoned Valerie to suggest that tonight might be a little messy, she got the secretary again. Val had finished early and gone to the gym. Life in personnel was so *tough*.

Peter gave her a lift home in the Saab – as he said, no point in struggling to find two car parking places. On the way there, he was keen to make conversation but Caz wasn't. She'd felt obliged to offer him somewhere to crash for half a shift but she really didn't need small talk. She was thinking about Pixie Walters and Claire Bullen. She was thinking about mud, about the river, now this poor woman, dead and not even named. How did people ever get to be that alone?

An evening without a serious drink loomed ahead of them. To Caz, that made it seem long. 'Do us both a favour,' she said suddenly to Peter. 'Carry on past the house. Take me to Shoreham.'

The DS had been edging the car over, ready to turn right. 'What for?' he said. This sounded like work.

'I'd appreciate it, all right? I'll show you some of the houseboats down there. You'll be fascinated.'

It was starting to rain. 'Like watching paint dry,' Mason said.

Peter was all right – he did as he was told. They drifted into the back of a small going-home jam and then, after a couple of stops, dropped over the bridge. They looked down to their right. Either Bob Moore or DI MacInnes had arranged for a 'jam sandwich' van to be parked very publicly inside the cordon. It was big, fat and white, with blue and red stripes enclosing a broad band of bright yellow day-glo, not-so-subtly reminding the locals 'Hey, look, *the police* are here!' As far as Caz could see, John Thingee, the PC, had taken refuge in it from the rain. With a shudder, she remembered more than one night like this. She didn't blame him for getting out of the rain. The first couple of years in uniform weren't easy.

When they got on to the island road, then off it, into the car park, they found they were sharing the space with half a dozen cars and vans. When they got closer, they upped the count to eight. There were two section cars parked nose to nose at the bottom of a set of steps. 'House-to-house?' Mason said.

'Guess so,' Caz said. 'They must be door-knocking the people who weren't there this morning.'

'So what you want t'do?'

'Let's go up top, take a look,' Caz said. 'Say hello to the uniforms. Meet a couple of the residents.'

'In case you hadn't noticed,' Mason said, 'it's pissing down!'

'This is true,' Caz said. 'Maybe we c'n wait five minutes.'

They gave it five, they gave it ten, but each time they looked at their watches and then looked out, as if on cue, a flash of water blasted against the windscreen. The DS decided to try the radio and was mizz when he found he couldn't get Ocean FM. Caz tried to tell him he should think himself lucky, but he wasn't impressed. He was fiddling with the tuner when the two drowning coppers came down the steps.

Peter flicked the headlights a couple of times at the two uniforms. Their faces were light-bleached, blue-white and eyes down, ducked from the beam, but Caz knew them straight away. The overweight PC in the big yellow waterproof was Harry Deans. The WPC with him was Julie Jones, a tough-as-boots little sweetie who did weights three times a week and lusted after Nick Berry. The pair splashed towards them. The DS leaned round to open the Saab's back door.

Harry was just in front of Julie. He leaned in, recognised Caz, and got in the back. Peter had just whacked the heater up to full belt and Harry groaned, pleasure and pain. By the time he had wiped the rain off his face and said 'Fuck!' fifteen times, Julie had got in, slammed the door and started trying to catch up.

'Wet, is it?' Caz said.

'It is fucking *evil*,' Julie said. 'You come to gloat?'

'No, actually,' Caz said, hurt. 'I came to help out a few of my oppos with the door-to-door. I've been to the boats before. Met a couple of blokes, a guy called Tim Hacht, and a Yank with gorgeous eyes.'

'Met him,' Julie said. 'Teaches night school; lives in that boat halfway down, near to the one with the teeth on the front.'

'And Hacht?'

'I said. Gorgeous eyes. Wood stove. Funny accent.'

'You're confusing me,' Caz said.

Seventy-Eight

The barge was in darkness, red and black, the windows unlit, staring glass. The rain worried across it, lashed to the back of the wind, sheets of silver-cold light waving across the deck, splashes of the folded rain spraying upwards against rushing gutters; the sea, the river, the night, the last grey before the beginnings of black.

Caz was in her Goretex jacket, proof to water but not to the hellish whipping effect of the cold. Her jeans had been wet in seconds; now they were dark and clinging, waving heavily from her hips like hanging ropes, only the dark ankles still able to flap, slapping in the wind, the wet eager and malevolent, looking for Caz's weakest spot, white-socked, unprepared, miserable.

She had managed to persuade Peter she would only be minutes; managed to persuade the others to wait in the car. There was no hood over her head, nothing between her and the storm. The rain ran off her, round her, curling into her neck. She could feel her nose running, reactive mucus quick-mixed with rainwater, rapid drips from the tip not quite a steady flow. When she wiped it, pointlessly but automatically, a faint smear of her body salt reached her mouth.

'A couple of minutes, OK? I'll be fine.'

'You're crazy, Caz. It's fucking *horrible* out there!'

'If you insist on being an arsehole, I'll come.'

'No!'

'Flood, Julie and me have done all the boats. What you wanta get wet for?' She had the door open.

'Five minutes, right? Four. Just let me check two boats.'

'Hacht isn't there, Caz.'

'Four minutes.' Then she had dived into the rain.

She stepped down on to the boat, flat steel, uncertain, hexed bolt heads, blue but dark with water. When she lifted her hand to the bell-press, the rain ran to her wrists, probing the elastic barrier. As she pressed, the light dimming as contacts were made, she listened for the rude buzzing inside. Perhaps she heard it, she wasn't sure. She heard the wind. She heard the patter-spatter of the rain.

There was no offered cooking, no hand to proffer wine. Even her rattled fist, banging on the door, failed to raise a response from Hacht. It was only when she kicked at the door in anger that she got anything, and that was movement, the door flucking wetly from the jamb. Still, all she could hear was rain.

She stepped to her right, right of the door frame, far right, far from the hinge. She looked out, away from the door, then pushed, her knuckles prodding just once at the door as if it lived. It swung maybe six inches, a wet sound, a heavy sound. Still, all there was was rain.

Peter and the others were in the car. They were so close they could be up those steps and with her in thirty seconds. Wet, yes, soaking wet, yes, but they'd be there, no question; they'd come straight away, to share her fear, to cut back on the doubt.

They were decent coppers. They were close by; but Caz knew that Peter, Harry, Julie were just far enough away that it didn't matter. This was where she was supposed to use her radio, supposed to use her wits, her common sense. She wasn't supposed to go in there.

The official line was crystal clear. 'If in doubt, call for back-up and wait.' Caz knew the official line. You toed the official line, you didn't go far wrong. You didn't go far either. You called in, you waited, a child died or a suicide made it over the red line. No one ever said anything. You were to code. Not far wrong, not far either.

The fear was the same whatever you eventually found. It was the unknown that was the problem. That was why the official line was 'call for back-up'. That was it. There was no other official line.

It was the unofficial lines that Caz was considering now; the copper's code that she worked to. Maybe there was something wrong in Hacht's barge. If there was, then Harry, Julie, Pete wouldn't give a shit about getting soaked, about being a bit freaked out for a minute or two. They would pile out of Mason's warm, dry car and be up behind Caz in half a minute, sort whatever it was, survive. Then they'd talk about it for a month maybe, coffees in the police lounge, doubles in the Grapes . . . But if there was nothing wrong . . . If Caz dragged three coppers, two blokes, out into the rain . . .

The unofficial, unwritten line two had to do with the split between the men and the boys, between the Moores and the Mortons. It had to do with the 'W' that WPCs no longer wore. If Caz called the others up on to the barge to find an innocent, empty wheelhouse, no one would say anything. She'd gone by the book; it was understandable; a WDC on her own, bit nervous? Of course she'd call out a few lads to help her; to be expected really. A *bloke* on his own might've done it different, but that's the difference with being a bloke. You'd expect it of a bloke.

Caz knew that the trick with the fear was to cut it up, to do each fearful thing in the smallest, bravest steps. She took a deep breath, reached a hand round the door jamb, felt for the light switch. The memory of too many horror movies in her teens helped to make her hand tremor. She had the sudden thought of another hand, a clammy hand, touching hers, grabbing her. If this was a film and not so frighteningly, freezingly shit-real, lightning would now flash across the sky, thunder would burst over her, her heartbeat would be picked out, amplified with her breath, secret music would creep to raise the stakes.

Her hand moved up and down the wood to find nothing. This was all she had promised herself she would do, switch the light on, run like fuck if she had to. Nothing. She moved her hand further in, up and down; the texture of old paint, year on year, the planked wall beneath. Nothing. When she stopped, she could feel her pulses, the seizure of her sympathetic nerves, air and saliva competing where her neck met her chest. Fuck, fuck, fuck-fuck-fuck.

A little further in . . . Now maybe she was missing the light switch, reaching past it, so dark, so stupid. Just find the switch, click, fuck off back to the car. Otherwise, it's the torch from your jeans, a little half-inch beam, another invented terror but this time you in focus, attached to the light.

She pressed her arm against the wood paint, the flesh of the inside waiting for the raised touch of plastic. And then, near her elbow . . .

It touched her, she retracted, her hand collapsing on to the switch. Another breath. Click – ready to see death-white, death-red, something hanging, something ripped. Not ready to see the soft domestic table, the book of poetry, spine up to keep the page, the wine glass, the bottle.

There were wellingtons in a corner, fat socks tucked into their tops. It was a farm kitchen. A winter night in Hereford. And empty.

Seventy-Nine

Caz heard the car horn, a couple of shorter beeps, then one three-second blast. She glanced again at the room, went out into the rain. She walked five yards along the towpath until she was in full view of the car, then she waved, flashed her light. The headlights blipped once. She went back to the barge.

The rain still ran freely on the painted metal deck. Her trainers squeaked, rubber on steel. She went back inside, calling Hacht's name, more for her own benefit than any realistic hello. The worst of the fear was gone now. She had light, a little familiarity, the table where she'd sat last night, Hacht's books, the red furnishings.

'Hello? Tim Hacht? DC Flood . . . We met last . . .'

This was utterly silly. Hacht could still be at work, in his car, on his way home. He said he worked at Lewes from eight thirty till five thirty. It wasn't even seven yet. The chances were he was sat in traffic on the bypass cursing the filthy weather and feeling sorry for himself. And Caz was cold now.

Caz didn't *want* to think weird thoughts. But Julie had described Tim Hacht as tall and good-looking. If she hadn't described him, tall, thin, short red hair, great eyes, Caz wouldn't have hesitated, wouldn't have said, 'You interviewed him? Where?'

Julie had been too wet. 'On his fucking boat. Where d'you think?'

Before Caz asked the question she knew the answer.

'Which boat, Jools?'

'Fer fuck's sake, Caz! His barge, of course. What is this?'

Caz had said, 'Nothing!' too quickly. She wasn't quite sure where she'd screwed up. Then she told them she was going up just to check a couple of things out.

So if Julie spoke to the American and he really was Hacht, why was he on a different boat the night before and calling himself Fred Kermy? If he was Fred then, and on the other boat, why was he on *Beached* this morning, impersonating Tim?

What had happened?

It had been dry that night. '*Looking for a chap called Tim Hacht.*'

'*Next door but one. Beached.*'

Could the American have been Hacht? Some nosy woman comes knocking and he just gets rid of her? But then later, the short man, the guy with piggy eyes, *he* had told Caz that *he* was Hacht. The American would have had to expect that.

'*Tim Hacht?*'

''*Oo wants to know?*'

And Caz had been back down to see Tom MacInnes at his car. She'd only been a minute, maybe a minute and a half, but that was just enough time for a phone call from one boat to another.

Had he actually said he was Tim Hacht? No. But he knew Claire Cook-Bullen. So, if the guy cooking steak on *Beached* wasn't Hacht, then he had to be buddies with the tall American, learnt a story in a minute, been prepared to lie. No way. Tim

Hacht was five seven and ordinary. The American, maybe he was called Fred Kermy, had only *said* he was Tim Hacht. Why? *Because he was on Tim Hacht's boat!*

That was why Caz had wanted to go up there now; some sudden intuition making her fear for Tim Hacht's safety. Julie had said she'd spoken to the American at eight o'clock in the morning. Caz didn't really expect to find him lurking, but she wasn't so sure she wouldn't find Tim Hacht; she'd made a habit recently of falling over bodies.

Julie hadn't been happy but she'd been insistent. 'Hacht said he'd be out today and out tonight. Said he was busy. Looking after his elf!'

'His health?'

'He said "elf". I reckon he was trying to be a Cockney. Trying to show off how British he'd become. It didn't work.'

Something had happened to Claire Bullen, something strange, something that made her lie, something that made her involve her husband who then lied too, something that persuaded Tim Hacht to continue the lies. Then a stranger spends time on Hacht's boat. He's surprised by a routine call from the police. Had Julie stumbled on a burglary in progress? Was the American looking for something? Or was Tim Hacht around too but maybe indisposed?

So Caz knew she had to go up and check out the boats. OK, so there could be an explanation – God knew what – but everything in her screamed that something weird was happening. When she had found the unlocked door she had been convinced. Fear had slowed her down, plus the feeling that whatever might have happened could long since have been tidied up. So she went in. To look at nothing. To see a place too normal, too tidy. The wheelhouse lounge-diner of *Beached* had looked abandoned, the local-paper version of the *Marie Celeste.* That was why Caz now needed to go down, into the boat's tight belly. She still had to convince herself that Tim Hacht was not there. She was certain that he wouldn't be coming home, wasn't stuck behind a row of wet red lights. She went downstairs.

Eighty

The floor, the wheelhouse deck, was old, foot-worn, foot-polished, what looked like oak or teak. Too many years of evening footfalls, spilled tea, wipes, paraffin waxes, buffing had removed the original tree, masked the tall trunk with layer upon layer of man-time.

The stairs to the lower deck – was she allowed to think stairs? – were just past the kitchen, steep, with hardwood handrails. She looked for a light switch before she lowered herself, not confident yet, still at least a little bit frightened. Outside, the wind rushed over the boat.

There was another switch, fat and brown, like something on the wall of a very old house. When she clicked it, a dull 'poot' preceded an equally dull light which cast up from the base of the stairs. At the foot there was a bedroom's feel, a bedroom smell, a faint warm dampness. Caz found herself leaning backwards as she went down, head-wary of, first the upper floor, then the steep ceiling, always just in front, always four inches further away than her instinct insisted. At the bottom, she turned away from the room that smelt empty and followed another feeling, another smell, into Tim Hacht's bedroom.

There was another switch, another 'poot' of old contacts,

another dismal light into dampness. Caz waited a second but there was no horror, no mystery, no sudden discovery. Hacht's cot was an old brass bedstead, half made up, the blankets pulled quickly over the sheets, the pillows still night-ruffled and awry. A couple of Laurie Lee paperbacks were on a wicker bedside table. There was a lamp to read them by, a phone on the floor nearby.

She peered in cupboards, alcoves behind sliding darkwood doors. They looked a bit empty; a few shirts, a pair of trousers, shoes . . . The shelves were bare, no underwear, no socks, just a squash racquet and a box of red-spot balls. Hacht was gone?

She went out, past the tiny bathroom and into the second sleeping quarter, slightly colder, faintly damper, a bare bed, blankets folded into a cube – a spare room. Behind the door was a washing machine, a load done, powders and softeners stacked on top, Domestos, aerosol air-fresheners, a multi-pack of blue loo-roll, a box of just-in-case candles, a cheap plastic torch. She went back upstairs.

The wheelhouse, third time round, was still rich and red. It was warmed by residual heat from the stove, the air with a whiff of woodsmoke and the more distant hint of oriental spices. Now she saw it as quite bare. The bookcases at the end of the room were emptied, a clear dust-line where, previously, spines had been displayed. Caz glanced up. The overhead shelf still displayed Hacht's passion for poetry. She looked harder. His tastes were not that specific. He seemed to have a range of pleasures from William Blake through to Spike Milligan. The books, tightly shoulder to shoulder, stretched ten feet. There was no gap to fit the book that had been left in the middle of the dining table. Caz picked it up, folded the corner of the open page, tucked the book into her jacket and left.

There was no real need to check out the American's boat but Caz decided to on principle. She hesitated at the rain-lashed door, then, with a deep breath, she ducked back into the night. The towpath was a river now. She stamped quickly down it. When she got to the other boat, she confirmed that there was no light, dropped down on to the deck anyway, and tried the door. She had expected it to be firmly locked. It was.

When she got back to the Saab, Peter Mason was smoking a cigar. The car was warm and dry, filling with the sweet darkness of rolled tobacco. Caz had never understood why she loathed cigarette smoke yet didn't mind this more expensive form of burning leaf. She was just about to say something about it when Mason got his retaliation in first. 'Don't you dare say a fucking *thing*, Flood!'

Instead of complimenting the cigar, Caz said, 'Looks like Hacht has done a runner. His wardrobes are cleaned out.'

The other two coppers had gone, no doubt to find some way of getting dry. Caz's feet were beginning to give off steam – she could make a good guess as to how they felt. Peter Mason was dry but in a soggy mood. As he re-clipped his seat-belt he said, 'Julie Jones thinks you've lost it. She thinks you've finally done one long run too many.'

'She could be right,' Caz said. 'What d'you know about poetry?'

'About *what*?'

'Poems, you know . . .'

'You want it in round figures?'

She grunted.

'Zero.'

Caz was starting to smell of warming water. 'Now why did I already guess that?' she said.

The DS suddenly thought, 'The boy stood on the burning deck?'

'Doesn't count.' Caz said.

'We were on the good ship *Venus*?'

'Same!'

'Zero was about right, then,' he said. With that he drove off, splashing from the car park and back out on to the island road.

'What's the time?' Caz said.

'Five past seven.'

'About average,' Caz said. 'I've got a visitor coming to the flat.'

'When?' Mason said.

Caz made a face. 'Five minutes ago.'

Eighty-One

They got to Inkerman Terrace at twenty-five past seven. The trip should have been quicker but half the length of the Shoreham to Brighton road was under water. The first time Peter came to serious flooding, he wheee-eed the Saab through it like a teenager. Eighty per cent of the way across, the engine coughed and threatened to die. After that, Peter took the aquatic bits more cautiously, high on the crown of the road, low gear and lots of revs.

When they arrived, the DS managed to park outside Caz's flat. Claire Bullen's yellow Metro was still there, just across the street, and a few yards down, opposite Mrs Lettice's. Caz's OAP neighbour would be in ecstasy now, peeking through her curtains at half-minute intervals, looking at the car and muttering, 'Still there, very strange. Not someone from the street, either. *Very* strange.'

Claire was either supremely patient or she was using Caz's late return as an excuse for not getting out of the car and going for her run. Here in the partial shelter of the town the wind was not quite so obvious but, even so, the rain was still filthy and cold. It was a terrible night for running. As Caz got out of the Saab, she waved lightly. A hand waved back. Then Claire opened her car door.

* * *

She was wearing a huge horse-rider's Driza-Bone coat and it looked like she had a tracksuit underneath. She walked towards Caz and the DS, who was now appearing from the driver's side. As she came closer, she glanced up at the sky as if to say, 'We're joking, right?'

'Hi-yah,' Caz said. Claire looked pointedly at Peter.

'Oh, Claire, this is Detective Sergeant Mason,' Caz explained. 'He's got accommodation problems. I'm letting him crash at my place.'

Claire nodded to the DS, then looked back at Caz. 'This weather!'

'Tell me about it!' Caz said. 'Come on inside.'

Ten minutes later they were all wrapped around hot toddies. The lemon juice was out of a plastic lemon, the whisky was cheap and the honey was from Cyprus, but Jeez! together they worked. The difficult decision was whether to drink from the glass or use it to warm their hands. In the end they compromised. They drank the first, cuddled the second while the central heating cut in.

Caz had set the drink ingredients out – even a DS can make a toddy – and had shot through to her bedroom to peel off her rain-soaked gear. This kind of wet was very rare for Caz. Dressed in even less, she could take the worst, provided that she was thrashing through muddy fields, one-two-three in a cross-country or chasing a 10K PB and a hundred quid or so first prize. But being cold-soaked like this, without the inner heat of running, was something else. She felt acutely miserable and under par. The last thing she could imagine tonight was finding some way to get around Claire Bullen's smoke screen.

She seriously wished the woman hadn't waited. To make it even worse, there was still the late-night stake-out on the Adur bridge. The idea of spending maybe six-seven hours banged up with Peter Mason did not exactly fill Caz with the joys of spring.

But Peter was happy. He couldn't believe his luck, two women under thirty and both of them runners! Absolutely no problem with the small talk, all personal bests and training schedules. He was still living off his PB in the Stubbington 10K, but he dropped a peg or two when he found that 'slow' Claire bested him at every distance beyond eight hundred metres.

Claire was choosing her words carefully, letting out stock answers quickly between long pauses, like a woman who has found herself stuck opposite a hopelessly wrong blind date. But it wasn't that – Claire wanted to talk, but to Caz and Caz alone. As long as Mason was around she wasn't likely to. The DS wasn't supposed to be there. Caz had to get rid. ASAP.

She fancied another body-warming drink so she went through to the kitchen. But when she glanced up at the clock she decided that tea was probably a safer bet than a third toddy. As she flicked the kettle on she shouted to Claire. Did she fancy putting something on the stereo?

'Anything in particular?'

'Whatever you like.'

Then she called Mason. Did he have a minute?

When Peter came through she touched her lips and pointed at a pad where she'd written, ME ALONE CLAIRE – URGENT. UFO?

He touched his chest and whispered, 'I've got to fuck off? In this weather?' Caz nodded. 'How long?' Caz made a cross of her fingers; half an hour. He grabbed three mugs. 'Oh, *wonderful*!' he said.

They came back through, three mugs of tea on a tray. Claire had managed to work out the NAD and stuck Phil Collins on – *Face Value*. Not a bad choice. You could listen to the old fella or ignore him, either way, the music slipped by easy.

Peter discovered that Claire had run 2.54 in the 1991 London. He was suitably impressed. He congratulated Claire, took a sip of his tea and said, 'I'm going to have to nip out at some time, Caz – get my shirts an' things. Soon as I've finished this, I'll go, that's all right with you.'

He lied smoothly. 'I'll cook something when you get back,' Caz said. 'How long d'you reckon you'll be?'

He stood up. 'Half an hour, forty minutes, say. You girls can talk about yer tubes while I'm out of it.'

Claire didn't react.

'Don't slam the door on your way out,' Caz said.

Eighty-Two

Once the man had left, the atmosphere between the women softened. Caz was taking a chance with later on, but she poured herself a small whisky anyway, a slightly larger one for Claire. The central heating had pumped up good and strong by now and the place was starting to fug nicely. She could feel the heat floating over her as she dropped into the softness of the sofa. Phil Collins honeyed away. 'I'm glad we scrubbed the run,' she said.

'Me too,' Claire said. 'I've got a high wimp factor.'

Caz passed over the stronger of the two drinks. Claire took it, slugged some of it straight away. Then she laughed. 'I don't drink whisky!'

'I do, but only when I'm depressed,' Caz said.

'So how often is that?' Claire asked.

Now *Caz* laughed. 'Two-three bottles a week . . .'

'Really?'

'No, not really. If I'm on my own, it's one strong one; lots of nights nothing. The boyfriend comes round, then it's a bit more, but he likes Southern Comfort and I like Chianti. My inspector drinks this.'

'He drinks with you?'

'Only days ending in Y.'

'Oh,' Claire said.

There were a few seconds of silence. Caz was expectant but trying to chant internally, cool, cool, cool. Claire was thinking, staring at the gold of her drink, the glass edge, Caz's piggies, now a threesome in the corner. She went over and picked up Vincent. When she spoke, it was to him, Caz overhearing. 'I don't know where to start, what to say.'

Caz trod carefully. 'Take your time.'

'You won't understand. Nobody could . . .'

'That's Vincent,' Caz said. 'He's a great listener.'

Claire turned round, still holding the pig. He was pulled into her stomach, soft and pink, his pug-friendly face nuzzling into her chest.

'I really don't know how to . . . what to . . . I . . .'

'Come and sit down,' Caz said softly. She tapped the cushion beside her. 'And bring yer friend.'

Claire still clung to the pig. She smiled from behind him, just a little foolishly. 'He's nice, isn't he?'

Caz tapped the cushion again. 'He has his moments.' Claire came and sat down, picked up her glass. 'I can top that up for you,' Caz said, 'but you'll need a taxi home if you have any more.'

'You don't know me and drink,' Claire said. She tried a little laugh. 'Another whisky and I'll be able to fly home!'

Caz pulled her legs up under her. 'Peter will be back . . .'

'I know,' Claire said.

She began with a question. Was marriage prostitution? Hadn't she read somewhere that it was a conspiracy? Was womankind not subjugated, chatteled, providing sex and services for security, for food? No, Caz said, she didn't think they were.

'So staying with a man, a pig, for money, that would be wrong?'

'I can't answer that,' Caz said. 'I don't know enough.'

But would she do it, ever do it? No, Caz said.

Claire's face flickered, some little internal adjustment being made. She sighed. Then she began. 'I was eighteen years old when I married Danny. He was nineteen. We started going out when I was fifteen, I was still at school. The first time we did it, he forced me. I didn't then, but now I'd say it was rape. Afterwards he was so kind, so loving. I just thought that was how it was.

'I was twenty-two before I knew enough to know that the things Daniel did to me weren't love. He used me. Hurt me. I never talked about it to anyone; it was like – I was like – under *control*. Then I began to think that these things happened because something about *me* made Daniel want to do them.

'Some time in 1987, something snapped and I just said "no more". I tried to get away but I didn't go far. I didn't keep my own money and both my parents were dead so I went to Daniel's parents. Dan's mum, Sarah, she seemed to understand me. She cuddled me, made a bed up for me in the box room, said I could stay as long as I liked.

'Dan's father was very straight-laced, very old-fashioned. He kept out of the way at first. Then he started to talk to me, arguing, analysing. Marriage was for ever, he said; I had to stay with my husband. He was a very strong man, very powerful, and he usually got his way. They told me I was unwell, that I needed help. Daniel was a kind man and if I couldn't see that, I must be ill.

'Somehow I ended up spending time in St Cadoc's. They put me on drugs; I even had ECT. Then one day Sarah came to take me home. She brought me back to their house, but when we arrived, Danny was there. While I was in hospital, he'd moved back to his parents' and they'd done out a double room for us. I was a bit of a zombie when I came back – I just let them do what they liked. I was back in Daniel's room, sleeping with him again, letting him use me. Again.

'Then Sarah died. One day she felt ill, three weeks later she was dead, rotten with cancer. I was left with the two of them. Then Arnold – Dan's father – he explained that he'd changed his will. We had to stay together until five years after his death – we had to be happy. If we were together, we would share the estate. If we weren't, the lot went to charity.

'The family were quite well off. Dan's grandfather had started a chain of newsagents and when he died, Dan's father had inherited the lot. The empire just grew. Then in 1989, Arnold died suddenly – of a heart attack. He left nearly three million to be split equally between me and Danny, but we couldn't touch a penny of it for that five years. The solicitor read a letter out, from Arnold to me. The old man felt that I had earned my half of the estate. We had to keep their house, their rooms, exactly as they were when he died, and we had to stay together – and everyone see us as happy – until the fifth anniversary of his death – until August 1994.

'I just went along with it. Daniel still manipulated me but in the background there was this thought that in five years I'd be worth one and a half million. I had this dream. I'd be thirty-two and I'd have enough money to get away.

'I'd always worked, but I was very quiet and withdrawn. That was another one of Daniel's control things. He had absolute charge over my money, gave me something every day, never let me go to works dos or anything like that.

'I'd been steadily putting on weight since I'd married and I put on even more when I came out of hospital. I think it was this self-image thing. I was the fat woman in the corner, the one everyone ignores. That was what I wanted. But the day the will was read, everything changed. I could see a different future.

'I started dieting the next day, walking for forty minutes every lunchtime instead of pigging out. Then I started swimming in the mornings. Daniel didn't like it but I was getting stronger inside. I told him it was so I'd look better, happier – so we could get our hands on that money. He liked that.

'In the November, I started running. I went out aiming to cover a mile and then turn round. It took me three weeks before I managed the whole mile without stopping; two weeks later I ran there and back. Then I found a four-mile route. Christmas Day I ran it all. I'd lost two stone in four months. In the New Year I got really serious.

'You're a runner, Caz; you understand. Have you ever been big?'

'No,' Caz said.

'Well, they're right when they say that people hide behind fat. The thinner I got, the harder I got. By June I was back into a size twelve and running forty miles a week. People at work thought I was ill but I wasn't. I'd never felt better. When I was running, I was free. When I was out there it was just me.

'Then I joined the running club. That was a shock. No one knew me as the fat woman in the corner or the woman who'd had mental treatment. I'd been there a week when I heard someone talking about me – "Skinny woman, quite quick, good-looking". I was high as a kite. I got back to the house and told

Daniel I would be sleeping in the box room. He tried to bully me but I moved in there anyway. He could see me growing stronger every day. The next night he got drunk, then he raped me. He stuck something over my mouth and raped me.'

She must have seen Caz's face drop slightly.

'You see, Caz, I was stronger, but I wasn't free. Daniel knew that there was something I wanted. I wanted that one and a half million. He knew that I wouldn't run away again.'

Despite herself, Caz whispered, 'Jesus!'

'It wasn't that bad, Caz. You'd be amazed what you learn to live with. Every time it happened, I repainted the room. I learned tricks to defuse things, found ways to avoid it happening. In three years it's happened maybe a dozen times.'

Caz looked at Claire, a face she couldn't read. 'You were painting Monday.'

'Yes,' Claire said. 'But that was something else.'

Eighty-Three

'I met Tim at the sports centre. He played squash there. I was with another runner in the bar, one of the girls from Worthing, and I was trying hard still, trying to improve my social skills. I heard him quote some poetry at someone and it really surprised me. When it had been really bad with Danny, I'd got into poetry. There were these really cheap books published by Dover in the States, less than a quid each. I read T. S. Eliot, Emily Dickinson, Christina Rossetti. Dickinson and Rossetti were recluses, maybe that's why I liked them.

'Anyway, I said, when I heard a man quoting poetry, it really surprised me. I went over. I made myself talk to him. He was really kind. I think he just sensed how difficult it was for me. He was with three other squash players and they were being typical blokes, all double meanings and vaguely sexual remarks. I tried to ignore them and asked him what was the poem he'd just quoted? He smiled, got off his bar stool, dug a book out of his sports bag, and asked me if I'd like to read it. I couldn't believe it. When he gave me the book, I could feel him through it. I said, "How will I get it back to you?" and he said, "Don't be silly, we'll find each other."

'It was a book of Liverpool poets, nothing at all like the

things I'd been reading. I carried it everywhere with me; my secret, my power over Danny. It was delicious, like forbidden fruit.

'I went to the sports centre every Tuesday and Thursday night after that but I didn't see him for a few weeks. I used to put his book inside my tracksuit, close to my skin. He was, like, my special secret; I carried him around everywhere.

'Then one night, he came in again. I was just sitting there, after a run, drinking an orange juice – it was about the time I'd started doing faster stuff round the island. He came over, gave me a little smile and said, "What did you think of the book?"

'Before Tim, I'd only really known two men. I don't remember my father – all I knew intimately of men was Danny and his father. Danny abused me and controlled me; his father abused me in a different way, tried to shape my life in a different way. But Tim was interested in *me*, what *I* thought, what I cared about.

'We met every Tuesday and every Thursday after that. I still did my run, but both nights I'd get back as quick as I could, get showered, go upstairs to the bar, grab an orange juice and wait for him; just like a schoolgirl. He was so kind.

'It was like that for three months, nothing else; we would just talk about books, about poets, about his boat. We did get closer, but not in a sexual way, and we never took our relationship outside the bar. We were having one, a relationship I mean, I suppose we were, but it was deeper somehow, because it *hadn't* gone on to being physical. On the sexual side, nothing happened at all. Is that strange, Caz?'

'No, Claire. It's sweet.'

Claire smiled and her eyes showed a bit of light. 'I think maybe Tim could sense that I had problems and he was trying to be gentle. But it was a funny little affair; Tim had never seen me in anything other than my running kit and I only ever saw him with the sweat of a squash game still on his shirt. Whatever else, no one could ever have accused us of dressing up for a date!'

'But it did develop, the relationship?'

'In the summer. I knew Tim lived on one of the houseboats down at Shoreham and I used to run down there when it was light, hoping I would see him. It was out of my way but not that bad. I used to have a long run which went down the towpath anyway, so I'd stop off for a stretch quite often, just hoping to catch a glimpse of him.'

Claire paused and looked across. 'Was I being stupid, Caz?'

'No,' Caz said. Claire was definitely not being stupid. Secretly, she wished she could recapture that innocence for herself, that splendid dreamy innocence of her teens. But she knew better; it was gone forever. Caz had given out and received a few too many scars since school. Now she couldn't respond to the lightweight, the delicate. Every scar she had received had healed but Caz knew how much harder scarred flesh finds feeling.

'It was a lovely evening. The sun was red, low in the sky, the river was up and the water was like liquid gold. I'd run about ten miles and I was coming along the towpath by the boats when I saw Tim. You know that feeling you get from LSD, that overall glow? Well, I was like that, feeling really good. Then I saw him. Not only was he out on deck, but he was working. He was in a pair of shorts, no top, doing something to one of his windows. I knew he was quite worked out but I hadn't really thought about it before. I was gawking at his body when I tripped over my own feet. I went head over heels, in a *very* unladylike fashion. Next thing I knew I was on my bum, picking bits of gravel out of a graze on my chin and looking up at him.'

Eighty-Four

'It happened that night; I don't remember the specifics. I remember Tim took me into his boat and I saw all his books. I was really surprised how efficient he was when he treated my cuts and bruises. He sat me down, went to his little kitchen and came out with a bowl of warm water, some Dettol in it. I really was sore and he was incredibly gentle with me, dabbing the blood away, picking out the bits of grit. Then he brushed the muck out of my hair and he kissed me. I started crying. That's almost all I remember but I know we went to bed. It was downstairs but all that is vague and misty. I just remember the *love*, the way he seemed to care about me.'

Caz waved the bottle half-heartedly. Claire shook her head.

'Tim wasn't like anything I'd ever known. He was a man but he didn't seem to be driven by the desire for sex. Often he'd just cuddle up, stroke my hair, be nice to me. Sometimes I felt like he was just looking after me, like I was a bird with a damaged wing that he was gently nurturing back to health. When the sex happened, not that often, it was – lingering – very tender, as if Tim didn't want to let rip and let out his animal side.'

'Tell me about him,' Caz said softly, 'what he looks like.'

'But you've met him, haven't you?'

'Tell me anyway,' Caz said.

'He's my height, your height, and wiry – that comes from climbing mountains – Tim says it gets rid of any excess weight. He's got short dark hair, a nice smile, and his eyes are dark, a bit too deep-set. But it's not what he looks like, Caz. It's the way he talks, the things he talks about, his kindness, his concern, that makes him special.'

'He plays squash, climbs – he plays football?'

'He doesn't play football.'

'But you said, your husband said, that—'

'I lied.'

'He doesn't play football?'

'Tim doesn't play football. There's a chap on one of the other boats that Danny knows – he plays football for Kingfisher. When we cooked up our story, that was why we said that Tim had played football. By accident, Danny had found out about Tim and he was worried that I might leave. I wasn't going to, but Danny didn't know that. We had to explain the weekend away and we had to maintain the charade that everything in our marriage was OK.'

'Ah!' Caz said. 'Well, that explains one thing. I saw the photograph of the Kingfisher team at your house and Tim wasn't in it.'

'This bloke that Danny knows is fairly tall and he's got sort of gingery-blond hair that he wears really short. Danny said he used to have it much, much longer but had it all cut off last summer. Him and Danny and another bloke from the team called Geoff White, they're into playing soldiers, wearing camouflage clothing, doing survival weekends and shooting these paintball things at each other.'

Caz grunted. 'I think I know the type.'

'Men and guns, the worst comes out, don't you think, Caz? It was always after a weekend that Danny would be his most aggressive. If he'd been away, he was far more likely to try and force me. He said once that Geoff had said he fancied getting a twelve-year-old, locking her up and training her to be the perfect sex machine. Geoff was probably joking but Dan was sick enough to imagine doing it.'

'But you stayed?'

Claire nodded. 'I told you that Tim was an engineer. That was a lie too. Danny's friend off the boats is the engineer. He works for the county council in Roads and Bridges Maintenance. Geoff works in the same department, that's how come they're in the same football team. He's some sort of engineer too.'

'They both work at Lewes?'

'Yes.'

'So where does Tim work?'

'For himself. He's got a shop in Brighton. He restores antiques and makes one-off furniture. The stuff he does is lovely but he won't have any of it on the boat because of the damp.'

'And when did you speak to him last?'

'On the phone, Monday. I rang him, said you might be calling in.'

'He seemed surprised to meet me.'

'He's a good actor.'

'I should have asked, but what does Daniel do for a living?'

'He keeps an eye on the newsagents. He has managers and senior chaps who run the day-to-day stuff so he handles the warehousing side. They buy in bulk and get better deals, like

Smith's. Danny drives a van round the outlets, delivering magazines and Twixes.'

'Sounds a bundle of laughs.'

'Danny doesn't need to do it. He says it gets him out of the house.'

'He works when, exactly?'

'It's a five-six-hour early-hours job. He usually starts about two a.m. and works through until eight. He gets home about nine o'clock – I'm usually already gone – has a sleep and does a bit of checking around in the afternoon.'

'And tonight he'll be playing football?'

'I doubt it. They won't play in this weather. Most of them will have gone home; maybe half a dozen or so will go to the Kingfisher for a few drinks.'

'Geoff?'

'Oh, definitely. Geoff and Danny are big buddies.'

'And Fred?'

'Who's Fred?'

Caz looked surprised. 'Danny's other footballing friend. The one off the houseboats.'

'Fred? His name is Jack! Where d'you get Fred from?'

'I must be getting mixed up,' Caz said.

'You must be,' Claire said.

If Caz was lucky, they might have another ten minutes before Peter Mason came back. He would probably arrive as Valerie was parking his Daimler-Jag. So far, Caz had hardly discovered anything except that the good-looking Yank had more than one name and liked to play cowboys. Ten minutes if they were lucky – and they still had to discuss the events of the weekend.

'So, Claire,' she said softly, as gentle as she knew how,

'something happened on Thursday. Do you want to tell me about it?'

Claire nodded. 'But I need to know something first.' She stopped and fixed Caz's face. 'Is Tim all right? Has anything happened?'

Eighty-Five

'Why would anything have happened to Tim?'

Claire looked worried. 'Has it?'

'Not that I know of. Why should it?'

'Do you know he's all right?'

'Not directly. Maybe if you explained what's going on . . .'

'There's nothing going on. It's just that I've rung Tim's boat today, three times. I've rung the shop. He hasn't come in and he never rang in with a message.'

'What do you think might have happened?'

'I just worry. Danny gets so angry. If he still thought that Tim and I might run off together, he might . . .'

'What, Claire? Hurt Tim? Do you think he could?'

'Not on his own.'

'Then why should you think anything's happened?'

'I don't. I just want to talk to Tim.'

'Tell me about Thursday, Claire.'

'I can't!' Claire said.

'I'm not worried about you, Claire. Tell me about Thursday and I'll help you find Tim.'

'How?' Claire said. Her eyes were filling up.

'Trust me,' Caz said.

Eighty-Six

New Year's Eve. Claire stormed from the house, angry at Danny, angry that he still wanted her to play those games, so angry that she forgot her keys. She had had enough. No she would *not* dress up, she would *not* smile for an audience, she would *not* hold hands at some stupid New Year party and be the quiet half of the happy couple.

She ran quickly at first, to get away, to feel a little pain in her muscles, to wash back the anger. After a mile she eased back, still tense but settling, settling into the rhythm of LSD. Then the worries drifted away, sailing on endorphins, and she thought of Tim.

If someone, something was following her, she didn't notice it then. But thinking back, whoever it was had to have been. In her anger she wandered, only generally heading for Shoreham. No one could have known where she would be, where she was going. Whocver it was couldn't have known beforehand that she would stop just half a mile from Tim's boat, and duck under the bridge for a quick wee. Whoever, whatever, it was, it was a blur of moving darkness, no face. There was just that sudden prick to her arm, her shoulder and then nothing.

She woke in darkness, complete darkness. Absolute, numbing fear.

It took time to adjust, to realise that the dream was not a dream, that the nightmare was real, the buzz in her body, the pain was real.

But the darkness, the faint movement of her cell, was so far from anything she had ever known, so null, that she feared for her mind. She closed her eyes, opened them, but saw nothing. She listened, listened, but there was nothing. Only the faint, faint sway of the room, the breathing darkness. She remembered a bang, like the slap from ECT, remembered faces, white coats leaning over; anaesthetic mist-people. Then, as the fear grew, she realised that her mind, like a dreaming brain, was searching for something, anything, to explain what was happening to her. But what was happening was nothing. It was the nothingness, the absolute nothingness that so terrified her.

Eventually she spoke, her voice removed from her, echoing round the hold. 'Hello. Is there anybody? Please.'

Then she heard, '*Tell me your name. Tell me your name.*'

It was a man but a machine. It reminded her of the sound of a karaoke player, false, heavily bass, with echoes rippling.

'*Tell me your name.*'

But she wouldn't. She was so frightened.

'*You are safe now, but you must tell me your name.*

'*Tell me your na-a-ame.*'

In her head she whispered, 'Claire, I'm Claire.'

'*Tell me your name. Is it Sally? No, you're not a Sally. Is it Joan? No, not Jo-o-an. Are you a Su-san? A Margaret? Zoe?*'

She stayed silent. The voice echoed, no breath, mechanical. With her eyes open, still surrounded by the utter blackness, she looked for, felt for the sound. It was then that she tried to reach, only then did she realise she was fettered. That was when she screamed out.

'I'm Claire! Who are you?'

Then the voice stopped. Then there was the darkness again. And silence. And sometimes, maybe, the faint swell of the sea.

It began then. The torture, the voice, then not the voice. Nothing else. The black was so black that her eyes began to invent sprinklings of gold dust, the random firing of her nerves powdery images only in her head. She thought of Peter Pan and Wendy. Then she began to feel cold. She said, 'I'm very cold. Will you help me?'

'*Will you love me?*' the voice said.

She said, 'What!'

'*Will you love me?*' the voice said again.

'Love you?'

'*Yes Claire. Love me. Then you can be warm.*'

She wanted to be angry. She wanted to lash out. But there was nothing to be angry at, nothing to strike at, nothing on which to project her venom. The anger turned inside, instead. She felt her old weaknesses, felt useless, suborned, fat.

'What can I do?' she said to darkness.

'*Love me,*' it said.

'Will you hurt me if I don't?'

'*No,*' the voice said. '*You are safe with me. I have made you safe. But I want you to love me.*'

'But I don't know you,' Claire said. 'Why do you think I would want to love you?'

'*Because I am protecting you. I have saved you from yourself.*'

'How?'

'*I know you. I know what you have done. I know your lover, the little man who lives on the river. I know you have betrayed*

Daniel Cook, betrayed holy vows. I can purge you. Save you. Love me!'

She stared into the black. Again she felt the slight lift of steel on water. For the first time she began to plan, to memorise, to consider an existence after this. The voice, what was it? She felt nothing. The words? Nothing except that someone knew her, saw her. The smell? Yes! Steel? The cold lick of rust? Salt? Paint?

A boat! A ship! She was inside, deep inside a ship! There! The swell again, very slight. A big ship, calm water. A harbour. Sheltered.

'*You have stopped talking to me, Claire. That is sad. I think I will go away now. Perhaps I will go away for a few days. Are you afraid of rats, Claire? Do you fear spiders?*'

'Where? When? Do you—? Please!' Claire said.

'*What is it, love? Are you frightened?*'

'Of course I'm fucking frightened, you bastard!'

'*Shush. Don't fret so. I will only be gone a few days. When I come back, I will wash you. If you are bitten, I will mend you. Claire?*'

She was cold, dying deep inside.

'Yes?'

'*Would you call me back, my footsteps, as they recede?*'

'Fuck you!'

'*In time, yes, but Claire, it must be love. It must be you who asks of me. I was sent to show you how you erred, to punish you, remove you from your sin. But I cannot, I need your love. Would you have me back?*'

'No.'

'*But Claire, not to call me back or say goodbye,*
And further still at an unearthly height,

One luminary clock against the sky,
Proclaimed the time was neither wrong nor right,
I have been acquainted with the night.'

'You're sick!'

'*I have walked out in rain – and back in rain,*
I have outwalked the farthest city light.'

'I'd rather die!'

'*No, Claire. You would not rather die. Who would rather die? Only those whose life is worse than death. Love me. I will keep you safe.'*

'Fuck off, sicko.'

'*Would you like some light? A blanket? Some water?'*

'Fuck off!'

'*I have looked down the saddest city lane,*
I have passed by the watchman on his beat,
And dropped my eyes, unwilling to explain.'

'Go away!'

'*I will visit with you soon, Claire. I promise. I always keep my promises.*' He moved for the first time, and for the first time the voice moved. It was moving away.

'*This place is lovely, dark and deep,*
But I have promises to keep,
And miles to go before I sleep . . .
And miles to go before I sleep . . .'

And she called out to him. After him. She called him back and not to say goodbye. Even an hour alone would be too much. She would rather have the voice than the darkness. She would rather love the voice. 'I want you,' she said. 'Will you let me love you?'

The footsteps changed.

'*Your juices drip?*
You want me so?
And I your furrow now to plough?'

' "Yes!" I said. I begged him yes, Caz. He whispered to me. I had to love him, talk to him. He had to be sure I loved him. Afterwards he played it back, the tape. He asked me, did I still love him? I said yes, and did he want to do it again? So help me God, Caz.'

Claire wasn't crying but her eyes were staring, pointed, soulless. Then she told Caz that all the way through she was telling herself, 'It's just a cock. It's just a cock.' She had been here before and she was determined to survive.

'Then he kissed me, Caz. He kissed me. Then he whispered, "Now, Claire, be true to your man." I felt him move away, then something touched my shoulder and I blacked out. I woke up in the river, an inch or two of water, between the railway bridge and the chain bridge. I was in my running kit, tights, sweat top, shoes and socks, but I was covered in mud. I was face down when I came out of it. I think I was probably lucky not to have drowned. I felt hung over and my armpits were incredibly sore, like someone had been deliberately pinching me.'

'And you went to Tim's boat?'

'He held me. Cuddled me. Then we had a couple of drinks. I asked if I could have a shower and I just stayed in there, washing my hair time after time, letting the shampoo run off and down me. Then something sort of clicked in my head. I got out, got dried, and went back to my man. I said I was stopping over and we would worry about it in the morning. I was still a bit confused but I was beginning to consider the idea of leaving Danny and forsaking all that money.'

'But Tim told the same story as you?'

'I asked him to. On the Saturday I told him about the will, about Danny's abuse. I was going to tell him about what happened in the ship but I didn't. I said someone had grabbed me and thrown me in a van. That I'd got away later and when I was running, I fell in the river. I don't think he believed me. He said, "Tell me what I have to say to Daniel."

'When I went back home on the Sunday, I wore some of Tim's stuff. He drove me there and I took all my muddy kit. Danny didn't seem all that surprised. I had been intending to just walk out on him and, if Tim would have me, become a houseboat person.

'But I suddenly had this cold feeling. That maybe Danny had been behind what had happened, that he had arranged for me to be terrorised, to be raped. I thought, if he had been, he might hurt Tim, have him hurt. At the last minute I changed my mind.

'I've thought about it since, Caz. My husband is a complete creep but I just can't see him having the intelligence to arrange something like that. We came up with that pathetic story because we thought it was vague enough to put you off the scent. Tim only went along with it after I begged him. I promised him we would sort it out but I needed these lies to give me time to think. He lied for me, Caz, but he isn't a dishonest man. He said he would lie for me but only once. He asked me never to lie to him again. All this was on the phone. Even though I couldn't see him, I knew he was hurt. I think I'd decided then that money was costing me love.'

'Did Daniel know what you were saying to each other?'

'He was on the extension. We needed all to know what we were going to say.'

'And then I called with my DI.'

'Danny said that you might believe we were lying but in the end what was there for the police to investigate? I was still trying to work things out in my head but I wasn't going to report what had happened on the ship.'

'Why not, for God's sake?'

'That man had taped everything I did, Caz. Everything. It was like the dialogue from a blue film. I'd heard it, remember? I sounded like I was loving every second. If they had ever caught him, found the tape, I could never have faced hearing it again. Never.'

'But you were raped, Claire. You know that.'

'I was coerced, yes. But he said he wouldn't hurt me. He just talked to me. He persuaded me to love him.'

'You were raped, Claire.'

'It felt like something else, like me and Danny.'

Caz sat up. 'It was rape, Claire. Any court would say so.'

'No court will, Caz. I won't testify. If ever, by some accident, I find this man, I will kill him or have him killed, but I won't ever stand up in a court, tell people what he made me do, listen to that tape.'

'You're not the only one, Claire.'

'What!'

'There's been at least one other victim.'

Claire was white. 'Oh, Caz, no . . .'

'And I'm not sure what's happened to Tim. It looks like he's done a runner but he's left his poetry, his squash gear.'

'He wouldn't do that.'

'Do a runner?'

'Leave his books.'

'That's what I thought. There was a poem left out, no

message, but I have to tell you, something may have happened to Tim.'

'What was the poem?' Claire said.

'It's in my bedroom. All I can remember is the first line, "After great pain, a normal feeling comes—" '

' "The nerves sit ceremonious, like Tombs—" '

'That was it!' Caz said.

' "First – Chill – then Stupor – then the letting go—" ' Claire looked up. Her eyes were overfull and she began to weep, very lightly. 'I didn't know Tim had any Dickinson,' she said.

'Have another drink,' Caz said. 'You're staying here tonight.'

She stood up to use the phone.

'Could I have the book?' Claire said.

Eighty-Seven

Caz got on the phone to John Street and asked for DCS Blackside. When they said he'd gone off for the night she asked that he be called out to contact her five minutes ago. She asked Control to get hold of DS Moore – could he come to her flat now – and DI MacInnes, would he ring her ASAP? She also asked for a WPC. Could they get one to her place urgently?

She had just put the phone down when Valerie pulled up outside. He had a key; Peter Mason didn't. Mason was still ringing the bell when Val clumped up the steps behind him. She went through to the kitchen, filled a kettle to the brim and flicked it on. Then she dug out the coffee-maker and filled that too. The phone rang. As she went back to answer it, Valerie came in, telling her what he had found on the door. DS Mason whiffed of a single pint. She picked up the phone. 'DC Flood.'

'Flood. Blackside.'

'Urgent as it gets, sir. Can you get to my flat?'

'What?'

'There's things already happening, sir. I'm with a member of the public waiting for a WPC.'

'Sexual assault?'

'Yes, sir. And the woman in the river was a murder.'
'Give me fifteen minutes.'

She put the phone down and turned to speak to Valerie. He had been expecting a quiet dinner *à deux* and looked a little peeved. Just as Caz raised her eyebrows to speak, the phone rang again. She waved her hands in apology and picked up the phone.

'Flood.'

'Bob Moore. What's up? I was just having tea.'

'Thanks for ringing, Sarge. I needed to talk to you. Something's come up, you won't have heard yet. The body this morning's now a murder and I've landed right in the middle of it. It's probably fucked up the operation we had planned. Can you come over?'

'What, your place?'

'The DCS is on his way and I've left a message for the DI. You already know DS Mason is here.'

'What's wrong with John Street?'

'It's just tricky, Sarge.'

'Give me half an hour,' he said.

'Peter, you've been introduced? This is Val; up to tonight, he was my boyfriend. Hello, Val.'

Val wasn't amused. 'Who wants tea?' he said.

'Start with everyone,' Caz suggested. 'And stick another kettle on straight away, I'm expecting my DCS.'

'Wonderful!' Valerie muttered.

'Shit happens, Val. I'm sorry, it goes with the territory.'

'*Your* territory,' he said as the phone rang again. While she was speaking he disappeared.

'Flood!'

The line crackled briefly – a Scots voice, the edge off, smoothed with Whyte & Mackay.

'Tom! Thanks for ringing so quickly. Can you get round? It's hit the fan in a big way and there's a personal that can't wait.'

'Ah'll have tee walk, ah'm well ovah.'

'Takes about ten minutes,' Caz said. 'I'll have the kettle on.'

'Ah'd rather a nice Whyte & Mackay.'

'The DCS will be here.'

'Make that a double then. It's still legal t'get pissed off duty.'

'Ten minutes.'

'See y'then, lass.'

Peter Mason was ferreting through the CDs. She tapped him on the head and said she didn't have any Slade. He grinned. She went through to see Val.

The kettle was blubbing, too full and blapping water on to the kitchen surface. Valerie had just turned to switch it off.

'It couldn't bc avoided,' she said. 'Some major shit just hit the fan.'

'And I've been offered a job in the States.'

'What!'

'Two-year contract. Double the money I'm on now.'

'Fuck!' Caz said.

'What's that mean?' he said.

'That you'll go?'

'I *came* to *talk* about it!'

'And walked into the middle of a murder!'

'Oil and water, isn't it?' Valerie said.

'What is?'

'Love and the law.'

The first few bars of *Sergeant Pepper* came through from the lounge. 'Oh, how *original*,' Caz said.

'I've got a week to think about it,' Valerie said. 'They're paying me enough money for two. I was going to suggest' – Caz went cold. *Please, God, don't let him mention marriage* – 'maybe we could get—Fuck! I've scalded myself!' The phone rang again and Caz escaped. 'I'll just get that.'

'Caz Flood.'

'Hi-yah, Caz! It's Moira. What's this overtime all about then? I thought me and Billy could come over your place a bit early, have a pizza before we went out snogging on overtime.'

'Moira you are fucking *hopeless*. You're supposed to *pretend* to be a couple. If you're at it when the villain shows, you're not likely to feel his collar, are you?'

'I was only joking, Caz.'

'Anyway, it might be off. There's bigger fish to fry.'

'But we need the overtime,' Moira said.

'Then just turn up, anyway, where we were going to meet. There's a good chance you'll be needed. Even if you're not, you'll still clock a few hours at time-and-a-half before they tell you you're not wanted.'

'So what's going on?'

'The G28, the woman in the river. Looks like it's just about to be upped to a murder. It's all happening.'

'We'll come round, then!'

'Not a good idea, Mo. We've got guests. From Southampton.'

'Oh,' Mo said.

Eighty-Seven

Tom MacInnes got there first, with just enough time to pour himself a massive whisky and wrap himself around it before the DCS arrived. Caz said they had to talk – a personal – and urgently. Valerie was doing his best to be human but it was difficult; he wasn't a copper. Claire had read and reread Tim's poetry selection and had managed to pull herself together. There was nothing on *Sergeant Pepper* to trigger fresh tears.

Valerie was sitting with Claire, trying to small-talk about poetry that he'd never read. Caz went to him, squatted on the floor, her hands in his lap. She was surprised by half an erection.

'Baby. I really wanted, you know, tonight. This big deal wasn't my idea. I'm sorry.' Half was now three-quarters. 'I'd like to come round later. When's too late?'

Seven eighths. 'Half past midnight.'

She looked at him, knowing how horrible it was loving someone you knew was going to leave you. He looked down. She mouthed, 'I love you.' Then for the room she said, 'It's a bit tricky, darling, but there's a police operation going on . . .'

'Maybe I'd be better off out of the way,' he said, on cue.

He stood up and she went with him to the door.

There was a dark brown ten seconds as she watched him go down to the hall, the music and the rat-a-tat-tat of conversation in a mist behind her. Then, as the top of his head reached the bottom of the stairs she turned back through the door and shut him out. Instantly the room was slightly lighter, the words clearer.

Tom MacInnes was saying something, something about being just thirty-summat when they brought out *Sergeant Pepper*. Caz did a quick sum; she'd been *two* when it came out. How come it felt like a song from her generation? 'This'n the *White Album*,' he was saying, slightly slurred, 's'goot, goot stoof.'

'I hate to split you two boys up,' Caz said, breaking in with a little laugh and nodding to Claire at the same time, 'but I need a minute with the DI. Right now.' Tom turned round and measured out a tiny nod of respect. 'And if DCS Blackside rings the bell,' she added for Peter, 'make him wait a minute. I'll let him in.'

'No probs!' said Peter. 'Have you got *Revolver*?'

They went through to Caz's bedroom. MacInnes was unsteady. Caz realised that she'd never seen him pissed; plenty of Whyte & Mackay down him, yes, but never fall-down pissed. She stood. He sat on her bed. The bedding underneath him was pastel light blue. He had bought it for her not so long ago, a house-reclaiming present.

She took a breath. 'Tom, have you ever looked the other way?'

'Course Ah have,' he said, 'five, six times mebbee.'

'For a copper?'

'Coupla times.'

'How serious?'

'Well, it wasnee murder.'

'But how did you decide?' Caz said.

'I went with ma gut, what felt reet,' MacInnes said. He had no control over his accent now. 'The book's never reet, things like tha'. Y'have t'follow what feels reet. D'what yer belly tells yer.'

Something finally made sense for Caz. She said thank you and touched the DI's arm. He looked up. His eyes were wet the way an old man's eyes are wet.

'A gidd decision, lass,' he said. 'Ah'd've done same.'

He stood to leave the bedroom.

'Tom?'

At the door he stopped, his hand on the jamb. 'He's a gidd copper, Caz. He jest med a mistake, s'all.'

'Thanks, Tom,' she said.

The DI left. She sat on the edge of the bed and dropped forward, her elbows on her thighs, making peace with herself. When she rose, through the en-suite door she could just see her reflection in the bathroom mirror. She went in, leaned forward to look at her reflected self. Her green eyes were a little flat, her blonde hair just a little dull, but not grey. There was a touch of hardness in the way she looked at herself. She thought of Valerie and wavered a little, but then she thought of Claire Bullen with nothing but a poem left; the grey, nameless woman on the oyster beds; Pixie Walters.

She washed her face, the cold tap running, the water a sharp shock. When she looked up she was pink. She pushed two open hands through her hair, squeezed it into a pony and pulled the tail until the roots screamed. As she looked at Caz Flood she saw her pupils narrow and darken. She let go and went through to the lounge. MacInnes was sitting with Claire. He had her book open in his hand. She had just said something and smiled. He replied.

'Ah, lassie! Freedom an' whisky gang thegither!'

Eighty-Eight

DCS Blackside arrived just as the Beatles were breaking in to 'Here There and Everywhere'. Caz went down to let him in, happy that she wasn't upstairs and able to dwell on the words. Blackside seemed to fill the doorway and the porch light pointed up a dark-angry face. 'This better be worth it, Flood!' he said. Before she could reply, two cars pulled up, their lights snaking over the pair of them.

'Who's that?'

'DS Moore, sir; and I asked for a female uniform.'

They waited until the sergeant got out of his car and scurried out of the rain. The section car was parked on the other side of the road and produced Harry Deans and Julie Jones. They were dried out and, Caz presumed, on a split shift. They hit the road and ran. When they were all in the hall, she sent them upstairs. All she had managed for the DS was a quick smile which he could have read as absolutely anything. She was last to go back up. Her hallway would need a clean if she ever got a half-day off.

Pete Mason should have known better but he didn't. He hadn't yet killed the CD and Norman Blackside walked into a chorus of 'Yellow Submarine'. The DS got to the off button quickly but the damage was already done. To make things worse, Tom MacInnes was quoting more Burns to a very drunk Claire Bullen. He raised his glass when he saw Blackside. The DCS glared.

Caz dived in. 'Would you give it a minute, sir?'

She turned to Julie and asked her to take Claire into the bedroom. The DI put his glass down and graciously helped her up. The instant she was out of the room, Blackside exploded. 'What the fuck is going on, Tom?'

MacInnes grinned. 'This is DC Flood's party, Norm.'

'Flood?'

'Take a seat, sir.'

She whisked the pink pig off the sofa and waved at the cushions. Blackside sat down, his huge arm spread along the back. Bob Moore had grabbed a dining chair from the kitchen and sat on it reversed.

'OK,' Caz said. 'First off, I apologise for bringing you all here. This should have happened at John Street but I had a distressed woman here who needed me. She was partly intoxicated and she wasn't prepared to go to the station.'

She could see Blackside trying to keep his cool.

'The lady's name is Claire Cook-Bullen. We had a misper report from her husband on Friday but she turned up back at home on Sunday. Mrs Bullen is a personal friend, sir. Tonight she came to see me and told me what happened to her this weekend. What she said makes it very likely, virtually certain, that the G28 we took out of the Adur this morning was a murder-rape.' She felt all of the men sit up. She took a breath. 'And I think the murderer has at least one woman still incarcerated. He has her now.'

Eighty-Nine

'Claire Cook-Bullen went for a run from her home in Hangleton on Friday afternoon. She was followed. She was heading for south Shoreham, the island, but stopped to duck under the chain bridge to relieve herself. Shortly afterwards she was accosted and quickly subdued. From her description of events, she may have been drugged.

'Mrs Bullen woke up in what she believes was the hold of a ship. Her abductor then used the crudest forms of sensory deprivation to terrify her, prior to coercing her into sexual intercourse and other sexual acts. Mrs Bullen was forced to overtly express an active desire to participate in these acts, all of which were tape-recorded. Her attacker subsequently played this recording back. For this reason, I doubt if Mrs Bullen will be persuaded to testify in court.

'After these various sexual acts, Mrs Bullen's attacker seemed sated and behaved almost decently towards her. Then, once again, Mrs Bullen was rendered unconscious. She woke to find herself on the mud flats close to the Adur bridge. She was able to crawl out of the river and seek help at a friend's close by.'

She spoke directly to Blackside. 'Obviously, sir, this MO

would produce this morning's G28. One drowned, one survived. I think we've got a pretty sick man to find.'

Caz hadn't finished but the DCS put a finger to his lips. He stood up and went to the phone, got through to the duty sergeant and issued orders. He wanted a dozen uniforms in an hour, half a dozen CID. Any sailings from Shoreham were stopped, *now* – get hold of the ACC – and they'd better close Newhaven, at least until the morning.

'Right, Flood!' he said as he put down the phone. 'What else?'

'The rest is not so definite, sir, but I've reason to believe one of the residents of the houseboats at Shoreham may be involved, may even be this rapist. I visited the boats yesterday to talk to a man called Timothy Hacht, a close friend of Mrs Bullen. I spoke to an IC-1 male, approx thirty years old, thin, short reddish hair, who said his name was Fred Kermy. Mrs Bullen knows him, but knows him as Jack, sir, and this morning, WPC Jones spoke to him. He was on Hacht's boat and gave Tim Hacht as his name.'

Harry Deans grunted uncomfortably. 'House-to-house, sir. We were following up on the oyster-bed woman.'

'I think this Jack or Fred may have been surprised by the uniform's visit. Said his name was Hacht to get rid of them.'

'We couldn't have known . . .' Harry started to say.

Bob Moore was closest. He muttered, 'Leave it, Harry.'

Caz had glanced that way. Harry was faintly pink. She continued. 'Mrs Bullen and Mr Hacht had been having an affair, sir. I went back to the boats tonight. Hacht is gone. His clothes have been taken but I'm not convinced he's done a runner.'

'Why not?'

'He's into poetry, sir and he's left his books. He plays squash and he's left his kit. I went on the boat. He hadn't locked up. It's iffy. There was no goodbye note, no *Dear John*, nothing. A poetry book was left out, open, some poem by Emily Dickinson, but it wasn't really an "I'm off" poem, more to do with Claire's problem.'

'What do you mean?'

'Claire has the poem, sir. It starts off about "great pain". She says it's about how she should deal with her rape. She said it *could* be about how if Tim had left her, she would feel dead for a while, but she says she knows that Tim wouldn't have left that book for her. She says that he didn't own any Dickinson. She said he would have left her something by Christina Rossetti.'

'*Remember me when I am gone away*,' MacInnes said, just loud enough for her to hear. Blackside's head didn't move but his eyes flicked that way, then back to Caz.

'I think we have just cause to suspect foul play, sir. I think there's a strong likelihood that something has happened to Tim Hacht.'

'Why would this chap do harm to Hacht?' Blackside said.

'He's a close friend of Daniel Cook, sir, Claire Cook-Bullen's husband. I believe he told Mr Cook about the relationship between Mr Cook's wife and Mr Hacht. Mr Cook wanted the affair stopped and hushed up. There are complicated money reasons for this, enough to make it worth getting rid of Mr Hacht.'

'What's enough, Flood?'

'One and a half or three million pounds, sir, depending on how you do the sums.'

'Jesus!' Mason slipped out.

'Do we have enough to go through both boats, sir?'

'Yes,' Blackside said.

Ninety

This time when Caz went back to the boats it was with team courage and flashing lights, a dozen men, noise, an incident van parked just down below. They approached the American's boat at the same time as half a dozen guys swooped on Tim Hacht's barge. Four uniforms, the DCS and DS Mason went for the Yank, Caz was with Bob Moore and four PCs checking out *Beached.* They had left Tom MacInnes in disgrace, crashed out on the sofa. Claire Bullen was flat out in Caz's bed and Julie Jones was watching the pair of them, listening to Sting and thinking about Nick Berry. That had cost Caz a big favour.

Hacht's boat was in darkness and had that eerie, abandoned feel Caz had experienced earlier. This time, though, tramping through his home with every light on, men's voices and a few size twelves around her for company, she felt obnoxiously powerful, a distinctly better emotion compared to the earlier one of barely controlled terror.

There was nothing new, no sign of Hacht's being or his leaving. The DS grunted at Caz and they went downstairs, leaving two uniforms in the wheelhouse and two outside. It had stopped raining so they were only cold and miserable, hold the wet. Downstairs, Moore spotted the loaded washing machine.

'Spot that, did we, Flood? No one leaves their washing.'

'I saw it, didn't clock it,' Caz said honestly. 'I was too scared, kept waiting for the Creature from the Black Lagoon to pop up.'

'Shouldn't have been on here anyway.'

'Maybe not, Sarge.'

'Took balls.'

'Bottle.'

'What?'

'Bottle, Sarge. Even Maggie Thatcher didn't have balls.'

'What the fuck you on about, Flood?'

God, he'd really missed it! 'Nothing, Sarge.'

When they went upstairs, one of the PCs had found Tim's watch.

'Anything?' Moore said.

'Yeah,' the uniform said. 'Found this under the table, by there.'

It was a TAG watch, and looked at least two hundred quid's worth, the sort of thing you don't misplace. The magazine ads always showed them strapped to the fleshless wrists of divers, climbers, yachtsmen and, lately, Grand Prix drivers. You don't lose those watches unless you're head-firsting it off a mountain, crashing your McLaren or falling foul of a blunt instrument wielded by a smooth American who maybe likes the Muppets.

'OK, Flood,' Moore decided. 'I'll give you "very iffy". Better hope your mate Bullen wasn't making long-term love plans.'

Caz was stunned; even for Moore, that was tasteless.

'For Christ's sake, Sarge!'

He looked at her. 'What, Flood?'

'Nothing.'

'You know what they say, Caz. If I didn't laugh, I'd cry.'

They left one of the PCs on *Beached* and went along to the other boat. Every window in the flotilla was lit up now, faces wondering, doors open, bits of music drifting out. A tethered dog barked, one end of the towpath.

They could see Blackside's head through glass. The PCs stayed on the path and formed a corral straight away, breaking out smokes. Caz and the DS stepped down on to the boat. The freezing uniform left guarding the gangplank turned momentarily to do a bit of work but saw straight away that there was no need to repel borders. He dropped back into his coat and the detectives went inside.

'Bob!' Blackside said neutrally as they stepped in. He was looking at a couple of magazines, Stateside gun books, with Peter Mason. They were open on a page marked 'Personal Protection' – screech alarms, pepper sprays, Tasers, stab-proof and bulletproof vests, Mace from $6.95. Ads were squared off with red marker pen, one with a fat exclamation mark in the margin. 'Know much about this shit, do you, Bob?' Moore looked and shook his head. 'How 'bout you, Flood?'

'There's been times when I wouldn't have minded a BP vest, sir.'

'All the time in the States,' he said. 'They don't dick about. Go to ground armed and they SWAT you, you're fucked.'

'They should legalise Mace, sir.'

'So bank-blaggers can use it?'

'They'll use it anyway, sir. So women like me can pay-back when some creep tries to grab us in the park.'

'What's wrong with a knee in the nuts?' Mason said.

'Easier said than done, Sarge. You know that.'

Blackside looked at the advertisements again. 'Shock machines, pepper juice in the face, Jesus! What else has this twat got?'

Ninety-One

Jack Gonz's framed photograph of Kingfisher FC was tacked up on the starboard wall. He smiled out, those special eyes changed by a fresh prejudice, not startling now but staring, maniacal. Nearby, a couple of pennants were displayed, the same victories, the same second places saved and savoured by Daniel Cook. On the same wall, a glossy picture of *Alcedo atthis,* iridescently green-blue-backed, with a chestnut belly and red feet. There was a note pinned beneath it, *When hunting, the kingfisher dives from a perch over water,* and later, *though beautiful, he is a merciless and efficient predator.*

There were finds; coils of rope, binoculars, a sleeping bag, torches, twine, tobacco tins packed with survival absolutes. But every one could be innocent; everything could be explained away by a walker, a camper, a man who lived on or near the sea. Scene of Crimes were on their way but they weren't going to find handcuffs, leather masks or incriminating tapes. Jack Gonz was clever as well as handsome.

They picked up his name from a notice board in the kitchen. Under 'Gonzo's Board' and a picture of Kermit's purple anteater friend was his business card with his works phone number and his title, Head of Maintenance, Bridges. There was a string of qualifying initials after his surname.

Bob Moore stood behind them. The DCS was looking at a little list of phone numbers and thinking. He was looking at the initials DC. Caz said, 'Daniel Cook.'

'And Mac?'

'No idea, sir.'

That was when Moore said, 'Jesus Christ!' and rushed back into the lounge. Both of them turned, surprised.

'I was right!' he shouted. 'I'd seen the bastard earlier, just didn't click. It's Billy McLintock – he's in this fucking football team photo, right behind the three dick'eads sat in the front with their hands on each other's knees. What's going on, Flood?'

'What d'you mean, "what's going on"?' Caz said as she followed his voice into the lounge. 'How am I supposed to know?'

The DCS stepped in. 'Would someone like to clue the boss in?'

Caz turned round. 'I'm sorry, sir. This American, Jack Gonz, plays soccer for Kingfisher Football Club. If you look at this photograph, this is Gonz but his hair is shaved now; this is Daniel Cook. This man is Geoff White who works with Gonz.'

Moore pointed at the photograph. 'And the big ugly bastard with the dark hair is William McLintock. He's been responsible with his brothers for a few shop break-ins and a ram-raid, Jan One.'

'This is the villain you were supposed to be going for tonight, Bob?'

'Yessir, until all this shit hit.'

'Does he work? When he's not knocking over shops?'

'He paints. He's not as thick as his brothers. Does industrial stuff. Contract jobs. Factories, that sort of thing.'

Caz felt something strange and frightening land in her gut. She could hear Pixie Walters now. She could feel panic rushing through her. And darkness, overwhelming darkness. Suddenly, she thought she knew something, but it was too wild. She stopped herself.

Caz felt the need for air. 'Would you excuse me, sir?'

She went out on deck without waiting for a reply.

She ignored the uniform skulking around at the back of the boat and went forward, breathing deeply, still feeling slightly sick. Out across the river there were lights, cars still drifting over the chain bridge, yellow windows and flickering TVs, people drinking cocoa . . .

'Flood? You all right?'

She turned round. Peter Mason.

'I'm OK,' she said, her voice wavering. 'Do you use a mobile, Pete?'

The DS fished a phone out of his inside pocket, a little Nokia. 'This do you?' Caz nodded, managed a smile.

'What's up?'he said, grinning. 'You want to order a pizza?'

Caz was looking in her bag. 'How did you guess?'

Mason stared out over the water.

'I appreciate this, Peter.' She pressed buttons.

'Come on, Flood,' Peter said. 'What you up to?'

'Booking a dinner date,' Caz said.

Someone picked up at the other end. 'Mariella?'

'This is David,' a voice said. 'She's out.'

Shit! 'When will she be back?'

'It's a girls' night out. Late. Midnight. Worse maybe.'

Shit! Double shit!

She took a huge breath, stamped. Looked wildly out over the water, bit her finger.

'David!'

'Yes?'

'David. This is as important as it gets. Can you get hold of Mariella?'

'What, now? Are you serious?'

'I'm deadly serious, David. Can you get hold of her. It's vital that we speak. Tell her, ring Caz Flood. Now!'

She turned to Peter. 'What's this number?'

He told her.

'David. Tell her to ring me. It is very, *very* urgent. I'll give you a mobile number. If for any reason she can't get me, tell her, ring my home number. There'll be someone there, let it ring. When she gets through, tell Mariella to tell whoever answers all about Medway.'

'What's your mobile?'

She gave him the number.

'David. Thanks. Get her to ring me.'

She rang off. The DS was next to her.

'What the fuck was that all about?'

'Don't ask,' Caz said.

'But I already did.'

'My DI once told me don't go saying things off the wall till I'm sure. What I'm thinking is so off the wall, it's a white-coat job.'

'Blackside's been talking to the dock authorities. Only thing last few days in Shoreham's been a dredger. It's still there. They've had dock police crawling all over it. Nothing.'

'Oh, shit,' Caz said.

'Shit what?' Mason said.

'I'm claustrophobic,' Caz said. 'What are you like with heights?'

Ninety-Two

The immediate danger of being sick was gone but Caz was close to shaking instead, adrenaline pumping too early around her. She could feel her skin prickling. They went back inside to see the DCS and Moore. She hit first. 'Sorry about that, sir. I missed lunch.'

'We need to go and see White and Cook,' Blackside said. 'Talk to them about our friend Mr Gonz.'

'Have we got White's address, sir?'

'We had his telephone, got the address from the exchange.'

'And he's where, sir?'

'Lancing, near the college.'

'Can I go?'

'Thought you felt rough?'

'Bit of fresh air, right as rain now, sir.'

'Bob?'

'DS Mason and Flood can go to Lancing if they want to, suh. I'm ready for my bed. Daniel Cook is a lot closer.'

'Right then!' Blackside snapped. 'We'll leave six uniforms here, two area cars. Have one bloke on each boat all the time, rotate them every hour. They stay till I tell 'em different.'

Bob Moore moved to go out. Caz turned to follow. 'A very quick word, Sarge?'

He stopped. She lowered her eyes. He clicked.

'Speak to you outside,' he said.

As she went out, Caz heard Peter Mason say something to the DCS. Blackside rumbled back. When she got on deck, Bob Moore was looking down at the mud. She went to his side. 'Sarge? Bob?'

Moore turned round, nothing in his eyes. She smiled.

'I've thought about it,' she said. She held out her hand.

He took it; they shook. 'Thanks,' he said, the tiniest of nods.

He let her go. 'Take care,' she said.

She walked away feeling all right.

Ninety-Three

Peter Mason drove out from the island, back up on to the road, and right towards Brighton. As soon as they'd crossed the chain bridge, Caz directed him left and they followed a narrow road up the side of the river. They ducked under the railway, passed an old toll bridge and then reached the A27. 'Don't get lost,' Caz said. 'Go wrong, it's like Spaghetti Junction by here.'

They took a left and slipped up on to the flyover, eight hundred feet of boxed bridge, girdered steel looping a hundred feet high over the Adur. Caz asked again, was Peter's phone definitely on?

'Yes,' he said. 'Just like it was half a minute ago!'

'And the batteries are OK?'

'Flood, it's plugged into the car!'

'That's the college,' Caz said. 'See the lights?'

White's place was down a track, an ill-kept cottage in a dead end, outhouses dropped haphazardly around, corrugated roofs, squalor. A large dog raged on the end of a chain, dashing madly thirty feet each way, each time choking to a halt that it never anticipated.

'Jesus!' Mason said. 'I hope that chain is strong!'

There were no lights, no cars parked. The house looked

cold and empty. They knocked for the sake of it, but an instinct told them both that there was no one home. After a few minutes they left. Coming down the lane, taking it gently, their lights picked out the frail red frame of a fox. He stopped, flashed his white neck as he took a look at them, then ducked away, into the hedge.

'When we get to the bridge, can we pull over?' Caz said. The Saab stopped. Mason looked at Caz as if she'd cracked. 'Trust me!' Caz said.

The fox was gone, slipped into the night. They slid from the lane on to a road and dropped back down towards the tarmac that flowed uphill and on into Brighton. Behind them the lit face of Lancing College church dominated everything. It made Caz think of Oxford spires and John le Carré. Next thing she'd be hearing Aled Williams and choirboys singing.

The road was quietening as midnight came closer, but cars still flacked by regularly, one every thirty or so seconds.

'Where d'you want me to pull over?' Peter said.

'There's a lay-by just before the first span of the bridge.'

Peter flicked his headlights to full beam. A few seconds later, he said, 'I see it.' There was a Transit van pulled up, three wheels, tilted by a jack. 'Some poor get's had a blow.'

They drew in behind the van, J-reg, no firm's logo. As they got out, both brandishing torches, two cars flashed past with a suck of air.

There was no one there. 'Must've had no spare,' Peter said. He went round the front. 'Yeah, there's a note on the windscreen. "Gone for a new tyre." Warra prat.' He came back round, his torch flicked off, its long barrel sloped on to his shoulders like a gun. Caz pointed down the bank with her light.

'I want to go down there,' she said.

Ninety-Four

Peter knew she was cracked now, especially when she said, 'Bring the phone.'

'Look,' he said, half falling his way down the bank after her, 'if it's sex you want, what's wrong with the back of the car?'

'Grow up!' she said.

They got to the bottom of the bank just as it started to rain again. Their torches were both halogen-bulbed serious beasts but even so there seemed to be an awful lot of darkness to beat back.

'It should be this way,' Caz said confidently and walked through dock leaves towards the river.

'What, exactly?' Peter said.

'Hollow abutment,' Caz said like a name-dropper. 'George Lindsell says there's bound to be one. You got that key you had?'

'That's not gonna be much use to you!'

'George says all the locks are the same. Otherwise the council staff would need hundreds of keys.'

'So where's the door?' he said.

Caz pushed back a bush. 'Here! Where's that key?'

* * *

George was right. Caz undid the big lock, lifted it out and pulled back the door. The rain drummed on metal. She was getting wet but it hardly mattered. She waved her torch at Peter. 'After you.'

Peter shook his head. 'You must be fuckin' joking!'

'Wimp!' Caz said.

She ducked in, surprised by the size. The room was more like a hall, sixty feet to the far side, forty feet deep and seven, maybe eight feet high. The walls were concrete strips and so was the ceiling.

'Fuck me!' Peter said from behind.

'Later! Later!' Caz said. 'We've got work t'do!'

She turned round. Peter had the torch under his chin, ghouling his face.

'Mind the door,' she said. 'If it shuts, you're a dead man!'

There were stacks of metal, old fencing, windbreaks with different-sized holes. She vaguely remembered now; once upon a time this was 'The Whistling Bridge' and the locals were complaining about ghosts and weirdies. It took a few scientists and engineers a while to find out the cause, the windbreaks. After a few months' experiments, they found out how to shut the bridge up. This was the residue.

Caz looked round very carefully, but apart from a few cans, a lot of metalwork and a dozen bags of cement, the place was clean. There wasn't even a trace of cats or pigeons. According to George Lindsell they were the first beasts to find a way in.

'At least it's dry,' she said.

Peter was just about to say something when his phone rang.

* * *

It was Mariella, ringing from the bottom of a barrel.

'What? No! You're breaking up!' Caz said. 'Ring me back in two minutes.'

'The reception's crap, Peter,' she said. 'We need to get up top.'

'It works better in the car,' Peter said.

'Right.'

They went out, locked up, then slipped-and-slid sideways up the grassy bank. It was pissing down now. When they got back into the car they squelched. 'Plug it in!' Caz squeaked. 'Quick!'

Peter started the car and whacked the heater and wipers on to full. After about a minute they had to turn the heat down one notch. Mariella still hadn't rung back and Caz was a bag of nerves. For something to do she radioed the van's number in for a vehicle check.

The girl in Control recognised her voice. 'Don't you sleep, Flood?'

'I can't,' Caz said. 'So many men, so little time . . .'

The woman laughed. 'Registered to a company, Arnold Cook's, that's the newsagent's, yeah? Not reported missing.'

Caz wasn't listening properly. She was looking up on to the crown of the bridge, the middle of the road, between the crash barriers, every sweep of rubber, just briefly, a yellow reflective jacket—

'Christ!' Peter said. 'What a time, what weather to be working . . .'

'Could you give me that again, please, Jackie . . .'

'Ford Transit-Van, registered to Arnold Cook's Wholesale News . . .'

'Thanks . . .' Everything slowed. 'Thanks . . . Jack . . .' She looked again at the road, each window freed of rain. A passing car bleared red taillights up the hill. There was no jacket. No workman.

Then she realised there were no warning triangles either.

She spoke into her radio again. 'Jack. Can you get me DS Moore?'

Ninety-Four

Caz got out of the car. The rain was greedy. She went to the van and tried the doors. She looked again at the note. Then she looked into the cab, her torch-yellow bouncing back off paper, a coil of rope, a tin.

She went round the back. Water ran down her face. This time the torch flashed over sacking, grey blankets, a lump.

'Peter!'

She looked back at the DS. Behind the windscreen and between the waves, his mouth formed a 'What?' Then he pointed to his chest. He was lit by the Saab's feeble interior light. She waved. When he didn't get out, she went to him. Through the electric side window she said, 'We need to get into that van.'

'There's a jemmy in the boot,' he said. She went round.

Finally, as she came out with the long spike of steel, he emerged from the dry car, looking up at the rain as if daring it to try that again. 'What's up?' he said, spluttering.

To look at him, Caz had to look into the wet. It hurt her eyes. She was shouting. '*I think we've found Tim Hacht!*'

Peter took the crowbar. He went to the Transit, heeled it between the doors, pushed. Caz was a yard away, his light.

The lock was surprising. The door didn't move.

'Try the bottom!' Caz said, more water in her mouth.

'That's no fuckin' good!'

'I can help. Bend the corner back!'

Mason slammed the iron under the bottom corner of the door. Instead of the door moving, the double skin curled back. Caz put her torch down. It rolled into the kerb. She put her hands under the door. Something cut her. She shouted, 'Have another go!'

Mason slapped in the crowbar again, scratches appearing on the Transit door. Caz pulled at the door's lower edge. Mason grunted and heaved. 'Fer fuck's—'

When the lock went it was with a bang, the bang of clacked metal.

Mason shouted, 'Yes!' Caz fell back into the road.

A car horn wailed past. Caz got up. Soaked. She picked up the torch. 'Can you see, Peter?'

The DS couldn't. He took the torch, then he waved it over the floor. When he waited, Caz climbed past him. Inside, there was a peculiar, musty smell. As she moved forward, she crossed the torch beam and cut her own light, suddenly blacking out the far wall. She gasped, 'Peter!' He moved. The dark was gone but the torch was shaking.

'Fer Christ's sake!' Peter said. 'Take a bloody look!'

'OK! OK!' Caz shouted. She grabbed the blanket, held a corner, jumped back.

She saw the clothes first. You always registered the clothes before you saw the body. 'Oh, God!' she said.

But there was no body, no gore. They had found Tim Hacht's books.

Ninety-Six

They went back to the Saab and tried Control again. She wanted Moore.

'No joy!' Jackie said. 'We've sent a PC round his house. Soon as he gets there.'

'Right!' Caz said. She thought for a moment. 'We're on the Brighton road, the bridge over the Adur. Can you let the DCS know? Get a couple of cars here?'

'Brighton road. Adur bridge. Good as done!' Jackie said.

Caz broke off. 'Right!' she said to Peter. 'Let's go and chat to those night-workers!'

She got out of the car, walked through the headlights, and round to the passenger door on the driver's side. She got in.

She tapped Peter's shoulder. 'Drive up on to the bridge in the right-hand lane. Slowly.'

'What for?'

'I want to see where those workmen are.'

'We'll get some night-shift tosser up our arse, we stop in the fast lane.'

'Put your hazards on!'

'Just what's the rush, Caz? Can't this wait until the morning?'

'No!' Caz said.

'Why the fuck not?'
'If you won't help me, I'll do it on my own!'
'Help you do *what*, Flood?'
'Find Pixie Walters,' Caz said.
'Who?' Peter said.

Ninety-Seven

Another minute wouldn't hurt. Caz told him.

'Billy McLintock was stashing stolen gear in a bridge, right?'

'Right.'

'Where'd he get the idea? Did *you* know some bridges were hollow?'

'Never thought of it.'

'Billy plays soccer for Kingfisher, with Gonz and White. They both work for the county as engineers, roads and bridges. *They* would have told McLintock. Claire Cook-Bullen was locked away. She thought, *we* thought, she was in a ship. Metal, paint, rivets. She said it moved, ever so slightly. So we thought, a *big* ship. Little bridges are fixed, Peter. Big bridges breathe.'

'Am I being thick or something?'

'No, Peter, you're being normal. People never look up. That's why snipers hide in trees. Our high streets are old, right? – the first floors, the second, higher up. But we only see the shiny bits, the ground floor, the stainless steel and glass. We see bridges as things we cross. Pigeons, rats, street kids, they see them as nests, dens, places to hide.'

'So you're saying?'

'Claire Bullen was *here.* Inside this bridge!'

They crept forward at walking pace. Caz leaned from the window with her torch, looking into the space between the double steel barriers. Every twenty yards was a rectangular manhole cover with rounded corners. In between was the flotsam and jetsam of the automobile, nuts, bolts, litter, bits of forgotten engineering, even paint cans and brushes.

She counted ten, eleven, twelve covers and was beginning to feel faintly car-sick. Then they came to a hole.

The manhole cover had been painted yellow. Even in the torchlight it was bright. It was heaved to the side, solid cast-iron, *very* heavy. Beside it, an inner cover, a lighter alloy, was also discarded.

'Stop the car!' Caz said breathlessly.

They got out, walked back five yards. This was where they had seen the yellow jacket. The silver reflecting, animal eyes in the night.

They climbed over the barriers. Between them was a yard wide, still debris-ridden, awkward. She heard Peter curse as he stepped on a bolt.

They were there. Peter bravely went by and with his torch looked down into what he thought would be the inside of the bridge.

'Jesus mother!' he said, falling backwards. He was white.

Caz came forward.

Peter was on his backside as if needing to feel the bridge.

'Fer Christ's sake, Caz! Be careful! It's not hollow. That manhole goes straight through the fuckin' floor! Straight down two hundred feet!'

She went forward on her hands and knees, flicking

metalware out of her way. When she got to the hole she looked in, down, through, straight at the sea, the river, fat and silver and a *long* way down.

'I don't understand . . .' she said, bewildered. 'If this is where the workman went through, then . . .'

That was when they heard the fart of an engine. A blupp. A two-stroke motor puttering. Out of context, it was bewildering, frightening. Then they heard the slow clank of a train, steel wheels on steel tracks. They looked at each other, different kinds of fear, different demons, as if any moment now they would be confronted by aliens.

Caz looked into Peter's white face. 'It's underneath!' They felt it trundle, the something, the train, the platform, moving underneath them, beneath the bridge. Then, through the hole, Caz saw metalwork, a steel-mesh floor, a ladder, paint cans, tool boxes. Then she saw a white plastic hat, the yellow coat, the man at the engine which powered the platform. She went cold.

Peter looked at her, still slightly shocked. Caz put her finger to her lips and pointed at her hips. The DS was still not with it, but when she took out her handcuffs, he nodded and produced his own. They both moved out of the workman's line of sight.

Ninety-Eight

The head came up. The hole was narrow and the workman moved carefully, brushing the hole sides with the muscles of his upper arms. His hands must have been on the ladder, for now, with his shoulders through, he glanced down, wriggled out his arms and brought his hands free. That was when the two detectives cuffed him, one from each side and behind. Caz flashed light in the man's face. Daniel Cook.

There was a brief, forlorn hope in the face, then Cook struggled, trying to drop back into the hole. The detectives merely moved backwards, spreading his arms out like a bug pinned to a board. He screamed.

'Come out now,' Peter said. 'Or we'll pull yer fuckin' arms *off*.'

Cook nodded.

'No, leave him there!' Caz hissed.

She moved so he could see but kept her arm stiff so he was still in pain.

'Who's down there?' she shouted, right in his face.

'No one!' Cook shouted back.

'Where's Pixie Walters, you bastard?'

'Who?'

'The girl. Where is she?'

Cook grinned. She felt disgusted. Then slowly he said, 'I don't know what you're talking about.'

'You fucking lowlife!' Caz spat. She stood up and ran behind him. His arm flew up and he roared as Caz got to the end of her reach. There was a snapping sound, then he whimpered, 'Jesus! Jesus!'

'Drag him out,' Caz said. She was already undoing her cuff. Her wrist was agony, she thought she might have damaged something.

Mason pulled Cook on to the surface. His head was tilted. The DS checked. 'I think you've dislocated his shoulder.'

'You've got a problem with that?' Caz said.

A car went by, slowing to look. Two blokes. Caz showed them the finger. 'I've got to go in and check for Pet Walters,' she said.

Mason was clipping Cook to the barrier. He unclipped Caz's cuffs and handed them over. 'Wait for back-up. We're talking minutes here.'

'You heard Cook,' Caz said. 'There's no one down there.'

'So wait.'

'I can't!' Caz said. She felt like crying. 'You wouldn't understand. That could be me in there!'

The DS looked at Cook. Quickly, he said, 'OK, I'll come.'

'You'll never make it on to the platform,' Caz said.

'I'll keep my eyes closed.'

'Thanks,' she said, 'but it'll be all right.'

She went back to Cook. 'Who is down there?'

'No one!' he said. She banged his arm with the torch. 'Christ! I *said*! There's no one. They went to—'

He stopped himself. Caz grabbed his shoulder. He looked like he was about to faint. 'Where have they gone, Danny?'

He was shaking with pain. Caz raised her torch.

'Newhaven,' he said.

Ninety-Nine

Caz put her torch by the side of the hole. She swung herself in, slipping on to the ladder. Leaning back, she looked down her chest, past her feet at the mesh floor. Below it she could see water. The drop was at least a hundred feet. She grabbed the torch. At the last second she asked Peter for his as a spare. She didn't know if she could do this.

She climbed down on to the floor of the cage. Either end, the square strength of the bridge closed her in, but between the platform and the side walls was a two-foot gap, straight down to the river. Peter would have freaked. He would never have made it.

She went to the edge, glanced down at the silver, looked up at the steel. It really was like a ship; metal, rivets, right-angled strengtheners, even, right in front of her, a four-by-three-foot door, fly-bolted shut.

She thought about opening it but then she thought that if Cook had used the moving cage to travel under the bridge, wherever he had come from might not be accessible this way.

She turned to the engine. It was hot and it stank. There was a button, originally red but rubbed to bare metal by rough hands. When she pressed it there was a putt and it started. It sounded like a small tractor.

She flicked the torch over the mechanism. There was a lever, 'E-W'. She guessed 'East-West' and chose West. There was a little jerk and then the platform began to move, ker-lank, clack-clack. She was quite proud of herself. She held on to something and trained her torch on to the wall.

The wall trundled east as she moved west. Most of the paintwork looked dry, old, untouched. All around her she was still aware that it was pouring with rain but right where she was, she was in a hidden, arid, separate world.

She looked more carefully. The cage moved so slowly it felt like an animal grumbling along, hanging from a tree. Rivets. Rivets. Bolted door. Door. Rivets . . .

She had got aboard the platform smack in mid-river. Now she was about fifty-sixty yards out from where she and Peter had looked inside the hollow abutment. She looked quickly back. Then she saw the bridge, a snake, roped across the river. It felt animal.

She turned to see the unlocked bulkhead. She knew straight away. She reached for the lever and pushed it into neutral. It stopped. There was the faintest sensation of a sway, but it was the bridge lifting, the wind still eager to feel it. She sat down. She'd done the easy bit.

It wouldn't be dark. She had a torch. She had *two* torches. It wouldn't be small. The doors were four by three, the tubes had to be at least ten by ten. She whispered to herself, 'It's not dark. It's not enclosed.'

She leaned over and flicked off the catches. They whacked away with a peculiar cast clack of cold metal. She put fingers underneath the door and pulled. Its weight surprised her. It swung open.

Inside was echoing black. She climbed up quickly, trying

not to think. Then she did think. Of Petula Walters.

She used it as a mantra. 'Hang on, Pixie. Hang on . . .'

She would never have predicted the shape inside the box. It was far taller than she could have guessed, tall enough for her torch to spread in the darkness, wasted on the distance. Eight feet, maybe ten wide, it was like a tall house without its floors, and it was dry. Electric cables ran along one wall about five feet from the bottom.

She stopped to listen. All she could hear was herself. She couldn't hear the rain, she couldn't hear traffic passing overhead. She was in a box, a big box but still a box. When she played the torchlight forward she saw a large oval hole, and behind, another box, more bridge.

She hadn't decided whether calling was a good idea. If there *was* someone down here, Gonz or White, then her calling would warn them. If there wasn't, it wouldn't matter and her shouts might just help Pixie Walters. She shouted, 'Hello?'

First time she hardly managed a croak. She suddenly remembered a film. She was a bugler and couldn't blow. An officer shouted, 'Spit, man! Spit!' She tried, filling her mouth with it, swallowing. A deep breath.

'Hello?' Now she realised the echoes, running away, running back, echoes on echoes, meeting where they crossed, slightly frightening as they changed who she was. She stopped calling and started walking.

In the third box she found bedding. She found a tape-recorder, a car battery, bottled water, a Gaz stove, rations. She found a first-aid tin, a tube of K-Y Jelly on top.

In the next box she found Pixie Walters. She was sitting on a crate, a brown blanket wrapped around her naked body.

She had a mug in her hand, something hot, steaming. When Caz caught her eyes she knew that she'd survived. She looked up at her rescuer and smiled. Then she returned to her drink.

'Don't jump to any conclusions,' a voice said from behind Caz.

Caz spun round, frightened enough to faint. Her torch picked out Billy McLintock just as his own light burned into her face. In his other hand he had a McLintock bat.

'It's not what you think,' he said. He put the bat on the floor.

Caz was still wary. She was so frightened she could feel herself losing control of her bladder. She concentrated on that, her dignity, for a second then she reached for the second torch, one for light, one for her protection.

'Who are you?' she said.

'Billy McLintock. One of the boys.'

'I've seen your photograph. You and Gonz. Cook, White.'

'I'm nothing to do with those sick bastards!'

'You're here,' Caz said.

'I know,' McLintock sighed. He moved towards Caz. She flinched and raised Mason's torch.

'Oh, fuck off, lass,' Billy said. 'If I'd wanted to hurt yer Ah'd've done so aw'riddy.'

He brushed past and went to the girl.

'See, hen, it's aw'reet. Wull soon as have yee outa here.' Pixie looked up. He stroked her head. He turned to Caz.

'Ah'm a villain, reet? Ah'll tek a pop atta poliss but that's fair enough. But this? A wee gurl? Ah'm a man, not an animal.

These blokes, Mother of Gad, they canna be normal.'

'So how come you're here?' Caz said.

'I got in here t'hide 'n' found the girl. The others think Ah'd join in withum. Ah've just bin waitin' on lettin' her go.'

Caz looked at the girl. She nodded. 'He's decent,' she whispered. 'He looked after me, made me some cocoa.'

Caz relaxed slightly. 'Did you sell Cook a TV, a stereo?'

'Aye.'

'He told you about the bridges?'

'Gonzo done that. The American.'

'So what was Daniel Cook doing here?'

'Thass t'do with the girl. They would be using huh 'ventually. Cook would wanta just have her, you know,' he mouthed 'rape', 'but Gonz, he says, no, he c'n make a gurl ask for him t'do it.'

'Did the others just go along with that?'

'No, but Gonz said he'd kill 'em if they so much as touched her.'

'And could he?'

'Oh, aye. Ah'm a street-fighter but Gonz, he's some sorta trained. He was in special forces, somethin' like tha'.'

Caz crouched. 'And Hacht? Anybody else?'

'Ah don't know no one called Hatch. Only know about this lassie, and Cook was joking with Gonzo about someone called Claire.'

'Joking!'

'Aye, 'bout how a real man puts a woman in place, you know.'

'Let's get out of here,' Caz said.

McLintock pawed at the floor. 'Ah'm not that keen on tha'.'

'You'll walk, Billy. I promise you.'

'What about ma bruthers?'
'They're nicked, Billy. No can do.'
He held out his hand. 'You're aw-reet!'
'Thanks,' Caz said.

One Hundred

They went out through the square boxes, found the door, climbed out on to the moving platform. McLintock was cuddling the girl through the blanket. He was so tender, Caz asked him why he didn't go straight.

'Ma bruthers,' he said. 'And 'sides, most've the time it's gidd fun.'

She restarted the engine and selected 'E'. The platform jerked, then edged back towards the middle of the river. She looked at the Scotsman and the little girl, Beauty and the Beast. Pixie suddenly decided to speak properly for the first time.

'They're slags. But I wouldn't do it. The smooth one said he would talk me round. I told him, not as long as there was a hole in my arse.'

Caz told her how brave she'd been. Caz wouldn't have held out.

'She's a cannie wee lassie,' McLintock said.

Caz stopped the platform. Above them the manhole gaped. She was at the bottom of the ladder. She shouted up, 'Peter? Sarge?' Whatever hit her, she didn't see.

She sat up, hurting. There was blood on her face. Her jaw ached. Pixie Walters was whimpering, not even able to scream.

White was trying to take her away from Billy McLintock who was holding her with one hand and brandishing the bat with the other.

She shook her head. As she did so, Gonz stepped over and touched Billy with something. He went down with a little grunt. Then the American turned round and looked at Caz. 'Be you a pirate?'

Caz ignored it. Her eyes were white. 'What is that?'

Gonz smiled. 'This?'

She nodded, submissive.

'Thirty thousand volts. Short, sharp shock treatment. Limeys won't have them, will they?'

'They kill people,' Caz said.

'Only sometimes,' Gonz said. 'Most of the time they just knock you down. There's a few side effects, like epilepsy, but hey, that's not my problem.'

'What have you done to my sergeant?'

'Same as Billy the Kid, here.'

'And Dan Cook?'

'Broken neck. He fell.'

She moved slightly. Her jaw felt broken. When she touched it, Gonz said, 'I am sorry about that. I dropped straight down. You were in the way.'

'So what now?' she said. 'You must know we've got cars on their way. I radioed in before I climbed down here.'

'Hey, is this where you say, "There's a man with a gun behind you" and I say something like, "Oh, yeah, I'm going to fall for that"?'

'It'd be nice,' Caz said.

'Oh, *you'd* be nice,' Gonz said. His eyes were suddenly

holes in the snow. For a second, Caz really saw him. 'Trouble is where to store you.'

He stepped towards White and the girl. White suddenly collapsed, Pixie with him. He looked at the prongs of the Taser. 'Wow! Two with one shot. How about that?'

Pixie moaned. Caz said, 'Is Tim Hacht dead?' She was thinking, how long did one of those things take to recharge?

'Soon will be,' Gonz said.

'So where is he?'

'Terrible taste in poetry. Hates American stuff. Not sure about Whitman, thinks Frost is too sweet, Dickinson too girlish.'

'Is he in a bridge?'

'Trussed up. Taped up. Nothing to do except think of his girl.'

'Jesus, you're sick!'

He thought a second, tilted his head. 'Well, yes.'

'They'll find you,' Caz said.

'Perhaps,' Gonz said. 'But we'll have *some* time together. There are so many places to hide. Lift shafts, ventilation systems, sewers.'

He came towards her. 'Shall we go?' Then he said, 'Ouch!'

When Pixie Walters hit him with the bat it was a girl's slap to the side of the head. Light enough to surprise him, but not enough to knock him down. He turned on her, black with rage. 'You little bitch!'

Caz came at him then, running, knowing that when she hit him, there was only one way to go. He grunted as she crashed into him and he half turned so their faces came together. He was grinning as they hit the side of the cage, still grinning as they tipped over together and fell towards the water.

'Kiss me!' he said as she tried to push him away. She saw his eyes, his teeth; then he let her go. The thought that she was free came as she turned over, the instant before she hit water. Stop.

Epilogue

Tim Hacht was found inside Newhaven swing bridge, folded into a recently painted part of the structure. He was very sore and he was suffering from the first signs of exposure, but he was alive. He was lucky. The section he was in was due to be repainted in 1998.

When Claire Cook-Bullen woke she was three million pounds poorer, but the house, its white room, automatically reverted to her. She thought that was a bit of luck. Once the house was sold, she had decided to bank the money. After all, living on a houseboat was cheap.

Billy and Moira waited until midnight before deciding to call it a night. Their luck was out. DCS Blackside turned down their claim for overtime. Peter Mason was lucky-ish. He woke at midnight with a mother and a father of a headache.

The six cars and twenty men who surrounded the Brighton road bridge at Shoreham jacked it in an hour after they had arrived. Someone decided to radio Control and asked for confirmation of DC Flood's message. Jackie Spring dug it out and repeated it, word for word. 'The bridge on the Brighton road. Where are you, then?'

They broke code then, swearing on the air. 'Maybe you

could try the other bridge,' Jackie said, helpfully. 'The big one on the A27.'

Valerie got to the hospital at one fifteen. DI MacInnes and DS Moore left the room to give them a minute. Caz had been told they'd found nothing wrong but she was trussed up like a turkey until morning, when they'd have another look.

Val said, 'About America . . .'

She gestured to him and mumbled something he didn't hear.

He leaned close. There was mud in her ear.

'I suppose,' she said, 'that a fuck is out of the question?'

More Compelling Fiction from Headline

Written in Blood

Caroline Graham

'Graham has the gift of delivering well-rounded eccentrics, together with plenty of horror spiked by humour, all twirling into a staggering *danse macabre*' *The Sunday Times*

It is clear to some of the more realistic members of Midsomer Worthy's Writers' Circle that asking bestselling author Max Jennings to talk to them is outrageously ambitious. Which is why Gerald Hadleigh, who knew Jennings many years before and for whom the prospect of seeing him again is the most appalling he can imagine, does not challenge the proposal. But, astonishingly, Jennings accepts the invitation and before the night is out Gerald is dead.

Summoned to the well-heeled village, Chief Inspector Barnaby finds that, despite the fact Hadleigh lived within a stone's throw of most of them, the polite widower was something of a mystery to his fellow group-members: as witnesses to his final hours they are little help. But the one thing they all agree on is that on the night of his murder Gerald was a deeply troubled man. The obvious cause of his distress was their guest speaker. So why did the wealthy and successful Max Jennings travel to Midsomer Worthy to talk to a small group of amateur writers? And, more to the point, where is he now?

'A wonderfully rich collection of characters . . . altogether a most impressive performance' *Birmingham Post*

FICTION / CRIME 0 7472 4664 5

More Crime Fiction from Headline

KATE CHARLES

Appointed to Die

A clerical mystery

Death at the Deanery – sudden and unnatural death. Someone should have seen it coming.

Even before Stuart Latimer arrives as the new Dean of Malbury Cathedral shock waves reverberate around the tightly knit Cathedral Close, heralding sweeping changes in a community that is not open to change. And the reality is worse than the expectation. The Dean's naked ambition and ruthless behaviour alienate everyone in the Chapter: the Canons, gentle John Kingsley, vague Rupert Greenwood, pompous Philip Thetford, and Subdean Arthur Bridges-ffrench, a traditionalist who resists change most strongly of all.

Financial jiggery-pokery, clandestine meetings, malicious gossip, and several people who see more than they ought to: a potent mix. But who could foresee that the mistrust and even hatred within the Cathedral Close would spill over into violence and death? Canon Kingsley's daughter Lucy draws in her lover David Middleton-Brown, against his better judgement, and together they probe the surprising secrets of a self-contained world where nothing is what it seems.

FICTION / CRIME 0 7472 4199 6